Tales of the Fays
Volume 2

Tales of the Fays
Volume 2

by
Marie-Catherine d'Aulnoy

Translated, annotated and introduced by
Brian Stableford

A Black Coat Press Book

ISBN 978-1-61227-837-7. First Printing. February 2019. Published by Black Coat Press, an imprint of Hollywood Comics.com, LLC, P.O. Box 17270, Encino, CA 91416.

TABLE OF CONTENTS

Introduction

This two-volume collection assembles all the published tales of the fays known to have been published by Marie-Catherine Le Jumel de Barneville, Baronne d'Aulnoy (1651-1705), presenting them as they appear to have been prepared by the author for publication. It is now impossible to determine with certainty the exact pattern of their actual publication; many modern reference books and critical studies assert that that originally occurred in 1697 and 1698, but none can name a publisher or give reliable details of the pattern of publication, because no copies of the supposed original volumes are accessible. The Bibliothèque Nationale does not have custody of any such editions, or any early reprints, and no copies can presently be located in any other library; all the bibliographical data in reference books appears to have been reconstructed by inference from the version of Madame d'Aulnoy's assembled works that was published in 1717, when Estienne Roger reproduced all the works included in the present collection in volumes 3-6 of his illicitly produced *Cabinet des Fées*. The same text was subsequently crammed into volumes 2-4 of Charles-Joseph Mayer's similarly illicit 1786 *Cabinet des Fées*.

Each of Roger's four volumes appears to have combined two volumes of the originally-planned editions, which were surely designed and perhaps issued as two pairs, a singleton and a three-volume work entitled *Le Nouveau bourgeois gentilhomme, ou fées à la mode* (tr. herein as "The New Bourgeois Gentleman"; the subtitle translates as "Fashionable Fays"). In the *Cabinet* versions the second couplet is separately titled *Les Contes de fées*, but no individual titles are attached to the first couplet or the singleton. That title has therefore been speculatively attributed to the first part of the assembly, while the rest are sometimes listed as *Nouveaux contes de fées* or as *Fées à la mode*. That is a highly unusual and rather puzzling dearth of information, about the possible reasons for which we can only speculate.

The first bibliographer who attempted to compile a definitive list of *contes de fées* was Nicolas Lenglet Du Fresnoy, in the second volume of *De l'usage des romans, où l'on fait voir leur utilité et leurs differents caracteres, avec une bibliothèque des romans* [On the Usage of Romances, which shows their utility and their different characteristics, with a library of romances], illicitly published in 1734, allegedly in Amsterdam, with the by-line "M. le C. Gordon de Percel." In the section devoted to Madame d'Aulnoy's *contes*, the bibliography records eight volumes under the collective title of *Les Contes de fées*, allegedly published in Paris in 1698, but Lenglet Du Fresnoy might not actually have seen any such volumes, and probably had not seen a reported reprint of 1708, published in Amsterdam either; the latter edition certainly does exist, although other sources record that the two volumes published in that year by Pierre Mortier only feature the contents of the first five hypothetical 1698 volumes, the remainder following from the same publisher in 1711, in a two-volume version of *Le Nouveau bourgeois gentilhomme*.

Lenglet Du Fresnoy mistakenly attributes *Histoires sublime et allegoriques* (1699; actually by the Comtesse de Murat) and *Les Chevaliers errans* (1710; actual author unknown) to d'Aulnoy as well, illustrating the difficulties in determining authorship that existed at the time, which were to become even more complicated thereafter.

In view of the absence of reliable documentation, one of two things must be true: either the alleged 1697-98 editions of Madame d'Aulnoy's work do not exist, evidently having been refused a royal privilege for publication, or, having been printed illicitly at that time, the copies were all destroyed, immediately or over time. We cannot know for sure—and the fact that we cannot is a significant datum in itself—but the likelihood is that Lenglet Du Fresnoy's recording of an eight-volume 1698

Paris edition is fictitious, and that the first editions of Madame d'Aulnoy's work, perhaps consisting of a compaction of eight intended volumes, were printed illicitly in 1708 and 1711. What is certain, however, is that if it were not for editions belatedly published without the benefit of the royal privileges necessary for licit publication, Madame d'Aulnoy's contributions to the genre she helped to invent and form would have been obliterated from the historical record.

Very little is known, either, about much of Madame d'Aulnoy's life. Joseph de La Porte, the indefatigable historian of literary works by French women, devoted abundant space in his the third volume of his history, compiled in 1769, to Madame d'Aulnoy's travelogues and historical fiction, but only gave brief and rather dismissive mention of three of her *contes de fées*, evidently working from a contemporary compilation, and he claimed to have been unable to discover anything about her biography other than a (mistaken) birth date and the year of her death.

Subsequent researchers ascertained without much difficulty that Marie-Catherine Le Jumel de Barneville had been born into the minor nobility of Normandy, and married off by her family at the age of fifteen to the much older François de La Mothe (or La Motte), Baron d'Aunoi (or d'Aulnoy). She had four children in rapid succession, two of whom died in infancy, but her marriage effectively ended when the Baron was arrested on a charge of lèse-majesté and was sent to the Bastille on 30 September 1669, on the order of Jean-Baptiste Colbert, one of Louis XIV's principal ministers.

Baron d'Aulnoy eventually turned the tables on his denouncers and was released, after claiming vociferously that he had been stitched up by his mother-in-law, with the collaboration of a lover and another accomplice. His wife was arrested, and might have been briefly imprisoned, but was soon released if so. The truth of the matter is now impossible to ascertain, but the accusation routinely flung around in later commentaries that Marie-Catherine was one of the instigators of a plot to frame her husband is pure speculation; the probability is that if the baron really was framed, the reasons were political and undisclosed; Colbert is unlikely to have lent his hand to a petty family dispute. At any rate, the Baronne's mother, who became the Marquise de Gudanes following her remarriage, fled to Spain, and although there does not appear to be any reliable information as to where the Baronne was during the 1670s and the early 1680s, she was probably with her mother for at least some of that time. During that period she had two more children, but the identity of their father, or fathers, is unknown.

The widely-published speculation that Baronne d'Aulnoy spent time in Holland and England is devoid of solid evidence, and might be based purely on the fact that she published works of fiction that masqueraded as memoirs of those nations. The suggestion that while she was there she worked as a spy for the French government is pure supposition, although she does appear to have had considerable credit with some influential individuals when she resurfaced in Paris late in the 1680s.[1] At that time she began to write fairly prolifically, producing a fictitious *Relation du voyage d'Espagne* [An Account of a Journey in Spain] (1691), a series of equally fictitious "memoirs" of the Spanish, English and French courts, a couple of *nouvelles espagnoles* [Spanish novellas] and two historical melodramas set in Tudor England, *Histoire d'Hypolite, comte de Duglas* [Hippolyte, Earl of Douglas] (1690; the spelling of "Hypolite" varies in different editions) and *Le Comte de Warwick* [The Earl of Warwick] (1692). The last-named titles were apparently popular—La Porte describes the former as a "masterpiece of its genre"—and by 1695 the author had a solid literary reputation.

From the early 1690s onwards d'Aulnoy was an active member of a literary salon hosted by Anne-Thérèse de

---

[1] Jean-Baptiste Colbert died in 1683, but whether that had anything to do with d'Aulnoy's return to Paris, there is now no way to know. She was, however, definitely acquainted with Colbert's long-serving secretary, Charles Perrault.

Marguenat de Courcelles, Marquise de Lambert (1647-1733), along with the poet Antoinette Deshoulières, the poet and dramatist Catherine Bernard, and the tutor to the young Duc de Bourgogne, François Fénelon. The most prestigious member of the salon was Marie-Anne de Bourbon (1666-1739), a princess of the blood, then known as the dowager Princesse de Conti; she was accompanied there one of the ladies of her household, Mademoiselle de La Force, and the salon was subsequently joined by the latter's cousin, the Comtesse de Murat. Lambert's salon was also joined by Antoine Houdar de la Motte, a writer who became very successful after the turn of the century—when the salon reached the peak of its celebrity—but he was at the outset of his career in the early 1690s; he was presumably related to Baron d'Aulnoy, but perhaps only distantly. Madame d'Aulnoy also hosted her own salon in the 1690s, and attended the long-running salon of Mademoiselle de Scudéry, by then hosted by the latter's protégée, Mademoiselle de L'Héritier, which had a regular membership overlapping Madame de Lambert's.

In part two of *Hypolite, comte de Duglas* one of the characters relates an allegorical *conte* [tale], "L'Île de felicité" [The Isle of Felicity]; it is set against the background of Classical mythology, but the narrator says by way of introduction that it is a "*conte approchant ceux des fées*" [a tale similar to those of fays], implying that the notion of *contes de fées* had already been introduced to the Parisian salons as early as 1690, probably as a kind of calculated exercise or game, like the games described in Mademoiselle de La Force's *Les Jeux d'esprit, ou la Promenade de la Princesse de Conti à Eu* [Witty Games; or, The Princess de Conti's Excursion to Eu] (written before 1700, published 1865) and Catherine Bernard's historical novelette set in the mid-sixteenth century, *Inès de Cordoue, nouvelle espagnole* (1697; tr. as "Ines de Cordova"). The latter might well have owed some inspiration to d'Aulnoy's exercises in that vein, although it is very striking in its refusal of the happy ending characteristically attached to such stories.

A key passage from *Ines de Cordoue,* in which the young queen of Spain, Elisabeth de France, proposes a storytelling contest, is often cited as a representation of the way in which *contes de fées* must have been invented:

"She proposed, in order to create a new amusement for herself, making up gallant tales. The order was received with pleasure by all the ladies who composed the little court; rules were agreed for those sorts of stories, of which the two principal ones were that the adventures should always counter plausibility and the sentiments should always be natural. It was judged that the charm of the tales should only consist of making visible what was happening in the heart, and that there should also be a kind of merit in the marvelous imaginations, which would not be retained by the appearances of verity."

It seems highly probable that some such suggestion must have been made in one of the literary salons in Paris, most likely by Mademoiselle de L'Héritier, who became an ardent propagandist for the writing of *contes de fées,* and that it was imported at some stage to Versailles—almost certainly by the dowager Princesse de Conti, who was Louis XIV's eldest and favorite daughter, and who had a court of her own within the king's court—where it apparently became something of a fad.

The importance of the Bernard representation is not restricted to the suggested "rules" for the writing of such stories, although the assertion that "the charm of the tales should only consist of making visible what was happening in the heart" certainly needs to be borne in mind is examining Madame d'Aulnoy's work, as well as the specification that they must contain "marvelous imaginations." The implication that there was an element of competition in their composition is equally significant. Some of the writers who dabbled in the genre would surely have said, if asked, that they were not competing with anyone, but merely dabbling for the joy of taking part, but even if they meant it, the fact remains that they were operating within a competitive framework of sorts.

Given that implication of competition, it must have rapidly become obvious to everyone involved in the game, and everyone tempted to get involved, that there were only two serious contenders for the hypothetical prize: Baronne d'Aulnoy and the Comtesse de Murat. If that was not obvious from the very beginning, it certainly became manifest when those two writers became the most prolific contributors to the genre, effectively in control of its development. It became blatantly obvious toward the end of the competition, when both writers deliberately undertook to produce new versions of two stories borrowed from Gianfrancesco Straparola's *Piacevoli notti* [Facetious Nights] (1551-53), "Galeotto" and "Pietro." Straparola's tales are both short, but the new versions produced by d'Aulnoy and Murat are much longer and greatly elaborated; they were probably the last *contes de fées* produced by either author, and represent the ultimate stage of development achieved by the process of evolution they had directed and contrived. D'Aulnoy's "Le Prince marcassin" (tr. as "Prince Marcassin") and "Le Dauphin" (tr. as "The Dolphin"), and Murat's "Le Roi porc" (tr. as "The Swine King") and "Le Turbot" (tr. as "The Turbot"), were evidently produced in parallel, in the context of an overt or covert literary duel.

In retrospect, it seems probable that the frame story in which d'Aulnoy's two Straparola-derived tales were embedded, *Le Nouveau bourgeois gentilhomme*, was produced at the same time—in 1698—and in the same spirit as the frame story of Comtesse de Murat's *Les Lutins du château de Kernosy* (tr. as "The Goblins of Kernosy Castle"), although the publication of the latter was long delayed, until a version eventually appeared, fugitively, in 1710, without the benefit of a royal privilege. D'Aulnoy embedded some of her earlier tales in two *nouvelles espagnoles*, and the competitive stimulation of Catherine Bernard might well be visible in the fact that two of those tales—"Le Mouton" (tr. as "The Sheep") and "Le Nain jaune" (tr. as "The Yellow Dwarf)—refuse happy endings, as Bernard's do: a rare circumstance in d'Aulnoy's work, and even rarer in Murat's, although the latter probably produced the similarly-exceptional "Anguilette" at the same time.

If the salon writers really did start the game of composing *contes de fées* as early as 1690, the stock of such tales would have had seven years to accumulate before the floodgates of publication were suddenly opened by the immense success in 1697 of Charles Perrault's *Histoires et contes du temps passé*, better known as *Contes de ma mère l'oye* (tr. as *Tales of Mother Goose*). The latter was originally its subtitle, but became its title in the reprint editions that followed post-haste—to the authorship of which Perrault rapidly owned up, having initially tried to pass off the first edition, apologetically, as the work of his son. When the success of Perrault's collection became spectacular, the printers of Paris raced to obtain privileges to publish the similar works, of which a considerable treasure-trove was awaiting their attention.

That change of fortune was very dramatic; it seems probably that *contes de fées* had previously been produced with no real expectation of publication, although Mademoiselle de L'Héritier had included two paradigm examples in a 1696 collection of *Oeuvres meslées* [Miscellaneous Works], buried among poems, historical fiction, essays and letters, and Catherine Bernard had embedded two in her Spanish novella.[2] It seems likely that Madame d'Aulnoy intended to use the same tactic as Bernard when she embedded tales in two *nouvelles espagnoles* of her own, but the packaging must have come to seem irrelevant before she rewrapped the two novellas within a further frame, as they appear in the 1708 Mortier collection and the 1717 *Cabinet*. There seems to be little doubt that the six long *contes de fées* embedded in the three projected volumes of *Le Nouveau bourgeois gentilhomme* were intended to be the selling point for their envelope rather than *vice versa*. That particular enclosure, which includes more wry commentary on the writing of such tales than the earlier portmanteau,

---

[2] Mademoiselle de L'Héritier's two exemplary *contes de fées* are translated in the Black Coat Press collection *The Robe of Sincerity*, and a translation of *Inès de Cordoue* can be found in the Black Coat Press anthology, *The Queen of the Fays*.

leaves no doubt as to the fact that it was difficult for *contes de fées* to be taken seriously even by their own writers, while they were regarded with sneering contempt by most "serious" people, as much because as in spite of the vogue that briefly boosted them to enormous popularity.

There is surely an element of disingenuousness in Madame d'Aulnoy's teasing protestations that her own works in that vein were mere play, essentially slapdash and rather silly, because she certainly poured a great deal of effort into them, and there is a naked determination in her later work not to be outshone by Murat, who was a more careful and more polished writer, and equally imaginative, although not as fluent or as rapid in production. Even if d'Aulnoy's earlier published stores are a trifle casual—but still brilliant in their fashion— her later work is certainly not lacking in application and intensity. If, as seems highly probable—although the order of composition of the works read in salons is impossible to determine—Charles Perrault stole freely from d'Aulnoy as well as L'Héritier and Bernard in shaping his much slighter and somewhat inept tales, it must surely have caused her immense chagrin to see him achieving astonishing popularity with material ineptly recycled from her superior endeavors, while she could not obtain a privilege from the royal censors to publish her own works.

In retrospect, d'Aulnoy and Murat can now be seen as the major contributors to the genre they helped to invent and largely took responsibility for shaping and developing, d'Aulnoy producing twenty-four *contes de fées* for intended, if not actual, publication in eight volumes, and the latter at least twelve, ten of which were published in three volumes in 1698-99, with two more added in 1710.[3] No one else managed to issue more than a single volume. Quantitatively, therefore, d'Aulnoy won the competition, and in terms of subsequent

---

[3] All of the *contes de fées* that Murat is known to have published during her lifetime are translated in the Black Coat Press collection *The Palace of Vengeance.*

popularity she held on to the laurels, although in terms of her influence on the writers of the second wave of production between 1735 and 1755, Murat was probably the more highly esteemed. That aspect of the competition is, however, of minor importance; the most interesting aspect by far is the effect that d'Aulnoy's endeavors had on Murat's, and vice versa. If they had not been consciously and manifestly in competition, listening attentively to one another reading their works and then trying to outshine them, *contes de fées* would not have undergone such a rapid and dramatic evolution, the nature and scope of which can very easily be seen by comparing the earlier stories in the present collection with the later ones, and comparing the six stories in Murat's first two published volumes with the four in the third. Although d'Aulnoy's stories were not necessarily written in the exact order that they appear herein, their sequence must be a close approximation of the order of their composition, and there can be no doubt at all that the stories in volume two of the present set were written later than those in volume one, in a markedly different frame of mind.

The extent of the fad for *contes de fées* and the rapidity of its spread is wryly indicated, albeit satirically exaggerated, in *Le Nouveau bourgeois gentilhomme*, set in d'Aulnoy's Norman homeland and featuring two deluded sisters addicted to the genre, one of whom calls herself Virginie, although her real name is Marie, and the other Marthonide rather than Marthe, in whom it is perhaps possible to find distant ironic echoes of d'Aulnoy and Murat as well as conspicuous echoes of Molière's scathing sexist satires of the salon culture promoted and shaped by Mademoiselle de Scudéry, *Les Précieuses ridicules* (1659) and *Les Femmes savantes* (1672). What the story could not contain, of course, is any comment on the fact that the production and publication of such stories in Paris soon came to a very abrupt end, and that from 1699 onwards, only a tiny handful of stories—five volumes in eighty years—received royal privileges, so that the entire genre was under effective proscription until the 1789 Revolution, and would have vanished entirely but for a trickle of illicit publications, at first unsteady but rebelliously robust for a while between 1735 and 1755.

Exactly why that sharp interruption happened, it is very difficult to determine, but it was certainly not spontaneous; the nascent genre was brutally crushed, and the complete absence of early editions of her works from the world's libraries leaves little doubt that d'Aulnoy was the principal victim, if not the primary target, of the suppression. As well as first editions of two of Murat's three volumes, the single volumes of *contes de fées* issued in 1698 by Mademoiselle de La Force, and two volumes nowadays attributed to Jean de Préchac and the Chevalier of Mailly are all in the Bibliothèque Nationale, but the absence of all eight of d'Aulnoy's alleged 1697-98 editions does occasion some pause to wonder whether other writers might have have been equally unfortunate. Lenglet Du Fresnoy's bibliography only lists one 1698 collection of *contes de fées* that seems to have vanished completely, by the historian Pierre de Lesconvel, which he dismisses as trivial (although he probably had not actually seen it and all other references seem to be copies of his allegation), but it is not impossible that other published volumes had left no detectable trace by 1734.

But what on earth happened to provoke that sudden suppression? What reason could Louis XIV's censors possibly have had for suddenly taking against *contes de fees* and maintaining that hostility for generations thereafter, leaving the genre to maintain a fugitive existence as literary contraband?

The first member of the coterie to suffer manifest persecution was Mademoiselle de La Force, who was banished from Paris even before her own collection appeared in December 1697, sent to a provincial nunnery from which she was not given permission to emerge for sixteen years. Some documentation survives of her protest against that imprisonment, including a letter addressed to the Prince de Conti, who had recently inherited that title from his brother, the late husband of her protectress—who was known as the "dowager" Princess de Conti because the new prince's wife was also a Princesse de Conti. Although La Force protests her innocence vigorously in the letter she does not actually specify what charges had been laid against her, nor does she name the individual responsible for her internment, although the suspicion is inevitably strong that it was probably either the dowager Princess or the Prince.[4]

Madame d'Aulnoy appears to have been the second of the three major writers of *contes de fées* to leave Paris for good, sometime in 1699, but no reliable information appears to be available as to why she left or where she went. Much was made by Charles-Joseph Mayer in the account of Madame d'Aulnoy that he included in volume 37 of the 1786 *Cabinet des fées* of the fact that an alleged friend of hers was executed for attempting to murder her abusive husband, and that the baronne might have feared implication as an accessory—and many subsequent commentaries copied that allegation—but it was mere gossip, and there does not appear to be any real evidence for the suspicion.

The Comtesse de Murat left the capital shortly after d'Aulnoy, having been under investigation for some while by the Lieutenant-General of Police, whose reports survive, and who continued to persecute her after she had left Paris, with the result that she was arrested in 1703 and committed to a state prison (without any formal charge or trial), where she spent the next seven years, only being released when her health had been comprehensively ruined. Why she was under investigation and who instigated the pursuit is unknown, but the Lieutenant-General's reports have survived; they consist

---

[4] The letter, along with the text of *Les Jeux d'esprit*, resurfaced in the mid-nineteenth century, when Louis-Philippe's personal library was sold at auction. It seems likely that both had been handed down from the possession of the Prince de Conti, although what that might imply about his relationship with Mademoiselle de La Force or his sister-in-law it is difficult to assess.

entirely of malevolent gossip, with not a shred of real evidence of any criminal conduct.

At the most, Murat seems to have been suspected of libertinism and lesbianism, but the former is an accusation to which few members of Louis XIV's court could have been immune, and the latter an inevitably vague suspicion. Some such suspicion might also have hung over Mademoiselle de La Force, Mademoiselle de L'Héritier and Catherine Bernard, none of whom ever married, but the "crime" was impossible to specify, let alone to prove, and it is not clear why, even if it were true, anyone should have cared very much. Mademoiselle de Scudéry had been calling herself "Sapho" for nearly fifty years, seemingly without attracting any particular hostility, or even comment. Baronne d'Aulnoy, who had borne six children, would seem to have had a ready-made defense against that particular charge, although the fact that two of her children had been born after her separation from her husband cannot have aided a reputation for virtue, and *Hypolite, comte de Duglas* includes a scene in which the heroine, who has attracted the passionate attentions of a marchionesss while disguised as a man, agrees to put on male attire again, briefly, purely for her benefit—a daring narrative move for the time. The frame story of *Le Nouveau bourgeois gentilhomme* includes some sly implications of lesbian lust on the part of Madame du Rouet and Madame de Lure, but they are not suggestive of anything except an awareness of its existence that must have been commonplace at the time.

It is not difficult to imagine a hypothetical scenario in which the relationships between the dowager Princess de Conti and her confidantes became suspect, and perhaps embarrassing, to the Prince—especially if the relationships in question became troubled—and that the suspicions then extended to the entire coterie, but it seems highly improbable that any such suggestion, no matter how well-founded, could have provoked such a blanket suppression. Mademoiselle de La Force, the Comtesse de Murat and Baronne d'Aulnoy must surely have been suspected of something worse than passionate amity with one another, or with a widowed princess of the blood, in order to provoke such sweeping reprisals. In any case, if their personal conduct was responsible for their exclusion from the court, that could hardly explain the extravagant subsequent persecution of the entire genre to which it belonged, which must have required a more general hostility.

One possibility is that it was not so much suspicions of lesbianism that attracted stern hostility to the salon coterie as suspicions of heresy, which had become subject to severe repression since the revocation of the Edict of Nantes in 1685. The ex-Huguenot Catherine Bernard had converted to Catholicism in order to avoid persecution, and Mademoiselle de La Force was also a convert, but such renegades were always open to the suspicion of merely putting on a show. A more relevant issue might be that the Château de Gudanes, to which d'Aulnoy's mother had fled, and where d'Aulnoy probably spent some time before her return to Paris, had long been the property of a powerful Huguenot family, and might well have served as a refuge for Huguenots fleeing France before and after 1685. It might also be significant, in this context, that one of the key features of the fictional world in which tales of fays are set is that it is utterly devoid of the Roman Church and its deity—with one significant exception.

The one prose tale that Charles Perrault published in advance of his 1697 collection was "La Belle au bois dormant" (tr. as "The Beauty in the Dormant Wood," but usually known in abridged English versions as "The Sleeping Beauty"), the opening sequence of which, when an evil fay gatecrashes an endowment party and sabotages the benevolence of a group of good fays, closely resembles scenes in d'Aulnoy's "Le Prince Lutin" (tr. as "The Sprite Prince") and "Serpentin vert" (tr. as "Green Worm"). Given Perrault's tendency to appropriate material, it seems highly likely that he stole that motif from d'Aulnoy rather than *vice versa*,[5] but either way, the signifi-

---

[5] D'Aulnoy was by no means above borrowing herself; "Finette Cendron" is a deliberate conflation of motifs borrowed

cant difference is that in Perrault's version of the scene the interrupted ceremony is a baptism, and when the princess eventually recovers from suspended animation she is married to the prince by her almoner; in d'Aulnoy's versions, there is no baptism, and no priest. In spite of the presence of fays, therefore, Perrault's tale might well have seemed far less offensive to the bigoted Churchmen in Louis XIV's court than the works of Madame d'Aulnoy, the narrative background of which is blatantly pagan, and in which the most important deity by far is Amour, although the temples at which characters occasionally go to worship are sometimes dedicated to the goddess Diana.

Whether or not the "rules" drawn up for the production of *contes de fées* in the context of the salon game actually specified the rigorous elimination of Christianity from the conventionally-adopted background, it certainly became a significant paradigm feature of such tales. Although the principal motivation for the placing of a new and idiosyncratic version of *fées* at the heart of the genre was undoubtedly feminist, permitting the construction of a hypothetical world in which the most powerful agents of virtue and evil alike are women, the construction of the particular idea of fays employed by the salon writers also avoided, almost entirely, all the ideological baggage associated with the terminology of "witchcraft." D'Aulnoy's mention in a couple of her stories of "the apparatus of the Sabbat," is atypical, and perhaps undiplomatic, although the characterization of her evil fays is blatantly similar to popular conceptions of the typical appearance and conduct of witches.

---

from Mademoiselle de L'Héritier's two paradigmatic tales, and "La Chatte blanche" (tr. as "The White Cat") deliberately recycles motifs from her own work as well as appropriating one from Mademoiselle de La Force, but d'Aulnoy never stooped to mere copying; she always wanted to extrapolate her recycled materials in order to draw more out of them. That cannot be said of Perrault.

The deliberate paganism of *contes de fées* might well have been instituted as a diplomatic move intended to deflect suspicions of Satanism, but if so, it might well have misfired badly, and made the tales seem more slyly suspect, and hence potentially more dangerous, in the eyes of devout readers. The royal censors were, of necessity "professionally devout," and perhaps the wonder is not that Madame d'Aulnoy was refused privileges for the publication of her work in the genre, but that other members of the coterie obtained a few in the wake of Perrault's breakthrough. Perhaps, had La Force and Murat not had the protection of a princess of the blood, at least temporarily, they would not have achieved that.

Given the forceful, if largely tacit, influence of the Church over the philosophy of censorship in the seventeenth and eighteenth centuries, and the inevitable wariness of the licensing bureaucracy in consequence, the taint of heresy is probably the likeliest hypothesis that could account for the almost complete removal of *contes de fées* from the protection of privileged publication. The overt feminism of *contes de fées*, although feeble by modern standards, might also have raised hackles on the part of Churchmen, who were notoriously misogynistic, and it is in that context that suspicions of lesbianism might have become a significant factor, infecting attitudes to the entire genre as well as occasioning particular reactions against its leading practitioners.

In terms of the feminist component of fay mythology, d'Aulnoy was not one of the more extravagant propagandists to begin with. In the early "Gracieuse et Percinet" (tr. as Gracieuse and Percinet") the agent of benevolent enchantment is male, and in "La Belle aux cheveux d'or" (tr. as "The Golden-Haired Beauty") the male hero is aided entirely by talking animals, without a fay in sight. Although the hero of "Le Prince lutin" makes abundant use of a fay gift, once he has received the gift in question, its benevolent donor disappears, and it is left almost entirely to his ingenuity to exploit it. In the fourth story in what was presumably her first collection, "L'Oiseau bleu" (tr. as "The Blue Bird"), which features the first of the grotesquely sadistic fays who were to become such a key feature of d'Aulnoy's work in the genre (Grognon, the archetypal harridan in "Gracieuse et Percinet," is not a fay), much of the magical opposition to the heroine's evil step-mother, repulsive stepsister and the latter's hagwife godmoth-er, is provided by a frankly misogynistic male enchanter, which leaves the poor heroine a trifle short of female support by comparison with many of her peers, until the conclusion of her woes.

That attitude underwent a definitive shift, however, in her later work, and d'Aulnoy eventually provided some of the most extravagant models of female empowerment. In the spec-tacular "La Princesse Carpillon" (tr. as Princess Carpillon") the character identified as "la fée Amazone"—which can be construed either as "the amazon fay" or "the fay [named] Amazone"—functions in much the same fashion as a twenti-eth-century superhero, clad in a shiny costume and popping up when required to save the innocent from seemingly certain disaster, and to slay monsters and villains with her fiery lance. In "Belle-Belle, ou Le Chevalier Fortuné," (tr. as "Belle-Belle; or, The Cavalier Fortuné"), the heroine, clad in male attire, effortlessly outshines her rival knights in the arts of dragon-slaying and seduction, although she does have a harem of male sidekicks, each of them endowed with a particular superhuman talent, at her beck and call. Those examples, and the enterprise of several other heroines featured in volume two of the present set surely make up for the relative dearth of female heroism in volume one.

At no stage in d'Aulnoy's career as a writers of *contes de fées* did her absolute commitment to the ideals of virtue, fideli-ty and altruism waver, and she also offers conspicuous support to the policy of forgiving one's enemies. One might imagine that a reasonable Churchman would approve of that whole-heartedly, but in fact, it is entirely possible that a devout critic would think it pernicious, and dangerous, precisely because the tacit argument of the stories is that Christ and the Christian God are utterly irrelevant to virtuous sentiment and action; the world of the fays is not only a world replete with evil and with appalling actions committed simply for the love of evil, but it is also a world that has no need of assisted redemption, where the crucial opposition to evil is provided entirely by instinctive decency and the effects of a particular, and perhaps peculiar, notion of Amour. In a strict interpretation of Catholic dogma, that is definitely heresy, and no matter how corrupt and licentious Louis XIV's court might have been beneath its ostentatiously polite surface, it had no shortage of outspoken dogmatists and bigots.

Madame d'Aulnoy could easily be seen at the time, as she still can be, as the most extreme promoter of the moral ideology of *contes de fées*, as well as the most prolific. She probably did not set out to be, but she had little alternative to taking up the challenge, simply because she was consciously engaged in a constant competition in extremism. None of the leading writers of *contes de fées*, either during the 1698 boom of the mid-seventeenth century revival seemed to know the meaning of the word "excess" when it came to managing their imaginative extravagance, but no one else was as flamboyant in that excess as d'Aulnoy. Because her work lacked a little of the polish and narrative organization of Murat's, it also lacked Murat's delicacy and discretion, and that could well have been the reason why pious observers apparently drew the conclusion that d'Aulnoy was the most dangerous of an inherently dangerous bunch: the writer whose works ought to be first in the queue for banning or burning. At any rate, their early editions really do seem either to have been aborted before publication or burned afterwards, silently but thoroughly.

By 1734, as Lenglet Du Fresnoy notes, d'Aulnoy was being promoted defensively, in the shadow of Perrault, as a writer primarily fit for reading by children, and the entire genre was often regarded by subsequent commentators in the same light, but in fact, Perrault and Fénelon were the only writers involved in the initial boom who designed their work for the consumption of children, and it is by no means difficult to make out a case for d'Aulnoy's work, in spite of the routine attachment of specific (but highly unconvincing) morals, being blatantly unfit for children from any ideological or esthetic viewpoint. Like almost all of the other members of the coterie, she was a renegade female aristocrat writing tales for the select consumption of other renegade female aristocrats about a world the corrupt glamour of which female aristocrats understood only too well, with a depth of sarcasm that the innocent could not be expected to comprehend.

Madame d'Aulnoy was not the only writer in the genre to feature sadistic fays who take great delight in torturing their victims most extravagantly and most ingeniously, but she set the standard for such horrors with such characters as Carabosse in "La Princesse printanière" (tr. as "Princess Springtime"), Magotine in "Serpentin vert," Lionne in "La Grenouille bienfaisante" (tr. as "The Benevolent Frog") and Grognette in "Le Dauphin." Nor was she the only writer to deal extensively in unrelentingly vicious and murderous ordinary women—mothers and sisters as well as stepmothers and scorned lovers—but no one else matched the sheer nastiness of Duchesse Grognon in "Gracieuse et Percinet", the king's sister in "Belle-Belle, ou Le Chevalier Fortuné," and the queen mother in "La Princesse Belle-Etoile et Prince Chéri" (tr. as "Princess Belle-Etoile and Prince Cheri"). Nor did any other writer take generic work as far into the esoterically perverse realms of surrealism as d'Aulnoy did in the remarkable triptych of tales constituted by "Babiole" (tr. as "Babiole"), "Serpentin vert" and "La Grenouille bienfaisante." In all of that work, innocence, although completely admirable, is something that cannot endure without the aid of miracles: specifically, the miracles provided by fays, whose non-existence thus becomes a tragedy for any reader capable of seeing that tales of faerie—tales of enchantment—are, in their essence, tales of deep and chagrined disenchantment.

It makes far more sense, therefore, to regard d'Aulnoy and Murat as significant writers in the development of Decadent fantasy literature than as writers for children, and one is bound to wonder what they might have done had they been allowed to continue with the process of evolution that they had begun and taken forward with such rapidity. Having already moved from the production of novelettes to novellas, it seems highly likely that one or both of them might have progressed to the writing of full-length novels, or even works of more epic length, with plots of a complexity to match. Given that both writers had extraordinary imaginative range, it is hard to imagine that they would have run out of inspiration any time soon, had they not been violently stopped in their tracks, even without the spur of their ongoing rivalry. It was not to be, however, and we have to be content to be grateful that they contrived to publish as much as they did during their brief window of opportunity, leaving behind fugitive material that could be recovered once worst of the tempest of repression had blown over.

Considered separately Madame d'Aulnoy and the Comtesse de Murat were both great writers of imaginative fiction, but seen as a competitive collective they are surely unique in literary history, and it is as part of that collective endeavor that Madame d'Aulnoy became fully entitled to her classic status, even though her modern reputation is somewhat misrepresentative of her actual ability and achievement. One thing that ought to be borne very much in mind while reading the present collection as that its contents first reached print as literary contraband, which the censors of the day attempted with the legal might at their disposal to suppress and annihilate, as a dangerous encouragement to freethinking—but it survived, and thrived in spite of that, and to some extent because of it. It deserves to be considered in that light, and not as a set of "fairy stories" fit for children.

All the translations were made from the versions contained in of volumes 2-4 of the 1786 *Cabinet des fées* reproduced on the Bibliothèque Nationale's *gallica* website.

Brian Stableford

PRINCESS CARPILLON

There was once an old king who, to console himself for a long widowhood, married a beautiful princess whom he loved very much. He had a son from his first wife, hunchbacked and cross-eyed, who felt a great deal of chagrin at his father's second marriage. *The quality of unique son*, he said to himself, *made me dreaded and loved, but if the young queen has children, my father, who can dispose of his realm, will no longer consider than I am the eldest; he will disinherit me in their favor.* He was ambitious, full of malice and dissimulation, with the consequence that, without giving any evidence of his anxiety, he went secretly to consult a fay who was reputed to be the most skillful in the world.

As soon as he appeared, she divined his name, his quality and what he wanted of hr. "Prince Bossu," she said to him—that was the name by which he was known—"you have come too late; the queen is pregnant with a son. I can't do him any harm, but if he dies or something happens to him I promise you that I'll prevent her from having any others."

That promise consoled the hunchback slightly; he implored the fay to remember it, and made the resolution to do his little brother a bad turn as soon as he was born.

After nine months the queen had a son, the most beautiful in the world, and it was remarked, as an extraordinary thing, that he had the form of an arrow imprinted on his arm. The queen loved her little infant to such an extent that she wanted to nurse him herself, by which Prince Bossu was very annoyed, because the vigilance of a mother is much greater than that of a nurse, and it is much easier to deceive the latter than the former.

However, the hunchback, who was thinking of nothing but making his coup, testified an attachment for the queen and a tenderness for the little prince, by which the king was charmed. "I would never have believed," he said, "that my son was capable of such good nature, and if he continues, I'll leave him a part of my kingdom."

Those promises were not sufficient for the hunchback; he wanted all or nothing, with the consequence that one evening, he presented the queen with some jam that contained opium. She fell asleep; immediately, the prince, who had hidden behind the tapestry, took the little prince very quietly, and put in his place a large cat, carefully swaddled, in order that the nursemaids would not perceive his theft. The cat cried, the nursemaids rocked it; eventually, it made such a strange racket that they thought it wanted to suckle.

They woke the queen who was still asleep, and, thinking that she was holding he dear baby, gave it her breast; but the malevolent cat bit it. She uttered a loud scream, and looked at it. What became of her when she perceived the head of a cat instead of that of her son? Her dolor was so intense that she nearly expired right away.

The noise of the queen's women woke the entire palace. The king put on his dressing-gown and run to her apartment. The first thing he saw was the cat, wrapped up in gold sheets that his son ordinarily had; it had been thrown to the ground and was making an astonishing racket. The king, very alarmed, asked what it signified, and he was told that no one understood anything, but that the little prince was not there, that they had searched in vain, and that the queen was badly wounded.

The king went into her bedroom; he found her in an unparalleled affliction, and, not wanting to augment it with his own, he controlled himself violently in order to console the poor princess.

Meanwhile, the hunchback had given his little brother to a man who was entirely his. "Take him into a distant forest," he said, "and put him, completely naked, in the place most exposed to ferocious beasts, so that he'll be devoured and no more mention will be heard of him. I'd take him there myself, so fearful am I that you won't carry out my commission well, but it's necessary that I appear before the king. Go, then, and be sure that if I reign, I won't be an ingrate."

He put the poor child into a covered basket personally, and as he was accustomed to caress him, the baby already knew him, and smiled at him, but the pitiless hunchback was less moved by that than a rock. He went promptly to the queen's room, almost undressed—by virtue, he said, of being in such haste—rubbing his eyes like a man still asleep, and when he learned the bad news of his stepmother's wound and the theft of the prince and saw the swaddled cat, he uttered cries to dolorous that everyone was also occupied in consoling him, as if he had really been very afflicted. He took the cat and wrung its neck with a ferocity that was very natural to him; he made it understood, however, that it was only because of the bite it had given the queen.

No one suspected him, even though he was malevolent enough to have done it; his crime was hidden under his feigned tears. The king and queen were grateful to that ingrate, and charged him with sending word to all the fays to ask what might have become of their child. In his impatience to put an end to the search he brought back several different and very enigmatic responses, which all agreed on one point: that the prince was not dead, that he had only been abducted for a time, for impenetrable reasons; that he would be brought back perfect in all ways; and that it was necessary not to search for him any longer, because the efforts would be futile. He judged that they would be tranquilized by that, and he judged correctly. The king and queen flattered themselves with recovering their son one day.

Meanwhile, the bite that the cat had inflicted on the queen's breast became so poisoned that she died of it, and the king, overwhelmed by dolor, remained in his palace for an entire year, always waiting for news of his son, but waiting for it in vain.

The man who had taken him away walked all night without stopping; when dawn began to appear, he opened the basket, and the amiable infant smiled at him, as he had been accustomed to do to the queen when she took him in her arms.

"Poor little prince," he said, "how unfortunate your destiny is, alas! You shall serve as fodder, like a tender lamb, for some hungry lion. Why did the hunchback choose me to aid him in dooming you?"

He closed the basket again in order no longer to see that object worthy of pity; but the child who had gone all night without feeding, started to cry with all his might. The man who was carrying him picked some figs and put them in his mouth. The sweetness of the fruit appeased him slightly, so he carried him all day until the following night, when he entered a vast and somber forest. He did not want to go into it deeply, for fear of being devoured himself, but the next day he advanced, with the basket, which he was still holding.

The forest was so large that, in whichever direction he looked, he could not see the end of it, but he perceived, in a place covered with trees, a rock that rose up in several different pinnacles. *That, no doubt,* he said to himself, *is the retreat of the cruelest beasts; it's necessary to leave the child there, since I'm not in a position to save him.* He approached the rock; immediately, an eagle of prodigious size emerged to fly around it, as if there was something dear to it there. In fact, it was its chicks that it was nourishing in the depths of a kind of grotto.

"You'll serve as prey for those birds, which are the kings of the others, poor child," the man said. Immediately, he unwrapped the baby and laid him in the middle of three eaglets. Their nest was large, sheltered from the insults of the air; he had a great deal of difficulty putting the prince inside because the side from which it could be approached was very steep and inclined over a frightful precipice. He drew away, sighing, and saw the eagle returning rapidly to its nest.

"There, it's done," he said. "The child will lose his life."

He drew away diligently, in order not to hear his last screams. He returned to the hunchback and assured him that he no longer had a brother.

At that news the barbaric prince embraced his faithful minister and gave him a diamond ring, assuring him that when he was king he would be the captain of his guards.

The eagle, having returned to her nest, was perhaps surprised to find that new guest there. Whether she was surprised or not, however, she observed the rights of hospitality better than many people have done. She placed herself next to her nursling, extended her wings over him and warmed him; it seemed that all her cares were now only for him; a particular instinct engaged her to go in search of fruits, to peck them and to pour the juice into the vermilion mouth of the little prince; in sum, she nourished him so well that the queen, his mother, could not have nourished him any better.

When the eaglets were a little stronger, the eagle took them one by one, sometimes on her wings, sometimes in her claws, and thus accustomed them to gazing at the sun without closing their eyelids. The eaglets sometimes quit their mother and flew a little way on their own, but for the little prince here was none of that, and when she lifted him into the air he ran a great risk of falling and being killed. Fortune mingled on that; it was her who had furnished him with such an extraordinary nurse, and it was her who made sure that she did not let him fall.

Four years passed thus. The eagle lost all her eaglets; they flew away when they were big enough; they no longer came back to see their mother and their nest. As for the prince, who did not have the strength to go far, he stayed on the rock, for the eagle, far-sighted and fearful, being apprehensive that he might fall into the precipice, took him to the other side, to a place so narrow that the wild beasts could not get into it.

Amour, who is depicted as perfect, was less so than the young prince; the ardor of the sun could not tarnish the lilies and roses of his complexion; all his features had something so regular that the most excellent painters would not have been able to imagine their like; his hair was already long enough to cover his shoulders, and his manner was so elevated that nothing more noble and grandiose has ever been seen in a child. The eagle loved him with a surprising passion. She only brought him fruits for his nourishment, making that species of difference between him and her eaglets, to whom she gave nothing but raw flesh.

She desolated all the shepherds in the surrounding area, stealing their lambs mercilessly; there was no talk of anything but the eagle's rapine. Finally, fatigued by nourishing her at the expense of their flocks, they resolved between them to search for her retreat. They split up into several groups, followed her with their eyes, and explored the mountains and valleys; they could not find her for a long time, but finally perceived that she alighted on the big rock.

The most determined among them tried to climb it, although there were a thousand perils. At that time she had two little eaglets that she nourished carefully, but however dear they were to her, her tenderness was still greater for the young prince, because she had seen him for a longer time.

When the shepherds had found her nest, as she was not there, it was easy for them to tear it to pieces and take everything there was inside. What became of them when they found the prince! There was something so extraordinary in that discovery that their limited minds could not comprehend it at all.

They took away the child and the eaglets; all of them cried. The eagle heard them, and came to swoop down on the thieves of her property. They would have felt the effects of her anger if they had not killed her with an arrow launched by one of the shepherds. The young prince, utterly ingenuous, seeing his nurse fall, uttered pitiful cries and wept bitterly.

After that expedition the shepherds matched toward their hamlet. On the way they performed a cruel ceremony, of which this was the subject.

That country had long served as a retreat for ogres. Everyone, desperate by virtue of such a dangerous proximity, had sought a means of driving them away without being able to succeed; the terrible ogres, angered by the hatred testified against them, redoubled their cruelties, and ate, without exception, all those who fell into their hands.

Finally, one day, when the shepherds had assembled in order to deliberate as to what they could do against the ogres, a man of frightful size appeared in their midst; half of his body had the form of a deer covered with blue fur, with the feet of a goat; he had a club over his shoulder and a buckler in his hand. "Shepherds," he said to them, "I am the Blue Centaur; if you will give me a child every three years, I promise to bring a hundred of my brothers here, who will make rude war on the ogres, whom we shall drive away, no matter what they do.

The shepherds had difficulty engaging themselves to do something so cruel, but the most venerable among them said. "Well, my companions, is it more useful to us that the ogres eat our fathers, our children and our wives every day? We would lose one in order to save several; let us not refuse the offer that the Centaur has made us, then." Immediately, everyone consented; they engaged themselves, with great oaths, to keep their word to the Centaur, and that he would have a child.

He departed and came back, as he had said, with his brothers, who were as monstrous as him. The ogres were no less brave than cruel; they delivered several combats, in which the centaurs were always victorious, finally forcing them to flee. The Blue Centaur came to demand the recompense for his pains; everyone said that nothing was more just, but when it was necessary to deliver the promised child there was no family that could resolve to give up theirs; the mothers hid their children in the bosom of the earth.

The centaur, who did not appreciate mockery, after having waited for twice twenty-four hours, told the shepherds that he intended that they would give him as many children as the days that he remained among them, with the consequence that the delay cost them six little boys and six little girls. Since that time, the great affair had been regulated; every three years there was a solemn fête to deliver the poor innocent to the Centaur.

It was the day after the prince had been taken from the eagle's nest that the tribute was due to be paid, and although the child had already been chosen, it is easy to understand that the shepherds gladly put the prince in his place; the uncertainty of his birth—for they were so simple that they sometimes believed that the eagle was his mother—and his marvelous beauty, determined them absolutely to present him to the Centaur, because he was so delicate that he did not want to eat children that were not very pretty.

The mother of the child that had been destined for him passed suddenly from the horrors of death to the joys of life; she was charged with ornamenting the little prince, as she would have done for her son; she combed his long hair well, gave him a crown of little red and white roses, which ordinarily came from the bushes, and dressed him in a long, trailing robe of fine white cloth, with a girdle of flowers.

Thus clad, he was marched at the head of several children that were to company him; but how can I describe the air of grandeur and nobility that already shone in his eyes? Having never seen anything but eagles, and being still at such a tender age, he appeared neither fearful nor savage; it seemed that all the shepherds were only there to please him.

"Oh, what a pity!" they said to one another. "What! That child is going to be devoured! Can we not save him?" Several wept, but in the end, it was impossible to do otherwise.

The Centaur was accustomed to appear on top of a rock, his club in one hand and his buckler in the other, and from there, in a terrible voice, he cried to the shepherds: "Leave me my prey and retire." As soon as he perceived the child he had been brought, he began to celebrate, and, shouting so loudly that the mountains trembled, he said in his terrible voice: "That's the best meal I've ever had in my life; I won't need salt or pepper to crunch that little lad."

The shepherds and shepherdesses cast their eyes on the poor child and said to one another: "The eagle has spared him, but this is the monster that will end his days." The oldest of the shepherds took him in his arms, kissed him several times and said: "Oh, my child, my dear child, I don't know you, and I sense that I haven't seen enough of you. Is it necessary that I witness your funeral? What is Fortune doing, then, to have protected you from the sharp claws and the hooked beak of the terrible eagle, since she is delivering you today to the carnivorous teeth of that horrible monster?"

While the shepherd was moistening the pink cheeks of the prince with the tears flowing from his eyes, the tender innocent passed his little hands through his gray hair, smiling in an infantile fashion, and the more pity he inspired, the less diligent the shepherd appeared to be in advancing.

"Hurry up!" cried the hungry Centaur. "If you make me come down and come to meet you, I'll eat more than a hundred."

In fact, impatience gripped him; he stood up and was whirling his club, when a huge ball of fire appeared in the air, surrounded by an azure cloud. As everyone remained attentive to such an extraordinary spectacle, the cloud and the globe descended slowly and opened. A diamond chariot immediately emerged, drawn by swans, in which there was one of the most beautiful women in the world. She had a helmet of pure gold on her head, covered by white plumes; the visor was raised and her eyes were shining like the sun. Her body, covered by a rich armor, and her hand, armed with a lance made entirely of fire, marked clearly enough that she was an amazon.

"What, shepherds!" she cried. "Have you the inhumanity to give such a child to the cruel Centaur? It is time to free yourselves from your word; justice and reason oppose such barbaric customs; have no fear of the return of the ogres; I will protect you from them. I am the Amazon Fay, and from this moment on I take you under my protection."

"Oh, Madame," cried the shepherds and shepherdesses, extending their hands to her, "that is the greatest good fortune that we could have."

They could not say any more, for the furious centaur challenged her to combat. He was rude and stubborn; the fiery lance burned him in every place that it touched him, and he uttered horrible cries, which only ended with his life. He fell, completely roasted; one might have thought that he was a collapsing mountain, so much noise did his fall make. The frightened shepherds had hidden, some in the nearby forest, others in the depths of rocks that had fissures, from which they could see without being seen.

It was there that the sage shepherd who was holding the little prince in his arms had taken refuge, far more anxious about what might happen to that lovely child than to everything regarding himself or the members of his family, although they merited that consideration.

After the death of the Centaur, the Amazon Fay took a trumpet, which she sounded so melodiously that the sick people who heard it got up full of health, and others felt a secret joy, the reason for which they could not express.

Eventually, the shepherds and shepherdesses reassembled to the sound of the harmonious trumpet. When the Amazon Fay saw them, in order to reassure them entirely she advanced toward them in her diamond chariot, gradually lowering it until it was only three feet from the ground. It was floating on a cloud to transparent that it seemed to be made of crystal.

The old shepherd, who was known as Sublime, appeared, clasping the little prince at his neck.

"Approach, Sublime," the fay shouted to him. "Have no fear; I want peace to reign in future in this place, and for you to enjoy the repose of which you came here in search. But give me that poor child, whose adventures have already been so extraordinary."

The old man, after having bowed profoundly to her, raised his arm and put the prince in hers. When she had him, she gave him a thousand caresses. She embraced him; she sat him on her knees, and spoke to him, although she knew that he did not did not understand any language and could not speak. He uttered cries of joy or dolor; he uttered sighs and accents that were not articulated, but he had never heard anyone speak.

Meanwhile, he was utterly dazzled by the Amazon Fay's brilliant armor. He climbed up from her knees in order to reach and touch her helmet. The fay smiled at him and said, as if he could understand her: "When you are in a state to bear arms, my son, I will not let you lack them."

After she had given him more great caresses, she returned him to Sublime. "Sage old man," she said to him, "you are not unknown to me, but do not disdain to give your cares to this child; teach him to scorn the grandeurs of the world and to put himself above the blows of fortune; he might have been born to have sufficient splendor, but I intend that he will be happier in being sage than in being powerful. The felicity of men ought not to consist in external grandeur alone; to be happy, it is necessary to be sage, and to be sage, it is necessary to know oneself, to know how to limit one's desires, to be content in mediocrity as in opulence, to seek the esteem of men of merit, not to scorn anyone, and always to be ready to quit without chagrin the possessions of this unfortunate life. But what am I thinking, venerable shepherd? I am telling you things that you know better than I do, and it is also true that I am saying them less for you than for the other shepherds who are listening to me. Adieu pastors, adieu shepherds; call upon me in your needs; the same lance and the same hand that have just exterminated the Blue Centaur will always be ready to protect you."

Sublime and all those who were with him, as confused as they were delighted, could not make any response to the obliging words of the Amazon Fay; in the trouble and joy they were in, they prostrated themselves humbly before her, and while they were kneeling, the globe of fire rose up slowly into the middle region of the air and disappeared, along with the Amazon and the chariot.

At first, the fearful shepherds dared not approach the Centaur; dead as he was, they nevertheless feared him. Finally, however, they were gradually emboldened, and resolved between them that it was necessary to built a great pyre and reduce him to ashes, for fear that his brothers, informed of what had happened to him, might come to avenge his death upon them. That opinion having been approved, they did not waste a moment, and delivered themselves thus of the odious cadaver.

Sublime carried the little prince into his cabin; his wife was ill therein, and his two daughters had not been able to quit her in order to come to the ceremony.

"Look, shepherdess," he said. "Here is a child cherished by the gods and protected by the Amazon Fay; it is necessary to regard him in future as our son and give him an education that can render him happy."

The shepherdess was delighted by the present that he gave her; she took the prince on her bed. "At least," she said, "if I cannot give him the great lessons he will receive from you, I can bring him up in his infancy and cherish him like my own son."

"That is what I ask of you," said the old man; and with that he gave him to her.

His two daughters ran to see him; they were charmed by his incomparable beauty and the graces that appeared in the rest of his little person. From that moment on they began to teach him their language, and no intelligence as quick and lively had ever been seen; he understood the most difficult things with a facility that astonished the shepherds, with the consequence that he was soon sufficiently advanced only to receive further lessons from Sublime.

The sage old man was in a state to give him good ones, for he had been the king of a good and flourishing realm, but a usurper, his neighbor and his enemy, had conducted secret intrigues successfully and gained certain restless spirits, who rebelled and furnished him with the means to surprise the king and his family. He had them imprisoned in a fortress where he wanted to let them perish in poverty.

Such a strange change did not prevail over the virtue of the king and the queen; they suffered all the outrages that he tyrant inflicted upon them with constancy, and the queen, who was pregnant when those disgraces occurred, gave birth to a daughter, whom she nursed herself; she already had two others, both very amiable, who shared her troubles as much as their age permitted them.

Eventually, after three years, the king gained one of the guards, who agreed with him to bring a small boat that he could use to traverse the lake in the middle of which the fortress was built. He furnished them with files to cut through the iron bars of their chambers, and ropes to descend therefrom. They chose a very dark night; everything went smoothly and without noise, and the guard helped them to slide down the walls, which were fearfully high.

The king descended first, then his two daughters, then the queen, and then the little princess in a large basket; but alas, it had been poorly attached, and they heard it fall suddenly into the lake. If the queen had not fainted from dolor, she would have awakened the entire garrison with her cries and laments.

The king, penetrated by that accident, searched as much as was possible in the obscurity of the night; he even found the basket and hoped that the princess would be inside, but she was no longer there, with the consequence that he started rowing in order to save himself and the rest of his family. They found horses ready on the shore of the lake, which the guard had brought there in order to carry the king wherever he wanted to go.

During his imprisonment the king and the queen had had time to moralize and to find that the greatest possessions of life are very small, when they are appreciated at their true value; that, combined with the new disaster that had just happened to them in losing their little girl, made them resolve not to seek shelter among the neighboring kings who were their allies, where they might perhaps have been a burden. Having made their decision, they established themselves in a fertile plain, the most agreeable of all those they could have chosen. In that location, the king exchanged his scepter for a crook, bought a large flock, and became a shepherd.

They built a little rustic cottage sheltered on one side by the mountains and situated on the other on the bank of a stream rich in fish. In that place they found themselves more tranquil than they had ever been on the throne. No one envied their poverty, they had no fear of traitors or flatterers; their days went by without chagrin, and the king often said: "Oh, if men could cure themselves of ambition, how happy they would be! I have been a king and am now a shepherd; I prefer my cabin to the palace where I reigned."

It was under that great philosophy that the young prince studied; he did not know his master's rank, and the master did not know the birth of his disciple, but the former king saw inclinations in the child so noble that he could not believe that he was an ordinary child. He remarked with pleasure that he almost always put himself at the head of his comrades, with an air of superiority that attracted their respect; he formed little armies incessantly; he built forts and attacked them.

Eventually, he went hunting, and confronted the greatest perils, whatever representation the royal shepherd could out to him. All those things persuaded the Sublime that he had been born to command. But while he is growing up and attaining the age of fifteen years, let us return to the court of the king, his father.

Prince Bossu, seeing his father already old, had almost no more regard for him; he became impatient waiting for such a long time for the succession. In order to console himself he requested an army in order to conquer a neighboring realm whose inconstant people were holding out their hands to him. The king agreed, on condition that, before his departure, he witnessed a document that he wanted all the lords of his realm to sign, to the effect that if the prince, his younger brother, ever returned, and that it could be ascertained that it was him, especially if the arrow marked on his arm was found, he would be the sole heir of the crown.

The hunchback not only wanted to witness the ceremony, he wanted to subscribe to the document, although his father thought that too hard to demand of him. As he believed himself to be certain of the death of his brother, however, he was not risking anything, and intended to make the most of that proof of his complaisance, with the result that the king assembled the estates, harangued them, shed many tears in speaking about the loss of his son, softened the hearts of all those who were listening to him, and after having signed and made the most notable sign, he ordered that the act should be put in the royal treasury and several authentic copes should be made in order that it should be remembered.

Then Prince Bossu took his leave of him, in order to go at the head of a fine army to attempt the conquest of the kingdom to which he had been summoned; and after several battles he killed his enemy with his own hand, took the capital city, left garrisons and governors everywhere and returned to his father, to whom he presented a young princess named Carpillon, whom he had brought back as a captive.

She was so extraordinarily beautiful that everything that nature had formed previously and everything that the imagination as able to depict did not approach her. On seeing Carpillon, the king was charmed, and the hunchback, who had seen her some time ago, had become so amorous that he had not had a moment of repose; but as much as he loved her, she hated him. As he only spoke to her as a master, and always reproached her that she was his slave, she felt her heart so opposed to his harsh manners that she did not neglect any opportunity to avoid him.

The king gave her an apartment in his palace and women to serve her; he was touched by the misfortunes of such a young and beautiful princess. When the hunchback told him that he wanted to marry her he replied: "I consent to that, on condition that she has no repugnance for it, for it seems to me that when you are with her, her expression is very melancholy."

"That is because she loves me," said the hunchback, "and dares not let it show; the constraint she is in embarrasses her. As soon as she is my wife, you will see her content."

"I want to believe it," said the king, "but are you not flattering yourself a little too much?"

The hunchback was very offended by his father's doubts.

"You are the cause, Madame," he said to the princess, "of the king showing me a harshness in his conduct that is not ordinary to him. Perhaps he loves you; tell me that sincerely, and choose between us the one that pleases you more; provided that I see you reign, I will be satisfied." He spoke thus in order to know her sentiments, for it was not that he had any design to change his own.

Young Carpillon, who did not know yet that the majority of lovers are cunning and deceitful animals, fell into the trap. "I confess to you, Sire," she said to him, "that if I were the mistress of it, I would not choose either the king or you, but if my ill fortune has subjected me to that harsh necessity, I prefer the king."

"And why?" replied the hunchback, controlling himself.

"Because," she added, "he is gentler than you, he reigns at present, and perhaps he will not live as long."

"Ha ha, little rascal," cried the hunchback, "you want my father in order to be the dowager queen in a short time; you certainly shall not have him. He isn't thinking of you; it's me that has that generosity—a generosity, to tell the truth, poorly employed, for you have an insupportable depth of ingratitude—but even if you were a hundred times more ungrateful, you will be my wife."

Princess Carpillon realized, but a little too late, that it is sometimes dangerous to say what one thinks, and in order to repair what she had just spoiled, she said to him: "I wanted to know your sentiments; I'm very glad that you love me enough to resist the harshness that I have affected. I esteem you already, Sire, work to make yourself loved."

The prince fell head first into the trap, crude as it was, but one is ordinarily stupid when one is very amorous, and one has a tendency to flatter oneself that is difficult to correct. Carpillon's words rendered him gentler than a lamb; he smiled, and squeezed her hands to the point of bruising them.

As soon as he had quit her she ran to the king's apartment and threw herself at his feet. "Protect me, Sire," she said to him, "from the greatest of misfortunes. Prince Bossu wants to marry me; I confess that he is odious to me. Do not be as unjust as him; my rank, my youth and the disgraces of my house merit the pity of a king as great as you."

"Beautiful princess," he said, "I am not surprised that my son loves you; that is a law common to all those who see you; but I would never pardon him for lacking the respect that he owes you."

"Oh, Sire," she said, "he regards me as his prisoner and treats me as his slave."

"It is with my army," replied the king, "that he vanquished the vanquisher of the king, your father; if you are a captive, you are mine, and I render your liberty to you, glad that at my advanced age, my white hair protects me from becoming your slave."

The grateful princess gave the king a thousand thanks and withdrew with her women.

The hunchback, however, having learned what had just happened, resented it keenly, and his fury increased when the king forbade him to think about the princess until he had rendered her services so essential that she could not help wishing him well.

"I would have to labor all my life, and perhaps uselessly," he said. "I don't like to waste my time"

"I'm sorry about that, for love of you," replied the king, "but it won't be in another manner."

"We shall see," said the hunchback, insolently, as he left the room. "You intend to take my prisoner from me; I would rather lose my life."

"The person you call your prisoner was mine," added the irritated king. "She is free now; I want to render her mistress of her destiny without making it depend on your caprice."

A conversation so sharp might have gone a long way if the hunchback had not made the decision to withdraw; he conceived at the same time the desire to render himself master of the kingdom and the princess. He had made himself loved by his troops while he had commanded them, and seditious spirits willingly seconded his evil designs, with the result that the king was warned that his son was working to dethrone him, and, as he was the stronger, the king had no other course to take than that of placating him.

He sent for him, and said to him: "Is it possible that you are ingrate enough to want to snatch the throne from me and set yourself upon it? You see me on the brink of the tomb; don't advance the end of my life; have I not had great enough displeasures by virtue of the death of my wife and the loss of my son? It's true that I'm opposed to your designs for Princess Carpillon; I'm thinking of you in that as much as her, for can one be happy with a person who doesn't love you? But since you want to run the risk, I consent to everything. Give me time to speak to her in order to resolve her to her marriage."

The hunchback wanted the princess more than the kingdom, for he already enjoyed the one he had just conquered, so he told the king that he was not as avid to reign as he believed him to be, since he had signed the act himself that would disinherit him if his brother returned, and that he would contain himself in respect provided that he married Carpillon.

The king embraced him and went to find the poor princess, who was in strange alarm as to what had been decided. She still had her governess with her; she took her into her cabinet and said to her, weeping bitterly: "Is it possible that after giving me his word, the king has the cruelty to sacrifice me to the hunchback? Certainly, my dear friend, if it is necessary for me to marry him, my wedding day will be the last of my life, for it is not so much the deformity of his person that displeases me as the evil qualities of his heart."

"Alas, my princess," the governess replied, "you are doubtless unaware that the daughters of the greatest kings are victims, whose inclination is almost never consulted; if they marry an amiable and well-made prince they can thank hazard for it; but between one ape and another, there is no thought of anything but the interests of the state."

Carpillon was about to reply when she was told that the king was waiting for her in her chamber. She raised her eyes to the heavens in order to request some aid.

As soon as she saw the king it was unnecessary for him to explain what he had resolved; she knew well enough, for she had an admirable penetration, and the beauty of her mind even surpassed that of her person.

"Oh, Sire," she cried, "What are you going to announce to me?"

"Beautiful princess," he said to her, "don't regard your marriage to my son as a misfortune; I implore you to consent to it with a good grace. The violence he is doing to your sentiments marks the ardor of his own well enough. If he did not love you he would have found more than one princess would have been delighted to share with him the kingdom that he already has and the one that he expects after my death. But he only wants you; your disdain and your scorn have not deterred him, and you ought to believe that he will not neglect anything to please you."

"I flattered myself that I had found a protector in you," she replied, "but my hope has been deceived; you are abandoning me, but the gods, the just gods, will not abandon me."

"If you knew everything I have done to protect you from this marriage," he added, "you would be convinced of my amity. Alas, Heaven had given me a son that I loved dearly; his mother nursed him; he was stolen from his cradle one night and a cat put in his place, which bit her so cruelly that she died of it. If that lovable child had not been stolen from me, he would now be the consolation of my old age; my subjects would fear him and I would have offered you my kingdom with him; the hunchback, who has now made himself master of it, would be fortunate if he were suffered at the court. I lost that lovable son, Princess, and that misfortune extends as far as you."

"It is me alone," she replied, "who has caused what has happened; since his life would have been useful to me, I have given him death. Sire, regard me as culpable; think of punishing me rather than marrying me."

"You were not in a state, beautiful princess," said the king, "to do either good or harm to anyone; I do not accuse you either of my disgraces, but if you do not want to augment them, prepare yourself to receive my son well, for he has rendered himself the strongest here, and he might put on a bloody play for you."

She only replied with tears. The king quit her, and as the hunchback was impatient to know what had happened, the king found him in his chamber, and told him that Princess Carpillon consented to her mirage and that he would give the orders necessary to render the ceremony solemn.

The prince was transported by joy; he thanked the king, and immediately sent in quest of all there were of lapidaries, merchants and embroiderers. He bought the most beautiful things in the world for his mistress and sent her large gold baskets filled with a thousand rarities.

She received them with some appearance of joy; afterwards, he came to see her and said to her: "Would you not be very unfortunate, Madame Carpillon, had you refused the honor that I wanted to make you? For, not to mention that I am lovable enough, people find that I have a great deal of intelligence, and I will give you so many clothes, so many diamonds and so many beautiful things that there will be no queen in the world like you."

The princess replied coldly that the misfortunes of her house permitted her less than any other to adorn herself and that she asked him, therefore, not to make her such great presents.

"You would be right," he said, "not to adorn yourself, if I had not given you permission, but you must think of pleasing me. Everything will be ready for our marriage in four days; amuse yourself, Princess, and give orders, since you are already the absolute mistress here."

After he had quit her, she shut herself away with her governess, and told her that she could choose between furnishing her with the means to run away, or those of killing herself on her wedding day. After the governess had represented to her the impossibility of flight and the weakness there was in killing herself in order to avoid the misfortunes of life, she tried to persuade her that virtue could contribute to her tranquility, and that without loving the hunchback recklessly, she esteemed him sufficiently to be content with him.

Carpillon did not yield to any of her remonstrations. She told her that until now she had counted on her, but that she knew how things stood; that if everyone else failed her she would not fail herself; and that to great ills it was necessary to apply great remedies. After that, she opened the window and looked out of it from time to time without saying anything.

Her governess, who was afraid that the desire might take her to throw herself out of it, threw herself at her knees and, looking at her tenderly, said: "Very well, Madame, what do you want of me? I will obey you, even at the expense of my life."

The princes embraced her, and told her that she begged her to buy her the clothes of a shepherdess and a cow, in order that she could escape to wherever she could; that it was necessary for her not to amuse herself trying to deflect her from her design, because it would be waste of time, and that she had scarcely had any; that it was also necessary, in order that she could get away, to coif a doll and lay it in her bed, and to say that she was ill.

"You can see clearly, Madame," the poor governess said to her, "to what I am exposing myself. Prince Bossu will have no doubt that I have seconded your design; he will inflict a thousand torments on me, in order to learn where you are, and then he will have me burned or flayed alive. Say after that that I do not love you."

The princess was very embarrassed. "I want you to run away yourself two days after me," she replied. "It will be easy for you to deceive everyone until then."

Finally, they agreed sufficiently that the same night, Carpillon had the costume and a cow.

All the goddesses descended from the heights of Olympus, those that went to find the shepherd Paris and twelve hundred others, would have appeared less beautiful in that rustic garment; she departed alone by moonlight, sometimes leading the cow on a rope, sometimes having it carry her. She went at hazard, dying of fear; if the slightest wind agitated the bushes, if a bird emerged from its nest or a hare from its form, she thought thieves or wolves were about to end her life.

She walked all night, and wanted to walk all day, but her cow stopped in order to graze in a meadow, and the princess, fatigued by her crude clogs and the weight of her coarse gray dress, lay down in the grass beside a stream, where she took off her bonnet of yellow cloth in order to pin up her blonde hair, which was escaping on all sides, falling in curls all the way to her feet.

She looked to see whether anyone could see her, in order to hide very quickly, but whatever precaution she took, she was surprised by a lady clad in full armor, except for her head, from which she had removed a golden helmet covered in diamonds.

"Shepherdess," she said to her, "I'm weary, would you care to draw me some milk from your cow in order to slake my thirst?"

"Gladly, Madame," replied Carpillon, "if I had a vessel in which to put it."

"Here is a cup," said the warrior. She presented her with a beautiful porcelain; but the princess did not know what to do in order to milk her cow.

"What!" said the lady. "Has your cow no milk, or do you not know how to milk her?"

The princess started to weep, being utterly ashamed to appear maladroit before such an extraordinary person. "I confess to you, Madame," she said, "that I have not been a shepherdess for long. My only concern is to take my cow to pasture; my mother does the rest."

"You have your mother, then," the lady continued. "What does she do?"

"She's a farmer's wife," said Carpillon.

"Near here?" added the lady.

"Yes, the princess replied, again.

"Truly, I feel affection for her, and am grateful to her for have given the light of day to such a beautiful daughter. I want to see her; take me there."

Carpillon did not know what to respond; she was not accustomed to lying, and she did not know that she was talking to a fay. Fays were not as common in those days as they have since become. She lowered her eyes; her complexion was covered with a vivid blush. Finally, she said: "Once I have left for the fields, I dare not return until the evening. I beg you, Madame, not to oblige me to annoy my mother, who might perhaps maltreat me if I do otherwise than she wishes."

"Oh, Princess, Princess," said the fay, smiling, "you cannot sustain a lie, nor play the character that you have taken on, if I do not help you. Look, here is a bouquet of wallflowers; be certain that as long as you are holding it, the hunchback you are fleeing will not recognize you. Remember, when you are in the great forest, to ask the shepherds who take their flocks there where Sublime lives. Go to him, tell him that you have come the part of the Amazon Fay, who begs him to put you with his wife and daughters. Adieu, beautiful Carpillon; I have been your friend for a long time."

"Alas, Madame," cried the princess, "how can you abandon me, since you know me, you love me and I have so much need of your help?"

"The bouquet of wallflowers will not fail you," she replied. "My moments are precious; it is necessary to let you fulfill your destiny."

As she finished speaking she disappeared from Carpillon's sight; the princess was so frightened that she nearly died of it.

After having recovered somewhat, she continued on her way. She had no idea where the great forest was, but she said to herself: *That clever fay, who appears and disappears, who knows me in the costume of a peasant, will guide me to where she wants me to go.*

She kept hold of her bouquet whether she was walking or when she stopped; but she did not get very far, her delicacy seconding her courage poorly. As soon as she found stones she stumbled; her feet were bleeding; it was necessary for her to lie down in the shelter of a few trees. She feared everything, and often thought, with a great deal of anxiety, about her governess.

It was not without reason that she thought about that poor woman; her zeal and fidelity had few examples. She had coiffed a large doll with the princess's night-cap; she had put it in fontanges and fine linen; she went about very quietly in her chamber, fearful, she said, of disturbing her; and as soon as anyone made any noise she scolded everyone.

Someone went to tell the king that the princess was ill; that did not surprise him; he attributed the cause to her displeasure and the violence that she was doing to herself. But when the hunchback heard the bad news he felt an inconceivable chagrin; he wanted to see her; the governess had a great deal of difficulty preventing him from doing so.

"At least," he said, "let my physician see her."

"Oh, Sire," she cried, "it wouldn't need any more to make her die; she hates physicians and remedies. But don't be alarmed; she only needs a few days' rest. It's a migraine that will pass while she sleeps."

She obtained thus that he would not disturb her mistress and left the doll in the bed. But one evening, when she was preparing to flee because she had no doubt that the impatient prince would make further attempts to enter, she heard him at the door, like a furious madman who was about to break it down without waiting for her to open it.

What had driven him to that violence is that one of the princess's women had perceived the deceit and, fearing to be maltreated, she had gone promptly to inform the hunchback. The excess of his anger is indescribable. He ran to the king, thinking that he was party to it, but by the surprise he saw on his face he realized that he knew nothing about it.

As soon as the poor governess appeared he threw himself upon her and seized her by the hair. "Return Carpillon to me," he said to her, "or I'll rip out your heart."

She only responded by tears, and, prostrating herself at his knees she implored him in vain to hear her. He dragged her personally to the depths of a dungeon, where he would have stabbed her a thousand times if the king, who was as good as his son was evil, had not obliged him to let her live in that frightful prison.

The amorous and violent prince ordered that the princess be pursued on land and sea; he departed himself and ran in all directions like an insensate. One day, when Carpillon was sheltering under a large rock with her cow because the weather was frightful, and the thunder, lightning and hail were making her tremble. Prince Bossu, who was soaked, along with all those accompanying him, came to take refuge under the same rock.

When she saw him so close to her, alas, he frightened her even more than the thunder; she took her bouquet of wallflowers in both hands, so fearful was she that ne might not be sufficient, and, remembering the fay, she said: *Don't abandon me, charming amazon.*

The hunchback looked at her. "What have you to fear, decrepit old woman?" he said. "If the thunder killed you, what harm would it be doing you? Are you not on the brink of the grave?"

The young princess was no less delighted than astonished to hear herself called old. *Doubtless*, she said to herself, *my little bouquet is operating marvelously*; and in order not to enter into conversation, she pretended to be deaf.

The hunchback, seeing that she could not hear him, told his confidant, who never abandoned him: "If I had a slightly more cheerful heart, I'd take that old woman up to the summit of the rock and throw her off, to have the pleasure of seeing her break her neck, for I'd find nothing more agreeable."

"But Sire," he scoundrel replied, "if it will give you pleasure, I'll take her there, wiling or not; you'll see her body bouncing like a balloon over all the points of the rock, and the blood would flow all the way to you."

"No," said the prince, "I don't have the time; I need to continue searching for the ingrate who is making all the misfortune of my life."

As he finished speaking, he spurred his horse and drew away at full tilt. It is easy to judge the joy that the princess felt, for assuredly, the conversation he had just had with his confidant was very appropriate to alarm her. She did not forget to thank the Amazon Fay, whose power she had just experienced.

Continuing her journey, she arrived in the plain where the pastors of the country had built their little houses; they were very pretty, each one had its garden and its spring. The valley of Tempe and the banks of the Lignon had nothing more elegant. The shepherdesses were mostly beautiful, and the shepherds did not neglected anything to please them; all the trees were engraved with a thousand different monograms and amorous verses. When she appeared they quit their flocks and followed her respectfully, for they were prejudiced by her beauty and by an extraordinary air of majesty; but they were surprised by the poverty of her garments. Although they led a simple and rustic life, they prided themselves nevertheless on being very neat.

The princess begged them to direct her to the house of the shepherd Sublime; thy hastened to escort her there. She found him sitting in a valley with his wife and daughters; a little river ran at their feet, making a soft murmur; he was holding marine rushes with which he was rapidly weaving a basket to contain fruit. His wife was spinning and his two daughters fishing with lines.

When Carpillon approached them she felt movements of respect and tenderness by which she was surprised, and when they saw her they were so emotional that they changed color several times. Saluting them humbly, she said: "I'm a poor shepherdess who has comes to offer you my serves on the part of the Amazon Fay, whom you know. I hope that consideration for her will enable you to be kind enough to receive me in your home."

"My daughter," said the king, standing up and saluting her in his turn, "that great fay has reason to believe that we will honor her perfectly; you are very welcome, and even if you had no other recommendation than what you bear with you, our house would certainly be open to you."

"Approach, beautiful girl," said the queen, extending her hand to her. "Come, let me embrace you; I feel full of good will for you, I want you to regard me as your mother and my daughters as your sisters."

"Alas, my good mother," said the princess, "I do not merit that honor; it is sufficient for me to be your shepherdess and to guard your flocks."

"My daughter," said the king, "we are all equal here; you have come on too good a part for there to be any difference between you and our children. Come and sit down next to us, and leave your cow to graze with our sheep."

She made some difficulty, still obstinate in saying that she had only come to be a servant; she would have been embarrassed if she had been taken at her word, but in truth, it was sufficient to see her to judge that she was made more to command than to obey, and it was hardly credible that a fay of the importance of the Amazon would have protected an ordinary person.

The king and the queen looked at her with an astonishment mingled with admiration difficult to comprehend. They asked her whether she had come very far. She said yes. Did she have a father and mother? She said no; and to all their questions, she only replied with monosyllables, to the extent that respect would permit.

"And what is your name, my daughter?" asked the queen.

"My name is Carpillon," she said.

"That's a singular name," said the king. "Unless some adventure has given rise to it, it's rare to have a name like that."

She made no reply, and picked up one of the queen's spindles in order to unwind the thread from it.

When she showed her hands they thought that she was drawing two snowballs out of her sleeves, so dazzling were they. The king and the queen exchanged a knowing glance, and said to her: "You coat is very warm, Carpillon, for the weather we're having and your clogs are very hard for a child like you. It's necessary for you to dress like us."

"My mother," she replied, "people dress like this in my country; as soon as it pleases you to order me to do it, I'll dress differently."

They admired her obedience, and especially the air of modesty that appeared in her beautiful eyes and throughout her face.

Supper time having come, they got up and all went into the house together. The two princesses had caught some nice little fish, and there were fresh eggs, milk and fruits.

"I'm surprised," said the king, "that my son hasn't returned; his passion for hunting takes him further than I'd like, and I always fear that some accident might happen to him."

"I fear that too," said the queen, "but if you agree, we'll wait for him to have supper with us."

"No," said the king. "It's necessary to refrain from that; on the contrary, I beg you, when he returns let no one speak to him and let everyone show him a great deal of coldness."

"You know his good nature," said the queen. "That's capable of giving him so much pain that it will make him ill."

"I can't do otherwise," said the king. "It's necessary to correct him."

They sat down at table, and some time before they left it, the young prince came in. He had a roe deer round his neck, his hair was damp with sweat and his face was covered with dust. He was leaning on a short spear that he usually carried. His bow was attached to his side, and his quiver full of arrows to the other. In that state he had something so noble and proud in his face and his bearing that one could not see him without attention and respect.

"Mother," he said, addressing the queen, "the desire to bring you this roe deer has made me run the mountains and plains today."

"My son," said the king, gravely. "You were seeking to give us anxiety rather than to please us; you know all that I have already said to you about your passion for hunting, but you're not in a humor to correct yourself."

The prince blushed, and what caused him additional chagrin was to see a young woman he did not know in the house. He replied that, another time, he would return at a better hour, or that he would not go hunting, no matter how much he wanted to do so.

"That's sufficient," said the queen, who loved him with an extreme tenderness. "Thank you for the present you've brought me, my son; come and sit down beside me and sup, for I'm sure that you don't lack appetite."

He was a little disconcerted by the serious manner in which the king had spoken to him and hardly dared raise his eyes, for he was intrepid in dangers but he was docile and very timid with those he ought to respect. He recovered from his trouble, though, sat down next to the queen, and cast his eyes upon Carpillon, who had not waited as long to look at him.

As soon as their eyes met, their hearts were so stirred that they did not know to what to attribute that disorder. The princess blushed and lowered her eyes; the prince continued to gaze at her. Then she raised her eyes slowly upon him, and kept them there for a long time. They were both in a mutual surprise and thought that nothing in the world could equal what they were seeing.

Is it possible, the princess said to herself, *that of so many people I have seen at court, not one approaches this young shepherd?*

How does it come about, he thought in his turn, *that this marvelous girl is a simple shepherdess? Oh, why am I not a*

*king, to set her on the throne, to render hr mistress of my es-
tates, as she would be of my heart?*

While dreaming, he was not eating. The queen, who
thought it was the pain of being poorly received, strove to caress him; she even brought him exquisite fruits of which she
was very fond. He invited Carpillon to taste one of them. She
thanked him but declined, and he, without thinking of the hand
that had given them to him, left them coldly on the table and
said "That's all I can do with them, then."

The queen did not notice, but the elder princess, who did
not hate him and would have loved him very much but for the
difference she believed there to be between his condition and
hers, remarked it with a sort of chagrin.

After supper, the king and the queen retired. The princesses ordinarily did what there was to be done in the little
household; one went to milk the cow, the other to make
cheese. Carpillon hastened to work too, following the example
of the others, but she was not so accustomed to it. She did
nothing worthwhile, with the result that the two princesses
called her, laughing, "the maladroit beauty," but the prince,
already amorous, helped her. He went to the spring with her;
he carried her pitchers for her, drew her water, and came back
fully laden, because he did not want her to carry anything.

"But what are you doing, shepherd?" she said to him. "Is
it necessary that I play the demoiselle here? Having worked all
my life, have I come to this plain to repose?"

"You can do whatever you please, lovely shepherdess,"
he said to her, "But don't deny me the pleasure of accepting
my feeble help in these sorts of occasions."

They came back together more promptly than he would
have liked, for although he hardly dared talk to her, he was
delighted to find himself with her."

They both spent an unquiet night, of which their inexpe-
rience prevented them from divining the cause; but the prince
waited impatiently for the hour when he would see the shepherdess again, and she already feared the one when she would
see the shepherd again. The new disturbance into which the

sight of him had cast her was some diversion from the other displeasures by which she was overwhelmed; she thought so often about him that she thought less about Prince Bossu.

Why, bizarre fortune, she thought, *have you given so many graces, good looks and charm to a young shepherd who is destined to guard his flock, and so much malice, ugliness and deformity to a great prince destined to govern a kingdom?*

Carpillon had not had the curiosity to look at herself since her metamorphosis from princess to shepherdess, but now a certain desire to please obliged her to look for a mirror. She found the one the princesses used, and when she saw her coiffure and her costume she was utterly confused.

"What a sight!" she exclaimed. "What do I look like? It isn't possible that I remain buried in this coarse fabric any longer." She took water, with which she washed her face and hands; they became whiter than lilies. Then she went to find the queen, and putting herself on her knees before her, she presented her with an admirable diamond ring—for she had brought precious stones—and said: "My good mother, I found this ring a long time age; I don't know it's value but I think it might be worth a little money. I beg you to receive it as proof of my gratitude for the charity you have for me. I also beg you to buy me clothes and underwear in order that I can resemble the shepherdesses of this region."

The queen was surprised to see such a beautiful ring in the possession of the young woman. "I want you to keep it," she said, "and not to accept it. In any case, you will have his very morning all you need."

In fact, she sent to small town that was not far away, and was brought the prettiest peasant girl costume that had ever been seen. The bonnet and the shoes completed the outfit; thus clad, she appeared more charming than the dawn.

The prince, for his part, had not neglected himself. He had put a cordon of flowers on his hat; the sash to which his basket was attached and his crook were ornamented by them; he brought a bonnet to Carpillon and presented it to her with the timidity of a lover. She received it with an embarrassed expression, although she had infinite intelligence.

As soon as she was with him she hardly spoke, and was always pensive; he was no less so. When he went hunting, instead of pursuing the hinds and the fallow deer he encountered, if he found a spot appropriate to think about the charming Carpillon, he suddenly stopped and remained in the solitary place, composing a few verses and singing a few couplets for his shepherdess, talking to the rocks, the woods and he birds. He had lost the good humor that made him search with the urgency of all shepherds.

However, as it is difficult to love a great deal and not to fear that which one loves, he was apprehensive to such a degree if irritating his shepherdess by declaring to her what he felt for her that he dared not speak to her, and all though she remarked well enough that he preferred her to all the others, and that that preference ought to assure her of his sentiments, she was nevertheless pained sometimes by his silence, and sometimes she was also glad of it.

If it's true that he loves me, she said to herself, *how could I receive such a declaration? By taking offense, I might cause him to die; by not taking offense, I would have reason to die myself of shame and dolor. What, born a princess, I could listen to a shepherd! Oh, unworthy weakness, I shall never consent to that! My heart ought not to change by virtue of the change in my costume, and I already have too many things or which to reproach myself since I came here.*

As the prince had a thousand natural charms in his voice, and perhaps, if he had sung less well, the princess, prejudiced in his favor, would have listened to him anyway, she often engaged her to sing her little songs; and everything he sang had such a tender character, his accents were so touching, that she could not help listening to him. He had composed words that he sang to her incessantly, of which she knew perfectly well that she was the subject:

Ah, if it were possible

That some other divinity
Could equal you in beauty,
And offered me the world to render me sensible
I would believe myself fortunate
To scorn her gifts in order to offer you my prayers.

Although she pretended not to pay any more attention to that one than the others, she accorded it nevertheless a preference that gave the prince pleasure. That inspired him to a little more boldness. He went expressly to a spot on the bank of the river shaded by willows and service trees. He knew that Carpillon took her lambs there every day. He took a graver and he wrote in the bark of a small tree:

In vain in this refuge
I see peace reign over all pleasures;
Where can I have a tranquil moment?
Amour himself draws sighs from me here.

The princess surprised him as he finished engraving those words; he affected to appear embarrassed, and after a few moments of silence, he said: "You see an unfortunate shepherd who laments the most insensible things, woes about which he ought only to complain to you."

While he was speaking she turned over in her mind the manner in which she ought to take what she heard from a mouth to which she was not indifferent, and her prejudice engaged her voluntarily to excuse him.

He does not know my birth, she told herself. *His temerity is pardonable; he loves me, he believes that I am not above him; even if he knew my rank, do not the gods, who are so elevated, want the hearts of man? Are they annoyed because they are loved?*

"Shepherd," she said to him, when he had ceased talking. "I feel sorry for you; that is all I can do for you, for I do not want to love; I have enough misfortunes already. Alas, what would be my fate if, to complete my disgrace, my sad days came to be troubled by an engagement?"

"Ah, shepherdess," he cried, "say rather that if you have some pains, nothing would be more appropriate to soothe them; I would share them all, my unique care would be to please you; you could repose on me the care of your flock."

"I wish to Heaven," she said, "that I only had that cause of anxiety."

"How can you have others," he said, in an urgent manner, "being so beautiful, so young, without ambition, not knowing the vain grandeurs of the court? But doubtless you love here; a rival renders you inexorable for me."

As he pronounced those words he changed color; he became sad; that idea tormented him cruelly.

"I have to agree," she said, "that you have a hated and abhorred rival; you would never have seen me without the necessity I had of fleeing his pressing pursuits."

"Perhaps, shepherdess," he said, "you would flee me in the same way, for if you only hate him because he loves you, I am in your regard the most hateful of all men."

"Either I do not believe that," she replied, "or I look at you more favorably, for I sense that I would not go as far to draw away from you than I have to get away from him."

The shepherd felt transported by joy by such obliging words, and from that day on she spared no cares to please the princess. He spent every morning searching for the most beautiful flowers in order to make garlands for her; he garnished her crook with ribbons of a thousand different colors. He did not leave her exposed to the sun; as soon as she came with her flock along the river bank or through the wood he bent branches, attached them together and made her covered arbors in which the grass immediately formed natural seats. All the trees bore his monograms; he engraved verses there that spoke of nothing but the beauty of Carpillon.

He only sang about her; and the young princess saw all that evidence of the passion of the young shepherd, sometimes with pleasure and sometimes with anxiety. She loved him, without knowing it very well; she dared not even examine herself in that matter, for fear of discovering sentiments that were too tender; but when one has that dread, is one not already certain of what one dreads?

The attachment of the young shepherd for the young shepherdess could not be secret; everyone perceived it; they applauded it. Who could have criticized it, in a place where everyone loved? People said that to look at them, they were born for one another; that they were both perfect; that they were a masterpiece of the gods that fortune had confided to their little country, and that it was necessary to do everything possible to retain them there.

Carpillon felt a secret joy in hearing the universal applause in favor of a shepherd she found very likeable, and when she came to think about the difference in their conditions, she was chagrined, and proposed to herself not making herself known, in order to leave more liberty to her heart.

The king and the queen, who loved her extremely, were not sorry about that nascent passion. They regarded the prince as if he had been their son, and all the perfections of the shepherdess charmed them no less than him.

"Was it not the Amazon who sent her to us?" they said to one another. "And was it not her who came to battle the Centaur in favor of the child? Doubtless that sage fay has destined them for one another; it is necessary to await her orders in order to follow them."

Things were in that state—the prince was still lamenting the indifference of Carpillon, because she hid her sentiments from him carefully—when, having gone hunting, he was unable to avoid a furious bear, which, emerging suddenly from the depths of a rock, threw itself upon him and would have devoured him if his skill had not seconded his valor. After having struggled for a long time on the summit of a mountain, they rolled to the bottom without quitting one another.

Carpillon had stopped in that place with several of her companions; they could not see what was happening up above,

and what became of those young women when they perceived
a man who seemed to be precipitating himself with a bear?
The princess recognized her shepherd immediately; she uttered screams full of fear and dolor; all the shepherdesses fled,
and she remained the sole spectator of the combat. She even
dared to thrust the iron of her crook boldly into the maw of the
terrible animal, and amour, redoubling her strength, gave her
sufficient to be of some help to her lover.

When he saw her, the dread of making her share the peril
he was running augmented his courage to such a point that he
no longer thought of preserving his own life provided that he
could guarantee that of the shepherdess. In fact, he killed the
bear almost at her feet, but he fell himself, half-dead by virtue
of two wounds that he had received.

Oh, what became of her when she perceived his blood
flowing and staining his garments? She could not speak; her
face was instantly covered in tears. She had leaned his head on
her knees, and, suddenly breaking silence, she said: "Shepherd, if you die, I shall die with you. In vain I have hidden my
secret sentiments from you; know them, and know that my life
is attached to yours."

"What greater good could I wish for, beautiful shepherdess!" he cried. "Whatever happens to me, my fate will always
be fortunate."

The shepherdesses who had fled returned with several
shepherds, whom they had told what they had just seen. They
helped the prince and the princess, for she was scarcely less ill
than him. While they were cutting tree branches to make a
kind of stretcher, the Amazon Fay suddenly appeared in their
midst.

"Don't worry," she said to them. "Let me touch the
young shepherd."

She took him by the hand, and, putting her golden helmet
on her head, she said to him: "I forbid you to be ill, dear shepherd."

Immediately, he stood up, and the raised visor of the
helmet allowed an entirely martial expression to be seen on his

face, and sharp and brilliant eyes that responded well to the hopes that the fay had conceived.

He was astonished by the manner in which she had just cured him, and the majesty that appeared throughout her person. Transported by admiration, joy and gratitude, he threw himself at her feet. "Great fay," he said to her, "I was dangerously wounded; a single one of your gazes, a word from your mouth has cured me, but alas, I have a wound in the depths of my heart of which I do not want to be cured; deign to soothe it and render my fortune better, in order that I might share it with this beautiful shepherdess."

The princess blushed, hearing him speak thus, for she was aware that the Amazon Fay knew her, and feared that she might criticize her for allowing such hope to a lover so far below her. She dared not look at her; sighs escaped her exciting the fay's pity.

"Carpillon," she said to her, "this shepherd is not unworthy of your esteem, and you, shepherd, who desire a change in your estate, know that a very great one will arrive very shortly."

She disappeared, as usual, as soon as she had pronounced those words. The shepherds and shepherdesses who had run to help them conducted them as if in triumph all the way to the hamlet; they had put the lovers in the middle of their company, and crowned them with flowers to mark the victory that they had just won over the terrible bear, which they bought after them. They sang these words about the tenderness that Carpillon had testified to the prince:

> *In these forests everything enchants us,*
> *We are going to see happy days!*
> *A shepherd, by his charming beauty,*
> *Will arrest here the daughter of the Amours.*

They arrived thus at Sublime's house, to whom they related everything that had happened, the courage with which the shepherd had defended himself against the bear, the generosity with which the shepherdess had aided him in the combat, and finally, what the Amazon Fay had done for him. The king, delighted by the story, ran to tell the queen.

"Undoubtedly," he said, "this boy and this girl have nothing vulgar about them; their eminent perfections, their beauty and the cares that the Amazon Fay takes in their favor designate something extraordinary."

The queen suddenly remembered the diamond ring that Carpillon had given her. "I always forgot," she said, "to show you a ring that the young shepherdess put in my hands with an air of uncommon grandeur, begging me to accept it and to furnish her for that with clothes such as are worn in this country."

"Is the stone beautiful?" asked the king.

"I only looked at it for a moment," said the queen, "but here it is. She presented the ring to him, and as soon as he cast his eyes upon it he cried: "O gods, what do I see? Have you not recognized a possession that I received from your hands?" At the same time he pushed a little spring, of which he knew the secret. The diamond was lifted up and the queen saw her portrait, which she had had painted for the king, and which she had attached to the neck of her little daughter to play with while she nursed her in the tower.

"Oh. Sire," she said, "What strange adventure is this? It renews all my dolors; but let us speak to the shepherdess, it's necessary to know more."

She called her, and said to her: "My daughter, I have awaited until now a confession from you, which would have even us a great deal of pleasure, if you had wanted to make it without being pressed, but since you continue to hide from us who you are, it is only just to tell you that we know it, and that the ring you gave me has enabled us to solve the enigma."

"Alas, my mother," replied the princess, putting herself on her knees in front of her, "it was not for lack of confidence that I was obstinate in hiding my rank from you; I believed that you would have difficulty in seeing a princess in the state I was in. My father was the King of the Peaceful Isles; his reign was troubled by a usurper, who confined him in a tower with the queen, my mother. After three years of captivity, they found the means to escape; a guard helped them.

"They lowered me in a basket by the favor of the darkness, but the rope broke; I fell into the lake, and without me knowing how I did not drown, fishermen who were extending their nets to catch carp found me enveloped in them. My size and weight persuaded them that I was one of the most monstrous carp in the lake; their hopes were disappointed when they saw me; they thought about throwing me back in the lake to nourish the fish, but finally, they left me in the nets and took me to the tyrant, who knew immediately by the flight of my parents that I was an unfortunate little princess abandoned of all aid. His wife, who had lived for some years without children, had pity on me; she took me in and raised under the name of Carpillon; perhaps she had the design of making me forget my birth, but my heart has always told me who I was, and that it is sometimes unfortunate to have sentiments so little in conformity with fortune.

"At any rate, a prince known as the hunchback came to conquer from my father's usurper the kingdom that he was enjoying tranquilly. The change of tyrant rendered my destiny even worse. The hunchback took me away as one of the most beautiful ornaments of his triumph and resolved to marry me against my will. In such a violent extremity I made the decision to flee, all alone, dressed as a shepherdess and leading a cow. Prince Bossu, who was searching for me everywhere would undoubtedly have recognized me if the Amazon Fay had not generously given me a bouquet of wallflowers capable of protecting me from my enemies.

"She rendered me an office no less charitable in addressing me to you, my good mother," the princess continued, "and if I have not declared my rank to you sooner, it is not because of a lack of confidence, but only with a view to sparing you chagrin. It is not that I am complaining; I have only known repose since the day when you received me in your home, and

I confess that the rural life is so mild and innocent that I would have no difficulty in preferring it to the one I led at court."

As she was speaking with vehemence, she did not notice that the queen had dissolved in tears and that the king's eyes were also very moist, but as soon as she had finished they both hastened to clasp her in their arms. They retained her there for a long time without being able to pronounce a single word. She was emotional too; she began to weep in their example, and it is not easy to describe the agreeable and dolorous sensations that passed between those three illustrious unfortunates.

Finally, the queen, making an effort, said to her: "Is it possible, dear child of my soul, that after so many regrets or your catastrophic loss, the gods have rendered you to your mother to console her in her disgrace? Yes, my daughter, you see the bosom that has borne you and nourished you in your most tender youth. This is the man from whom you obtained the light of day. O light of our eyes! O princess that wrathful Heaven stole from us, with what transports can we solemnize your blissful return!"

"And I, my illustrious mother and my dear queen," cried the princess, prostrating herself at her feet, "by means of what terms, and what actions, can I make known to you both all that the respect and love that I owe you makes me feel! What! I have found you, dear refuge of my woes, when I no longer dared flatter myself that I would ever see you again?"

Then the caresses were redoubled between them, and they spent several hours thus. Carpillon retired thereafter; her father and mother forbade her to speak about what had just happened; they were apprehensive of the curiosity of the local shepherds, and although they knew that the majority were rather coarse, it was to be feared that they might penetrate mysteries that were not made for them.

The princess did not say anything to indifferent individuals, but she could not keep the secret from her young shepherd; what means is there of keeping silent when one is in love? She had reproached herself a thousand times for having concealed her birth from him. *What obligation would he not owe me*, she said to herself, *if he knew that, being born on the throne, I am lowering myself as far as him? But alas, how little difference amour puts between the scepter and the crook! Can that chimerical grandeur, of which we are so proud, fill our soul and satisfy it? No; virtue alone has that right; it puts us above the throne and detaches us from it; the shepherd who loves me is sage, intelligent and amiable; what can a prince have above him?*

As she abandoned herself to her reflections, she saw him at her feet; he had followed her to the river bank, and, presenting her with a garlands of flowers, the variety of which was charming, he said: "Where have you been, beautiful shepherdess? I've already been searching for you for hours and waiting for you with impatience."

"Shepherd," she said to him, "I have been occupied with a surprising adventure; I would reproach myself for not telling you about it, but remember that this mark of my confidence demands an eternal secrecy. I am a princess, my father was a king, and I have just found him, in the person of Sublime."

The prince was so troubled and confused by that news that he did not have the strength to interrupt her while she told him her story with the utmost good will. What subjects did he not have to dread? The sage shepherd who had raised him might refuse him his daughter, since he was a king, or she, reflecting on the difference there was between a great princess and him, might distance herself one day from the initial generosity she had shown him.

"Oh, Madame," he said to her, sadly, "I'm a doomed man; it's necessary that I renounce life. You were born on the throne, you have found your nearest relatives, whereas I'm a wretch who knows no country or fatherland. An eagle served as my mother, her nest as a cradle. If you have deigned to cast a few favorable glances upon me, they will be turned away in future."

The princess thought for a moment without replying to what he had just said; then she took a pin that was retaining a part of her beautiful hair and she wrote on the bark of a tree: *Do you love a heart that loves you?*

The prince immediately engraved the line: *With thousands of fires I am inflamed?*

The princess put below them: *Enjoy the supreme good fortune of loving, and you will be loved.*

Transported by joy, the prince threw himself at her feet and, taking one of her hands, he said: "You flatter my afflicted heart, adorable princess, and by virtue of these new bounties, you conserve my life; remember what you have just written in my favor."

"I am not capable of forgetting it," she said to him, graciously. "Rely on my heart; it is more in your interests than mine."

Their conversation with undoubtedly have lasted longer if they had had more time, but it was necessary to bring back the flocks they were leading, and they hastened to return.

Meanwhile, the king and the queen had conferred together as to the conduct they ought to adopt with regard to Carpillon and the young shepherd. So long as she had been unknown to them, they had approved of the nascent fires that had ignited in their souls; the perfect beauty with which Heaven had endowed them, their intelligence, the grace with which all their actions were accompanied had made them with that their union might be eternal, but they looked at it with a different eye when they envisaged that she was their daughter and that the shepherd was doubtless an unfortunate who had been exposed to wild beasts to spare the care of nourishing him. Finally, they resolved to tell Carpillon that she should no longer maintain the hopes with which he had flattered himself, and that she should declare to him seriously that she did not want to establish herself in the country.

The queen summoned her very early and spoke to her with a good deal of kindness; but what words are capable of calming such a violent disturbance? The young princess tried in vain to constrain herself; her face, sometimes covered with a bright redness and sometimes paler than if she were on the point of death, and her eyes, extinguished by sadness signified al to clearly what state she was in. Oh, how she regretted the confession she had made! However, she assured her mother, with a great deal of submission, that she would follow her orders. Having retired, she hardly had the strength to throw herself on her bed, where she dissolved in tears, uttering a thousand laments and a thousand regrets.

Finally, she got up in order to take her sheep to the pasture, but instead of going toward the river she plunged into the wood, where, lying down on the moss, she supported her head, and started thinking profoundly.

The prince, who could not be in repose where she was not, ran to find her; he suddenly appeared before her. At the sight of him she uttered a loud cry, as if she had been surprised, got up precipitately, and drew away from him without looking at him. He was bewildered by conduct so unusual; he followed her and stopped her.

"Beautiful shepherdess," he said to her, "do you want, in causing my death, to rob yourself of the pleasure of seeing me expire before your eyes? You have changed for your poor shepherd; you no longer remember what you promised yesterday."

"Alas," she said, looking at him sadly, "alas, of what crime are you accusing me? I am unfortunate; I am submissive to orders that it is not permitted to me to elude; pity me, and go away from all the places where I shall be; it is necessary."

"It is necessary!" he cried, putting his hands together with an expression full of despair. "It is necessary that I flee you divine princess! Can an order so cruel and so unmerited by pronounced to me by you? What do you expect to become of me? Can the flattering hope to which you permitted me to abandon myself be extinguished without my losing my life?"

Carpillon, as afflicted as her lover, let herself fall, devoid of a pulse and a voice. At that sight, he was agitated by a thousand different thoughts; the state that his mistress was in told him clearly enough that she had had no part in the orders that had been given to her, and that certainty diminished his displeasures somewhat.

He did not waste a moment in helping her. A spring that flowed slowly through the undergrowth furnished him with water to throw in the face of the shepherdess, and the amours that were hiding behind a bush told their little comrades that he dared to steal a kiss. At any rate, she soon opened her eyes; then, pushing her lovable shepherd away, she said: "Flee, get away from me. If my mother came, would she not have reason to be annoyed?"

"It is necessary, then, that I leave you to be devoured by the bears and the wild boars?" he said. "Or, during a long faint, alone in this solitary place, that some viper comes to bite you?"

"It is necessary to risk everything," she said, "rather than displeasing the queen."

While they were having that conversation, in which there was so much tenderness and concern, the fay, their protectress, suddenly appeared in the king's bedroom. She was armed as usual; the precious stones with which her breastplate and her helmet glittered less than her eyes. Addressing the queen, she said: "You are scarcely grateful, Madame, for the gift I made you in returning your daughter to you, who would have drowned in the nets but for me, since you are on the point of causing the death of the shepherd I confided to you. Do not think any longer about the difference there might be between him and Carpillon; it is time to unite them." To the king she said: "Think, illustrious Sublime, about their marriage; I wish it, and you will never have reason to repent of it."

With those words, without awaiting their response, she quit them; they lost sight of her, and only remarked after her a long trace of light similar to sunbeams.

The king and the queen were equally surprised; thy even felt joy that the fay's orders were so positive. "There can be no doubt," said the king, "that the unknown shepherd is of a birth appropriate to Carpillon; his protectress has too much nobility to want to unite two people who are not suited to one another.

She is the one, as you see, who saved our daughter from the lake in which she would have perished; by what right have we merited her protection?"

"I have always heard it said," replied the queen, "that there are good and evil fays, that they take families in amity or in aversion, in accordance with their genius, and apparently that of the Amazon Fay is favorable to us."

They were still talking when the princess returned; her expression was dejected and afflicted. The prince, who had only dared to follow her at a distance, arrived some time afterwards, so melancholy that it was sufficient to look at him to divine a part of what was happening in his soul. Throughout the meal, the poor lovers, who made the joy of the house, did not say a word, not even daring to raise their eyes.

As soon as the meal was over the king went into his little garden, and told he shepherd to come with him. At that order the shepherd went pale; an extraordinary frisson ran through his veins, and Carpillon thought that her father was about to send him away, with the result that she had no less apprehension than him.

Sublime went into an arbor; he sat down, gazing at the prince. "My son," he said, "you know with what love I have brought you up; I have kept you as a present from the gods to sustain and console my old age, but what will prove my amity more is the choice I have made of you for my daughter Carpillon. She is the one of whom you have sometimes heard me deplore the loss; Heaven, which has returned her to me, wants her to be yours, and I want it too, with all my heart. Will you be the only one who does not want it?"

"Oh, my father," cried the prince, putting himself at his feet, "Dare I flatter myself with what I am hearing? Am I fortunate enough that your choice falls on me, or do you only want to know the sentiments I have for that beautiful shepherdess?"

"No, my dear son," said the king, "don't float between hope and dread. I'm resolved to make the marriage in a matter of days."

"You are heaping me with benefits," the prince replied, embracing his knees, "And if I am explaining my gratitude poorly, the excess of my joy is the cause of it."

The king obliged him to get up; he made him a thousand amities, and although he did not mention the grandeur of his rank, he let him glimpse that his birth was far above the state to which fortune had reduced him.

But the unfortunate Carpillon had had no repose, because she had not gone into the garden after her father and her lover; she was watching them from afar, hidden behind some trees. When she saw him at the king's feet she thought he was begging him not to condemn him to such a rude expulsion, with the result that she did not want to know any more.

She fled into the depths of the forest, running like a fawn pursued by dogs and hunters. She had no fear either of the ferocity of wild beasts or the thorns that scratched her on all sides. The echoes repeated her sad plaints; it seemed that she was only seeking death, when her shepherd, impatient to tell her the good news that had just been announced to him, hastened to follow her.

"Where are you, my shepherdess, my lovely Carpillon?" he cried. "If you can hear me, don't flee; we're going to be happy!"

As he pronounced those words, he perceived her in the depths of a valley, surrounded by several hunters who were trying to put her on horseback behind a little hunchbacked and ill-made man. At that sight, and the cries of his mistress, calling for help, he advanced more rapidly than a forcefully unleashed arrow; having no other weapons than his sling, he launched a shot so accurate and terrible at the man who was abducting his shepherdess that he fell from his horse with a frightful wound in his head.

Carpillon fell too; the prince was already beside her, trying to defend her against her abductors, but all his resistance was futile; they captured him, and would have killed him on the spot if Prince Bossu—for it was him—had not made a sign to his men to spare him. "Because," he said, "I want to make him die under several different tortures."

They contented themselves, therefore, with binding him with stout cords, and the same cords also served for the princess, in such a manner that they could talk to one another.

A stretcher was made to carry away the malevolent hunchback. As soon as they had finished, they all departed, without any of the shepherds having seen the misfortune of the young lovers, in order to render an account of it to Sublime.

It is easy to judge his anxiety when he did not see them return at nightfall. The queen was no less alarmed. Several days passed with all the shepherds in the region searching for them in vain and mourning them.

It is necessary to know that Prince Bossu had not forgotten Princess Carpillon; time had only weakened his idea. When he was not diverting himself by committing a few murders and cutting the throats indifferently of all those who displeased him, he went hunting, and sometimes did not come back for a week. He was on one of those long hunting expeditions when he suddenly saw the princess crossing a path. Her dolor had so much vivacity, and she was paying such scant attention to what might happen to her that she had not taken the bouquet of wallflowers, with the result that he recognized her as soon as he saw her.

"Oh, of all misfortunes, the greatest misfortune," the shepherd whispered to his shepherdess, "is that we were reaching the fortunate moment of being united forever." He told her what had happened between Sublime and him.

It is easy to comprehend Carpillon's regrets. "So I am going to cost you your life," she said, dissolving in tears. "I am leading you to the torture myself—you, for whom I would give all my blood! I am the cause of the misfortune that is overwhelming you, and by virtue of my imprudence I have fallen into the hands of my cruelest persecutor."

They talked thus until they reached the city where the good old king was, the father of the horrible Bossu. He was told that his son was being brought back on a stretcher, because a young shepherd trying to defend his shepherdess had struck him with a stone from his sling with such force that he was in danger. At that news, the king, moved by the knowledge that his unique son was in that state, said that the shepherd should be put in a dungeon.

The hunchback gave a secret order that Carpillon should be no better treated. He had resolved that either she would marry him or she would die in torment. The result was that the two lovers were only separated by a door, whose poorly joined cracks preserved for them the sad consolation of seeing one another when the sun was at its zenith; for the rest of the day and at night they could only glimpse one another.

What tender and passionate things did they not say? Everything that the heart can feel and everything that the mind can imagine, they expressed, in terms so touching that they dissolved in tears, and perhaps would have made anyone weep in repeating them.

The hunchback's confidants came every day to speak to the princess, to threaten her with imminent death is she did not ransom her life by consenting with a good grace to her marriage. She received those propositions with a firmness and a scornful attitude that made them despair of their negotiation, and as soon as she was able to talk to the prince she said: "Have no fear, my shepherd that the fear of the most cruel torments will lead me to an infidelity; at least we shall die together, since we cannot live together."

"Do you think you are consoling me, beautiful princess?" he said. "Alas, would it not be preferable for me to see you in the arms of that monster than in the hands of the executioners with whom you are threatened?"

She did share his sentiments; she accused him of weakness, and always assured him that she would set him an example of dying with courage.

The hunchback's wound being slightly improved, his amour, irritated by the princess's continual refusals, caused him to make the resolution to sacrifice her to his anger, along with the young shepherd who had maltreated him. He marked the day for that lugubrious tragedy, and invited the king to come, with all the senators and noblemen of the realm.

He was in an uncovered litter, in order to feast his eyes on all the horror of the spectacle. The king, as I have already said, did not know that Princes Carpillon was a prisoner, with the result that when he saw her dragged to the torture, with the poor governess, whom the hunchback had also condemned, and the young shepherd more beautiful than the day, he ordered that they be brought on to the terrace, where the entire court was surrounding him.

He did not wait for the princess to open her mouth to complain of the unworthy treatment to which she was being subjected; he hastened to cut the cords by which she was bound. Then, looking at the shepherd, he felt his entrails stirred by tenderness and pity.

"Reckless young man," he said to him, making a violent effort not to speak rudely to him, "what inspired you to attack a great prince and to reduce him to death?"

The shepherd, seeing that venerable old man ornamented by the royal purple, experienced movements of respect and confidence on his part, which he had not yet known. "Great monarch," he said, with an admirable firmness, "The peril in which I saw this beautiful princess is the cause of my temerity. I did not know your son, and how would I have known him, in an action so violent and so unworthy of his rank?"

As he spoke in that manner he animated his discourse with gesture and tone; his arm was bare; the arrow with which it was marked was too visible for the king not to perceive it.

"O gods!" he cried. "Am I deceived, or shall I rediscover in you the dear son that I have lost?"

"No, great king," said the Amazon Fay from the air above, where she appeared mounted on a superb winged horse, "No, you are not mistaken; that is your son. I conserved him for you in the eagle's nest to which his barbaric brother had him taken. It is necessary that this one consoles you for the loss you are about to suffer of the other."

As she finished speaking she fell upon the culpable Bossu, and struck him with her ardent lance in the heart. She did not allow him to envisage the horrors of death for long; he was consumed as if he had been burned by lightning.

Then she approached the terrace and gave arms to the prince. "I promised them to you," she said. "You will be invulnerable with them, and the greatest warrior in the world."

Immediately, the fanfares of a thousand trumpets were heard, and all the instruments of war imaginable; but that din ceded shortly thereafter to a sweet symphony, which sang the praises of the prince and the princess melodiously.

The Amazon Fay descended from her horse, placed herself beside the king, and asked him to order promptly everything necessary for the pomp of the marriage of the prince and the princess. She commanded a young fay, who appeared as soon as she had called her, to go in quest of the shepherd king, the queen and his daughters. The fay departed instantly, and came back immediately with those illustrious unfortunates.

What satisfaction after such long tribulations! The palace resounded with cries of joy, and nothing has ever equaled those of the kings and their children.

The Amazon Fay gave orders everywhere; every single one of her instructions activated more than a hundred thousand people. The wedding was completed with such great magnificence that its like has never been seen. King Sublime returned to his estates; Carpillon had the pleasure of taking him there with her dear husband. The old king, delighted to see a son so worthy of his amity, was rejuvenated; or, at the very least, his old age was accompanied by so much satisfaction that he lived much better.

Youth is an age in which the human heart
Acquires all the movements it is intended to make;
It is a soft wax
Obedient to the hands;
Character is formed there easily,
Either vices or virtues.

Whatever efforts one makes,
As soon as it is engraved it is never effaced.
On a sea so difficult
Fortunate is the man with a skillful pilot
Who traces him a fortunate route.
The prince I have just depicted.
Had no reef to fear,
While the shepherd king governed his destiny.
That master instructed him in all the virtues;
It is true that Amour out him under his empire,
But flee, odious censors
Who want a hero to resist tenderness;
Provided that reason is always his mistress,
Amour gives splendor to glorious exploits.

THE BENEVOLENT FROG

There was once a king who sustained a war against his neighbors for a long time. After several battles, his capital city was besieged. He feared for the queen, and, because she was pregnant, he begged her to retire to a castle that he had had fortified, to which he had only ever been once. The queen employed her prayers and tears in order to persuade him to let her remain with him; she wanted to share his fortune and uttered loud cries when he put her in his carriage to make her depart. However, he ordered his guards to accompany her and promised to steal away secretly when he could, in order to come to see her. That was a hope with which he flattered her, for the castle was far away, surrounded by a dense forest, and unless one knew the roads well, one could never arrive there.

The queen departed, very upset at leaving her husband in the perils of war. She was taken in small stages, for fear that the fatigue of such a long journey might make her ill. Finally, she arrived at the castle, very anxious and very chagrined.

After she had rested she wanted to explore the surroundings, and found nothing there that could divert her. She looked in all directions; she saw great deserts that gave her more chagrin than pleasure. She gazed at them sadly, and sometimes said to herself: *What a contrast there is between the abode where I am and the one in which I have been all my life! If I stay here much longer, I shall die. Who is there to talk to in this solitary place? With whom can I soothe my anxieties? What have I done to the king to be exiled? It seems that he wants me to feel all the bitterness of his absence, when he has relegated me to such a disagreeable castle.*

It was thus that she lamented, and although he wrote to her every day and gave her very good news of the siege, she became more and more afflicted, and made the resolution to return to the king. But as the officers that he had given her had orders only to bring her back when he sent a courier expressly, she did not give any evidence of what she was meditating, and had a small carriage made in which they was only room for her, saying that she wanted to go hunting sometimes. She guided the horses herself and followed the dogs so closely that the huntsmen did not go as quickly as her. By that means she rendered herself mistress of her carriage, and could leave whenever she wished.

There was only one difficulty, which was that she did not know the forest roads, but she flattered herself that the gods would bring her safely to port, and after having made them a few petty sacrifices, she said that she wanted to undertake a great hunt, and that everyone should come; that she would mount her carriage and that everyone would follow different routes in order not to leave any retreat for the wild beasts. Thus, everyone split up. The young queen, who thought she would soon be with her husband, had put on a very advantageous costume; her capeline was covered with plumes of different colors, her jacket garnished with precious stones and her beauty, which had nothing common about it, made her appear a second Diana.

At the moment when everyone was most occupied by the pleasure of the hunt, she let her horses off the bridle, and animated them with her voice and a few cracks of the whip. After having trotted quickly, they began to gallop, and fled with the bit between their teeth. The carriage seemed to be drawn by the winds; eyes would have had difficulty following it.

The poor queen repented of her temerity, but too late. *What have I done?* she thought. *Can it be a good thing for me to be drawn by horses so proud and indocile, at their own whim? Alas, what will happen to me? Oh, if the king knew that I have exposed myself to the peril I am in, what would become of him? He loves me so dearly, and only sent me away from his capital in order to put me in greater security. This is how I have responded to his tender cares, and the dear child that I am carrying in my womb is going to be a victim, like me, of my imprudence.*

The air resounded with her dolorous plaints; she invoked the gods and summoned the fays to her aid, but the gods and the fays had abandoned her; the carriage turned over; she did not have the strength to throw herself to the ground promptly enough. Her foot remained caught between the wheel and the axle; it is easy to believe that it would require nothing less than a miracle to save her after such a terrible accident.

Finally, she lay extended on the ground at the foot of a tree; she had neither a pulse nor a voice; her face was covered in blood. She remained in that state for a long time.

When she opened her eyes, she saw a woman of gigantic stature beside her, clad only in a lion skin. Her arms and legs were bare, her hair bound with the dried skin of a snake, the head of which hung over her shoulders. There was a stone club in her hand, which she used as a walking-stick, and a quiver full of arrows at her side.

A figure so extraordinary persuaded the queen that she was dead, for she did not believe that after such a serious accident she ought still to be alive. Speaking in a low voice, she said: "I am not surprised that people have so much difficulty in resolving themselves to die, when one sees that the other world is so frightful."

The giant, who was listening, could not help laughing at the idea she had that she was dead. "Recover your spirits," she said. "Know that you are still among the number of the living, but your fate is scarcely less sad. I am the fay Lionne, who lives close by. It is necessary that you come to spend your life with me."

The queen looked at her sadly, and said: "If you wish, Madame Lionne, to take me back to my castle and prescribe to the king what he must pay you for my ransom, he loves me so dearly that he would not even refuse half of his kingdom."

"No," she replied. "I'm sufficiently rich; it has irritated me for some time to be alone; you have intelligence, perhaps you can divert me."

As she finished speaking, she took on the form of a lioness, and, loading the queen on her back, she carried her into the depths of her terrible grotto. As soon as she was there, she cured her with a liquid with which she rubbed her.

What a surprise and what dolor for the queen, to find herself in that frightful abode! One descended to it by ten thousand steps, which went all the way to the center of the earth. It had no other light than that of several large lamps, which was reflected from a lake of quicksilver. It was covered with monsters, the different forms of which would have frightened a less timid queen.

Owls of various species, a few crows and other birds of sinister omen could be heard there. In the distance, a mountain was visible from which almost dormant waters flowed; they were all the tears that unfortunate lovers had ever shed, of which the sad Amours had made reservoirs. The trees were always devoid of leaves and fruits, the earth covered with marigolds, brambles and nettles. The nourishment was appropriate to the climate of such an accursed place: a few dry roots, horse-chestnuts and rose-apples were all that was offered to relieve the hunger of unfortunates who fell into the hands of the fay Lionne.

As soon as the queen was in a state to work, the fay said that she could build herself a cabin, because she would remain with her for the rest of her life. At those words the princess did not have the strength to hold back her tears.

"What have I done to you," she cried, "that you should keep me here? If the end of my life, which I sense approaching, causes you pleasure, kill me—that is all I can hope for from your pity—but don't condemn me to spend a long and deplorable life without my husband."

Lionne did not care about her dolor, and told her that she advised her to dry her tears and try to please her; that if she adopted any other conduct, she would be the most unfortunate person in the world.

"What is it necessary to do, then," replied the queen, "to touch your heart?"

"I like fly pies," she said. "I want you to find the means of having enough to make me a very large and very excellent one."

"I can't see any here," said the queen, "and even if there were any, there isn't enough light to catch them, and even if I caught them, I've never made pastry, so you're giving me orders that I can't carry out."

"It doesn't matter," said the pitiless Lionne "I want what I want."

The queen made no reply. She thought that, in spite of the cruel fay, she only had one life to lose, and in the state she was in, what could she have to fear? Instead of going in quest of flies, therefore, she sat down under a yew tree and commenced her sad laments.

"What will be your dolor, my dear husband," she said, "when you come to seek me and no longer find me? You will believe me dead or infidel, and I'd rather you wept for my death than that of my tenderness. Perhaps my carriage will be found in the forest, in pieces, and all the ornaments I had put on to please you. At that sight, you will no longer doubt my death, and how do I know whether you will not accord to another the part that you had given me in your heart? But at least I will not know, since I shall never return to the world."

She would have continued to talk to herself in that manner for a long time if she had not heard the sad croaking of a crow above her head. She looked up, and by favor of the paltry light that illuminated the shore she did indeed see a large crow, which was holding a frog with the intention of eating it

Although nothing presents itself here to relieve me, she thought, *I cannot neglect saving a poor frog, which is as afflicted in its species as I am in mine.*

She made use of the first stick that came to hand, and made the crow let go. The frog fell, remained stunned for some time, and then recovered its batrachian spirits.

"Beautiful queen," it said to her, "you are the only benevolent person I have seen in this place since curiosity brought me here."

"By what marvel can you speak, little frog?" the queen replied. "And who are the persons you have seen here, for I haven't yet perceived any?"

"All the monsters with which the lake is covered," said the little frog, "have been in society, some on the throne and others in the confidence of their sovereigns; there are even the mistresses of a few kings, who have cost the state a good deal of blood; they are the ones you see metamorphosed into leeches. Destiny has sent them here for some time, without any of them returning better and corrected."

"I understand," said the queen, "that several wicked individuals gathered together do not aid one another to mend their ways, but in your regard, my dear frog, what are you doing here?"

"Curiosity engaged me to come here," she replied. "I'm half-fay; my power is limited in certain ways, and very extensive in others. If the fay Lionne recognized me in her estates, she would kill me."

"How is it possible," the queen said to her, "that, being fay or half-fay, the crow was about to eat you?"

"A few words will enable you to understand," replied the frog. "When I have my little hood of roses over my head, in which my greatest virtue resides, I fear nothing, but unfortunately, I had left it in the marsh when the accursed crow swooped down upon me. I confess, Madame, that without you, I would be no more, and since I owe you my life, if I can do anything for the relief of yours, you can order me to do anything you please."

"Alas, my dear frog," said the queen, "the evil fay who is keeping me captive wants me to make a fly pie. There are none here, and even if there were, there isn't enough light to catch them, and I'm running a great risk of dying under her blows."

"Leave it to me," said the frog. "Before long, I'll furnish you with it."

She immediately rubbed herself with sugar, and more than ten thousand frogs, her friends, did the same; she was soon in a place filled with flies; the evil fay had a store of them there expressly to torment certain unfortunates. As soon as they scented the sugar, they attached themselves to it, and the obliging frogs returned at a fast gallop to where the queen was. There had never been such a catch of flies, nor a better pie than the one she made for the fay Lionne.

When she presented it to her she was very surprised, not understanding how she had been able to trap them.

The queen, who was exposed to all the inclemency of the atmosphere, which was poisoned, cut a few cypress branches in order to begin building her cabin. The frog came to offer her generous services, and put herself at the head of all those who had gone in quest of the flies. They helped the queen to make a little building, the prettiest in the world, but she had scarcely lain down inside it when the monsters of the lake, jealous of her repose, came to torment her with the most horrible racket that had ever been heard. She got up, very frightened, and fled; that was what the monsters wanted. A dragon, once the tyrant of one of the most beautiful kingdoms of the world, took possession of it.

The poor afflicted queen tried to complain, but they did not care about her at all; the monsters jeered her and the fay Lionne said to her if she deafened her with her lamentations again she would beat her. It was necessary to shut up and have recourse to the frog, who was the best person in the world. They wept together, for as soon as she had her hood of roses she was capable of laughing and weeping just like anyone else

"I have such a great amity for you," she told her, "that I want to recommence your building, when all the monsters of the lake will be in despair. She cut wood immediately, and the queen's little rustic palace was constructed in such a short time that she retired therein that same night.

The frog, attentive to everything the queen needed, made her a bed of wild thyme. When the malevolent fay heard that the queen was no longer lying on the ground she sent for her. "Who are the men or gods who are protecting you?" she said. "That soil, always washed by a rain of sulfur and fire, has never produced a worthwhile leaf of sage. I hear that in spite of that, odorant herbs grow under your feet."

"I don't know the cause, Madame," the queen said to her, "and if I attribute it to anything, it's to the child with which I'm pregnant, which might perhaps be less unfortunate than me."

"The desire takes me," said the fay, "to have a bouquet of the rarest flowers; see whether the fortune of your brat can furnish you with them. If it fails, you won't lack a beating, for I often give them, and I always give them marvelously."

The queen started to weep; such threats scarcely pleased her, and the impossibility of finding flowers put her in despair.

She returned to her little house; her friend the frog arrived. "How sad you are," she said to the queen.

"Alas, my dear friend, who wouldn't be? The queen wants a bouquet of the most beautiful flowers; where could I find them? You can see those that are born here; it will cost my life, though, if I don't satisfy her."

"Amiable princess," said the frog, graciously, "it's necessary to try to get you out of the embarrassment you're in. There's a bat here who is the only one with which I've linked commerce; she's a good creature and she can go much quicker than me; I'll give her my hood of roses; with that help, she'll find you the flowers."

The queen bowed profoundly, for there was no means of embracing the little frog.

The latter went immediately to speak to the bat, and a few hours later she came back, hiding admirable flowers under her wings. The queen took them very quickly to the evil fay, who was even more surprised than she had been previously, unable to comprehend by what miracle the queen was so well served.

The princess thought incessantly about means of being able to escape. She communicated her desire to the good frog, who said to her: "Madame, permit me, before anything else, to consult my little hood, and we'll act then in accordance with its advice. She took it, and having put it on a stick, she burned a few sprigs of juniper, capers and two little green peas in front of it; she croaked five times, and then, the ceremony over, putting on the hood of roses again, she began to speak like an oracle.

"Destiny, master of everything," she said, "forbids you to leave this place. You will have a princess more beautiful than the mother of the amours; don't go to any trouble regarding anything else; time alone can relieve you."

The queen lowered her eyes; a few tears flowed therefrom, but she made the resolution to believe her friend. "At least," she said, "don't abandon me; be at my childbed, since I'm condemned to give birth here." The honest frog promised to be her Lucina,[6] and consoled her as best she could.

But it is time to talk about the king.

While his enemies were holding him under siege in his capital city, he was unable to send couriers incessantly to the queen; having made several sorties, however, he obliged them to withdraw, and he felt glad of that event less for his own sake than of his dear queen, of whom he could go in quest without fear. He was unaware of her disaster; none of her officers had dared to go and inform him.

They had found the carriage in pieces in the forest, with the escaped horses and the amazon attire that the queen had put on in order to go in search of him. As they did not doubt that she was dead, there was only a question between them of persuading the king that she had died suddenly. At that fatal news he nearly died of dolor himself; hair torn out, tears shed, pitiful cries and other meager rights of widowhood were not spared in that occasion.

After having spent a few days without seeing anyone and without wanting to see anyone he returned to his great city, trailing after him a long mourning, which he wore more in his heart than in his garments. All the ambassadors of the neighboring kings came to give him their compliments, and after the ceremonies inseparable from catastrophes of that sort, he at-

---

[6] Lucina was the Roman goddess of childbirth.

tached himself to giving repose to his subjects by exempting them from war and procuring them a great commerce.

The queen was unaware of all these things. The time for her to give birth arrived; she did so very fortunately. Heaven gave her a little princess as beautiful as the frog had predicted. They named her Mousette, and the queen had a great deal of difficulty obtaining permission from the fay Lionne to nourish her, for she had a great desire to eat her, so ferocious and barbaric was she.

Mousette, the marvel of her age, was already six months old, and the queen, gazing at her with a tenderness mingled with pity, said incessantly: "Oh, if the king your father could see you, my poor child, how much joy he would have; you would be so dear to him! But perhaps, at this very moment, he's beginning to forget me. He believes us buried forever in the horrors of death; perhaps another is occupying in his heart the place he had given to me."

These sad reflections cost her many tears; the frog, who loved her in good faith, seeing her weeping thus, said to her one day: "If you wish, Madame, I will go to find the king, your husband. The journey is long, and I travel slowly, but in the end, sooner or later, I hope to arrive."

That proposition could not have been more agreeably received than it was. The queen put her hands together and even joined them with Mousette's, to mark to the frog the obligation she would have to her for undertaking such a journey. She assured her that the king would not be ingrate. "But," she continued, "Of what utility would it be to him to know that I am in this dismal abode? It will be impossible for him to get me out of it."

"Madame," said the frog, "it is necessary to leave that care to the gods, and do for our part what depends on us."

Immediately, they bid one another adieu. The queen wrote to the king in her own blood and a small piece of linen, for she had no ink or paper. She begged him to believe everything that the virtuous frog was about to tell him of her news.

The frog took a year and four days to climb the ten thousand steps there were from the black plain where she left the queen to the world. She took another year making her equipage, for she was too proud to want to appear in a great court like a wretched marsh frog. She had a litter made large enough to accommodate two eggs comfortably; it was covered with tortoiseshell outside and lined with the skin of young lizards. She had fifty maids of honor; they were little green frogs that hopped in the fields; each one was mounted on a snail with an English saddle and one leg over the bow in a marvelous attitude. Several water rats dressed as pages preceded the snails, to which she had confided the guard of her person.

In sum, nothing had ever been so pretty, especially her rosy hood, always fresh and blooming, which suited her perfectly. She was a little coquettish in her métier, which had obliged her to put on rouge and beauty spots; it is even said that she was wearing make-up, as the majority of ladies of that country did, but on looking into the matter, it was found that only her enemies said that of her.

She took seven years to make the journey, during which the poor queen suffered inexpressible woes and pains, and without the beautiful Mousette to console her, she would have died hundreds of times. That marvelous little creature did not open her mouth and did not say a word without charming her mother; there was not even the fay Lionne that she could not tame; and finally, after the queen had spent six years in hat horrible abode, she agreed to take her hunting, on the condition that everything she killed would be for her.

What a joy it was for the poor queen to see the sun again! She had so completely lost the habitude of it that she thought she would go blind. As for Mousette, she was so adroit that at the age of five or six, nothing escaped the arrows that she launched. By that means, the mother and daughter softened the fay's ferocity slightly.

The little frog traveled over mountains and through valleys, day and night, and finally arrived in the vicinity of the capital city where the king made his abode. She was surprised only to see dancing and festivities everywhere; people were laughing and singing, and the closer she came to the city, the more joy and jubilation she found.

Her marshy equipage surprised everyone; everyone followed her, and the crowd became so large when she entered the city that she had great difficulty reaching the palace. It was there that everything was in magnificence. The king, a widower for nine years had finally decided to yield to the pleas of his subjects; he was about to marry a princess, less beautiful, in truth, than his wife, but very agreeable nevertheless.

Having descended from her litter, the benevolent frog entered the king's apartment, followed by her cortege. She had no need to request an audience; the monarch, his bride-to-be and all the princes had too much desire to know the reason for her coming to interrupt it.

"Sire," she said, "I do not know whether the news I am bringing you will give you joy or pain; the marriage that you are about to make persuades me of your infidelity to the queen."

"Her memory is still dear to me," said the king, shedding a few tears that he could not retain, "but it is necessary for you to know, amiable frog, that kings cannot always do as they wish; for nine years my subjects have been pressing me to remarry; I owe them heirs, so I have cast my yes upon this young princess, who appears to me to be very charming."

"I advise you not to marry her," said the frog, "For polygamy is a hanging offence; the queen is not dead; here is a letter written in her blood, with which she has charged me. You have a little princess, Mousette, who is more beautiful than all the heavens put together."

The king took the rag on which the queen had scribbled a few words. He kissed it, washed it with his tears, and showed it to the entire assembly, saying that he recognized the character of the woman clearly. He asked the frog a thousand questions, to which she replied with as much intelligence as vivacity.

The princess, his fiancée, and the ambassadors charged with seeing the celebration of the marriage made ugly grimaces. "What, Sire," said the most celebrated among them. "Can you break such a solemn engagement on the word of a toad like this one? This marsh scum has the insolence to come to your court and savor the pleasure of being heeded!"

"Sire Ambassador," replied the frog, "Know that I am not marsh scum, and since it is necessary to display my science here let my vassal lords[7] appear. All the frogs, rats, snails, lizards did, in fact, appear, with her at their head, but they no longer had the form of those little animals; their stature was tall and majestic, their face agreeable, their eyes more brilliant than stars. Each bore a crown of precious stones on the head and a velvet royal mantle lined in ermine on the shoulders, with a long train borne by dwarfs of both sexes. At the same time, trumpets, timpani and oboes pierced the clouds with their agreeable and martial sounds. All the vassal lords commenced a ballet so lightly danced that the lightest gambol lifted them up as far as the vault of the hall.

The attentive king and the future queen were no less surprised when they saw those honorable strolling players suddenly metamorphose into flowers, which performed no less: jasmines, jonquils, violets, carnations and tuberoses now provided with legs and feet. It was an animate flower-bed, all the movements of which gave as much pleasure to the sense of smell as to that of sight.

An instant later, the flowers disappeared; several fountains took their place; their jets rose up rapidly and fell back into a wide channel that formed at the foot of the castle; it was covered with little painted and gilded galleys, so pretty and so elegant that the princess invited the ambassadors to enter one with her in order to take a ride. They were very willing, think-

---

[7] The original has *fées et féos*, wordplay that is clearly deriving the former term and a hypothetical masculine equivalent from the word "féodal" [feudal], hence my translation.

ing that it was all only a game that would soon be concluded by a happy wedding.

As soon as they had embarked, the galley, the river and all the fountains disappeared; the frogs became frogs again. The king asked where the princess was. The frog reappeared. "Sire," she said, "You ought not to have any other wife than the queen; if I were less her friend I would not have interfered with the marriage you were about to, but she has so much merit, and your daughter, Mousette, is so lovable, that you ought not to waste a moment before trying to liberate them."

"I confess to you, Madame Frig," said the king, "that if I had not believed that my wife was dead, there is nothing the world I would not have done to have her back."

"After the marvels that you have just seen me contrive before you," she said, "it seems to me that you ought to be persuaded of what I say. Leave your kingdom with good orders and don't delay your departure. Here is a ring that will furnish you with the means of seeing the queen and taking to the fay Lionne, although she is the most terrible creature there is in the world.

The king, no longer seeing the princess who had been destined for him, sensed that his passion for her had diminished considerably, and that, by contrast, the passion he had had for the queen was taking on new force. He departed without wanting to be accompanied by anyone, and made very considerable presents to the frog.

"Don't be discouraged," she said to him. "You will have terrible difficulties to overcome, but I hope that you will succeed in what the desire to do."

Consoled by those promises, the king took no guides other than the ring in order to go in search of his dear queen.

As Mousette grew up, her beauty was perfected to such an extent that all the monsters of the quicksilver lake fell in love with her. Dragons of frightful form were seen coming to crawl at her feet. Although she had always seen them, her beautiful eyes could not become accustomed to them; she fled and hid in her mother's arms.

"Will we be here for a long time?" she asked her. "Will our misfortunes never end?"

The queen gave her hopes in order to console her, but deep down, she had none herself. The absence of the frog, her profound silence, and so much time having passed without any news of her, all afflicted her to excess.

The fay Lionne gradually become accustomed to taking them hunting; she was greedy, and loved the game that they killed, and for their only recompense she gave them feet or the head; but it was great deal for her to permit them to see the daylight again. The fay took on the form of a lioness; the queen and her daughter sat astride her, and they roamed the forests thus.

The king, guided by his ring, having stopped in a forest, saw them pass by like an unleashed arrow. He barely perceived them, and when he tried to follow them they disappeared absolutely from his sight.

In spite of the queen's continuing troubles, her beauty had not diminished; she seemed lovelier than ever. All his fires were reignited, and, not doubting that the young princess who was with her was his dear Mousette, he resolved to perish a thousand times rather than abandon the design of seeing them again.

The obliging ring conducted him into the dismal abode where the queen had been for so many years. He was not a little surprised to descend so far into the depths of the earth, but everything he saw there astonished him much more. The fay Lionne, who was not unaware of anything, knew the day and the hour when he was due to arrive; what would she not have done in order for destiny, in intelligence with her, to have ordered otherwise? But she resolved at least to combat its power with all her own.

In the middle of the quicksilver lake she built a palace of crystal, which floated like a wave; she imprisoned the poor queen and her daughter there; then she harangued all the monsters that she believed to be in love with Mousette.

"You will lose that beautiful princess," she said to them, "if you do not interest yourself with me in defending her against a knight who is coming to abduct her."

The monsters promised not to neglect anything of what they could do. They surrounded he crystal palace. The lightest placed themselves on the roofs and the walls, others at the doors, and the rest in the lake.

The king, advised by his marvelous ring, went first to the fay's cabin. She waited for him there in the form of a lioness. As soon as he appeared, she threw herself upon to him. He drew his sword with a valor that she had not anticipated, and as she stretched out her paw, he cut it off at the joint, exactly at the elbow. She uttered a loud scream and fell. He approached her, put his foot on her throat, and swore by his faith that he would kill her. In spite of her invulnerable fury, she did not lower herself to being afraid.

"What do you want of me?" she said. "What are you asking of me?"

"I want to punish you," he replied, proudly, "for having abducted my wife, and I want to oblige you to return her to me, or I'll kill you right away."

"Cast your eye on that lake," she said "and see whether she is in my power."

The king looked in the direction she had indicated to him; he saw the queen and his daughter in the crystal castle, which was floating like a galley on the quicksilver, without oars or tiller. He nearly died of joy and dolor. He shouted to them with all is might, and he knew that he was heard, but how could he join them?

While he was searching for a means, the fay Lionne disappeared.

He ran along the shore of the lake: when he was on one side, close to reaching the transparent palace, it was drawn away with frightful rapidity; and his hopes were always disappointed thus.

The queen, who feared that he would eventually weary, cried out to him, in order to give him courage that the fay Lionne wanted to fatigue him, but that a veritable amour cannot be repelled by any difficulties. With that, she and Mousette extended their hands toward him, adopting a supplicant manner.

At that sight, the kind was penetrated by further arrows; He raised his voice and swore by the Styx and the Acheron, to pass over, and that he would rather spend the rest of his life in that bleak location rather than leave without her.

He had to be endowed with a great perseverance; he spent his time as badly as any king in the world; the earth, full of brambles and covered with thorns, served as his bed; he had no lack of wild fruits, as bitter as bile, and he had incessant combats to sustain against the monsters of the lake.

A husband who adopts that conduct in order to see his wife again is assuredly of the time of the fays, and his procedure testifies well enough to the epoch of my story.

Three years went by without the king having had any reason to promise himself any advantage. He was almost desperate. He made the resolution a hundred times to throw himself into the lake, and would have done it if he had been able to envisage that last coup as a remedy for the difficulties of the queen and the princess.

He was running, as usual, from one side to another, when a frightful dragon called to him and said: "If you care to swear to me on your crown and scepter, your wife and daughter, to give me a certain morsel to eat of which I'm very fond, and for which I shall ask you when I have the desire, I'll take you on my wings and in spite of all the monsters covering the lake and guarding the crystal castle, I promise you that you'll get the queen and Princess Mousette out."

"Oh, dear dragon of my soul," cried the king. "I swear to you and all your dragon species that I will give you anything you like to eat, and will forever remain your petty servant."

"Don't engage yourself," replied the dragon "if you have any desire not to keep your word, for misfortunes so great would happen to you that you'd remember them for the rest of your life."

The king redoubled his protestations; he was dying of impatience to deliver his dear queen. He climbed on to the dragon's back as he would have done the finest horse in the world. At the same time, the monsters came toward him to block his passage; nothing could be heard but the shrill hissing of snakes, and nothing could be seen but fire, sulfur and saltpeter falling pell-mell. Finally the king arrived at the castle; efforts were renewed there; bats, owls and crows all tried to deny him entry, but the dragon tore the boldest to pieces with its claws, teeth and tail.

For his part, the king, seeing that great battle raging, broke the walls with a kick and made weapons out of the fragments to aid his dear wife. They were finally victorious; they came together and the enchantment ended with a lightning bolt that fell upon the lake, which dried it up.

The obliging dragon had disappeared with all the rest, and without the king being able to divine by what means he had been transported into the capital city he found himself there with the queen and Mousette, sitting in a magnificent hall at a delectably served table. There had never been an astonishment similar to theirs, nor a greater joy.

All their subjects ran to see their sovereign and the young princess, who, by virtue of a series of prodigies, was so superbly clad that people could hardly sustain the glare of her precious stones

It is easy to imagine that all the pleasures occupied that fine court; there were masquerades, ring races and tournaments that attracted the greatest princes in the world, and Mousette's beautiful eyes arrested them all. Between those who seemed the best made and the most adroit Prince Mousy held the advantage everywhere; nothing was heard but applause; everyone admired him, and Mousette, who had been until then with the serpents and dragons of the lake, could not help rendering justice to Mousy's merit. He did not let a day go by without making new gallantries to please her, for he loved her passionately, and, having put himself in the ranks to establish his pretentions, he made the king and queen understand that his principality had a beauty and extent that merited fully a particular attention.

The king said that Mousette was free to choose a husband for herself, and that he did not want to constrain her at all, that he should work to please her, which was the only means of being fortunate. The prince was delighted with that response; he had known in several encounters that she was not indifferent to him; and when he had finally explained himself to her, she said if he were not her husband she would never have another. Mousy, transported by joy, threw himself at her feet and implored her in the most tender terms to remember the word that she had given him.

He ran immediately to the apartment of the king and queen; he gave them an account of the progress that his amour had made with Mousette, and begged them not to defer his happiness. They consented to that with pleasure. Prince Mousy had such great qualities that he seemed to be the only one worthy to posses the marvelous Mousette. The king agreed to affiance them before Mousy returned home, where he had to go to give orders for his marriage, but he would never have departed if he had not had certain assurances of being happy on his return.

Princess Mousette could not bid him adieu without shedding abundant tears; she had presentiments of some kind that afflicted her, and the queen, seeing the prince overwhelmed by dolor, gave him a portrait of her daughter, begging him, for the sake of their love, that the entrance he was about to organize would not be so magnificent as to delay his return.

"Madame," he said to her, "I have never taken so much pleasure in obeying you than I shall on this occasion; my heart is too interested for me to neglect what can make me happy."

He departed post-haste, and Princess Mousette, while awaiting his return, occupied herself with music and instruments that he had learned to play a few months ago and which she played marvelously well.

One day, when she was in the queen's chamber, the king came in, his face covered in tears. Taking his child in his arms, he cried: "Oh, my child! Oh, unfortunate father! Oh, unfortunate king!"

He was unable to say more; sighs cut off the thread of his voice. The queen and the princess, frightened, asked him what was wrong. Finally, he told them that a giant of immeasurable height had just arrived, who was the ambassador of the dragon of the lake, which, in accordance with the promise that he had demanded of the king in exchange for its aid in combating and vanquishing the monsters, had come to demand Princes Mousette, in order to eat her in a pie; and that he had promised by frightful oaths to give him whatever he wanted.

In those days, people were not able to break their word.

On hearing that sad news, the queen uttered frightful screams; she hugged the princess in her arms. I would rather have my life taken away," she said, "than resolve to deliver my daughter to that monster. Let him take our kingdom and all that we possess. Unnatural father, how could you lend your hand to such a great barbarity? What! My child will be baked in a pie! Ha! I can't sustain the thought. Send this barbaric ambassador to me; perhaps my affliction can touch him."

The king made no reply. He went to talk to the giant and finally took him to the queen, who threw herself at his feet; she and her daughter implored the giant to have pity on them, and to persuade the dragon to take everything they had and to spare Mousette's life. He replied that that did not depend on him at all, and that the dragon was too stubborn and too greedy; that once it took it into his head to eat some nice morsel, all the gods put together could not take away the desire; and that he advised them as a friend to do the thing with a good grace, because greater misfortunes might yet arrive."

At those words the queen fainted, and the princess would have done likewise if she had not had to help her mother.

That sad news had scarcely spread through the palace that it was all over the city, and nothing could be heard but tears and groans, for Mousette was adored, The king did not know what response to make to the giant, and the giant, who had already been waiting for several days, was beginning to weary of it and making threats in a terrible manner,

Meanwhile, the king and the queen said "What can happen to us that is worse? If the dragon of the lake came to devour us, we'd be no more afflicted. If we put our poor Mousette in a pie we're doomed."

With that, the giant told them that he received news from his master, and that if the princess wanted to marry a nephew he had, he would consent to let her live; that the nephew was also handsome and well made, that he was a prince, and that she could like quite content with him.

That proposition soothed Their Majesties dolor slightly; the queen spoke to the princess, but she found her even more averse to that marriage then to death. "I am not capable, Madame," she said, "of conserving my life by an infidelity. You have promised me to Prince Mousy; I will never belong to anyone else. Let me die; the end of my life will assure the repose of yours."

The king arrived; he said to his daughter all that the strongest tenderness can provoke the imagination. She remained firm in her sentiments; and by way of conclusion, it was resolved to transport her to the top of a mountain to which the dragon of the lake would come to take her.

Everything was prepared for the sad sacrifice; those of Iphigenia and Psyche had not been so lugubrious. Nothing could be seen but black coats and pale, consternated faces. Four hundred young women of the first quality were clad in long black garments and were crowned with cypress, in order to accompany her. She was carried in an uncovered back velvet litter, in order that everyone could see the masterpiece of the gods; her hair was scattered over her shoulders, attached by crepes, and the crown she had on her head was of jasmines, mingled with a few marigolds.

She did not appear to be touched by the dolor of the king and the queen, who were overwhelmed by the utmost sadness. The giant, fully armed, was marching alongside the litter in which the princess was sitting, and gazing at her with an avid eye, seemingly assured of eating his share. The air resounded with sighs and sobs; the road was inundated by the tears that were shed.

"Oh, frog, frog," cried the queen, "have you really abandoned me? Alas, why did you give me your help in the somber plain, since you are denying it to me now? How fortunate I would be to have died then. I would not be seeing all my hopes deceived now. I would not be seeing my dear Mousette on the point of being devoured."

While she was making these plaints, they were still advancing, although they were walking slowly; finally, they reached the top of the fatal mountain. In that place, the cries and regrets redoubled with such force that nothing has ever been so lamentable.

The giant invited everyone to make their adieux and withdraw. It was necessary to do it, because people were very simple in those days, and did not seek remedies for anything.

Drawing away, the king and the queen climbed another mountain with their entire court, because they could see from there what was going to happen to the princess.

In fact, they had not been there long when they perceived a dragon in the air that was nearly half a league long. Although it had six huge wings it was almost unable to fly, so heavy was its body, covered with large blue scales and long blazing spines. Its tail was coiled fifty times and a half. Each of its claws was the size of a windmill, and in its gaping mouth three rows of teeth were visible as long as an elephant's tusks.

But while it was advancing slowly, the dear and faithful frog, mounted on a sparrow-hawk, flew rapidly to Prince Mousy. She was wearing her hood of roses, and although he was shut in his cabinet she entered without a key.

"What are you doing here, unfortunate lover?" he said to him. "You're dreaming about the beauty of Mousette, who is exposed at this moment to the most rigorous catastrophe. Here is a rose leaf; by blowing on it, I can make it into a rare horse, as you shall see."

Immediately, a green horse appeared; it had twelve feet and three heads, one of which spat fire, the second one bombs and the third one cannonballs. She gave him a sword that was eighteen aunes long and was lighter than a feather. She dressed him in a single diamond, into which he entered as if in a coat, and although it was as hard as rock it was so flexible that it did not hamper him at all.

"Go," she said, "run, fly to the defense of the woman you love. The green horse I have given you will take you to where she is; when you have delivered her, let everyone know the part that I have played in it."

"Generous fay," cried the prince, "I cannot testify all my gratitude to you at present, but I declare that I am your faithful slave forever." He mounted the horse with three heads, immediately started its twelve feet galloping, and made more diligence than three of the best horses, with the result that he arrived in very little time at the top of the mountain where he saw his dear princess all alone, and the frightful dragon that was approaching her slowly.

The green horse started spitting fire, bombs and cannonballs, which were no mediocre surprise to the monster. It received twenty cannonballs in the breast, which bit into its scales somewhat, and the bombs punctured one of its eyes. It became furious and tried to hurl itself upon the prince, but the eighteen-aune sword was so well-tempered that he could manipulate it as he wished, sometimes plunging it in all the way to the hilt, or using it like a whip. The prince would have felt the effect of its claws nevertheless, had it not been for the diamond coat, which was impenetrable.

Mousette had recognized him from far away, for the diamond that covered him glittered brilliantly, with the result that she was seized by the most mortal apprehension of which a mistress can be capable; but the king and the queen began to sense in their hearts a few rays of hope, for it was quite extraordinary to see a horse with three heads and twelve feet spitting fire and flames, and a prince sheathed in diamond, armed with a formidable sword, arriving at such a necessary moment and fighting with so much valor.

The king put his crown on his cane and the queen attached her handkerchief to the end of a stick in order to make signals to the prince and encourage him. All their retinue did likewise. In truth, there was no need, his heart alone, and the peril in which he saw his mistress, sufficed to animate him.

What efforts he made! The ground was covered with the dragon's spines, claws, horns, wings and scales; blood was flowing in a thousand places—his was all blue and that of the dragon all green, which made a singular shade on the earth. The prince fell five times, but he always got up again; he took his time to remount his horse, and then there were cannonades and Greek fire, to which nothing has ever been similar.

Finally, the dragon lost its strength; it fell, and the prince delivered a thrust to the belly that inflicted a frightful wound. What one might have difficulty believing, but which is as true as the rest of the tale, is that the most handsome and charming prince that has ever been seen emerged from that wound; his coat was blue velvet on a golden backcloth, embroidered with pearls; on his head he had a small Greek morion shaded by white plumes. He ran with open arms to embrace Prince Mousy.

"What do I not owe you, my generous liberator," he said to him. "You have just delivered me from the most frightful prison in which a sovereign could ever be interned: I had been condemned to it by the fay Lionne. I've been languishing there for sixteen years, and her power was such that, in spite of my own will, she was forcing me to devour this beautiful princess. Take me to her feet, in order that I can explain my misfortune to her."

Prince Mousy, surprised and charmed by an adventure so astonishing, did not want to cede in anything to the civilities of that prince; they hastened to join the beautiful Mousette, who, for her part, rendered a thousand thanks to the gods for such an unexpected good fortune. The king, the queen and the entire court were already surrounding her; everyone was speaking at the same time, and no one could hear anything; they were weeping almost as much in joy as they had done in grief.

Finally, in order that the celebration should not lack anything, the good frog arrived in the air, mounted on a sparrow-hawk that had little golden bells on its feet. When they were heard jingle-jangling everyone looked up; they saw the hood of roses shining like a sun, and the frog was as beautiful as the dawn. The queen advanced toward her and took her by one of her little feet; immediately, the sage frog metamorphosed and appeared as a great queen; her face was the most agreeable in the world.

"I have come," she cried, "to crown the fidelity of Princess Mousette; she preferred to expose her life rather than change; that example is rare in the century in which we are living, but it will be even rarer in centuries to come."

Immediately, she took two crowns of myrtle, which she placed on the heads of the two lovers who adored one another, and when she tapped three times with her wand all the dragon's bones were seen to rise up to form a triumphal arch, in memory of the great adventure that had just occurred.

Then that beautiful and numerous troop headed toward the city, singing wedding marches with as much gaiety as the sadness with which they had celebrated the sacrifice of the princess. Her marriage was only deferred until the following day; it is easy to judge the joy that accompanied it.

The queen that I have just depicted,
Amid the horrors of an infernal abode,
For her days had nothing to dread;
For her, amity combined with amour.
The frog and the king marked their zeal
By communal efforts.

In spite of the cruel Lionne
They snatched her from that baleful place.
Spouses so constant, friends so sincere,
Belonged to the time of our ancestors;
They no longer exist today;
The century of faerie in all its glory,
By the feature I cite here,
Of the epoch of my story,
One can be sufficiently enlightened.

THE WOODLAND HIND

There was once a king and a queen whose union was perfect; they loved one another tenderly and their subjects adored then, but all of them lacked the satisfaction of seeing that they had an heir. The queen, who was convinced that the king would love her even more if she had one, did not fail in spring to go to drink waters that were excellent. Crowds flocked to them, and the number of foreigners was so great that people from all parts of the world could be found there.

There were several springs in a large wood to which people went to drink; they were surrounded by marble and porphyry, for everyone took pride in embellishing them.

One day, when the queen was sitting on the edge of a spring, she told her ladies to go away and leave her alone. Then she commenced her usual laments.

"Am I not very unfortunate," she said, "not to have a child? The poorest women have them; for five years I have been asking the gods for one, and I have not been able to touch them. Am I going to die without having had that satisfaction?"

As she was speaking thus she noticed that the water of the spring was agitated. Then a large crayfish appeared and said to her: "Great queen, you shall have what you desire. I can inform you that there is a superb palace near here that the fays have built, but it is impossible to find because it is surrounded by dense clouds that the eyes of a mortal person cannot penetrate. However, as I am your very humble servant, if you care to confide yourself to the conduct of a poor crayfish, I offer to lead you there."

The queen listened to her without interrupting, the novelty of seeing a crayfish talk having surprised her greatly. She told her that she would accepted her offer gladly, but that she did not know how to walk backwards like her. The crayfish smiled, and immediately took on the form of a beautiful little old woman.

"Well, Madame," she said, "let's not go backwards, I consent to that; but above all, regard me as one of your friends, for I don't think anyone can be more advantageous to you."

She emerged from the fountain without being wet. Her garments were white, lined with crimson, and her gray hair was bound with green ribbons. Old ladies with such elegance have rarely been seen. She bowed to the queen and was embraced by her; then, without wasting any more time she led her into a path through the wood that surprised the princess, for, although she had been there thousands of times, she had never entered that one. How could she have entered it? It was the path that the fays used to go to the spring; it was ordinarily closed by brambles and thorns; but when the queen and her guide appeared, the brambles immediately grew roses and jasmines, and orange trees interlaced their branches to form an avenue covered with foliage and flowers; the ground was strewn with violets; a thousand different birds sang competitively in the trees.

The queen had not yet recovered from her surprise when her eyes were struck by the unparalleled splendor of a palace entirely made of diamond: the walls, the roofs, the ceilings, the floor, the stairways, the balconies, and even the terraces, were all diamond. In the excess of her admiration, she could not help uttering a loud cry and asking the elegant old woman who was accompanying her whether what she saw was a dream or a reality.

"Nothing is more real, Madame," she replied.

Immediately, the doors of the palace opened. Six fays emerged—but what fays! They were the most beautiful and the most magnificent that had ever appeared in their empire. They all came to make a profound reverence to the queen, and each of them presented her with a flower of gems in order to make a bouquet; there was a rose, a tulip, an anemone, a columbine, a carnation and a pomegranate.

"Madame," they said to her, "we could not give you a greater mark of our consideration than permitting you to come to see us here, but we are very glad to announce to you that you will have a beautiful princess, whom you will name Désirée, for it must be admitted that you have desired her for a long time. Don't fail to call us as soon as she comes into the world, because we want to endow her with all sorts of good qualities; you will only have to pick up the bouquet that we have given you and name each flower while thinking about us; be certain that we will be in your chamber immediately.

Transported by joy, the queen threw her arms around them, and the embraces lasted a good half-hour. After that they invited the queen to enter their palace, of which a sufficiently beautiful description cannot be given. In order to build it they had employed the architect of the sun; he had made on a small scale what the sun is on a large one. The queen, who could only sustain the glare with difficulty, was continually closing her eyes.

They took her into their garden; there have never been such fine fruits; the apricots were larger than her head, and one could not eat a cherry without cutting it into four. Their taste was so exquisite that after the queen had eaten one she did not want to let anything else as long as she lived. There were all sorts of artificial trees in the orchard, which were nevertheless alive, and grew like the others.

I shall not attempt to describe all the queen's transports, how she talked about little Princess Désirée, and how she thanked the amiable individuals who had announced such agreeable news, but in sum, no terms of tenderness and gratitude were forgotten. The Fay of the Spring had the part in it that she merited. The queen remained in the palace until the evening; she loved the music, and the voices she heard that appeared to her to be celestial. She was laden with presents, and after having thanked the great ladies she returned with the Fay of the Spring.

The entire house was in distress in her regard; people had been searching for her everywhere. No one could imagine where she was; it was even feared that some audacious foreigner might have kidnapped her, for she had beauty and youth. The result was that everyone expressed an extreme joy at her return, and as she felt on her part an infinite satisfaction in the hopes that she had just been given, she had an agreeable and brilliant conversation that charmed everyone. The Fay of the Spring had quit her close to home; the compliments and caresses redoubled at their separation.

The queen stayed at the waters for further week, not failing to return to the palace of the fays with the coquettish old woman, who appeared initially as a crayfish and then took on her natural form.

The queen left, she became pregnant, and brought into the world a princess she named Désirée. Immediately, she took the bouquet she had received; she named the flowers one by one, and saw the fays arrive right away. Each had a chariot of a different sort; one was ebony, drawn by white pigeons, others ivory, drawn by little crows, and others of cedar and calambora. That was their equipage of alliance and peace, for when they were annoyed it was nothing but flying dragons and snakes that projected fire from the mouth and eyes, lions, leopards and panthers, that transported them from one end of the earth to the other in less time than it takes to say good day or good night; but this time, they were in the best possible humor.

The queen saw them enter her room in a cheerful and majestic manner; their dwarfs of both sexes followed them, laden with presents. After they had embraced the queen and kissed the little princess, they deployed her layette, the fabric of which was so fine and so good that one could make use of it for a hundred years without wearing it out; the fays spun it in their leisure hours. As for the lace, it surpassed even what I said about the cloth; the entire history of the world was represented there, either by means of the needle or the spindle.

After that they displayed the linen and coverlets that they had embroidered expressly; a thousand different games with which children amuse themselves were represented there.

Nothing so marvelous has been seen since there have been embroiderers; but when the cradle appeared the queen cried out in admiration, for it surpassed everything that she had seen until then. It was of a wood so rare that it cost a hundred thousand écus a pound. Four little amours were sustaining it; they were four masterpiece, the artistry of which so far surpassed the material, although it was diamonds and rubies, that one cannot say enough about it. Those little amours had been animated by the fays, so that when the child cried they rocked her and put her to sleep; that was marvelously convenient for the nursemaids.

They fays took the little princess on to their knees themselves; they wrapped her up and gave her a thousand kisses, for she was already so beautiful that one could not see her without loving her. They remarked that she needed to suckle; immediately they struck the floor with their wands and a nurse appeared such as the lovable child required. There was nothing left to do but endow the child; the fays hastened to do that. One gave her virtue, another intelligence, the third a miraculous beauty, the one after a happy fortune; the fifth desired a long health for her, and the last that she should do everything she attempted well.

The delighted queen was thanking them thousands of times for the favors they had just done her when a crayfish was seen entering the room so large that the door was scarcely large enough for her to pass through.

"So, ingrate queen," the crayfish said, "you have not deigned to remember me? Is it possible that you have forgotten the Fay of the Spring so soon, and the good offices I have rendered you in taking me to see my sisters? What! You have summoned them all, and I'm the only one that you neglect? It's certain that I had a presentiment of it, which is what obliged me to take the form of a crayfish when I spoke to you for the first time, wanting to mark thus that your amity would be able to advance backwards."

The queen, inconsolable for the fault she had committed, interrupted her and begged her pardon. She told her that she believed she had named her flower like the others; that it was the bouquet of gems that had deceived her; that she was incapable of forgetting the obligations that she had to her; that she begged her not to take back her amity, and, in particular, to be favorable to the princess.

All the fays, who feared that she might endow her with misery and misfortune, seconded the queen in order to mollify her. "My dear sister," they said to her, "let Your Highness not be annoyed against a queen who never had the design to displease you; please quit this form of a crayfish, and enable us to see you with all your charms."

I have already said that the Fay of the Spring was something of a coquette; the praise that her sisters gave her soothed her somewhat. "Oh well," she said, "I shan't do Désirée all the harm that I had resolved, for I certainly had a yen to doom her, and nothing could have prevented me from doing it. However, I want to warn you that if she sees daylight before the age of fifteen years she'll have reason to repent of it; perhaps it will cost her life."

The queen's tears and the prayers of the illustrious fays did not change the sentence she had just pronounced; she retired backwards, for she had not wanted to quit her crayfish attire.

As soon as she was out of the room, the sad queen asked the fays for a means to preserve her daughter from the misfortunes that menaced her. They held council immediately, and after having discussed several different possibilities they settle on this one: that it was necessary to built a palace without doors or windows, to make a subterranean entrance, and to nourish the princess in that place until the fatal age when the threat would expire.

Three taps of a wand commenced and completed that great edifice. It was made of white and green marble outside; the ceilings and floor were diamond and emerald, which formed flowers, birds and a thousand agreeable things. Everything was carpeted with velvet of different colors, embroidered by the hands of fays; and as they were knowledgeable in history, they took pleasure in tracing the most beautiful and most remarkable things. The future was no less present than the past; the heroic actions of the greatest king in the world filled several wall-hangings.

> *Here, of the demon of Thrace*
> *He has the victorious bearing,*
> *The redoubled lightning that emerged from his eyes*
> *Marks his bellicose audacity.*
> *There, more tranquil and serene,*
> *Governing France in a profound peace,*
> *He makes seen by his laws that the rest of the world*
> *Ought to envy his design.*
> *By the painters with the most artful hands,*
> *He appears depicted with his various traits;*
> *Redoubtable in taking cites,*
> *Generous in making peace.*[8]

The sage fays had imagined that means for teaching the young princess more easily the various events in the lives of heroes and other men.

One could only see in her abode by candlelight, but there was such a great quantity of candles that they made a perpetual daylight. All the masters of whom she had need to render her perfect were conducted to the place; her intelligence, her vivacity and her skill almost always anticipated what they wanted to teach her, and each of them remained in a continual admiration of the surprising things she said, at an age when others were scarcely able to name their nurse—but one is not endowed by the fays to remain ignorant and stupid.

---

[8] The reference of this gratuitous insertion is obviously to Louis XIV, but the first lines, with credit him with the bearing of "the demon of Thrace" are a trifle enigmatic; the reference is probably to Thrax, the archetypal Thracian, regarded by Classical authors as a son of Ares, the god of war, or as Ares himself.

If her intelligence charmed all those who approached her, her beauty had no less powerful effects; she delighted the most insensible, and the queen, her mother, would never have taken her eyes off her if her duty had not attached her to the presence of the king.

The good fays came to see the princess from time to time; they brought her unparalleled rarities, and clothes so well-designed, rich and elegant that they seemed to have been made for the wedding of a young princess no less lovely than the one of whom I am speaking. Among all the fays who cherished her, however, Tulip loved her most and recommended most carefully to the queen not to let her see daylight before the age of fifteen.

"Our sister of the spring is vindictive," she told her. "Whatever interest we take in the child, she will do her harm if she can; so, Madame, you cannot be too vigilant in this matter."

The queen promised her to watch incessantly over such an important matter, but as her dear daughter approached the time at which she would emerge from the castle, she had her painted, and her portrait was taken to the greatest courts in the world. At the sight of it there was not a single prince who could help admiring her, but there was one who was so touched that he no longer wanted to be separated from her. He took the portrait into his cabinet and locked himself in with it, talking to it as if it were sensible, and as if it could hear him; he said the most passionate things in the world to her.

The king, who hardly saw his son any longer, enquired about his occupations and what could have prevented him from seeming as cheerful as he usually was. A few courtiers in too much haste to speak—for there are many of that character—told him that it was to be feared that the prince had lost his mind, because he spent entire days locked in his cabinet, where he could be heard talking by himself as if someone were with him.

The king received that news anxiously. "Is it possible," he said to his confidants, "that my son is losing his reason? It has always been so evident; you know the admiration that people have had for him until now, and I don't find anything amiss in his gaze; he merely appears to me to be more melancholy. I need to talk to him; perhaps I'll be able to determine what sort of folly is afflicting him."

In fact, he sent for him, commanded everyone to withdraw, and after several things to which he paid no great attention and to which he responded rather poorly, the king asked him what could be wrong with him in order for his humor and his person to have changed so much.

The prince, thinking the moment favorable, threw himself at his feet. "You have resolved," he said to him, "to make me marry Princess Noire; you find advantages in the alliance that I cannot promise you in Princess Désirée, but Sire, I find charms in the latter that I shall never encounter in the former."

"Where have you seen them?" asked the king.

"Portraits of both of them have been brought to me," replied the Warrior Prince—that was what he was called since he had won three great battles—"and I confess to you that I have conceived such a strong passion for Princess Désirée that if you do not retract the promise you have given to Noire, I will surely die, fortunate to cease to live in losing hope of the person that I love."

"So it's with her portrait," said the king, gravely, "that you've taken it into your head to hold conversations that are rendering you ridiculous to all the courtiers. They believed you to be insane, and if you knew what they have reported to me on that subject, you would be ashamed to have given evidence of so much weakness."

"I cannot reproach myself for such a beautiful flame," he replied. "When you have seen the portrait of that charming princess you will approve of what I feel for her."

"Go and fetch it immediately, then," said the king, "with an impatience that made his chagrin obvious enough."

The prince would have had difficulty doing it if he had not been certain that nothing in the world could equal Désirée's beauty. He ran to his cabinet and came back to the king's apartment; the later was almost as enchanted as his son.

"Oh, my dear Warrior," he said to him. "I consent to what you wish. I'll be rejuvenated when I have such a lovable princess in my court. I'll send ambassadors to Noire immediately to retract my promise; even if I have to fight a rude war against her, I'd rather resolve myself to it."

The prince kissed his father's hands respectfully and embraced his knees more than once. He was so joyful that he was scarcely recognizable. He pressed the king to dispatch ambassadors, not only to Noire but also to Désirée, and wanted him choose for the latter mission the most capable and richest msn, because it is necessary to put on an appearance on such an important occasion and to be persuasive in what one desires.

The King cast his eyes upon Becafigue; he was a very eloquent young lord who had an income of a hundred millions. He loved the Warrior Prince passionately; in order to please him he put together the mot grandiose equipage and the most beautifully liveried that he could imagine. His diligence was extreme, for the prince's amour augmented every day and he implored him incessantly to depart.

"Think," he said, confidently, "that my life is at stake, that I go out of my mind when I think that the father of that princess might make an engagement with someone else without wanting to break it in my favor, and that I would be doomed forever."

Becafigue reassured him in order to gain time, for he intended that his expense would do him honor. He took eighty carriages glittering with gold and diamonds; the best finished miniature did not approach the one that ornamented them; there were fifty more carriages, twenty-four thousand mounted pages more magnificent than princes, and the rest of the great cortege did not let him down in any fashion.

When the ambassador had his audience to take his leave of the prince, he embraced him tightly. "Remember, my dear

Becafigue," he said, "that my life depends on the marriage that you are going to negotiate; do not neglect anything to persuade and bring back the lovely princess that I adore."

He charged him with a thousand presents, the gallantry of which equaled their magnificence; there was nothing but amorous devices engraved on diamond signet rings, watches inside carbuncles changed with Désirée's monogram, ruby bracelets cut in hearts—in sum, everything imaginable to please.

The ambassador carried the portrait of the young prince, which he had painted by such a knowledgeable painter that it could talk and make little compliments full of wit. In truth, it did not respond at all to what anyone said, but that was scarcely necessary. Becafigue promised the prince not to neglect anything for his satisfaction, and added that he was taking so much money that if the princess were refused to him he would find a means of gaining one of her women and abducting her.

"Oh!" cried the prince, "I can't resolve myself to do that; she'd be very offended by such a disrespectful procedure."

Becafigue said nothing in response to that, and departed.

The rumor of his journey preceded his arrival; the king and the queen were delighted by it. They held his master in high esteem and knew about the Warrior Price's great deeds; but what they knew even better was his personal merit, with the consequence that if they had searched the whole world for a husband for their daughter they could not have found one more worthy of her. A palace was prepared to lodge Becafigue, and all the necessary orders were given for the court to appear in the utmost magnificence.

The king and queen had resolved that the ambassador should see Désirée, but the fay Tulip came to find the queen and said to her: "Refrain carefully, Madame, from taking Becafigue to the abode of our child"—that was what she called the princess—"it's necessary for him not to see her so soon, and don't consent to send her to the home of the king who is requesting her until she has passed her fifteenth year, for I'm sure that if she departs sooner, some misfortune will overtake her."

The queen embraced the good Tulip, and promised to follow her advice. They went to see the princess right away.

The ambassador arrived; his equipage took twenty-three hours to go past, for there were six hundred thousand mules whose bells and hooves were gold, their blankets velvet and brocade embroidered with pearls; there was an unprecedented blockage in the streets, everyone having run to see it. The king and queen went to meet him, so glad were they of his coming.

There is no point in talking about the speech he made and the ceremonies that took place on either part; they can easily be imagined. When he asked to salute the princess, however, he was very surprised that the favor in question was denied him.

"If we refuse you something that seems so just, Sire Becafigue," the king said to him, "it's not by virtue of a caprice particular to us. It's necessary to tell you about our daughter's strange adventure, in order that you should take it in good part. A fay took an aversion to her at the moment of her birth and threatened her with a very great misfortune if she saw the daylight before the age of fifteen years; we keep her in a palace in which the most beautiful apartments are underground. When we made the resolution to take you there, the fay Tulip prescribed us to do nothing of the sort."

"What, Sire!" replied the ambassador. "Shall I have the chagrin of returning without her? You're according her to my master, the king, for his son; she's awaited with a thousandfold impatience. Is it possible that you pause at bagatelles such as the predictions of fays? Here is the portrait of the Warrior Prince that I was ordered to present to her. The resemblance is so perfect that I believe I am seeing him when I look at it."

He unfurled it immediately. The portrait, which was instructed only to talk to the princess, said: "Beautiful Désirée, you cannot imagine the ardor with which I await you. Come soon to our court, to ornament it with the graces that render you incomparable."

The portrait said nothing more, but the king and queen were so astonished that they begged Becafigue to give it to them, in order to take it to the princess. He was delighted by that, and placed it in their hands.

The queen had not spoken to her daughter until then about what was happening; she had even forbidden the ladies that were with her to say anything to her about the arrival of the ambassador. They had not obeyed her, and the princess knew that it was a matter of a great marriage, but she was so prudent that she had not said anything about it to her mother. When the queen showed her the talking portrait of the prince, which made her a compliment as tender as it was gallant, she was very surprised, for she had never seen anything to equal it.

"Would you be sorry," the queen said to her, laughing, "to have a husband who resembled this prince?"

"Madame," she replied, "it is not for me to make a choice; thus, I shall always be content with the one that you destine for me."

"But after all," said the queen, "If the lot fell to him, would you not consider yourself fortunate?"

She blushed, lowered her eyes, and made no reply.

The queen took her in her arms and kissed her several times; she could not help shedding tears when she thought that she was on the point of losing her, for in three months' time she would be fifteen. Hiding her displeasure, she told her everything that regarded her in the embassy of the celebrated Becafigue; she even gave her the rarities that he had brought to present to her. She admired them, and praised with an abundance of good taste what was most curious about them; but from time to time hr gaze escaped in order to attach itself to the portrait of the prince with a pleasure that had been unknown to her until then.

The ambassador, seeing that he was making futile entreaties for the princess to be given to him, and that he would have to be content with her being promised—but so solemnly that there was no reason to doubt it—did not remain with the king long, and returned post-haste in order to render his masters an account of his negotiation.

When the prince discovered that he could not hope to see his dear Désirée for three more months, he uttered laments that afflicted the entire count. He no longer slept, he no longer ate; he became sad and pensive; the vivacity of his complexion changed to the color of anxiety. He spent entire days lying on a sofa in his cabinet gazing at the portrait of his princess. He wrote to her continually and presented his letters to the portrait, as if it were capable of reading them. In the end his strength gradually diminished; he fell dangerously ill, and it did not require physicians to divine the cause.

The king was in despair; he loved his son more tenderly than any other father had ever loved his. He saw that he was on the point of losing him: what agony for a father! He could not see any remedy that could cure the prince. He wanted Désirée; without her, he would die. He therefore made the resolution, in such a great extremity, to go and see the king and queen that had promised her, in order to implore them to have pity on the state to which the prince was reduced, and not to defer a marriage that would never take place if they were obstinate in waiting until the princess was fifteen.

That step was extraordinary, but it would have been even more extraordinary if he had allowed such a lovable and dear son to perish. However, he found a difficulty that was insurmountable, which was that his great age only permitted him to go in a litter, and that vehicle was ill-suited to his son's impatience, with the result that he sent the faithful Becafigue post-haste and wrote the most touching letters in the world to engage the king and queen to do as he wished.

In the meantime, Désirée had scarcely less pleasure in seeing the portrait of the prince than he had in gazing at hers. She went continually to the place where it was, and whatever care she took to hide her sentiments, they were penetrated nevertheless. Among others, Wallflower and Longthorn, who were her maids, perceived the small anxieties that were beginning to torment her.

Wallflower loved her passionately and was faithful to her; Longthorn incessantly felt a secret jealousy of her merit and her rank; her mother had brought the princess up; after having been her governess she had become her maid of honor; she would have loved her, as the most lovable thing in the world, but she cherished her daughter madly, and, seeing the hatred she had for the beautiful princess, she could not wish her well.

The ambassador that had been dispatched to the court of Princess Noire was not well received when the compliment with which he was charged was known. That Ethiopian was the most vindictive creature in the world; she thought it was treating her in a cavalier fashion, after having made engagements with her, to send word that they were being retracted. She had seen a portrait of the prince, with whom she was infatuated, and Ethiopians, when they dabble in amour, love with more extravagance than others.

"What, Sire Ambassador!" she said. "Does your master not think me rich enough and beautiful enough? Travel in my estates, you will scarcely find any vaster; come into my royal treasury and see more gold than all the mines in Peru have ever furnished. Finally, look at the blackness of my head; are not this squashed nose and these thick lips all that is necessary in order to be beautiful?"

"Madame," replied the ambassador, who feared the bastinado even more than those we send to the Sublime Gate, "I criticize my master to the extent that is permissible for a subject; if Heaven had put me on the foremost throne in the world it would certainly be you to whom I would offer it."

"That speech will save your life," she said. "I had resolved to commence my vengeance with you, but there would be injustice in that, since you are not the cause of your prince's bad procedure. Go and tell him that it gives me pleasure to break with him because I do not like dishonest people."

The ambassador, who wanted nothing more than to be given leave to depart, had no sooner obtained it than he took advantage of it.

But the Ethiopian was too piqued against the Warrior Prince to pardon him; she mounted an ivory chariot drawn by six ostriches, which could cover ten leagues in an hour. She went to the palace of the Fay of the Spring, who was her godmother and her best friend. She told her about her adventure and begged her, with the utmost insistence, to serve her resentment. The fay was sensible to the dolor of her goddaughter; she looked into the book that says everything and immediately discovered that the Warrior Prince had only quit Princess Noire for Princess Désirée; that he loved her madly and that he had even fallen ill solely by virtue of impatience to see her.

That knowledge reignited her anger, which was almost extinct; and as she had not seen her since the moment of her birth, it can be assumed that she would have neglected to do her any harm if the vindictive Noire had not implored her to do so. "What!" she exclaimed. "So that wretched Désirée still wants to displease me! No, charming princess, no, my darling, I mill not suffer that anyone insults you; the heavens and all the elements are interested in this affair; return home and rely on your dear godmother."

Princes Noire thanked her and made her presents of flowers and fruits, which she received very agreeably.

Ambassador Becafigue advanced in all diligence to the capital where Désirée made her abode; he threw himself at the feet of the king and the queen; he shed abundant tears and told them in the most touching terms that the Warrior Prince would die if they refused him much longer the pleasure of seeing the princess, their daughter; that only three more months were required for her to be fifteen years of age; that nothing unfortunate could happen to her in such a short span of time; and that he took the liberty of informing them that such a great credulity for petty fays was injurious to royal majesty.

In the end, he spoke so well that he was able to persuade them. They wept with him, imagining the sad state to which the young prince was reduced, and then told him that they would need a few days to make up their minds and reply to him. He replied that he could only give them a few hours; that his master was at the extremity; that he imagined that the princess hated him and that she was the one delaying her journey; he was therefore assured that he would know that evening what could be done.

The queen ran to her dear daughter's palace; she told her everything that had happened. Désirée felt an unparalleled dolor then; her heart constricted and she fainted. The queen knew then the sentiments that she had for the prince.

"Don't be afflicted, my dear child," she said. "You can do everything for his cure, and I am only anxious about the threats that the Fay of the Spring made at your birth."

"I flatter myself, Madame," she replied, "that, by taking a few precautions, we can cheat the malevolent fay. For instance, can I not travel in a closed carriage in which I cannot see the daylight? It can be opened by night in order to give us something to eat; thus, I shall arrive safely at the Warrior Prince's home."

The queen liked that expedient very much; she told the king about it, who also approved of it, with the consequence that they send word to Becafigue to come promptly. He received certain assurances that the princess would depart as soon as possible, so that he had only to return to give that good news to his master, and that in order to hasten it further, they would neglect to give her the equipage and rich clothes appropriate to her rank.

The ambassador, transported by joy, threw himself at Their Majesties' feet again to thank them. He departed afterwards without having seen the princess.

Separation from the king and queen would have seemed insupportable to her if she had been less prejudiced in favor of the prince, but there are certain sentiments that stifle almost all the others.

A carriage was made of green velvet outside, ornamented by large plates of gold and inside by silver brocade embroidered with pink. It had no mirrors, it was very large, sealed better than a box, and one of the foremost lords of the realm was charged with the keys that opened the locks that had been fitted to the door.

> *Around her were seen the graces,*
> *Laughters, pleasures and games,*
> *And the respectful Amours*
> *Hastened to follow her tracks;*
> *She had a majestic air,*
> *With a celestial mildness.*
> *She attracted all prayers,*
> *Without counting here the rest,*
> *She had the same attractions*
> *That made Adelaïde shine,*
> *When, hymen serving as a guide,*
> *She came to this place to cement peace.*[9]

Few officers were appointed to company her, in order that a numerous retinue would not embarrass her, and after giving her the most beautiful precious stones in the world and a few rich garments, after adieux that nearly caused the king to choke, she was locked in the somber carriage with her maid of honor, Wallflower and Longthorn.

It might perhaps have been forgotten that Longthorn did not love Princess Désirée, but she did love the Warrior Prince, for she had seen his portrait. The arrow that had wounded her had been so sharp that, on the point of departure, she told her mother that she would die if the marriage of the princess were accomplished, and that if she wanted to conserve her, it was absolutely necessary for her to find a means of breaking that

---

[9] The reference is to Marie-Adélaide de Savoie, who married the Duc de Bourgogne in December 1697 (a few days after her twelfth birthday), in order to seal the Treaty of Turin; the event is referenced in three stories by the Comtesse de Murat published in her 1699 collection.

affair. The maid of honor told her not to be afflicted, that she would try to remedy her pain by rendering her fortunate.

When the queen sent her dear child away, she recommended her above all that can be said to that wicked woman. "What a deposit I am confiding to you!" she said to her. "She is more than my life; be careful of my daughter's health, but above all be careful to prevent her from ever seeing daylight, for all would be lost; you know with what woes she is threatened, and I have agreed with the Warrior Prince's ambassador that until she is fifteen years old she will be put in a castle where she will not see any light except candlelight." The queen heaped the woman with presents in order to engage her to the greatest exactitude. She promised to watch over the conservation of the princess and to render her a good account as soon as they had arrived.

Thus the king and queen, relying on her cares, should have had no more anxiety for their dear child; that served to some degree to moderate the pain that the separation caused them.

But Longthorn, who learned from the officers of the princess who opened the carriage every evening in order to serve her supper, that they were approaching the city where they were awaited, pressed her mother to execute her design, fearing that the king or the prince might come to meet her and there would no longer be time. In consequence, toward midday, when the sun darts its rays most forcefully, she suddenly cut through the imperial of the carriage in which they were enclosed with a large knife that she had brought expressly for that purpose.

Then, for the first time, Princess Désirée saw daylight. Scarcely had she looked at it and uttered a profound sigh than she was precipitated from the carriage in the form of a white hind, and started running toward the nearby forest, where she plunged into a dark place, in order to regret without witnesses the charming form that she had just lost.

The Fay of the Spring, who was leading the strange adventure, seeing that of all those who were accompanying the princess, some set out to follow her and others to go to the city to inform the Warrior Prince of the misfortune that had just occurred, immediately seemed to overturn nature. Lightning and thunder frightened the most assured, and by means of her marvelous knowledge she transported all those people far away, in order to distance them from the place where their presence displeased her.

No one remained but the maid of honor, Longthorn and Wallflower. The last-named ran after her mistress, making the woods and the rocks resound with her name and her laments. The other two, delighted to be at liberty, did not lose a moment in doing what they had planned. Longthorn put on Désirée's richest garments. The royal mantle that had been made for her wedding was of unparalleled richness, and the crown had diamonds three or four times as large as a fist. Her scepter was a single ruby; the orb that she held in her other hand was a pearl larger than her head; it was rare and very heavy to carry; but it was necessary to persuade people that she was the princess, and not to neglect any of the royal ornaments.

In that equipage, Longthorn, followed by her mother, who carried the train of her mantle, walked toward the city. The false princess marched gravely; she had no doubt that they would be met, and, indeed, they had scarcely advanced when they perceived a large troop of cavalry, in the middle of which were two litters brilliant with gold and precious stone, borne by mules ornamented with long sprays of green plumes—green was the favorite color of the princess.

The king, who was in one of them, and the sick prince, who was in the other were only able to judge the two ladies who were coming toward them. The most urgent galloped toward them and judge by the magnificence of their garments that they must be persons of distinction. They dismounted and approached them respectfully.

"Oblige me by informing me," said Longthorn, "who is in those litters."

"Mesdames," they replied, "It is the king and the prince, his son, who are coming to met Princess Désirée."

"Go tell them, please," she said, "that she is here. A fay who is jealous of my happiness has dispersed all those who were accompanying me by means of a hundred thunderclaps, lightning and surprising prodigies, but this is my maid of honor, who is charged with letters from the king, my father, and my gems."

Immediately, the cavaliers kissed the hem of her robe and went diligently to inform the king that the princess was approaching.

"What!" he cried. "She's coming on foot in broad daylight!"

They told him what she had said to them.

The prince, burning with impatience, called to them and without asking them any questions, said to them: "Admit that she is a prodigy of beauty, a miracle, a very accomplished princess."

The made no reply, which surprised the prince. "For having to praise her too highly," he said, "you prefer to keep quiet?"

"You will see her, Sire," said the boldest among them. "Apparently, the fatigue of the voyage has changed her."

The prince remained surprised; if he had not been so weak he would have leapt out of the litter in order to satisfy his impatience and his curiosity. The king descended from his and, advancing with all his court he joined the false princess. But as soon as he had cast his eyes on her he uttered a loud cry and recoiled several paces. "What do I see?" he said. "Some perfidy!"

"Sire," said the maid of honor, advancing boldly. "This is Princess Désirée, with letters from the king and the queen; I am also putting in your hands the casket of gemstones with which I was charged on departure."

The king looked at all that in a bleak silence, and the prince, leaning on Becafigue, approached Longthorn. O gods, what became of him, after having considered that young woman, whose extraordinary stature frightened him! She was so tall that the princess's garment hardly came down to her knees; she was frightfully thin; her nose, more hooked than a parrot's, shone a brilliant red; there had never been teeth blacker and more badly arranged. In sum, she was as ugly as Désirée was beautiful.

The prince, who was only occupied with the charming idea of his princess, remained transfixed, as if paralyzed, at the sight of her. He did not have the strength to proffer a single word. He looked at her in astonishment, and then addressed the king. "I have been betrayed," he said. "The marvelous portrait on which I engaged my liberty is nothing like the person who has been sent to us; they sought to deceive us; they have succeeded, and it will cost me my life."

"What do you mean, Sire," said Longthorn, "that someone has sought to deceive you? Know that you will never be deceived in marrying me." Her effrontery and conceit were unexampled.

The maid of honor outdid her. "Oh, my beautiful princess," she cried, "where have we come? Is it thus that a person of your rank is received? What inconstancy! What procedure! The king our father will obtain a reckoning for it."

"It is us who will have it," relied the king. "He promised us a beautiful princess and he sends us a skeleton, a frightening mummy. I'm no longer astonished that he has kept this fine treasure hidden for fifteen years. He wanted to attract some dupe; it is on us that the lot has fallen, but it is not impossible to exact revenge."

"What outrages!" cried the false princess. "Am I not very unfortunate to have come on the word of such people? Is it a great wrong to have oneself painted slightly more beautiful than one is? Does it not happen every day? If princes sent away their fiancées for such inconveniences, few would be married."

The king and the prince, transported by anger, did not deign to respond. They each climbed back into their litter. Without further ceremony, a guardsman put the princess on his horse behind him; and the maid of honor was treated in the same way. They were taken into the city on the king's order and locked in the Castle of Three Spires.

The Warrior Prince had been so downcast by the blow that had just struck him that his affliction was all concentrated in his heart. When he had enough strength to lament, what did he not say about his cruel destiny? He was still in love, and he had no object for his passion but a portrait. His hopes no longer subsisted; all the charming ideas he had formed about Princess Désirée had capsized; one would rather have died than marry the person he took to be her. In sum, no despair had ever equaled his. He could no longer suffer the court, and he resolved to go away secretly as soon as his health permitted, and to go to some solitary place in order to spend the rest of his sad life there.

He only communicated his design to the faithful Becafigue, he was so convinced that he would follow him anywhere, and he chose to speak to him more frequently than any other about the bad turn that had been done to him. Scarcely had he begun to feel better than he departed, leaving on the table of his cabinet a long letter for the king, assuring him that as soon as his mind achieved a little tranquility he would return to him, but begging him in the meantime to think about their common vengeance and to keep the ugly princess prisoner.

It is easy to judge the dolor that the king felt when he received that letter. Separation from a son so dear nearly killed him.

While everyone was occupied in consoling him, the prince and Becafigue drew away, and after three days they found themselves in a vast forest, so somber by virtue of the density of its trees and so agreeable by virtue of the freshness of its grass and the streams that ran through it in all directions, that the prince, fatigued by the long journey—for he was still ill—dismounted and threw himself sadly to the ground, his hand beneath his head, almost unable to speak, so weak was he.

"Sire," Becafigue said to him, "While you rest, I'll go in search of a few fruits to refresh you, and reconnoiter a little the place where we are."

The prince made no reply, but only gave him permission with a gesture.

It was some time ago that we left the woodland hind—by which I mean the incomparable princess. She wept like a desolate creature when she saw her form in a spring that served her as a mirror. *What, that's me!* she said to herself. *It's today that I find myself reduced to suffering the strangest adventure that can happen by virtue of the reign of the fays to an innocent princess like me! How long will my metamorphosis last? Where can I retire, in order that the lions, bears and wolves won't devour me? How will I be able to eat grass?*

In sum, she asked a thousand questions, and felt the cruelest dolor possible. It is true that if anything could console her, it is that she was as beautiful a hind as she had been a princess.

Hunger pressing Désirée, she grazed the grass with a good appetite, and was surprise that that was possible. Then she lay down on the moss; night surprised her, and she passed through inconceivable terrors. She heard ferocious beasts nearby, and, forgetting that she was a hind, she tried to climb a tree. Daylight reassured her slightly; she admired its beauty and the sun seemed to her something so marvelous that she never wearied of looking at it; everything that she had heard said about it seemed far below what she saw; that was the unique consolation that she could find in such a deserted pace. She remained alone there for several days.

The fay Tulip, who had always loved the princess, felt her misfortune keenly, but she had a veritable chagrin that the queen and she had paid such little heed to her advice, for she had told them several times that if the princess left before she was fifteen, she would find herself in trouble. However, she did not want to abandon her to the fury of the Fay of the Spring, and it was her who guided Wallflower's steps toward the forest, in order that the faithful confidante could console her in her disgrace.

The beautiful hind was passing slowly along a stream when Wallflower, who could hardly walk, lay down in order to rest. She was wondering sadly which way she ought to go to find her dear princess. When the hind perceived her she promptly crossed the stream, which was wide and deep, came to throw herself into Wallflower's arms, and gave her a thousand caresses. She was surprised by that; she did not know whether the animals in the area had some particular amity for human, which rendered them humane, or whether it knew her—for, in sum, it was very singular that a hind should take it into her head to do her the honors of the forest so well.

She looked at the hind attentively, and saw, with an extreme surprise, large tears flowing from her eyes; she no longer doubted that it was her dear princess. She took her feet and kissed them, with as much respect and tenderness as she had kissed her hands. She spoke to her, and knew that the hind understood her, but that she could not reply to her. The tears and sighs redoubled on either side. Wallflower promised her mistress that she would not quit her; the hind made her a thousand little signs with her head ad eyes, which marked that she was very glad about that, and that it consoled in her part for her troubles.

They had remained together almost all day; the hind was afraid that her faithful Wallflower might need something to eat, and guided her to a part of the forest where she had remarked wild fruits, which were nevertheless good. She took a quantity of them, for she was dying of hunger, but after that snack was finished, she fell into a great anxiety, not knowing where they could retire in order to sleep, for it was not possible for her to resolve to remain in the middle of the forest, exposed to all the perils they might run.

"Are you not afraid, charming hind," she said to her, "to spend the night here?"

The hind raised her eyes toward the heavens, and sighed.

"But you've already explored a part of his vast solitude," Wallflower continued. "Are there no cottages, a charcoal-burner's hut, a woodcutter's cabin, or a hermitage?"

The hind marked, by the movement of her head, that she had not seen any.

"O gods!" cried Wallflower. "I shall not be alive tomorrow; if I have the good fortune to avoid the tigers and the bears, I'm certain that the fear will be sufficient to kill me—and don't believe, my dear princess, that I'm regretting life with regard to myself; I'm regretting it with regard to you. Alas, to leave you in this desolate place deprived of all consolation! Can there be anything sadder?"

The little hind began to weep, sobbing almost like a human.

Her tears touched the fay Tulip, who loved her tenderly; in spite of her disobedience, she had always watched over her conservation. She suddenly appeared. "I don't want to scold you," she said. "The state you are in gives me too much pain."

The hind and Wallflower interrupted her by throwing themselves at her knees; the former kissed her hands and caressed her as prettily as was possible; the latter implored her to have pity in the princess and return her to her natural form.

"That doesn't depend on me," Tulip said. "The one who did her so much harm has a great deal of power; but I'll shorten the time of her penitence, and make it milder. As soon as night replaces day she'll quit the form of a hind, but as soon as dawn appears, it will be necessary for her to resume it and roam the plains and forests like the others."

It was already a great deal to cease to be a hind by night, and the princess testified her joy by laps and bounds that gave Tulip joy. "Advance along this little path," she told them; "you'll find a cabin that is clean enough for a rustic abode."

As she finished speaking, she disappeared.

Wallflower obeyed; she entered with the hind into the path they had been shown and found an old woman sitting on her doorstep, finishing a wicker basket. Wallflower saluted her. "Would you allow me to retire with my hind, my good mother? I only need a small room."

"Yes, my beautiful girl," she replied, "I'll gladly give you shelter here. Enter with your hind." She took them right away to a very pretty room paneled with cherry-wood. There were two small beds of white cloth, with fine sheets, and everything appeared so simple and neat that the princess said thereafter that she had never found anything more to her taste.

As soon as night had fallen completely, Désirée ceased to be a hind; she embraced her dear Wallflower a hundred times over, thanked her for the affection that had engaged her to follow her fortune, and promised that she would render her very happy as soon as her penitence was over.

The old woman knocked gently on their door, and, without coming in, she gave excellent fruits to Wallflower, which the princess ate with great appetite; then they went to bed.

As soon as daylight appeared, Désirée, having become a hind again, started scratching at the door in order that Wallflower would open it. They expressed a sensible regret at separating, although it would not be for long; and, the hind having launched herself into the densest part of the wood, she commenced running, as usual.

I have already said that the Warrior Prince had stopped in the forest, and that Becafigue was roaming around in order to find a few fruits. It was rather late when he found the cottage of the old woman that I have mentioned. He spoke to her civilly and asked her for the things of which he had need for his master. She hastened to fill a basket, and gave it to him.

"I fear," she said," that if you spend the night here without a retreat, some accident might befall you. I can only offer you a poor one, but at least it will shelter you from the lions."

He thanked her, and told her that he was with one of his friends, and that he would go to propose to him that they spend the night in her house. In fact, he convinced the prince so easily that he allowed himself to be led to the good woman's cottage. She was still at the door, and without making any noise, she led them to a room similar to the one that the princess occupied, so close to it that they were only separated by a partition.

The prince spent the night with his usual anxieties; as soon as the first rays of the sun had brightened his windows he got up, and in order to distract himself from his sadness he went into the forest, telling Becafigue not to come with him. He walked for a long time without following any definite route; eventually, he arrived in a rather spacious area covered with trees and moss; immediately, a hind set off therefrom.

He could not help following her; his dominant penchant was for hunting, but it was no longer so keen since the passion he had in his heart. in spite of that, he pursued the poor hind, and from time to time he unleashed arrows at her that nearly caused her to die of fright. Although she was not wounded by them, because her friend Tulip protected her, it required nothing less than the helpful hand of a fay to save her from perishing under such accurate shots. No one has ever been a weary as the hind princess was; the exercise she was doing was entirely new to her.

Finally, she turned into a path so fortunately that the dangerous hunter lost sight of her, and, finding himself extremely fatigued, did not persist in pursuing her.

The day having passed in that manner, the hind saw with joy the hour to retire approaching. She directed her steps toward the house where Wallflower was waiting for her impatiently. As soon as she was in her room she threw herself down on the bed, Wallflower gave her a thousand caresses; she was dying of the desire to know what had happened to her. The hour of transformation having arrived, the beautiful princess resumed her original form and threw her arms around her favorite's neck.

"Alas," she said, "I thought I had nothing to fear but the Fay of the Spring and the cruel guests of the forest, but I was pursed today by a young hunter, whom I scarcely glimpsed, so intent was I on fleeing; a thousand arrows unleashed after me threatened me with inevitable death; I don't know by what good fortune I was able to get away."

"It's necessary not to go out again, my princess," Wall-flower replied. "Spend the fatal time of your penitence in this room. I'll go into the nearest town to buy books to divert you; we'll read the new tales that have been written about the fays, we'll have verses and songs."

"Shut up, my dear girl," said the princess. "The charming idea of the Warrior Prince is sufficient to occupy me agreeably; but the same power that reduces me during the day to the sad condition of a hind forces me, in spite of myself, to do what they do: I run, I jump and I eat grass like them; at that time a room would be insupportable to me"

She was so harassed by the hunt that she asked promptly for something to eat. Then her two beautiful eyes closed until daybreak. As soon as she perceived it, the usual metamorphosis occurred and she returned to the forest.

For his part, the prince had come back in the evening to rejoin his favorite. "I've spent the time," he said, "running after the most beautiful hind I've ever seen. It deceived me a hundred times with a marvelous skill. I fired so accurately that I don't understand how it avoided my shots. As soon as daylight comes, I'll go to look for it again, and I won't fail."

In fact, the young prince, who wanted to expel from his heart an idea that he thought chimerical, not being displeased that the passion for hunting was occupying him, returned at an early hour to the same place where he had found the hind; but she had carefully refrained from going back there, fearing an adventure similar to the one she had had.

He looked in all directions, and walked for a long time, and when he became hot he was delighted to find apples, the color of which pleased him. He picked some and ate them, and almost immediately fell profoundly asleep, lying on the fresh grass under trees in which a thousand birds seemed to have arranged a rendezvous.

While he was asleep, the fearful hind, eager to seek out remote spots, passed through the one where he was. If she had perceived him sooner she would have fled, but she found herself so close to him that she could not help looking at him, and his torpor reassured her so much that she took the time to consider all his features. O gods, what became of her when she recognized him! Her mind was too full of the charming idea of him to have lost it in such a short time.

Amour, Amour, what do you want, then? Is it necessary that the hind should risk losing her life at her lover's hands?

Yes, she would risk it; there was no longer any means of thinking of her safety. She lay down beside him, and her eyes, delighted to see him, could not turn away for a moment. She sighed. She uttered little moans; finally, becoming bolder, she approached even more closely; she touched him, and he woke up.

His surprise seemed extreme. He recognized the same hind that had given him so much exercise, and for which he had been searching for a long time, but to find it so familiar appeared to him to be a rare thing. She did not wait for him to try to catch her; she fled with all her might, and he followed her with all of his. From time to time she stopped in order to recover her breath, for the beautiful hind was still weary from having run the day before, and the prince was no less tired than she was; but what relented the hind's flight more, alas— is it necessary to say it?—was the difficulty of drawing away from the man who had wounded her more by his merit than by the arrows he launched at her.

He often saw her turn her head toward him, as if to ask him whether he wanted her to perish under his shots, but when he was on the point of catching up with her, she made new efforts to run away.

"Oh, if you could understand me, little hind," he shouted at her, "you wouldn't avoid me. I love you; I want to nourish you; you're charming; I'd take care of you."

The wind carried his words away; they did not reach her.

Finally, after having made an entire circuit of the forest, the hind, unable to run any more, slowed down; the prince accelerated, and caught up with her, with a joy of which he would not have believed himself to be capable. He could see clearly that she had exhausted all her strength; she was lying down like a poor little half-dead animal, and was only waiting to see her life ended by the hands of her conqueror. But instead of being cruel to her, he began caressing her.

"Beautiful hind," he said to her, "have no fear; I want to take you with me, and for you to go everywhere with me." He cut tree-branches, folded them adroitly and covered them with moss; he threw roses, with which a few bushes were covered, on to them. Then he took the hind in his arms, leaned her head on his neck and laid her down gently on the branches. Then he sat down beside her, searching from time to time for delicate herbs, which he presented to her, and which she ate from his hand.

The prince continued to talk to her, although he was convinced that she could not understand him. She became anxious because nightfall was approaching. What *will he do*, she said to herself, *if he sees me suddenly change form? He'll be frightened and will flee; or, if he doesn't flee, what would I not have to fear, alone like this in the forest?*

She was still wondering in what manner she could get away when he furnished her with the means; for, being afraid that she might need to drink, he went to see whether he could find a stream in order to take her to it; while he was searching, she slipped away promptly and came to the small house where Wallflower was waiting for her.

She threw herself on her bed again; night fell; her metamorphosis ceased, and she told her about her adventure.

"Would you believe, my dear," she said to her, "that my Warrior Prince is in this forest? It's him who has hunted me for two days, and who, having caught me, gave me a thousand caresses. Oh, the portrait they sent me is not very faithful; he's a hundred times better made; all the disorder that one sees in hunters took away nothing from his good looks, and conserves charms for him that I can't express. Am I not very unfortunate to be obliged to flee that prince, who is destined for me by my parents, who loves me, and whom I love? A wicked fay had to conceive an aversion to me on the day of my birth and is troubling all those of my life."

She started to weep. Wallflower consoled her, and enabled her to hope that in time, her pains would be changed into
pleasures.

The prince had returned to his dear hind as soon as he
had found a spring, but she was no longer in the place where
he had left her. He searched for her everywhere in vain, and
felt as much chagrin against her as if she had been rational.

"What!" he exclaimed. "Shall I only ever have reasons
for complaint against that deceptive and infidel sex?"

He returned to the home of the good old woman, full of
melancholy. He related the adventure of the hind to his confidant and accused her of ingratitude. Becafigue could not help
smiling at the prince's anger; he advised him to punish the
hind when he encountered her again,

"I'm only staying here for that," the prince replied. "Afterwards, we'll leave, in order to go further on."

Daylight returned and with it the princess resumed the
form of the white hind. She did not know what to resolve,
whether to go to the same places where the prince ordinarily
roamed, or to take an opposite route in order to avoid him. She
chose the latter course, and went far away, but the young
prince, who was as clever as her, did the same, believing that
she would employ that little ruse, with the result that he discovered her in the densest part of the forest. She thought that
she was safe there when he perceived her. Immediately, she
bounded, leapt over bushes, and as if she feared him more
because of all that she had done the previous evening, she fled
as lightly as the wind; but as she was crossing a path, he
launched an arrow so accurately that it penetrated her leg. She
felt a violent pain, and having no more strength to flee, she let
herself fall.

Cruel and barbaric Amour, where were you, then? What!
You allow an incomparable young woman to be wounded by
her tender lover?

That sad catastrophe was inevitable, because the Fay of
the Spring had attached herself to the end of the adventure.

The prince approached; he had a sensible regret at seeing the hind's blood flowing. He picked herbs and bound them to the leg in order to soothe it. He made her another bed of branches. He held the hind's head on his knees.

"Are you not the cause, fickle little thing," he said "of what has happened to you? What did I do yesterday for you to abandon me? It won't be the same today; I'll take you away."

The hind made no reply. What would she have said? She was wrong and could not speak—for it is not always a consequence that those who are wrong keep silent. The prince gave her a thousand caresses.

"How I'm suffering for having wounded you," he said to her. "You'll hate me, and I want you to love me." It seemed, in hearing him, that a secret genius was inspiring everything he said to the hind.

Eventually, the hour to return to the home of his aged hostess approached. He loaded himself with his quarry, finding it not a little awkward to carry her, to lead her. and sometimes to drag her.

She had no desire to go away with him. *What will become of me?* she thought. *What! I'm going to find myself alone with this prince? Oh, let's rather die.* She made herself a dead weight and wearied him. He was sweating all over with so much fatigue, and although he did not have far to go to the little house, he felt that without some help he would not be able to reach it.

He went in quest of Becafigue, but before quitting his prey he attached her with several ribbons to the foot of a tree, in the dread that she might flee.

Alas, who would have been able to think that the most beautiful princess in the world would one day be treated thus by a prince who adored her? She tried in vain to escape from the ribbons; her attempts to untie them only made the knots tighter. She was ready to strangle herself with a slip knot that he had unfortunately made when Wallflower, weary of being always shut up in her room, came out to get some air and went past the place where the white hind was struggling. What became of her when she perceived her dear mistress? She could not make haste enough to untie her; the ribbons were knotted in different places. In the end, the prince arrived with Becafigue, as she was about to take the hind away.

"Whatever respect I have for you, Madame," the prince said to her, "permit me to oppose a larceny that you are attempting to commit. I have wounded this hind, she is mine, I love her. I beg you to leave me the master of her."

"Sire," replied Wallflower, politely—for she was well brought-up and gracious—"this hind was mine before she was yours; I would renounce life sooner than her; and if you want to know how well she knows me, I only ask that you give her a little liberty. Come on, my white darling," she said, "embrace me." The hind threw herself at her neck. "Kiss me on the right cheek." She obeyed. "Touch my heart." She placed her foot upon it. "Sigh." She sighed.

It was no longer permissible for the prince to doubt what Wallflower said. "I yield her to you," he said, honestly, "but I confess that it is not without chagrin."

She went away immediately with the hind."

They did not know that the prince was residing in their house. He followed them at a distance, and was very surprised to see them entering the old woman's cottage. He arrived there shortly thereafter and, urged by an impulse of curiosity of which the white hind was the cause, he asked her who the young woman was.

She replied that she did not know, that she had taken her into her home with her hind, that she paid well and lived in great solitude. Becafigue asked where her room was; she said that it was next to his own, only separated from it by a partition.

When the prince had retired, his confidant told him that either he was the most mistaken of men or that young woman had lived with Princess Désirée, that he had seen her in the palace when he had gone there as an ambassador.

"Of what fatal memory are you reminding me?" the prince said to him. "And by what hazard would she be here?"

"That's what I don't know, Sire," added Becafigue. "But I have a yen to find out, and since we are only separated by mere woodwork, I'll make a hole in it."

"That's a very unnecessary curiosity," said the prince, sadly, for Becafigue's words had renewed all his dolors. In fact, he opened his window, which overlooked the forest, and started meditating.

Meanwhile, Becafigue worked, and had soon made a hole big enough to see the charming princess dressed in a robe of silver brocade mingled with a few red flowers embroidered with gold and emeralds. Her hair was falling in long curls over the most beautiful breasts in the world; her complexion shone with the brightest colors, and her eyes were ravishing. Wallflower was on her knees before her, bandaging her arm, from which the blood was flowing abundantly. They both seemed rather embarrassed by the wound.

"Let me die," said the princess. "Death would be milder for me than the deplorable life I'm leading. What! To be a hind all day long, to see the man for whom I am destined without being able to speak to him, without telling him about my fatal adventure. Alas! If you knew all the touching things he said to me during my metamorphosis, what a tone of voice he had, what noble and engaging manners, you would feel even more compassion for me than you do, for not being in a state to enlighten him as to my destiny."

One can easily judge Becafigue's astonishment at everything he had just seen and heard. He ran to the prince, he tore him away from the window with transports of inexpressible joy.

"Oh, Sire!" he said. "Don't defer approaching that petition; you'll see the true original of the portrait that charmed you."

The prince looked, and recognized his princess immediately. He would have died of pleasure if he had not feared being deceived by some enchantment—for, in sum, how could such an encounter be reconciled with Longthorn and her mother, who were imprisoned in the Castle of Three Spires and who claimed, one to be Désirée and the other her maid of honor.

However, his passion flattered him; one has a natural penchant to be persuaded of what one wishes, and in such an occasion it is necessary to die of impatience or be enlightened. Without delay he went to knock gently on the door of the room where the princess was.

Wallflower, not doubting that it was the good old woman and needing her aid to help her bandage her mistress's arm, hastened to open it, and was very surprised to see the prince, who threw himself at Désirée's feet. The transports that animated him hardly permitted him to speak coherently, so I have had difficulty determining what he said in those first moments; I have not found anyone who can enlighten me clearly.

The princess was no less embarrassed in her responses, but Amour, who often serves as an interpreter to the mute, became a third party, and persuaded both of them that they had never said anything more intelligent, or, at least, that they had never said anything more touching and tender. Tears, sighs, oaths and even a few gracious smiles, everything was there.

The night passed thus; the daylight appeared without Désirée thinking about it, and she no longer became a hind. She perceived that; nothing equaled her joy. The prince was too dear to her to defer sharing it with him. At the same time she commenced her story, which she told with a grace and a natural eloquence that surpassed that of the most expert.

"What, my charming princess!" he cried. "It's you that I wounded in the form of the white hind? What can I do to expiate such a great crime? Would it be sufficient to die of dolor before your eyes?"

He was so afflicted that his displeasure was visibly painted on his face. Désirée suffered from that more than from her wound; she assured him that it was almost nothing and that she could not help loving an injury that had procured her so much good.

The manner in which she spoke was so obliging that he could not doubt her generosity. In order to enlighten her in her turn of everything, he told her about the fraud that Longthorn and her mother had attempted, adding that it was necessary to hasten to send word to his father of the good fortune he had had in finding her, because he was about to wage a terrible war in order to obtain a reckoning for the affront he had received.

Désirée begged him to write to him via Becafigue. He was about to obey her when a piercing sound of trumpets, clarions, timpani and drums spread through the forest. It even seemed to them that they heard many people passing close to the little house. The prince looked out through the window; he recognized several officers, his flags and his pennants. He commanded them to stop and wait for him.

No surprise has ever been more agreeable than that of the army; everyone was convinced that the prince was about to lead them and take vengeance on Désirée's father. The prince's father was leading them himself, in spite of his great age. He arrived in a velvet litter embroidered with gold; it was followed by an uncovered carriage; Longthorn was in it with her mother. The Warrior Prince, having seen the litter, ran to it, and the king held out his arms to embrace him with a thousand testimonies of paternal amour.

"Where have you come from, my dear son?" he cried. "Is it possible that you have delivered me from the dolor your absence has caused me?"

"Sire," said the prince, "deign to listen to me."

The king immediately descended from his litter, and, moving a little way aside, his son told him about the fortunate encounter he had had, and the knavery of Longthorn.

The king, delighted by that adventure, raised his hands and eyes to the heavens in order to render thanks; at that moment, he saw Princess Désirée appear, more beautiful and more brilliant than all the stars put together. She was mounted on a beautiful horse, which only went in curvets; a hundred plumes of different colors decorated its head and the largest diamonds in the world had been added to her costume; she was dressed as a hunter. Wallflower, who was following her, was no less ornamented than her.

Those were the effects of the protection of Tulip, who had guided everything with care and with success. The pretty wooden house had been made in favor of the princess, and in the form of an old woman she had regaled her for several days. As soon as the prince had recognized his troops and had gone to find the his father she had gone into Désirée's room; she blew on her arm to heal her wound; then she gave her the rich garments in which she appeared to the eyes of the king, who remained so charmed that he had a great deal of difficulty believing that she was a mortal individual.

He told her everything that one can imagine of the most obliging in a similar occasion and implored her not defer giving his subjects the pleasure of having her for their queen. "For I am resolved," he continued, "to cede my kingdom to the Warrior Prince, in order to render him more worthy of you."

Désirée replied to him with all the politeness that one ought to expect of a person so well brought-up; then, casting her eyes on the two prisoners who were in the carriage, and who hid their faces in their hands, she had the generosity to ask for clemency for them, and that the same carriage in which they were should serve to take them wherever they wanted to go. The king consented to what she wished, not without admiring the goodness of her heart and giving her great praise.

The army was ordered to turn back. The prince mounted a horse in order to accompany his beautiful princess. They were received in the capital with a thousand cries of joy. Preparations were made for the wedding day, which became very solemn, by virtue of the presence of the six benign fays who loved the princess. They gave them the richest presents that were ever imagined; among others, the magnificent palace where the queen had been to see them suddenly appeared in the air, carried by fifty thousand amours, which placed it in a beautiful plain on the edge of the river. After such a gift, none more considerable could be made.

The faithful Becafigue asked his master to speak to Wallflower and to unite her with him when he married the princess; he agreed. The lovely young woman was very glad to find such an advantageous establishment on arriving in a foreign kingdom. The fay Tulip, who was even more liberal than her sisters, gave her four gold mines in India, in order that her husband would not have the advantage of saying that he was richer than her.

The prince's wedding celebrations lasted for several months, every day furnishing a new fête, and the adventures of the white hind have been sung all over the world.

> *The princess was too hasty*
> *To emerge from that somber place,*
> *Where a sage fay wanted*
> *To hide her from the light of the sky;*
> *Her misfortunes, her metamorphosis*
> *Make it evident to what danger*
> *A young beauty is exposed*
> *When she dares to engage in society too soon!*
> *You, to whom Amour with a liberal hand,*
> *Has given attractions capable of touching,*
> *Beauty is often fatal,*
> *You cannot hide it too much.*
> *You think you can always defend yourself*
> *From feeling amour by making yourself loved;*
> *But know that in one's turn,*
> *By dint of giving, one can often be taken.*

THE NEW BOURGEOIS GENTLEMAN

A gentleman, the son of a merchant in the Rue Saint-Denis, who wanted to be quality and play the fop, because he was very rich in ready money and furniture, finding that his new nobility was insufficiently revered in a quarter were several people had seen him measuring cloth, took it into his head to distinguish himself in the provinces, by making himself a savant man of good taste. He bought the library of an academician who had just died, not doubting that he would soon know as much as him, since he had so many excellent books. He even learned how to bear arms, wanting to pass for brave, but his courage responded poorly to his boasting.

When it was a question of choosing the province in which the new gentleman wanted to establish himself, he cast his eyes on Normandy and departed for Rouen. He found all his father's correspondents there, who strove to regale him well, but they were only merchants, after all, and he had a great deal of trouble comparing himself with them, saying that he was a man of high quality, and in order to persuade people of that, he told everyone ridiculous lies; his head was strangely cracked and full of all sorts of imaginations.

When he enquired about lands that were for sale in the region, one was indicated to him that was on the shore of the sea, the description of which pleased him greatly. He went to see it and bought it, but the house did not seem sufficiently beautiful to him, with the result that he immediately hired workmen to demolish it, and as he prided himself on knowing everything, he did not want any architect other than himself to built his little château.

He chose a location that was, in fact, very agreeable. It was on the edge of the sea, which, when it was slightly irritated, came all the way to the foot of its walls. A fairly wide river emptied into it at that point, with the result that he had a great arcade constructed on which he built his modern palace. One climbed up to it on either side by way of sixty steps of carved stone with iron rails, and when it rained, or the wind was strong, it was an admirable feat; before one reached the house one was soaked to the skin, paralyzed by cold or roasted by the sun. It was necessary not to complain, though, and if anyone did, they were never pardoned.

Our bourgeois gentleman, having quit his paternal name, wanted to call himself Monsieur de La Dandinardière. The length of that name seemed appropriate to impose upon his neighbors, who were, for the most part, only barons and vicomtes, not very rich and unaccustomed for a long time to going to court. It was also necessary to see how he wanted to impose on them; his pockets were full of letters from persons of the highest quality; he composed them and wrote them himself, God knows with what style—but he filled them with news, which was highly esteemed in the province, and the king was always worried about the state of his health. On the strength of his great credit, he had half a dozen nasty little dogs, which he called his "pack," and a valet called Alain, who was titled with the names most suitable to the tasks for which his master employed him, such as secretary, maître d'hôtel, cook, steward and valet de chambre.

That valet led his master's pack on to the lands of his neighbors, where he often killed game at his ease, without La Dandinardière fearing that anyone might think that bad, or that anyone might take him to task for it; but a gentleman of impatient humor, having encountered the shooter in his wheat-field making rude war on innocent grouse, beat him mercilessly, and in response to the threats he made that his master would reckon with him before his best friends, the Maréchals de France, the countryman said: "Ah! You think you can frighten me; know that I know your Monsieur de La Dandinardière; here, here's four blows of my fist, take them to him on my behalf and ask him whether he's ever measured anything like them with his yardstick."

The valet returned with two black eyes, an aching head and devoid of game, although his master had been relying on him to have something to give at dinner to three honest local clergymen. When Alain told him about his sad adventure and the nasty joke made by Villeville—that was the gentleman's name—he flew into a terrible anger, for he was a refractory little man, coarse, fat and quick-tempered, who found it very bad that anyone lacked respect for him.

"I'll avenge myself," she said, "by staying in his hat, and we'll see whether it's better to be in peace or at war with me. Am I not important, then? I have a river that passes under my house, the sea outside my windows, and a château roofed with slate, while that rogue only has walls of mud and a cottage covered in thatch."

He was pacing back and forth proudly, his hands behind his back, when Baron de Saint-Thomas arrived. He rendered himself useful throughout the canton by virtue of his good manners; there was scarcely any dispute that he did not settle, any marriage about which he was not consulted, or any lawsuit in which he was not summoned. He had birth but little wealth; in addition to that, he was married to a tall, stiff, thin, dark woman who wanted to be beautiful at any price, so she made much more expenditure than was appropriate to the state of his affairs. She had two daughters, very well made, whom she did not love at all because they had grown up a little too soon and all the connoisseurs found a considerable difference between them and their mother; because of that they were kept locked up in a little pavilion at the end of the garden.

In that solitude they read as many romances as they wished, and, finding themselves pretty and very unhappy, they imagined themselves as unfortunate princesses always awaiting some hero to get them out of their enchanted castle. The scant acquaintance they had with society, combined with the chimeras they forged to soothe their ennui, soon rendered them *précieuses* of a sort, who, instead of the common sense that the Lord had given them, acquired a very singular turn of mind.

Their mother, who did not have the wherewithal to perceive that and remedy it, tranquilized herself in that regard. In fact, as long as they cost her almost nothing and all her expenditure was for herself, she let their imagination run to a thousand extravagances. Monsieur Saint-Thomas had a better sense of the oddities that his daughters got into their heads, and if he had enjoyed a greater fortune he would have worked usefully on theirs, but as his daughters could only find themselves fortunate in ideas, he left them mistress at least of making themselves agreeable ones.

Baron de Saint-Thomas was surprised by the furious expression that he remarked in Monsieur de La Dandinardière. "I don't know you today," he said, smiling. "Is something wrong?"

"What's wrong, my neighbor," he replied, "I shall soon tell you, and if you don't fall dead on the spot, at least you'll be very ill. Sieur de Villeville has insulted me; he has insulted me, he has killed my dogs, he has assassinated my huntsman. He is jeering at me; in truth, it's too much, for between ourselves...I shall say no more; we shall see, we shall see."

"What!" said Monsieur de Saint-Thomas interrupting. "You want to measure your sword against his?"

"Yes, I want to, Monsieur, "cried La Dandinardière. "I want to kill him with the first shot, at least, or I won't be content."

"It's necessary to moderate yourself," said the baron. "You know the cruel destiny of duelists, and you'd have to think of leaving the country promptly if your design were known to one of your enemies."

"Honor has always been dearer to me than life," said La Dandinardière. "If I suffer jeers and sneers patiently I'll have to desert my château. These Norman dogs are treating me lightly—I don't call them dogs, Monsieur le Baron, to give you any pain, but only in relation to the anger I have against Villeville."

"I don't take things so literally," replied Monsieur de Saint-Thomas, "and to show that I'm your servant, if it's true that you really have a desire to fight, I'm entirely ready to issue the summons."

La Dandinardière was surprised by that proposition; peril was entirely appropriate to diminish his wrath, and his friend's zeal appeared to him at that moment to be the most insupportable thing in the world.

After having meditated for some time, he said to him: "Do you believe in all conscience that if find myself on the dueling-ground with that bumpkin that I'll end up in court?"

"It's necessary to be wary of an encounter," the baron replied. "I know Villeville; you'd have no difficulty engaging him to fight."

"Is he brave?" said La Dandinardière, anxiously.

"To the point of temerity," replied the baron. "He's killed more men in his life than many another has killed flies."

"I'm delighted to hear it," he said maintaining the best countenance he could. "That's what I need. I'll remember all my life the tenth duel I fought, when I sliced up a kind of braggart before anyone could stop it."

"Oh, I've always suspected that you're not an apprentice," added the baron, "But after all, make up your mind, in order that I can have the pleasure of being useful to you."

"I'm quite determined," said La Dandinardière. "However, it's necessary not to do anything in a hurry. In a few days I'll have the honor of seeing you." And, immediately changing the subject, he talked about several items of news sent to him from Paris and the army.

Monsieur de Saint-Thomas had too much desire to laugh to stay for long in the home of our bourgeois. Although he was no longer young, he had lost nothing of a certain natural gaiety that made him imagine rather pleasant things. He understood La Dandinardière's embarrassment completely, and that he was less annoyed with Villeville for insulting him than with himself for having boasted. He wanted to push the affair for his own entertainment.

He had a rather well made valet who had come to him from the depths of Gascony; he had not lost the boastful attitude natural to the people of that region. He instructed him marvelously and sent him two days later to see La Dandinardière. He had a leather coat, a cravat of black taffeta, a hat with a brim as broad as a parasol turned up in a mutinous fashion, a broad leather belt, a multicolored sash and the most formidable sword that had appeared in the region since William the Conqueror.

La Dandinardière, full of anxiety, was walking along the sea shore when he suddenly saw that swashbuckler so close to him that whatever desire he had to avoid him, he could not manage it.

"Are you not," he said to him in a thunderous voice and almost without saluting him, "Monsieur de La Dandinardière?"

"Perhaps," he replied, fearfully.

"Perhaps?" the other continued. "What does that mean?"

"I mean that I don't know you," added La Dandinardière, "And that I can easily do without making new acquaintances, so I'll respond to you briefly that I might be La Dandinardière and I that might have another name."

"That's your perhaps explained, then," said the bravo. "Personally, I'll tell you without any other ceremony that Monsieur de Villeville, having been informed of the nasty remarks you've been making on his account, finds it appropriate to see you face-to-face in three days' time in the nearby wood. I'll serve as his second; you'll take care to bring one."

La Dandinardière was so surprised that the eater of little children had had time to draw away before he had recovered from his fright. He looked in all directions to see where he might be, but could not see him, because he had slipped behind a cliff that rose up at that spot. La Dandinardière, who preferred in such a case to be dealing with a demon rather than a man, convinced himself as best he could that it had been a vision, that the evil spirit had taken on a fantastic appearance in order to come to trouble him, and that, if he were mistaken in that conjecture, he would at least persuade himself of it in public and thus get himself out of the affair honorably.

He went home so pale and distraught that he would have had no need to compose himself in order to make people believe that he had had a terrible scare. He found the prior of Richecourt and the Vicomte de Berginville, who had come to see him, and who did not notice it, because they had been occupied in the meantime in gazing at the old heroes with which Monsieur de La Dandinardière had ornamented his drawing room. He had written beneath then their names and principal deeds, but in characters so small they were hardly legible, with the consequence that the prior and the vicomte were arguing with one another, one saying that it was Gillet, the other Gillot.

At that point our bourgeois gentleman came in. "Ah, Monsieur," they said to him, "please put us in accord; what is the name of the person whose portrait this is?"

"Gilles, Messieurs," he replied. "Gilles de La Dandinardière. He was my ancestor; he was nourished by Louis XI, King of France,[10] at the Château d'Amboise, with his son Charles VIII, who was a very pretty and sage little king; that little king loved my ancestor Gilles madly. Louis XI feared, as history says, that his son might do him some bad turn, and in order to protect himself from that he brought him up very badly and nourished him on coarse meat, but Gilles, his favorite, always had good game and shared it with his master, with the consequence that in order to recompense him, he made him, I no longer know what, but I believe that it was Constable."

"I sustain," said the vicomte, "that we have never had one of that name."

"No matter," said La Dandinardière. "If he wasn't Constable he was at least a land admiral, for it's certain that there he is with a commander's baton and that isn't insignificant." He then explained to them all that was written about the history of his ancestors, which he knew by heart, and he would

---

[10] Louis XI reigned from 1461-1483; his son Charles VIII succeeded him at the age of thirteen.

have continued, in spite of the condition in which the swash-buckler had put him, but for the vicomte, who cast his eyes upon him, and seeing him blue, green and yellow, suddenly exclaimed: "Alas, my good Monsieur, are you about to die? I find you strangely changed."

"After what has just happened to me," he said, "It's a stroke of luck that I'm still alive, and if I had less courage, it's certain that I'd have died on the spot. Can you imagine, Messieurs, the state in which a man finds himself who has just been accosted by a demon, in human form, in truth, but who nevertheless had eyes full of an infernal malice, his feet on backwards and huge hooked fingernails?"

He told them what had happened on the sea shore, but however serious the prior and the vicomte affected to be, they could not help laughing at that chimerical fear. They nudged one another and gave one another sly winks, which signified their sentiments well enough. Finally, after great acclamations on such an extraordinary adventure, they advised him to have himself bled, and he consented to that with pleasure, because however the matter turned out, at least he would gain a few days' respite.

He sent for the surgeon, and in the meantime they dined. La Dandinardière was tempted not to eat, even though he was very hungry, because sea air gives one an appetite that one does not have elsewhere, but his friends told him that he need-ed to keep his strength up in order to resist men or demons. He approved of the advice and followed it so exactly that he ate as much by himself as his two guests and the rest of his domes-tics.

As the surgeon lived some distance from the house of our bourgeois, the prior and the vicomte left before he arrived, admiring the folly of wanting to descend from a favorite of Charles VIII and claiming that a demon would take the trouble to give him a scare. They agreed with one another that there must be some kind of joke underneath it, and that the Baron de Saint-Thomas would be able to clarify the enigma. They there-fore went to sleep over at his house, and found him with his usual gaiety, although he did not always have any great reasons for having any. His wife and his two daughters, as I have said, often mingled wormwood with the charms of his good humor.

He could not help confessing to his friends the trick he had played on La Dandinardière; he showed them the man who had frightened him so much, and told them that it was necessary to enjoy themselves further at his expense, and that he would go to offer his services against Villeville and render them an exact account of the violent state to which he could reduce him by means of the proposition of a duel. Everyone imagined in that regard something that would render the joke more amusing, and the next day, the Baron did not fail to go to our bourgeois gentleman's little château.

The surgeon who has come in response to his order had not found him disposed to shed a single drop of blood; he believed that it was sufficient to spread the rumor that he had been bled; he begged him to say so and paid him liberally enough to lend himself to a more considerable lie. He ordered his servants to say the same as the surgeon, and after having his arm bandaged he went to bed.

Baron de Saint-Thomas arrived early enough to find him still there. His faithful domestic Alain told him that he had not yet woken his master up, because he was ill.

"I have things too important to say to him to go away without seeing him," he replied. "Open his bedroom to me, Alain; I need to talk to him."

The valet obeyed, and the baron found La Dandinardière lying down, clad in a black camisole, which had once been close-fitting but from which the superfluity had been removed, with which his red woolen bonnet was covered. The rest of his attire corresponded well enough with that state of undress.

"What!" said the baron. "You're sleeping while Villeville is on campaign to exterminate you? He says that he sent a bravo here yesterday to call you out, and that he wants to fight, at any cost. I don't believe," he continued, "that you can refuse him that satisfaction."

La Dandinardière listened with a fearful expression that he was no longer the master of hiding. "I confess to you," he said, "that I haven't come to settle in this province in order to cross swords with anyone; I might as well have stayed in Paris, with is a rather murderous city, and where there is no lack of people capable of tormenting one another. I sought out this canton in order to live here peacefully. I have wealth and no reason to hate life; why are you advising me to risk two things that seem so precious to me?"

"I'm advising you as your friend," the baron said. "You're obliged to march in the tracks that your ancestors have frayed so gloriously. Would you want to lose your honor to save yourself three or four sword-cuts? If the word duel displeases you, let's call it an encounter; I'm ready to serve you. I'll be your second with regard to and against anyone, although I'm risking a good deal, for I have a wife and two daughters—but what would I not do for a friend? I'd give my very soul."

Seeing himself hard pressed, La Dandinardière had recourse to a feint that did not come off. He let himself fall back on his bed, crying with all his might: "I'm dying; I was bled too much yesterday evening; my arm is numb; I lost two buckets of blood last night; at least, I'm feeling faint." With that, closing his eyes, he lay down, resolved not to open them again for four hours.

The baron, who knew what he was dealing with, tickled him, and flicked him a few times, which the placid moribund suffered with an admirable patience. Then he went to fetch a jug, from which the threw water so rudely in his face that La Dandinardière, fearing a fecund inundation, opened his little eyes and went red with anger.

"I beg you, Monsieur," he said, "that if you ever find me unconscious again, let me die rather than relieve me as you've just done."

"My zeal is poorly repaid," replied the baron, "but no matter; I am your friend and your servant; provided that you fight, I'll be content."

"My God, Monsieur," leave me the time to calm down," replied La Dandinardière. You're almost as pressing as Villeville."

"Do you want him to assassinate you" added the baron. "That's the destiny of the majority of men who refuse the assignations that are given to them."

That threat worried our little man. "It's necessary that I give a little thought to this affair," he said. "I'll give you a positive response afterwards."

Monsieur de Saint-Thomas judged that he would fatigue him too much if he harassed him any further, and after having embraced him as if to stifle him, he returned home, in spite of La Dandinardière's entreaties to stay for lunch.

As soon as he was alone, the latter thought very seriously about the engagements of honor in which he found himself. He thought he had a marvelous secret for saving his reputation and his skin, which was to make Alan fight Villeville, clad in his beautiful armor, and to appear at the baron's house and elsewhere clad in the same armor himself, in order that people would believe that it was him.

He summoned his faithful Alain.

"I don't doubt your affection," he said to him, "but there are certain things that don't depend absolutely on us; for example, it's no good wanting to be brave if one is a coward; all the efforts one makes will be futile. Personally, I was born with the heart of a king or a emperor full of courage and resolution; if I have a flaw, it's that I have too much. Now you know, Alan, that that wretch Villeville wants to fight me; if I resolve to do it, it's a man dead at a stroke. I have wealth; it would vex me to lose it, and as he's brutal, he might be able to kill me before I can arrange myself to prevent it. The sole remedy that I can imagine in the affair is for you to appear on the dueling-field in my place, while I say prayers for you."

Alain was the meekest of all men; that proposition seemed to him to be the cruelest things in the world and the most distant from common sense. He thought about it for a moment in order to be able to give his master an acceptable excuse, and finally said to him: "Unless I'm given your face, your bearing and your stature, how do you expect me to resemble you and deceive Monsieur de Villeville?"

"If I smooth out that difficulty," replied La Dandinardière, "will you promise me to fight?"

"Yes, Monsieur," said Alain, believing the thing to be impossible.

"And if you fail, what shall I do to you?"

"Anything you like," the good Alain continued.

"Well, we'll soon see whether you have courage and honor" added La Dandinardière.

Alain, listening to him, started trembling so forcefully that he could scarcely stand up; he thought immediately that the same demon that had talked to his master on the sea shore might have taught him some extraordinary secret.

"At least, Monsieur," he said to him, "unless the devil is mixed up in it, if you please. I don't want to be damned for anyone. I hate sorcerers and all their tricks; I renounce the pact, and if there is one, I don't want to fight, even if there are a hundred pistoles to earn."

La Dandinardière, in despair at Alain's cowardice, took a stick and beat him. "You can count on receiving similar treatment every day," he said to him, "until you've made the resolution to obey me."

Alain ran away, deeply chagrined, and firmly resolved to quit his master.

La Dandinardière was agitated by a thousand worries. The time of the rendezvous was approaching, without him having taken measures to avoid it. He had bought two breastplates, two helmets, gauntlets and the rest of the equipment of a man of war from old stock, so he wanted to dress Alain in it, thinking that with the visor lowered, Villeville would not be able to recognize him. He searched everywhere for his valet, and found him sitting sadly in a small cellar soothing his woes beside a barrel whose liquor seemed to be excellent for curing wounds inflicted by a stick.

"Come on, rogue," he shouted at him from the top of the stairs, "Come and see whether I'm a sorcerer or whether you're a madman."

Alain hastened to finish his jar and went up more cheerful than he had come down, for he had obtained a little joy in the subterranean vault. He followed his master to his bedroom, and was very frightened by the iron costume. La Dandinardière commanded him to put it on.

"Where shall I put it, Monsieur? I know as little about all that as the law of the Great Turk."

"I'll help you, bumpkin," he replied, "for if I don't serve as your valet de chambre you'd never have the intelligence to get dressed."

At the same time, he fitted the breastplate, which was so tight that Alain had to take off his doublet and shirt, with the consequence that the armor scratched his skin.

"That," said La Dandinardière," is what the greatest kings wear when they go to war."

"Those kings," said Alain, "don't have much sense, when they could have as much velvet and satin as they please, to put on nasty stuff like that. I'd rather dress in a feather bed."

"Oh, the scoundrel!" cried La Dandinardière. "You'll never succeed; in the small things as in the great, one knows the inclination of men of quality or wretches. For example, I, as a man of quality, would like to eat, drink and sleep with my body in harness."

"Yes," said Alain, "but you don't want to fight Monsieur de Villeville, and it's for me, thank God, that you reserve combat."

La Dandinardière, very annoyed, made no reply; he took the helmet and stuck it on poor Alain's head with so much force and so little care that he nearly died of it, for being as inexpert as his valet, he had put the visor behind the head. The worthy Alain, ready to expire, cried out, and even howled, in vain; La Dandinardière, convinced that it was pure malice and lack of habitude, only laughed. Finally, he perceived his mistake; he remedied it promptly. Alain was already much changed, but the joy of breathing caused him to say quite pleasant things.

After he was armed, his master armed himself in his turn, and, dragging him before a large mirror, said: "Who are you, in your opinion?"

"Eh? I'm Alain, Monsieur."

"You're an idiot," said his master. Can't you see that you're Monsieur de La Dandinardière? When the visors of our helmets are lowered, there's no difference between us, and I'm sure that Villeville will never see any. Have a little courage, then, my poor lad," he continued. "I don't intend you to fight *gratis*; I promise you a good recompense, dead or alive. If you're killed you'll be interred honorably, like a lord of the parish, and if you come back I'll marry you to Richarde, whom it seems to me that you don't hate. Look, here's three five-sol pieces in advance, and some small change, you can see that your fortune will be made."

Alain, who had drunk a few cups too many, seeing his master's money, combined with his promises, allowed himself to be touched. In the tone of a hero he cried: "Let's go fight, then, since that's necessary in order to be rich and to please my Richarde."

La Dandinardière, penetrated by joy, gave him further caresses.

Baron de Saint-Thomas was awaited impatiently at his home by the vicomte and the prior. They were rejoicing great-ly together at the state to which our bourgeois was reduced, and resolved that it would cost him something to have peace. La Dandinardière, sure of his Alain, did not fail to go to Baron de Saint-Thomas's home. He had ornamented his helmet with an old bouquet of plumes, and to render himself even more terrible he cut off the tail of a rather pretty horse he had and allowed it to float like a panache over his shoulders; his sword was one of the most ancient. One could have taken him in that rig for the younger brother of Don Quixote, and one can say with no lie that he was just as crazy, if less brave. He was fol-lowed by Alain, a worthy imitator of Sancho Panza.

La Dandinardière dreaded an unfortunate encounter with Villeville, even though he had a great confidence in the visor of his helmet, which was lowered, through which he could scarcely breathe.

"It's impossible that I can be recognized by my enemy," he said to Alain. "In any case, if he approaches me, I shall tell him right away that he's mistaken, and that I'm not La Dandinardière. After such a declaration, he'd be very impertinent to push me to the end."

The valet approved strongly of his prudence.

They continued to talk, when it suddenly struck him that the good Alain might reveal what he wanted to keep hidden, for he was not armed like him, and Villeville had beaten him not long ago; that he would surely have the same idea and give another thrashing, by which he would be only too fatigued.

He stopped promptly in order to command Alan to go home, and to say that if he did not come back that evening, he was not to worry, that he would sleep at the baron's house, but that for his own account he should not fail to exercise with weapons, because that might be necessary before very long.

Alain was surprised by that order; he had already taken enough air to dissipate a part of the good humor that his sojourn in the cellar had inspired in him. He replied, in a sullen manner, that he had no desire to fight and that no man would ever be newer at that métier than he was.

La Dandinardière was no longer listening, which was just as well, for blows of the stick would not have been lacking. He was following the route along the shore when, approaching a small pavilion that terminated a rather large garden, he suddenly heard a women's voice saying; "Marthonide, my sister, come, hurry up; there's a fully armed knight going by."

La Dandinardière, having no doubt that the reference was to him, gravely raised his head, being very glad to have inspired curiosity, but what became of him when he perceived two young and beautiful women at a barred window? He bowed to them so profoundly that without his visor he would have bruised his nose on his saddle-bow. Immediately, they both returned his salute with interest. They were the daughters of Baron de Saint-Thomas, whom La Dandinardière had never seen, although he had visited the house several times. As they were new to one another, it would be difficult to express the reciprocal admiration they inspired.

Little La Dandinardière was susceptible enough to tenderness, and gallant enough to be delighted by such an unexpected and agreeable encounter; as for the demoiselles, their heads were full of so many extraordinary adventures of knights errant, heroes and princesses that they were much less astonished to see La Dandinardière in that burlesque outfit than he was to find two such amiable demoiselles living on the edge of the sea in a little pavilion apart from society.

Virginie, who was the elder of the two sisters, and who called herself Virginie instead of Marie—which was her real name, just as Marthonide was really named Marthe—broke the silence first.

"Although it is easy to judge, Sire," she said to the bourgeois, "that you have urgent business that summons you to some important place, permit us to stop you in order to ask you by what chance you are passing before our windows?"

La Dandinardière, delighted to be called Sire, and not wanting to cede anything in civility, replied: "Since Your Divine Highnesses deign to rest your eyes on an unfortunate like me, I will tell you that an affair of honor obliges me to render here."

"What, noble knight!" cried Marthonide, interrupting him. "You're going to fight! And who is the reckless individual who dares to go into the closed field with you?"

La Dandinardière was transported by the pretty things he heard; never in his life had he found so much wit in a woman.

"I cannot name my adversary, Mesdames," he said. "Good reasons prevent me from doing so. I only assure you that I shall no sooner have cut off his head than I will hang it on your windows as a homage that I owe to your beauty."

"Oh, Sire, refrain from that," cried Virginie, "You'll make us die of fright."

He replied that he would rather die himself than displease them; that he had sentiments so vivid and delicate for them that no one had ever made so much progress in such a short time, and that he was in despair that his affairs obliged him to quit them."

It is true that he wanted, before taking his leave of them, to make his horse perform a few maneuvers of dressage; he applied his spur to the belly, and pulled the bridle so rudely that the poor horse, not knowing what was being asked of it, bucked, and La Dandinardière, seeing the peril without knowing the remedy, gave it an even more violent jerk, at which the horse overturned completely on top of him.

Anyone who heard the cries of the two imprisoned princesses would easily have deduced that their new hero was in peril; he was, in fact, for his heavy horse was stifling him, and the pebbles covering the shore were breaking his ribs. His poorly-attached helmet fell off his head, and his head struck a small rock that unfortunately happened to be there, bruising it cruelly. At that sight, Marthonide lost patience and told Virginie to stay that the window while she went to warn someone about the knight's disaster.

She ran to her father's room; he was there with the vicomte and the prior, who were drinking coffee. "Oh, Monsieur," she said, "Come to the shore promptly. A knight errant, a hero, armed from head to toe, is dangerously wounded and has need of your help.

The baron, accustomed to his daughters' follies, believed that there was a vision in what she was saying to him. "Is it a Knight of the Round Table or one of Charlemagne's twelve peers?" he asked, smiling.

"I don't know," she said, in a sad and serious manner. "All that I know is that he has a little gray horse with a mane tied up with green ribbon and the right ear cut off."

By those signs, the baron and the vicomte recognized poor La Dandinardière. They looked at one another, astonished by what Marthonide was telling them. Without pausing to question her further, they hastened to go to the place that she indicated to them.

They found our unfortunate bourgeois, veritably unconscious. His equipage surprised them. "What folly," they said, "can such a singular metamorphosis be?"

Finally, with the help of the Queen of Hungary's water and everything they could imagine, they brought him round. He seemed astonished by the state he was in, and took the path to Monsieur de Saint-Thomas's house leaning on him and the vicomte.

Virginie and Marthonide, who were at their windows, wondered by what hazard their father knew that brave knight, since he was evidently not native to the area. They went into Madame de Saint-Thomas's room, to which her husband came to tell her about the adventure of their good neighbor La Dandinardière. She asked whether he would be staying for a long time, and if he intended to be cured at their expense, for she was as miserly with others as she was prodigal with herself.

He told her that she need not worry, that he was a very rich man and would treat them well. Then taking her aside into her cabinet, he said: "The Vicomte de Berginville has communicated to me a thought that had occurred to him, which I don't find bad, which is to try to get La Dandinardière to marry Virginie or Marthonide. I'm not in a state to give them much, and if he liked that affair, I'd be very pleased."

"But Monsieur," replied Madame de Saint-Thomas, who also had her visions, "you know what our ancestors were; would we be capable of misallying our blood and debasing its nobility by an unequal marriage?"

"Believe me, Madame," he said, "quality without wealth rings very hollow, and I'd like this bourgeois, very bourgeois as he is, to become infatuated. Don't go talking in another tone to your daughters; you're capable of spoiling what I'll have guided with so much difficulty."

"Am I not their mother, as you're their father?" she cried, changing color. "Ought I not to be consulted in such a matter, and isn't my advice as judicious as yours? No, Monsieur, my daughters will only marry a marquis or a comte, who will furnish twelve quarters or more."

"Courage," said Monsieur Saint-Thomas, coldly. "Courage, Madame; sustain the dignity of your ancestors and keep your daughters for another fifty years."

The baronne, desperate, stated to cry insult; the racket that they made drew the vicomte and the prior into the cabinet.

"I take these messieurs as judges," said the baron.

"And I recuse them," said the baronne. "Apart from the fact that they're more your friends than mine, they're the ones who have advised this fine marriage to you; they wouldn't want to contradict themselves."

Those messieurs, who had intelligence, entered into the dispute without bitterness, and begged her to act without passion in the easiest matter in the world to regulate, since she consented to everything, provided that her son-in-law had birth, and they could testify that his hall was full of portraits of all his grandparents. They had remarked one in particular, called Gilles de La Dandinardière, who had been at least a constable under Charles VIII.

At those words, the baronne calmed down considerably; she closed her mouth in order to make it smaller, and gave her word that if that were the case, she would not trouble the fête. The messieurs advised her to go and see the poor wounded man, in order to offer him the help that is needed in the case of such accidents.

She never wanted to appear until she was under arms—which is to say, fully dressed—so she changed her bodice, her dress, her skirts, her bonnet, her hair-style and her ribbons, and after having spent several hours at her dressing table, she went into La Dandinardière's room.

He had already been bandaged by the village surgeon, who was utterly ignorant, and who always said that it was necessary to dread shutting the wolf in the sheepfold, with the result that he cut off arms, legs and, if necessary, heads in order to evade the redoubtable wolf. He wanted to apply the scalpel to the poor wounded man, but as soon as the later perceived it in his hand he shouted at the top of his voice: "Monsieur de Saint-Thomas, I place myself under your protection; don't suffer anyone doing me any more harm than I already have."

After that, the baron prevented Maître Robert from doing him any.

Madame la Baronne found herself more anxious than the invalid, for his wound was not as serious as it might have been, given the horrible blow that he had received. She offered obligingly to keep him in her home until he was healed, to keep him company, and even to bring her daughters into his room to entertain him.

"I dare say," she added, "without too much vanity, "that they have intelligence and delicate taste. They like reading, and they know how to profit from it; they can recite Amadis of Gaul to you by heart."

"Madame," said La Dandinardière, "I believe everything you tell me, but, hazard having enabled me to encounter two young highnesses of an incomparable beauty, my ideas are so full of them that I would be glad not to see any others who might efface them from my memory. What I say is not to lack respect for mesdemoiselles your daughters, but rather out of fear of finding them too beautiful."

The baronne went red with chagrin and puffed herself up slightly. "Wills are free, Monsieur," she said. "I thought I would give you pleasure, but in fact it is not necessary that my daughters come here."

She got up immediately, and as she was in a bad mood she nearly strangled her husband and the vicomte, reproaching them for the futile step that she had just made. "For in sum, I have certain presentiments," she continued, "which are never mistaken. I suspected that I wouldn't be content with my visit; that little man is in love with two or three princesses; truly, he wouldn't care to think of Virginie."

Monsieur de Saint-Thomas, who liked peace in his house, not wanting to embitter his wife, went for a walk in the garden with the vicomte and he prior, and told them about La Dandinardière's extravagances.

"Who can he mean?" he said. "Where has he seen these charming princesses? It's necessary that his head has turned absolutely."

"It's on your conscience," said the vicomte. "Since the challenge your servant made on Villeville's behalf, he hasn't had a moment of common sense, and that armor he's wearing is convincing proof of it."

The next morning, all those messieurs visited him in his bedroom, and after a few moments of conversation he testified that he wanted to talk to the baron in private. The others withdrew and he remained alone with him; he took his hands between his own and pressed them. "Can I count on you," he said, "as one counts on an inviolable friend?"

"Undoubtedly you can," replied the baron. "I make a profession of being yours."

"It's necessary that you know, then," said La Dandinardière, that I had the design of finding myself at the rendezvous with Villeville fully armed, for I never arm myself otherwise, and if that does not suit him, he has only to leave me in peace; I don't take back a gauntlet. I was coming to see you to ask you to inform him, in order that he might seek similar arms, if by hazard he lacks them, being incapable of wanting any advantages over him, and holding to the rules of honor and chivalry written on my forehead. In sum, in order not to bore you with too long a speech, I shall open my heart to you and tell you in three words that I'm in love."

"You're in love!" cried he baron, interrupting him. "For how long?"

"Twenty-four hours," he said, "and a few minutes, if my count is accurate; but I haven't always been insensible to the charms of beauty. I have loved, and I have made coups of gallantry that astonished All Paris and swelled the *Mercure galant*. In sum, a few duchesses, whom I shan't name, did me a bad turn and committed thirty atrocious adulteries. I confess to you that I took the bit between my teeth, and piqued against my star, I departed to go and throw myself into the depths of the sea, but having found a beautiful location, I preferred to build my château almost in the air, and to live in a philosophical lethargy.

"That, Monsieur, is the state that I was in, devoid of amour, devoid of ambition, full of joy and health, when my first misfortune commenced with the brutality of Villeville and the impertinence of Alain, in blabbing about it. That rogue has involved me in an affair of honor, which, between us, weighs upon me like a mountain, for I have no desire to lose my wealth and exile myself from France. I nevertheless resolved myself to that accursed duel, on condition, as I said, of being armed. I was coming to inform you of my design when, passing along the sea shore, I heard two young women talking rather loudly. Their voices had a sweetness and charm. I looked around, and I saw a small pavilion, the windows of which were barred, and princesses who delighted me, in particular the one who was pale and blonde, who won my heart entirely.

"They spoke to me with a politeness, a daintiness, an energy, a...I would never end if I wanted to express the charm of what they said to me; and when they called me *Sire*—which made it evident that they only had commerce with kings and princes—it seemed to me that they were carrying away my soul as a merlin caries away a pigeon. In the movements of respect and admiration that they inspired in me, I had so little idea of what I was doing that instead of giving myself the air of a man on horseback I fell awkwardly on to the stones, where my head came to grief—with the result that I am, at the present moment, amorous, ill, charged with a procedure against Villeville, and the most unfortunate of all men."

La Dandinardière fell silent at that point in order to sigh three or four times like a man overwhelmed by dolor. The baron had listened without interrupting him; then he raised his hands and his eyes toward the heavens, marking a great deal of surprise at the great events that had just been recounted to him, and sighed in his turn, for he was not miserly with his sighs.

"Have courage, my dear friend," he said. "It is necessary to hope for everything of time."

"Oh, Monsieur le Baron," said La Dandinardière, "this is a strange chaos to disentangle, but the most urgent matters at the present moment are my amour and my health. I beg you to send in quest of a surgeon more skilled than Robert and to write a letter for me to the beautiful person about whom I have just spoken to you."

"Provided that you dictate it," replied Monsieur de Saint-Thomas, "I will gladly serve as your secretary."

"I would spare you that trouble," added La Dandinardière, "if my head were in a better state, and I don't even know how I can get a thousand pretty things out of it that I want to send them."

"It's unnecessary in that matter to consult anyone," said he baron. "You're touched, and you have a great deal of intelligence; let's begin."

He picked up a writing tablet. While he was preparing to write, La Dandinardière meditated and bit his fingernails. This is what he dictated:

Imprisoned highnesses, who set the world ablaze, it seems to me that you are two suns, which, striking the optic crystal of my eyes, reduce my heart to ashes. Yes, I am ash, charcoal, a furnace, since the fatal and blissful moment when I perceived you at the grille, my beauties, and my reason became irrational, evaporating to the point of sacrificing my tender heart to you. I lost all tramontane then; you were the culpable witness of my fall; I shed my blood beneath your walls, and I would spread my soul there if the sacrifice were agreeable to you. I am, Mesdemoiselles your most submissive slave, Georges de La Dandinardière, descendant of Gilles de La Dandinardière, favorite of Charles VIII and constable, or something approaching.

"Ah!" he cried, after having read and reread the letter. "That's a letter, to tell the truth, that has cost me a little, but it's also excellent. I can see that I haven't entirely lost the style that was admired so much at court, and which distinguished me rather advantageously."

"I'm so confused," said the baron, "in seeing with what facility you have made that true masterpiece, that I have a desire to get angry. Yes, Monsieur, I would sooner at the inkwell, ink, quill and paper than do as much in a month. How fortunate it is when one has intelligence!"

"Ho ho ho," said the bourgeois, "don't praise me so much, my dear baron; you'll give me too much vanity. I confess, nevertheless, that the comparison with optical glass pleases me infinitely; that is what is known as a new thought."

"Add to that quite sublime," said the baron.

"Did you like the little play on words, *grill* and *grille*? Nothing suits the subject more," continued poor La Dandinardière. "I can only hide in those sorts of things; I have a superior genius. But let's seal the letter in such a gallant manner that it responds to what it contains. It needs green silk and a device; I have a seal in my pocket that is appropriate: it's a woman leaning on an anchor, breast-feeding a little Amour, and the words of the caption are: *Hope nourishes amour*.

"I remember having one similar," said Monsieur de Saint-Thomas.

"In whatever place you had it, it came from me," said La Dandinardière, boldly. "The entire court admired it; the king had it engraved, and nothing was good, in the matter of devices, if they weren't made in my fashion."

"I can easily believe it," the baron continued. "You have a fire and a vivacity that would enable you to succeed in something even more difficult; but by the way, I doubt that my wife can furnish you with flat silk."

"No matter," said La Dandinardière. "As long as it's green, I'll be content."

Monsieur de Saint-Thomas went out, and sent the Gascon, who dared not come in, for fear that La Dandinardière might recognize him as his swashbuckler, to search for it. After having rummaged through twenty different drawers, he decided to go to Mesdemoiselles de Saint-Thomas's pavilion; he told them that the wounded gentleman was asking for green silk and wax in order to seal a letter. As they had not been able, on any pretext, to go into his room, they were delighted by the one that was offered. "Don't wait," they said to him, "we don't have any silk or wax."

The Gascon returned to ask everyone in the house, while the two beautiful young women slipped along the hornbeam hedge in the garden, in order not to be seen by their mother, holding a little tortoiseshell box garnished with thin silver leaf, in which they had put wax, brilliant powder, gilded paper and balls of silk of all colors. They went into La Dandinardière's room and approached his bed before their father, whose back was turned, had perceived them; but the little man, who recognized them at first glance, uttered a great cry, and, shivering in his bed, he said: "Make way for the princesses."

It is certain that the baron thought then that he was completely insane; however, the noise that he heard behind him obliged him to turn his head, and he was surprised to see his daughters.

"Here are Virginie and Marthonide," he said, "who have come to see you; they doubtless knew that I was in your room."

"Father," said the elder, "someone came to tell us on your behalf that this young stranger needed silk to seal a letter; we've brought him some."

La Dandinardière, confused by such a great favor, made no reply; he was agitated by a thousand different thoughts; he believed that he loved a highness and it was necessary to come down several degrees; he had written the letter in that spirit, and it no longer seemed appropriate to provincial demoiselles. He had a mortal regret in losing the applause that it merited. He had made a pleasure out of conducting that gallant intrigue, and of having a man of quality for a confidant, the father of his mistress. The thing, according to him, could not have been more mysterious; it had changed species considerably. That was a subject of despair; on the other hand, he was delighted to rediscover the charming strangers; their eagerness to come to his room flattered his vanity and his heart greatly. All those different things agitated him to such a point that he could not speak.

The baron, who had not doubted, while writing the letter, that it was for his daughters, soon extracted him from his embarrassment. He said to him, cheerfully, that he could no longer doubt the merit of Virginie and Marthonide, since they had made such a strong impression on him, and that he did not want them to miss reading the most gallant note that had been written for a century, of which they had enough taste to sense the fine passages.

Our *précieuses* had no need to be prepared to fall into ecstasy; they were struck by the optical glass, and cried a hundred times: "Oh, how beautiful that is! What thought! What finesse! It isn't permitted to write thus."

In the meantime, La Dandinardière readjusted his nightcap, and, feeling ashamed of having a head swathed in napkins, abruptly picked up his helmet, which was on a chair beside him and tried to put it on "in order," he said, "to be more decent before these demoiselles."

The baron could not help laughing wholeheartedly at such a novel extravagance. He allowed him to try the impossible task, for his head was now too large to go into the helmet.

"At least receive my respectful intentions," he said.

"We take account of everything, Sire," replied Virginie, "and in the fear of inconveniencing you, I think we ought to retire."

"Oh, beautiful suns," cried our bourgeois, in the tone of Phoebus, "are you going to darken the room by your eclipse?" He turned toward the baron. "Monsieur," he said, "Oblige these charming goddesses to remain, I implore you."

"No," said the baron, "You've already talked too much, for which I reproach myself. Rest a little, you're wounded sufficiently to need to be spared. Adieu, we'll leave you; be sure that Maître Robert will no longer appear, and that you'll have another."

The father and the two daughters were about to quit La Dandinardière thus when he said to them: "At least don't refuse me a few books, the reading of which might soften your absence, for I'm not so ill as to be unable to read."

"I'll send you a tale that my sister finished yesterday evening," said Marthonide."

"I don't want tales," he replied. "As I make heavy expenditure, my merchants sent me them too frequently."

"You don't know this one, Sire Chevalier," said Virginie. "These kinds of tales are in fashion, everyone is writing them, and as I pride myself on imitating people of intelligence, even though I'm in the depths of a province, I nevertheless want to send my little work to Paris; but if it could please you, how delighted I would be! I'd be sure of the approval of connoisseurs."

"I've already given you my suffrage, adorable Virginie," replied the little La Dandinardière, "and I intend to send that pretty tale to the court tomorrow, if you find it good. There are five or six princesses there who permit me to write to them and the regale them with my verses."

"Oh, what are you saying, Sire?" cried Marthonide. "You make verses! I'm crazy about them! Please let us have the pleasure of hearing them."

"It won't be at present, at least," said the baron, pushing them to make them leave. "You're just chatterboxes, and you'll be the case of my friend's death."

As soon as they had returned to their pavilion, they charged a chambermaid with taking the tale to the knight errant; he seemed delighted by so much evidence of good will, but as he could not read for long in the state that he was in, he sent word to the prior that he was asking for him urgently.

That news made the whole house anxious; everyone thought that he was worse, with the result that everyone came, but he seemed so tranquil that they judged correctly that it was a false alarm. The prior asked him what he wanted, La Dandinardière showed him the notebook that had just been brought to him, and begged him to soothe the illness he was feeling with an agreeable reading.

He began the following tale immediately.

THE WHITE CAT

There was once a king who had three sturdy and courageous sons. He was afraid that the desire to reign might grip them before his death; certain rumors were even running around that they were seeking to acquire creatures, and that it was to take away his crown. The king felt old, but his intelligence and capability having not diminished, he had no desire to cede a place that he filed so worthily. He thought, therefore, that the best means of living in repose was to amuse them with promises whose effect he could always elude.

He summoned them to his cabinet, and after having talked to them with an abundance of good will, he added: "You'll agree with me, my dear children, that my great age doesn't permit me to apply myself to the affairs of my State with as much care as I once did; I fear that my subjects might suffer in consequence, and I want to put the crown on the head of one of you; but it's only just that, for such a present, you seek means to please me, in the design that I have to retire to the country. It seems that a clever, pretty and faithful dog would keep me good company, so, rather than choosing my eldest son rather than the youngest, I declare to you whichever of you brings me the most beautiful little dog will immediately become my heir."

The princes were surprised by the inclination of their father for a little dog, but the younger two thought that they might be able to find their opportunity that way, and they accepted with pleasure the commission to go in search of one; the eldest was too timid or too respectful to represent his rights. They all took their leave of the king; he gave them money and precious stones, adding that they in a year, without fail, they should come back on the same day at the same hour, bringing him their little dogs.

Before leaving, they went to a castle that was a league from the city. They took their closest confidants there and held great feasts, in which the three brothers promised one another eternal amity, that they would act in the affair in question without jealousy and without chagrin, and that the most fortunate would always share his fortune with the others.

Finally, they departed, having agreed that they would meet on their return in the same castle, in order to go together to see the king. They did not want to be followed by anyone, and changed their names in order not to be known.

Each one took a different route. The elder two had a great many adventures but I shall only attach myself to those of the youngest. He was gracious, he had a lively and joyful spirit, an admirable head, a noble stature, regular features, good teeth and a great deal of skill in all the exercises that befit a prince. He sang agreeably, and he played the lute and the theorbo with a charming delicacy. He knew how to paint. In a word, he was very accomplished, and as for his valor, it went as far as intrepidity.

Scarcely a day went by when he did not buy dogs: large ones, small ones, greyhounds, hunting dogs, spaniels, barbets and lap-dogs. As soon as he had a beautiful one he found one that was more beautiful; he let the first one go in order to keep the other, for it would have been impossible for him to lead thirty or forty thousand dogs all on his own, and he did not want gentlemen, valets de chambre or pages in his retinue.

He was still going forward on his route, without having determined exactly where he was going when he was surprised by nightfall, thunder and rain in a forest where he could no longer recognize the paths.

He took the first path and after having walked for a long time he perceived a glimmer of light, which persuaded him that there was a house nearby where he could shelter until the following day. Guided by the light he could see, he arrived at the door of a castle, the most superb ever imagined. The door was made of gold, covered with carbuncles, the bright and pure light of which illuminated the surroundings. That was what the prince had seen from a distance. The walls were transparent porcelain, mingled with several colors, which represented the history of all the fays from the creation of the world until the present day: the famous adventures of Donkeyskin, Finette, Orange Tree, Gracieuse, the Beauty in the Dormant Wood, Green Worm and a hundred others were not forgotten. He was charmed to recognize the Sprite Prince, who was a distant relative.

The rain and the bad weather prevented him from stopping any longer in a place where he was drenched to the bone, apart from the fact that he could not see anything at all in places that the light of the carbuncles did not reach.

He returned to the golden door he saw the foot of a roe deer attached to a diamond chain; he admired that magnificence, and the security with which those in the castle lived. *For, in sum*, he thought, *what prevents thieves from coming to cut that chain and tearing away the carbuncles? They'd be rich forever.*

He tugged the roe deer foot, and immediately heard a bell chiming, which appeared to be gold or silver, to judge by the sound it rendered. After a moment the door opened, without him perceiving anything except a dozen hands in the air, each of which was holding a torch. He was so surprised that he was hesitating to go forward, when he felt other hands pushing him from behind rather violently. He therefore walked, very anxiously, and at hazard he put his hand on the hilt of his sword. When he entered a vestibule encrusted with porphyry and lapis, he heard two delightful voices singing these words:

At the hands that you see don't take umbrage

He could not believe that he was being invited with such good grace in order to do him harm; so, feeling himself pushed toward a large coral door, that opened as soon as he approached it, he entered into a room of nacre and pearls, and then several rooms ornamented differently, and so rich in paintings and gemstones, that it was as if he were enchanted. Thousands of lights attached from the vault of the hall to the floor partly illuminated other apartments, which were no less filled with chandeliers, candelabras and steps covered in candles. In sum, the magnificence was such that it was not easy to believe that it was possible.

After having passed through sixty rooms, the hands that were conducting him stopped. He saw a large, comfortable armchair, which approached the fireplace of its own accord. At the same time the fire was lit, and the hands, which seemed to be very beautiful, white, small, fleshy and well-proportioned, undressed him—for he was soaked, as I have said, and it was to be feared that he might catch a cold.

Without him seeing anyone, he was presented with a chemise as beautiful as for a wedding day, with a dressing gown of a fabric glazed with gold, embroidered with little emeralds, which formed figures. The bodiless hands propelled him toward a table on which grooming-equipment was set out. Nothing was more magnificent. They combed his hair with a lightness and a skill with which he was very content. Then he was dressed again, not with his own clothes but with others that were brought, much richer. He admired everything that happened, silently, and sometimes made little movements of fright, of which he was not entirely the master.

After he had been powdered, curled, perfumed, attired, ornamented and rendered more beautiful than Adonis, the hands conducted him to a hall superb by virtue of its decoration and furniture. All around, the history could be seen of the most famous cats: Rodillardus hung by the feet at the council of rats;[11] Puss-in-Boots, the Marquis de Carabas, the Cat who wrote, the cat who became a woman, sorcerers who became cats, the Sabbat and all its ceremonies; in sum, nothing was more singular than those pictures.

There were two places set at the table, each garnished with a golden side-plate; the sideboard was surprising in the quantity of vases of rock crystal and a thousand rare stones. The prince did not know for whom the places were set.

He saw cats placing themselves in a little orchestra expressly designed; one held a book with the most extraordinary notes in the world, another a scroll of paper with which he beat the measure, and the others had little guitars. Suddenly, they all started mewling in different tones and scraping the strings of the guitar with their claws; it was the strangest music that had ever been heard. The prince might have believed that he was in Hell if he had not thought the palace too marvelous to give him such an implausible thought; but he blocked his ears and laughed wholeheartedly on seeing the different postures and grimaces of those novel musicians.

He was meditating on the various things that had already happened to him in the castle when he saw a little figure enter that was only a cubit high. That puppet was covered by a long veil of black crepe. Two cats were leading it; they were dressed in mourning, in mantles, with swords at their sides; a numerous cortege of cats came after them; some were carrying rat-traps full of rats, others mice in cages.

---

[11] Rodillardus seems to be employed here as an alternative spelling of Robilardus, a name often applied to cats pejoratively, after being employed by Rabelais. D'Aulnoy's spelling had reportedly been employed, perhaps significantly, in a satirical mock-heroic text in the Dauphinois dialect printed in the late sixteenth century by Benoist Rigaud entitled *Le Banquet des fées*, translated into French as *La Bataille fantastique des rois Rodillardus & Croacus,* but Rodillardus is a rat therein, not a cat.

The prince could not get over his astonishment; he did not know what to think. The black figurine approached, and when the veil was lifted he saw the most beautiful white she-cat there had ever been and ever will be. She seemed to be very young and very sad; she began a mewling so soft and charming that it went straight to the heart.

"Son of a king, be welcome," she said to the prince, "My Mewling Majesty sees you with pleasure."

"Madame Cat," said the prince, "you have been very generous to give me such a fine welcome, but you do not seem to me to be an ordinary animal; the gift you have of speech and the superb castle you possess are evident enough profs of that."

"Son of a king," the white cat replied, "Cease to pay me compliments, I beg you. I am simple in my discourse and my manners, but I have a good heart. Let's go," she continued, "serve, and let the musicians shut up, for the prince can't understand what they're saying."

"Are they saying something, Madame?" he asked.

"Of course," she said. "We have poets of infinite intelligence here, and if you stay with us for a while you'll have reason to be convinced of it."

"It's only necessary to hear you to believe it," said the prince, gallantly, "But also, Madame, I regard you as a very rare cat."

Supper was brought; he hands whose bodies were invisible served. Two bisques were put on the table first, one of pigeon and the other of fattened mouse. The sight of the latter prevented the prince from eating the former, imagining that the same cook had accommodated both; but the little cat, who divined by the expression on his face what he was thinking, assured him that that the kitchen was separate and that he could eat what was presented to him with the certainty that there were neither rats nor mice therein.

The prince did not have to be told twice, believing firmly that the beautiful little cat would not want to deceive him. He remarked that she had a miniature portrait in her paw; that surprised him. He asked her to show it to him, thinking that it was master Minagrobis.[12] He was astonished to see a young man so handsome that it was scarcely credible that nature had been able to form his like, and which resembled him so strongly that he could not have been painted better. She sighed, and, becoming even sadder, maintained a profound silence. The prince saw clearly that there was something extraordinary behind it, but he dared not enquire further for fear of displeasing the cat or causing her chagrin. He talked to her about all the news he knew, and found her very well-informed about the different interests of princes and other things happening in the world.

After supper, White Cat invited her guest to go into a drawing room where there was a stage, on which twelve cats and twelve monkeys were dancing a ballet. Some were dressed as Moors, the others in the Chinese style. It is easy to imagine the leaps and capers they made, and from time to time they swiped one another with their claws; it was thus that the soirée concluded. White Cat bid her guest good night.

The hands that had conducted him thus far took charge of him again and led him to an apartment entirely opposed to the one he had seen. It was less magnificent than elegant; everything was covered with butterfly wings, the various colors of which formed a thousand different flowers. There were also feathers of very rare birds, which had never been seen anywhere but in that place. The beds were gauze, attached by a thousand knotted ribbons. There were large mirrors from the ceiling to the floor, and the frames of sculpted gold represented a thousand little amours.

The prince lay down without saying a word, for he had no means of making conversation with the hands that were serving him.

---

[12] An evident contraction of Raminagrobis, a name applies to several cats by Jean de La Fontaine.

He did not sleep much, and was woken up by a strange noise. The hands immediately extracted him from his bed and dressed him in hunting garb. He looked into the courtyard of the castle and saw more than five hundred cats, some of which had greyhounds on leashes, others sounding horns; it was a great fête. White Cat was going hunting; she wanted the prince to come too.

The obliging hands presented him with a wooden horse that was running flat out and had a marvelous stride. He had some difficulty mounting it, saying that it was all he needed to be a knight errant like Don Quixote, but his resistance was futile; he was planted on the wooden horse. It had a blanket and a saddle embroidered with gold and diamonds. White Cat was mounted on a monkey, the most beautiful and most superb that had ever been seen; she had quit her large veil and was wearing a dragoon's bonnet, which made her seem so resolute that all the mice in the vicinity were afraid.

There had never been a more agreeable hunt; the cats ran faster than the rabbits and the hares, with the result that when they were caught. White Cat had the spoils divided before her, and there were a thousand enjoyable feats of skill. The birds, for their part, were not entirely secure, for the cats climbed trees and the master ape carried White Cat all the way to the nests of eagles in order to dispose at will of Their Little Highnesses the eaglets.

When the hunt ended, she took a horn that was as long as a finger, but which rendered a sound so clear and loud that it could easily be heard ten leagues away; as soon as she had sounded two or three fanfares she was surrounded by all the cats in the region; some appeared in the air mounted on chariots, other came by water in boats; he had never seen so many. They were almost all clad in different styles. She returned to the castle with that pompous cortege, and invited the prince to come in. He was glad to do so, although it seemed that so much feline company was reminiscent of the Sabbat and witchcraft, and that the talking cat was even more astonishing than all the rest.

As soon as she was inside, her long black veil was replaced. She had supper with the prince; he was hungry and ate with a good appetite. He was brought liqueurs that he drank with pleasure, and immediately they took away the memory of the little dog that he was supposed to take to the king. He no longer thought about anything but mewling with White Cat—which is to say, keeping her good and faithful company.

He spent days in agreeable fêtes; sometimes they went fishing or hunting, sometimes there were ballets, tournaments and a thousand other diversions. Often, the beautiful cat composed verses and songs in a style so passionate that it seemed that she had a tender heart and that one could not talk like that without being in love; but her secretary, who was an old cat, wrote so poorly that, even though those works have been conserved, it is impossible to read them.

The prince had almost forgotten his homeland. The hands that I have mentioned continued to serve him. He sometimes regretted not being a cat, in order to spend his life in that good company.

"Alas," he said to White Cat, "how much dolor I would have in quitting you, I love you so dearly! Either become a young woman or make me a cat."

She thought his desire very humorous, and only made him obscure responses, in which he understood almost nothing.

A year goes by very quickly when one has no cares or troubles, when one is enjoying oneself and is good health. White Cat knew the time when he was supposed to return, and as he was no longer thinking about it, she reminded him of it.

"Do you know," she said, "that you only have three days to search for the little dog that your father wants, and that your brothers have found very beautiful ones?"

The prince returned to himself and was astonished by his negligence. "By what secret charm," he cried, "have I forgotten the most important thing in the world? My glory and my fortune depend on it. Where shall I find a dog such as is necessary to win a kingdom and a horse diligent enough to travel so far?" He became anxious and very afflicted.

"Son of a king," White cat said to him, soothing him, "don't be chagrined; I'm your friend; you can stay here for another day, and although it's five hundred leagues from here to your homeland, the good wooden horse can take you there in less than twelve hours."

"Thank you, beautiful Cat," said the prince, "but it isn't sufficient for me to return to my father; Í have to take him a little dog."

"Look," White Cat said to him, "this is an acorn in which there is one more beautiful than the dog-days."

"Oh, Madame Cat, Your Majesty is making fun of me."

"Put the acorn to your ear," she continued, "and you'll hear it yapping."

He obeyed. Immediately, the little dog went "Yap! Yap!"—at which the prince was transported by joy, for any dog that can be contained in an acorn has to be very tiny. He wanted to open it, so much did he desire to see it, but White Cat told him that it might be cold on the roads, and that it was better to wait until he was in the presence of his father, the king. He thanked her a thousand times, and bid her a very tender adieu.

"I assure you," he added "that days have never seemed so short to me as with you, and I regret leaving you here, in a way, and although you are sovereign here and all the cats pay court to you, having more intelligence and gallantry than ours, I invite you nevertheless to come with me."

White Cat only replied to that proposition with a profound sigh. They separated.

The prince arrived first at the castle where the rendezvous with his brothers had been arranged. They arrived there shortly afterwards, and were surprised to see a wooden horse in the courtyard that jumped better than all those in academies.

The prince came to met them. They embraced several times, and gave one another accounts of their voyages, but our prince disguised from his brothers the truth of his adventures and showed them a wretched dog that served as a turnspit, saying that he thought it so pretty that it was the one he was taking to the king. Whatever amity there was between them, the two elder brothers felt a secret joy at the poor choice of their junior. They were at table, and walked on tiptoe as if to say to one another that they had nothing to fear from that direction.

The next day they left together in the same carriage. The king's two elder sons had little dogs in baskets, so beautiful and so delicate that one scarcely dared touch them. The youngest was carrying the poor turnspit dog, which was so dirty that no one could suffer it.

When they were in the palace, everyone surrounded them to wish them welcome; they went into the king's apartment, he did not know in whose favor to decide, for the little dogs presented by the two elder brothers were almost equal in beauty, and they were already disputing the advantage of the succession when the youngest put them in accord by taking out the acorn the White Cat had given him.

He opened it promptly, and everyone saw a tiny dog lying on cotton. It passed through the middle of a ring without touching it. The prince put it on the floor and immediately it commenced to dance a saraband with castanets as lightly as the most famous Spaniard. It was a thousand different colors; its silky hair and ears trailed on the floor.

The king was very confused, for it was impossible to find anything to criticize in the beauty of the pooch. However, he had no desire to give up his crown. The smallest fleuron of it was dearer to him than all the dogs in the world. He therefore told his sons that he was satisfied with their efforts, but that they had succeeded so well in the first thing he wanted of them that he wanted to test their skill again before keeping his promise; thus, he gave them a year to search on land and sea for a piece of cloth so fine that it could pass through the eyes of a needle, in order to make Venetian point lace.

All three of them were very afflicted to be obliged to return to a further quest, but the two princes whose dogs were less beautiful than their younger brother's consented to it. Each departed in a different direction without showing as much amity as the first time, for the turnspit incident had chilled them slightly.

Our prince mounted his wooden horse, and without wanting to seek any other aid than that he hoped to obtain from the amity of White Cat, he departed in all diligence and returned to the castle where he had been so well received. He found all the doors open; the windows, the roofs, the towers and the walls were brightly illuminated by a hundred thousand lamps, which made a marvelous effect. The hands that had served them so well advanced to meet him, took the bridle of the excellent wooden horse, which they led to the stable while the prince went into White Cat's room.

She was lying in a basket on a very neat mattress of white satin. She was wearing a negligent night-bonnet, but when she saw the prince she made a thousand leaps and as many gambols to testify to the joy she was experiencing.

"Whatever reason I had to hope for your return, son of a king," she said to him, "I confess that dared not flatter myself with it, and I am ordinarily so unfortunate in the things for which I wish that this one surprises me."

The grateful prince gave her a thousand caresses; he told her about the success of his journey, which she might well have known better that he did; that the king wanted a piece of fabric that could pass through the eye of a needle; that in truth, he believed such a thing to be impossible, but that he nevertheless had to attempt it. promising himself everything of her amity and aid.

White Cat, adopting a more serious expression, told him that it was an affair requiring some thought; that, fortunately, she had cats in her castle that spun very well; that she would even put a claw to it herself; that she would carry the work forward; and that he could thus remain tranquil without going any further to search for what he would find more easily in her house than anywhere else in the world.

The hands appeared bearing torches, and the prince, following them with White Cat, entered a gallery that extending along a great river, over which there was a surprising firework display. Four cats were due to be burned there, the trial of which had been conducted formally. They were accused of having eaten the roast meat, cheese and milk of White Cat's supper, and to have conspired against her person with Martafax and Lhermite, famous rats of the country, held as such by La Fontaine, a very truthful author. With all that, however, it was known that there was a good deal of conspiracy in the affair and that the majority of the witnesses were suborned. At any rate, the prince obtained mercy for them. The fireworks did no harm to anyone, and such beautiful rockets had never been seen.

A midnight supper was served thereafter, which gave the prince as much pleasure as the fireworks, for he was very hungry, and his wooden horse had carried him so rapidly that there had never been such diligence.

The following days passed like those that had preceded them, with a thousand different fêtes, with which White Cat regaled her guest. He was probably the first mortal who had been so well diverted with cats without having any other company.

It is true that White Cat had an agreeable, engaging and almost universal intelligence. She was more knowledgeable that it is permitted for a cat to be. The prince was sometimes astonished by that.

"No, he said, "it's not a natural thing, all that I remark of the marvelous about you. If you love me, charming puss, tell me by what prodigy you think and talk so well that you could be received in the famous academies of the finest minds."

"Cease your questions, son of a king," she said to him. "It isn't permitted to me to reply to them, and you can push your conjectures as far as you like without my opposing them; let it suffice that I always have a velvet paw for you and that I am tenderly interest in everything that concerns you."

That fecund year went by, insensibly, like the first. The prince scarcely wished for something before the diligent hands brought it to him right away, whether it was books, gems, paintings or antique medallions. In sum, he only had to say that he wanted some jewel, which was in the cabinet of the Mogul or the King of Persia, or some statue from Corinth or Greece, and he immediately saw what he desired before him, without knowing either who had bought it or where it came from. It had its charms nevertheless, and in order to relax it is sometimes very pleasant to find oneself master of the most beautiful treasures on earth.

White Cat, who was always watching over the prince's interests, warned him that the time of his departure was approaching, and that he could be tranquil with regard to the piece of cloth he desired, because she had had a marvelous one made. She added that this time she wanted to give him an equipage worthy of his birth, and without waiting for his response she obliged him to look into the great courtyard of the castle.

There was an uncovered caleche there made of gold, enameled with the color of flame, with a thousand gallant devices, which satisfied the mind as much as the eyes. Twelve horses as white as snow, attached in front, four by four, pulled it, charged with flame-colored velvet harness embroidered with diamonds and garnished with gold plaques. The lining of the caleche was similar, and a hundred eight-horse carriages, all filled with lords of grandiose appearance, superbly dressed, followed the caleche. It was also accompanied by a thousand guards, whose coats were so covered with embroidery that the cloth could not be seen, and there were portraits of White Cat everywhere, in the devices of the caleche, in the uniforms of the guards and attached by ribbons to the garments of those making up the cortege, like a new Order with which they had been honored.

"Go," she said to the prince. "Appear at your father's court in such a sumptuous manner that your magnificent airs will serve to impose upon him, in order that he can no longer refuse you the crown that you merit. Here is a walnut; refrain from breaking it except in is presence; you will find within it the piece of cloth you have requested of me."

"Amiable Blanchette," he said to her, "I confess to you that I am so penetrated by your generosity that if you would like to consent to it, I would prefer spending my life with you to all the grandeurs that I have reason to promise myself elsewhere."

"Son of a king," she replied, "I am persuaded of the generosity of your heart; it is a rare merchandise among princes; they want to be loved by everyone and to love no one, but you show clearly enough that the general rule has its exception. I give you credit for the attachment you testify for a little white cat, which is fundamentally good for nothing but catching mice."

The prince kissed her paw and departed.

One would have difficulty believing the diligence that he made if one did not know already the manner in which the wooden horse had carried him, in less than two days, more than five hundred leagues from the castle; with the consequence that the same power that animal had pressed the others so forcefully that they were only on the road for twenty-four hours; they did not stop anywhere until they had arrived at the king's palace.

The two elder brothers had already arrived, and not seeing their younger brother appear, they had applauded themselves for his negligence and said to one another: "That's very fortunate; he's dead or ill and he won't be our rival in the important affair that is about to be settled."

Immediately, they deployed their fabrics, which were in truth so fine that they passed through the hole of a large needle, but could not pass through the eye of a small one. The king, very glad of that pretext for dispute, showed them the needle that he had proposed, and the magistrates, by his order, brought the treasure of the city from where it had been carefully locked up.

There was a great murmur regarding that dispute. The friends of the princes, particularly those of the eldest—for his was the more beautiful fabric—said that it was a mere quibble, into which entered a great deal of cleverness and Normanism. The king's creatures sustained that he was not obliged to hold to conditions that he had not proposed.

Finally, to put them all in accord, a charming sound of trumpets, timpani and oboes was heard; it was our prince, who was arriving in pompous apparel. The king and his two sons were as astonished as one another by such great magnificence.

After he had saluted his father respectfully and embraced his brothers, he took the walnut out of a ruby-encrusted box, which he broke. He thought he would find the much-vaunted piece of cloth inside, but instead there as a hazelnut. He broke that, and was surprised to see a cherry-stone.

Everyone looked at one another, and the king laughed very quietly, mocking his son, who had been credulous enough to believe that he could bring a piece of cloth a nut-shell; but why should he not have believed it, since he had already given him a little dog that had been contained in an acorn? He therefore broke the cherry-stone, which was filled with its kernel. Then a loud noise went up in the chamber, and nothing else could be heard but: "the youngest son is the dupe of the adventure."

He did not make any reply to the courtiers' bad jokes. He opened the kernel and found a grain of wheat, and then, inside the grain of wheat, a grain of millet.

Oh! He began to mistrust the truth, and muttered between his teeth: "White Cat, White Cat, you've made a fool of me." At that moment, he felt the paw of a cat on his hand, by which he was scratched so hard that he bled. He did not know whether that clawing was intended to give him courage or make him lose it.

However, he opened the millet seed, and the astonishment of everyone was not small when he took out a bolt of cloth four hundred aunes long, so marvelous that all the birds, animals and fish on earth were painted thereon, along with the all trees, the fruits and the plants, the rocks, the rarities and the sea-shells, the sun, the moon, the stars and the planets of the heavens. There were also portraits of the kings and other sovereigns who had reigned on earth thus far, their wives, their mistresses, their children and all their subjects, without the smallest brat being forgotten. Everyone in his estate was represented appropriately, in the fashion of his country.

When he king saw that piece of cloth went as pale as the prince had gone red from searching it for such a long time. The needle was presented, and it passed through it, back and forth, six times. The king and the two older princes maintained a bleak silence, although the beauty and rarity of the fabric forced them from time to time to admit that nothing in the universe was comparable.

The king uttered a profound sigh, and, turning toward his children, said to them: "Nothing can give me as much consolation in my old age as recognizing your deference for me. I therefore want you to put you to a further proof. Go and travel for another year and the one who brings back the most beautiful young woman at the end of that year will marry her and be crowned king on his marriage; it's also a necessity that my successor be married. I swear, I guarantee, that I will not defer again the recompense that I have promised.

All the injustice flowed over our prince. The little dog and the piece of cloth merited ten kingdoms rather than one; but he was so well-born that he did not want to oppose his father's will, and without delay he climbed back into his caleche. His entire equipage followed him, and he returned to his dear White Cat.

She knew the day and the moment when he would arrive; the whole road was strewn with flowers; a thousand cassolettes were smoking on all sides, and especially in the castle.

She was sitting on a Persian carpet under an awning of gold cloth, in a gallery from which she could see him returning. He was received by the hands that had always served him.

All the cats climbed on to the gutters in order to congratulate him with a desperate mewling.

"Well, son of a king," she said to him, "you've come back without a crown, then?"

"Madame," he replied, "Your generosity has put me in a state to earn one, but I'm convinced that the king would have more difficulty letting go of it than I would have pleasure in possessing it."

"No matter," she said. "It's necessary not to neglect anything in order to merit it; I'll serve you in that occasion; and since it's necessary for you to take a beautiful young woman to your father's court, I'll search for one who will win you the prize. Meanwhile, let's rejoice; I've ordered a naval combat between my cats and the terrible rats of the country. My cats might perhaps have difficulty, for they fear the water, but they would otherwise have too much advantage, and it's necessary, as far as one can, to equalize everything."

The prince admired the prudence of Madame Puss. He praised her abundantly, and went with her to a terrace overlooking the sea.

The cats' ships consisted of large pieces of cork, on which they could navigate quite comfortably. The rats had joined several eggshells together, and those were their ships. The combat was cruelly determined; the rats threw themselves into the water and swam far better than the cats, with the consequence that twenty times over they were victors and vanquished, but Minagrobis, the admiral of the feline fleet, reduced the rodent genre to the utmost despair. He ate the general of their fleet greedily, who was an experienced old rat who had gone around the world three times in fine ships on which he was nether captain or crewman but merely vermin.

White Cat did not want those poor unfortunates to be destroyed entirely. She had a knack for politics, and thought that, if there were no longer and rats or mice in the land, her subjects would live in an idleness that might become prejudicial.

The prince spent that year as he had spent the others—which is so say, hunting, fishing and playing games, for White

Cat was a very good chess player. He could not help asking her further questions from time to time, to know by what miracle she could talk. He asked her whether she was a fay, or if she had been rendered a cat by some metamorphosis, but, just as she only ever said what she wanted to say, she only ever responded what she wanted to respond, and that was with so many brief comments that signified nothing that it was easy to discern that she did not want to share her secret with him.

Nothing goes by so quickly as days that are passed without difficulty and without chagrin, and if the Cat had not been careful to remember the time when he had to return to the court, it is certain that the prince would have forgotten it absolutely.

She warned him the day before that he only had to take back one of the most beautiful princesses on earth; that the hour to destroy the fatal work of the fays had finally arrived; and that it was necessary for that that he resolve to cut off her head and tail and throw them promptly in the fire.

"Me!" he cried. "Blanchette! My amour! Could I be barbaric enough to kill you? Oh, you doubtless want to test me heart, but be certain that I am incapable of lacking the amity and gratitude that I owe you."

"No, son of a king," she continued, "I don't suspect you of any ingratitude; I know your merit; it is neither you nor I who regulate our destiny in this affair. Do as I wish and we well both commence to be happy, and you will know, faith of a good and honorable Cat, that I am veritably your friend."

Tears came to the eyes of the young prince two or three times, merely at the thought that it would be necessary to cut off the head of his little Puss, who was so pretty and gracious. He said everything he could imagine of the most tender in order that she might dispense him of it, but she replied stubbornly that she wanted to die by his hand, and that it was the only means of preventing his brothers from having the crown; in brief, she pressed him with so much ardor that he drew his sword, tremulously, and with a ill-assured hand he cut off the head and tail of his good friend the Cat.

At the same time he saw the most charming metamorphosis imaginable. The body of White Cat grew and suddenly changed into that of a young woman, in an indescribable fashion. There was none as accomplished as her in the world. Her eyes delighted the heart and her mildness retained it; her figure was majestic, her attitude noble and modest, her mind and manners engaging; in sum, she was above everything there is of the most lovable.

On seeing her, the prince was so surprised, and his surprise was so agreeable, that he thought he was enchanted. He could not speak, his eyes were not wide enough to gaze at her and his tied tongue could not explain his astonishment; but it was something else entirely when he saw an extraordinary number of lords and ladies enter, whose cat skins were thrown over their shoulders, come to prostrate themselves at the queen's feet and testify their joy at seeing her in her natural state again. She received them with testimonies of good will that marked the character of her heart sufficiently.

After having maintained the circle for a few minutes, she ordered that she be left alone with the prince, and she spoke to him thus: "Don't think, Sire, that I have always been a cat, or that my birth among humans was obscure. My father was the king of six kingdoms. He loved my mother tenderly and left her in entire liberty to do as she wished. Her dominant inclination was to travel, with the consequence that, while pregnant with me, she decided to go and see a certain mountain about which she had heard surprising things.

"As she was in the road, she was told that near the place she was passing there was an ancient fay castle, which was the most beautiful in the world, or was believed to be by tradition, for as no one could enter it, no one could judge; but it was known for sure that those fays had in their garden the best, most flavorsome and most delicate fruits that had ever been eaten.

"Immediately, my mother had such a violent desire to eat that she turned aside. She arrived at the door of that superb edifice, which shone with gold and azure on every side, but she knocked in vain; no one appeared and it appeared that everyone within was dead. Her desire augmented by the difficulties, she sent people in quest of ladders, in order that someone could pass over the garden wall; and they could have done that if the walls had not been so high, although no one was working there. The ladders were attached together, but they broke under the weight of those who tried to climb them, and they were crippled or killed.

"The queen was in despair. She could see tall trees laden with fruits that she believed to be delicious; she wanted to eat some or die, with the consequence that she had rich tents pitched outside the castle and remained there for six weeks with her entire court. She did not sleep or eat; she sighed incessantly and did not talk about anything except the fruits of the inaccessible garden. Finally, she fell dangerously ill, without anyone being able to bring the slightest remedy to her malady, for the inexorable fays has not even appeared since she had been established close to their castle. All her servants were extraordinarily afflicted; nothing was heard but tears and sighs, while the dying queen demanded fruits from all those who served her; but she did not want any others than those she was refused.

"One night, when she was drowsy, she saw as she awoke an ugly and decrepit little old woman sitting in an armchair beside her bed. She was surprised that her women had allowed a stranger to get so close to her, when she said to her: 'We find Your Majesty very importunate, to want to eat our fruits with so much obstinacy, but since your precious life depends on it, my sisters and I consent to give you as much as you can carry away, and as much while you remain here, provided that you make us a gift.'

"'Oh, my good mother, speak,' cried the queen. 'I'll give you my kingdoms, my heart my soul, provide that I have the fruits; I can't buy them too dear.'

"'We want Your Majesty to give us the child you are carrying in your womb,' she said. 'As soon as she is born we shall come in quest of her. She will be nourished among us; there will be no virtues, beauties and sciences with which we will not endow her; in a word, she will be our child; we will render her happy, but observe that Your Majesty will not see her again until she is married. If the proposition is agreeable to you, I will cure you right away and bring you into our orchards; in spite of the night, you will be able to see clearly enough to choose what you want. If what I say doesn't please you, good night, Madame, I'll go to sleep.'

"'Hard as the law you're imposing on me is,' the queen replied. 'I accept it, rather than dying; for it's certain that I don't have a day to live, so I'd doom my child in dooming myself.. Cure me, savant fay, and don't leave me a moment without enjoying the privilege you've just granted me.'

"The fay touched her with a little golden wand, saying: 'May You Majesty be quit of all the ills that retain you in his bed.'

"It seemed to her immediately that a very heavy and harsh robe was removed, by which she had felt crushed, and which had clung harder in places, where the malady had apparently been greatest. She summoned all her women and told them with a cheerful expression that she felt marvelously well, that she was going to get up, and that the worm-eaten and barricaded doors of the fay castle would be opened, in order that she could eat the marvelous fruits and take away as many as she pleased.

"None of the women believed that the queen was not delirious and dreaming about the fruits she had desired so much, with the consequence that instead of replying to her they began to weep and had all the physicians woken up to see what state she was in. That delay made the queen desperate; she demanded her clothes, but they were refused to her. She became angry and went very red. They thought that it was an effect of her fever, but the physicians, having come in, taken her pulse and performed their usual ceremonies could not deny that she was in perfect health. Her women, who realized the mistake that their zeal had caused them to make, tried to repair it by dressing her promptly. Everyone begged her pardon; all was appeased, and she hastened to follow the old fay, who was still waiting.

"She went into the palace, to which nothing could be added to make it the most beautiful place in the world; you will easily believe that, Sire," Queen White Cat added, "when I tell you that it was the one where we are at present. Two other fays, slightly less aged than the one conducting my mother met them at the door and gave her a very favorable welcome. She begged them to take her to the garden promptly, and to the espaliers where she would find the best fruits. 'They are all equally good,' they said, 'and if you do not want to have the pleasure of pick them yourself we would only have to summon them for them to come here.

"'I beg you, Mesdames,' said the queen, 'to give me the satisfaction of seeing such an extraordinary thing.'

"The oldest one put her fingers in her mouth and whistled three times, and then she shouted: 'Apricots, peaches, cling-peaches, nectarines, cherries, pears plums, melons, Muscat grapes, apples, oranges, lemons, redcurrants, strawberries and raspberries, run to my voice.'

"'But all those you have just summoned,' said the queen, 'come in different seasons.'

"'It's not like that in our orchards,' they said. 'We have all the fruits there are on earth, always ripe and always good, and they never spoil.'

"At the same time, they arrived, rolling and crawling pell-mell, without being spoiled or dirtied; with the consequence that the queen, impatient to satisfy her desire, threw herself upon them and took the first that came to hand; she devoured them rather than eating them.

"After having sated herself somewhat she asked the fays to let her go to the espaliers in order to have the pleasure of choosing them by eye before picking them. 'We consent willingly,' said the three fays, 'but remember the promise you have made us; it will no longer be permissible for you to take it back.'

"'I am convinced,' she replied, 'that it is so good with you, and this palace seems so beautiful, that if I did not love the king, my husband, dearly, I would offer to live here too; that is why you need have no fear that I shall retract my word.'

"The fays, quite content, opened all their gardens to her, and all their enclosures. She stayed there for three days and three nights without wanting to leave, so delightful did she find them. She collected fruits for her provision; and as they never spoiled she had four mules loaded with them, which she took away. The fays added to their fruits golden baskets of exquisite workmanship in which to put them, and several rarities of excessive price. They promised to raise me as a princess, to render me perfect and to choose me a husband; that they would inform her of the wedding and that they hoped that she would come to it.

"The king was delighted by the queen's return; the entire court testified its joy; there was nothing but balls, masquerades, ring-races and feasts, in which the queen's fruits were served as delicious fate. The king ate them in preference to everything that could be presented to him. He did not know about the treaty that she had made with the fays and he often asked her to which country she had gone to bring back such good things. She replied that they were found on an almost-inaccessible isle, another time that they came from valleys, and then from a garden or a great forest. The king was surprised by so many contradictions. He questioned those who had accompanied her, but she had forbidden them so strictly to tell anyone about her adventure that they dared not talk about it.

"Eventually, the queen, worried about what she had promised the fays and seeing the time of her childbirth approaching, fell into a frightful melancholy; she sighed continually and was visibly changed. The king became anxious; he pressed the queen to tell him the reason for her sadness, and after extreme difficulties she told him everything that had happened between the fays and her, and how she had promised them the daughter that she was about to have. 'What!' cried the king. 'We have no children, you know how much I desire one, and, in order to eat a few apples, you've been capable of promising your daughter? It's necessary that you have no amity for me.'

"With that he heaped her with a thousand reproaches, of which my poor mother nearly died of dolor; but he was not content with that. He had her imprisoned in a tower and put guards all round it in order to prevent her from having any commerce whatsoever with society. He even changed the servants she had from those who had been with her at the fays' castle.

"The bad intelligence of the king and the queen threw the court into an infinite consternation. Everyone quit their rich clothes in order to put on ones in conformity with the general dolor. The king, for his part, seemed inexorable; he no longer saw his wife, and as soon as I was born he had me brought into the palace to be nursed, while she remained a prisoner and very unhappy.

"The fays were not unaware of anything that had happened; they became irritated; they wanted to have me; they regarded me as their property and considered that it was committing a theft to retain me. Before seeking a vengeance proportionate to their chagrin thy sent a celebrated embassy to the king to warn him to set the queen at liberty, to return her to his good graces and also to beg him to hand me over to their ambassadors in order to be nourished and raised among them. The ambassadors were so small and ill-made—for they were hideous dwarfs—that they did not have the gift of persuading the king to do as they wished. He refused them rudely and if they had not departed diligently he might perhaps have done worse to them.

"When they fays knew what my father had done they were as indignant as it is possible to be, and after having sent into his six kingdoms all the evils that could desolate them, thy unleashed a frightful dragon that filed with venom the places through which it passed, which ate men and children and caused trees and plants to die with the exhalations of its breath.

"The king found himself in the utmost desolation; he consulted all the sages of his realm as to what he ought to do to preserve his subjects from the misfortunes by which he saw them overwhelmed. They advised him to send throughout the world for the best physicians and the most excellent remedies, and on the other hand, that it was necessary to promise life to any criminals condemned to death who were prepared to fight the dragon.

"The king, satisfied with that advice, followed it, but did not receive any consolation, for the mortality continued and no one who went against the dragon was not devoured by it, with the result that he had recourse to a fay who had protected him since his earliest youth. She was very old and could hardly get out of bed any more. He went to see her, and made her a thousand reproaches for allowing destiny to persecute him without helping him.

"'What do you expect me to do?' she said. 'You've irritated my sisters; they have as much power as I do, and we rarely act against one another. Think of appeasing them by giving them your daughter; that little princess belongs to them. You have put the queen in a narrow prison; what has that lovable woman done to you to be treated so badly? Resolve yourself to keep the word she gave you, and I assure you that you will be heaped with benefits.'

"My father loved me dearly, but, seeing no other means of saving his kingdoms and delivering himself from the fatal dragon, he told his friend that he was resolved to believe her, that he wanted to give me to the fays, since she assured him that I would be cherished and treated as a princess of my rank; that he would also bring back the queen; and that she had only to tell him to whom to confide me in order to carry me to the fay castle.

"'It's necessary,' she said, 'to take her in her cradle to the mountain of flowers; you can even stay in the vicinity to witness the celebrations that will take place.'

"The king told her that in a week, he would go with the queen, that she should inform her sisters the fays, in order that they should do whatever they judged appropriate.

"As soon as he had returned to the palace he sent for the queen, with as much tenderness and pomp as he had put anger and haste into her imprisonment. She was so dejected and so changed that he would scarcely have recognized her if his heart had not assured him that it was the same person that he had cherished so much. He begged her with tears in his eyes to forget the displeasures that he had caused her, assuring her that they would be the last she would ever experience with him. She replied that she had attracted them by the imprudence she had had in promising her daughter to the fays; and that if anything could render her excusable it was the state that she was in. Finally, he declared that he wanted to put me in their hands.

"The queen, in her turn, opposed that design; it seemed that some fatality was mingled with it and that I would always be a subject of discord between my father and my mother. After she had moaned and wept a great deal without obtaining what she wanted—for the king could see too many fatal consequences in that, and our subjects were continuing to die, as if they were culpable of the faults of our family—she consented to anything he desired, and preparations were made for the ceremony.

"I was put into a mother-of-pearl basket ornamented with everything that art can imagine of the most gallant. There was nothing but garlands of flowers and festoons hang around it, and the flowers were precious stones, the different colors of which, struck by the sun, reflected rays so brilliant that one could not look at them. The magnificence of my apparel surpassed, if possible, that of the cradle. All my swaddling clothes were made of large pearls; twenty-four princesses of the blood carried me on a kind of light stretcher; their adornment had nothing of the commonplace, but it was not permitted to them to mingle any other colors therein but white, as a symbol of my innocence. The entire court accompanied me, everyone in accordance with their rank.

While they were climbing the mountain, a melodious symphony was heard approaching; eventually, the fays appeared, thirty-six in number; they had invited their good friends to come with them; each of them was seated in a pearl shell larger than the one in which Venus emerged from the sea; marine horses that hardly ever come on to land were drawing them more pompously than the first queens of the world, but they were old and excessively ugly. They carried an olive branch to signify that his submission had found mercy before them; and when they held me there were caresses so extraordinary that it seemed that they only wanted to live any longer in order to render me happy.

The dragon that had served to avenge them against my father came after them, with diamond chains. They took me in their arms, gave me a thousand caresses, endowed me with several advantages, and then commenced the fay swing, which is a very gay dance; it is incredible how those old women leapt and gamboled. Then the dragon that had eaten so many people approached, crawling. The three fays to whom my mother had promised me sat down on it, placing my cradle in between them, and struck the dragon with a wand. It immediately deployed its huge scaly wings; finer than crepe they mingled a thousand bizarre colors; they returned thus to the castle.

"My mother, seeing me in the air, exposed on that furious dragon, could not help uttering loud cries. The king consoled her by mans of the assurance that his friend had given him that no accident would happen to me and that they would take the same care of me as if I had remained in his own palace. She calmed down, although it as very painful for her to lose me for such a long time, and to be the sole cause of it, for if she had not wanted to eat the fruits from the garden, I would have remained in my father's kingdom, and I would not have had all the displeasures that it remains for me to relate to you.

"Know, then, son of a king, that my guardians had built a tower expressly, in which there were a thousand beautiful apartments for all seasons of the year, magnificent furniture and agreeable books, but there was no door and it was always necessary to enter through the windows, which were prodigiously high. There was a beautiful garden around the tower, ornamented with flowers, fountains and arbors, which provided protection from the heat in the most ardent heat-waves. It was in that place that the fays raised me with cares that surpassed everything that they had promised the queen. My garments were more fashionable and so magnificent that if anyone had seen me they would have thought that it was my wedding day.

"They taught me everything that was appropriate to my age and my birth; I did not give them much difficulty, for there were very few things that I did not understand with an extreme facility. My meekness was very agreeable to them, and as I had never seen anyone but them, I could have lived tranquilly in that situation for the rest of my life.   .

"They always came to see me mounted on the furious dragon that I have already mentioned; they did not talk to me either about the king or the queen; they called me their daughter, and I believed that I was. No one remained with me in the tower except a parrot and a little dog that they had given to me to divert me, for they were endowed with reason and talked marvelously.

"One of the sides of the tower was built over a sunken road full of ruts and cluttered with trees, with the consequence that I had never seen anyone on it since I had been shut away; but one day, as I was at the window chatting with my parrot and my dog, I heard a noise. I looked around and I perceived a young knight who had stopped to listen to our conversation; I had only ever seen one in paintings.

"I was not sorry that an unexpected encounter had furnished me with that opportunity, with the consequence that, not suspecting the danger that was attached to the satisfaction of seeing a likeable object, I leaned forward to look at him, and the more I looked, the more pleasure I obtained. He made me a profound reverence, attached his gaze to mine and appeared to me to be in great difficulty as to the manner in which he ought to converse with me, for my window was very high and he was fearful of being heard, because he knew full well that I was in a fay castle.

"Night fell rather suddenly—or, to be more accurate, it arrived without our perceiving it; he sounded his horn two or three times, and entertained me with a few fanfares, and then he departed without my being able to distinguish which way he went, so great was the obscurity. I remained very pensive, and no longer felt the same pleasure in chatting with my parrot and my dog. They said the nicest things in the world to me, for enchanted animals become intelligent, but I was preoccupied, and I did not know the art of constraining myself. Parrot remarked that, but because he was subtle, he did not give any evidence of what was passing through his mind.

"I did not fail to get up with the dawn. I ran to my window; I was agreeably surprised to see the young knight at the foot of the tower. He was wearing magnificent clothes; I flattered myself that I was partly responsible for that, and I was not mistaken. He spoke to me with a kind of trumpet that carries the voice, and with its aid he told me that, having been insensible until then to all the beauties he had seen, he had suddenly felt so sharply struck by mine that he could not understand how he could forsake, without dying, seeing me every day for the rest of his life.

"I was very content with that compliment, and very anxious about not daring to respond to it, for it would have been necessary to shout at the top of my voice and run the risk of being heard even more clearly by the fays than by him. I was holding some flowers, which I threw to him; he received them as a signal favor, with the consequence that he kissed them several times and thanked me. Then he asked me whether I found it good if he came every day at the same hour beneath my window, and that if I wanted that I should throw him something. I had a turquoise ring, which I took off my finger abruptly, and which I threw to him with a great deal of precipitation, making him a sign to go away diligently. That was because I could hear the fay Violente mounting her dragon on the other side of the tower in order to bring me breakfast.

"The first thing she said on entering my room was: "I smell the voice of a man here, search, dragon!' Oh, what became of me? I was paralyzed by the fear that it might pass through the other window and follow the knight, in whom I was already very interested. 'In truth, my good Mama,' I said—for that was what the old fay wanted me to call her— 'you're joking when you say that you smell the voice of a man; does a voice have an odor? If it it did, who is the mortal reckless enough to try to climb into this tower?'

"'What you say is true, my daughter,' she replied. 'I'm delighted to see you reasoning so nicely, and I imagine that it's the hatred I have for all men that sometimes persuades me that they aren't far away from me.' She gave me my breakfast and my distaff. 'When you've eaten, don't fail to spin,' she said to me, 'for you did nothing yesterday and my sisters are annoyed.' In fact, I had been so occupied with the stranger that it had been impossible for me to spin.

"As soon as she had gone, I threw away the distaff with a mutinous gesture and went up on to the terrace in order to see further into the countryside. I had an excellent telescope; nothing limited my view. I looked in all directions, and I discovered my knight on the top of a mountain. He was reposing under a rich awning of golden cloth, and he was surrounded by a large court. I did not doubt that he was the son of some king who was a neighbor of the fays' palace. As I feared that if he returned to the tower he might be discovered by the terrible dragon, I came to get Parrot and I told him to fly to that mountain, find the man who had talked to me, and beg him on my part not to return, because I feared the vigilance of my guardians, and that they might do him a bad turn.

"Parrot acquitted his mission like an intelligent parrot. Everyone was surprised to see him arrive at high speed to perch on the prince's shoulder and whisper into his ear. The prince felt the joy and the pain of that embassy. The care that I had taken flattered his heart, but the difficulties he would encounter in talking to me depressed him, without being able to turn him away from the design he had formed to please me. He asked the parrot a hundred questions, and Parrot asked him a hundred in his turn, for he was naturally curious.

"The prince gave him a ring for me in place of my turquoise; it was another one, but much more beautiful than mine; it was cut in a heart shape, with diamonds. 'It is only just,' he added, 'that I treat you as I would treat an ambassador; this is my portrait, which I am giving you; only show it to your charming mistress.' He tucked the portrait under his wing and brought the ring back in his beak.

"I waited for the return of my little courier with an impatience that I had not previously known. He told me that the person to whom I had sent him was a great king, who had received him as well as possible, and that I could be sure that he only wanted to continue living for me; that even though there was a great deal of peril in coming to the base of my tower he was resolved to anything rather than renounce seeing me.

"That news intrigued me greatly; I started to weep. Parrot and Toutou did their best to console me, for they loved me tenderly. Then Parrot presented me with the prince's ring and showed me the portrait. I confess that I had never been as glad as I was to be able to consider at close range the man I had only seen at a distance. He seemed to me to be even more lovable than he had before.

"A hundred thoughts came into my mind, some agreeable and others sad, which gave me an extraordinary expression of anxiety. The fays who came to see me perceived it. They said to one another that I was doubtless bored, and that it was necessary to think of finding me a husband of the fay race. They talked about several and settled on little King Migonnet, whose kingdom was five hundred thousand leagues from their palace.

"Parrot overheard that fine conference; he came to render me an account of it and said: 'Oh, how I pity you, my dear mistress, if you become Queen Migonnette! He's an ape who scares everyone, I regret to tell you, but in truth, the king who loves you would not want him for his footman.'

"'Have you seen him, Parrot?'

"'I believe so, yes.' he continued. 'I was brought up on a branch with him.

"'What do you mean, on a branch?' I said.

"'Yes,' he said, 'it's because he has the feet of an eagle.

"Such a story afflicted me strangely; I looked at the charming portrait of the young king. I thought that he had only regaled Parrot in order to give me the opportunity to see him, and when I made the comparison between him and Migonnet, I no longer hoped for anything of my life, and I resolved to die rather than marry him.

"I did not sleep all night. Parrot and Toutou chatted with me; I dozed off when morning came, and as my little dog had a good nose he caught the scent of the king when he was at the foot of the tower. He woke Parrot. 'I'll wager,' he said, 'that the king is down below.'

"Parrot replied: 'Shut up, chatterbox; because you almost always have your eyes open and your ear alert you're a nuisance to the repose of others.'

"'But let's wager,' said the little dog, again. 'I know that he's there.'

"Parrot replied: 'And I know that he isn't. Haven't I forbidden him to come, on the part of our mistress?

"'Oh, truly, you make me sick with your forbidding,' cried the dog, 'a passionate man only consults his heart.' And with that he began to tease his wings so forcefully that Parrot became annoyed.

"I woke up at their cries; they told me what the argument was about and I ran—or, rather, I flew—to the window. I saw the king, who was holding his arms out to me, and who told me with his trumpet that he could no longer live without me, that he implored me to find a means of getting out of my tower, or of enabling him to enter it; that he attested by all the gods and all the elements that he would marry me immediately and that I would be one of the greatest queens in the world.

"I commanded Parrot to go and tell him that what he wanted seemed to me to be impossible, that nevertheless, on the word that he had given me and oaths that he had sworn, I would apply myself to what he desired; that I implored him not to come very day, that someone might see him eventually, and that there was no quarter with the fays.

"He retired, overwhelmed by joy, in the hope with which I flattered him, and I found myself in the greatest embarrassment in the world when I reflected on what I had just promised. How could I get out of the tower, which had no door, and where the only aid I had was Parrot and Toutou? To be so young, so inexperienced and so fearful! I therefore made the resolution not to attempt something in which I could never succeed, and I sent Parrot to tell the king. He wanted to kill himself before his eyes, but in the end he charged him with persuading me, either to come to see him die or to soothe him. 'Sire,' my feathered ambassador cried, 'my mistress is sufficiently persuaded, she only lacks the power.'

"When he rendered me an account of what had happened, I was more afflicted than I had yet been. The fay Violente came; she found me with red and swollen eyes; she said that I had been weeping, and that if I did not confess the reason, she would burn me, for all her threats were always terrible. I replied, trembling, that I was tired of spinning, and that I had a desire for little nets in which to catch the little birds that came to peck the fruits in my garden. 'What you wish, my daughter,' she said, 'won't cost you any more tears. I'll bring you cords, as many as you want; and in fact, I had them that same evening, but she warned me to think less about working than making myself beautiful, because King Migonnet was due to arrive shortly. I shivered at that bad news, and made no reply.

"As soon as she had gone I started two or three fragments of nets, but what I applied myself to doing was making a rope-ladder that was very well made without ever being seen. It is true that the fay had not furnished me with as much as I needed, and she incessantly said: 'But my daughter, your work is like that of Penelope, it makes no progress, and you never weary of asking me for the wherewithal to work.'

"'Oh, my good Mama, it's easy for you to talk; all that you see is that I don't know how to do it, and keep ruining everything.'

"'How can you be afraid of ruining a piece of string?'

"My air of simplicity made her laugh, even though she had a very disagreeable and very cruel humor.

"I sent Parrot to tell the king to come under the windows of the tower one evening, that he would find a ladder there, and that he would know the rest when he arrived. In fact, I attached it very firmly, resolved to run away with him, but when he saw it, without waiting for me to descend, he climbed up in haste and threw himself into my room as I was preparing everything to flee.

"The sight of him gave me so much joy that, I forgot the peril we were in. He renewed all his oaths and implored me not to defer receiving him for my husband. We took Parrot and Toutou as witnesses to our marriage; never has a marriage been made between persons of such high rank with so little splendor and fuss, and no hearts have ever been more content than ours.

"Daylight had not yet come when the king quit me; I told him the terrible design the fays had of marrying me to little Migonnet; I gave him a description, which horrified him as much as it did me. Scarcely had he gone than the hours seemed to me to be as long as years. I ran to the window and followed him with my eyes in spite of the obscurity, but what was my astonishment to see in the air a chariot of fire drawn by winged salamanders, which was making such diligence that the eye could scarcely follow it? That chariot was accompanied by several guards mounted on ostriches. I did not have enough leisure to consider the ape that was traversing the atmosphere thus, but I concluded easily that it was a fay or an enchanter.

"Shortly thereafter the fay Violente entered my room. 'I'm bringing you good news,' she said. 'You lover arrived a few hours ago. Prepare yourself to receive him. Here are clothes and jewels.'

"'Eh! what tells you,' I cried, 'that I want to be married? That's not my intention at all. Send King Migonnet away. I won't put on another pin; whether he finds me beautiful or ugly, I'm not for him.

"'Yes, yes,' said the fay, 'what a little rebel, what a head without a brain! I don't intend to be mocked, I…'

"'What will you do to me?' I said, all red at the names she had called me. 'Can he be more badly nurtured than I am, in a tower with a parrot and a dog, seeing the horrible figure of a frightful dragon several times a day?'

"'Ha! Little ingrate," said he fay, 'do you merit so many cares and pains? I've told my sisters over and over again that we'd have a sad recompense.'

"She went to find them, and told them about our dispute; they were all as surprised as one another.

"Parrot and Toutou made me great remonstrations, that if I were any more mutinous they foresaw the sharp displeasures would ensue for me. I felt so proud of possessing the heart of a great king that I scorned the fays and the advice of my poor comrades. I didn't get dressed and I put up my hair wrongly, in order that Migonnet would find me disagreeable.

"He arrived in his chariot of fire. Never since there have been dwarfs has one been seen as small. He walked on his eagle's feet and his knees at the same time, for he had no leg bones, with the consequence that he sustained himself with diamond crutches. His royal mantle was only half an aune long, and a third of it was the train. His head was as large as a bushel and his nose so long that he carried a dozen birds on it, whose songs entertained him. He had such a furious beard that canaries built their nests in it, and his ears stick up a cubit above his head, but one did not perceive that because of a high pointed crown that he wore in order to seem taller. The flame of his chariot roasted the fruits, desiccated the flowers and dried up the fountains in my garden.

"He came toward me, his arms open to embrace me. I stood up very straight and his principal squire had to lift him up, but as soon as he approached I fled into my room, and closed the door and windows, with the result that Migonnet went back to the fay's residence, very indignant against me.

"They begged his pardon a thousand times for my abruptness, and in order to appease him—for he was redoubtable—they resolved to bring him to my room at night while I was asleep, and to bind my hands and feet in order to put me in his burning chariot, so that he could take me away. Having settled the matter thus, they hardly scolded me for the abruptness I had shown. They only said that it was necessary to think of repairing it. Parrot and Toutou were surprised by such great mildness.

"'Do you know, my mistress,' said the dog, 'that my heart doesn't announce anything good; the fays are strange individuals, especially Violente.'

"I mocked those alarms and waited for my husband with a thousand impatiences; he was too eager to see me to be late. I threw out the rope ladder, firmly resolved to return with him. He climbed up lightly, and said things to me so tender that I dare not recall them to my memory.

"As we were talking together with the same tranquility as if we had been in his palace, we suddenly saw the windows of my room staved in. The fays entered on their terrible dragon, Migonnet followed them in his chariot of fire, and all his guards with their ostriches. Unafraid, the king drew his sword, only thinking of protecting me from the most furious adventure that had ever happened—for in sum, Sire, what can I tell you? Those barbaric creatures pushed their dragon at him, and it devoured him before my eyes

"In despair at his misfortune and mine, I hurled myself into the maw of that horrible monster, wanting it to swallow me as it had just swallowed everything that I loved in the world. It wanted that as well, but the fays, even crueler, did not want it. 'It's necessary,' they cried, 'to reserve longer pains for her, a prompt death is too mild for that unworthy creature,' They touched me, and I immediately saw myself in the form of a white cat.

"They brought me into this superb palace, which was my father's; they metamorphosed all the lords and ladies of the realm into cats; they left other people of whom only the hands could be seen, and reduced me to the deplorable state in which you found me, making me know my birth, the death of my father, that of my mother, and that I would only be delivered from my feline form by a prince who resembled perfectly the husband hey had stolen from me.

"It is you, Sire, who have that resemblance," she continued. "The same features, the same bearing, the same tone of voice. I was immediately struck by it when I saw you; I was informed of everything that had to happen and I also know everything that will happen. My troubles are about to end."

"And mine, beautiful queen?" said he prince, throwing himself at her feet. "Will they be of long duration?"

"I love you more than my life already, Sire," said the queen. "It's necessary to depart to go to your father; we shall see his sentiments for me, and whether he will consent to what you desire."

They went out; the prince gave her his hand; she climbed into a carriage with him; it was much more magnificent than those he had had thus far. The rest of the equipage responded to it, to such a degree that all the horseshoes were emeralds and the nails diamonds. That has probably never been seen except for that time.

I shall not say anything about the agreeable conversations that the queen and the prince had together; if she was unique in beauty, she was no less so in intelligence, and the young prince was as perfect as she was, with the consequence that they thought of utterly charming things.

When they reached the castle where the prince's two older brothers were to meet him the queen entered into a little crystal rock, of which all the points were garnished with gold and rubies. There were curtains all around, in order that she could not be seen, and it was carried by young men, very well-made and superbly dressed. The prince remained in the carriage; he perceived his brothers, who were walking with princesses of an excellent beauty.

As soon as they recognized him they advanced to greet him and asked him whether he had brought a mistress; he told them that he had been so unfortunate that throughout his journey he had only encountered very ugly ones, but that he had brought the rarest, who was a little white cat.

They started to laugh at his simplicity. "A cat?" they said. "Are you afraid that the mice might eat our palace?"

The prince replied that it was, in fact, unwise to want to make such a present to his father. With that, they all took the road to the city.

The older princes climbed with their princesses into caleches that were all gold and azure. Their horses had plumes and sprays on their head. Nothing was more brilliant than that cavalcade. Our young prince came after them, and then the crystal rock, at which everyone gazed admiringly.

The courtiers hastened to tell the king that the three princes had arrived.

"Have they brought beautiful ladies?" asked the king

"It's impossible to see anything that surpasses them."

At that response he seemed annoyed. The two princes hastened to show themselves with their marvelous princesses. The king received them very well and did not know to which to give the prize. He looked at his youngest son and said: "Have you come alone this time?"

"Your Majesty will see in this rock a little white cat," replied the prince, "which mewls so sweetly and has such velvet paws that it will please him."

The king smiled, and went to open the rock himself, but as soon as he approached it the queen activated a spring that caused it to fall apart and appeared like the sun that has been enveloped for some time in a cloud. Her blonde hair was scattered over her shoulders, falling in long curls all the way to her feet; her head as circled by flowers, her dress was a light white gauze, lined with pink taffeta. She stood up, and bowed profoundly to the king, who could not help crying out, in the excess of his admiration: "This is the incomparable one and the one who merits my crown."

"Sire," she said to him, "I have not come to take a throne from you that you fill so worthily. I was born with six kingdoms; permit me to offer you one, and that I give as much to each if your sons. I only ask you as recompense for your amity, and this young prince for a husband. We shall have enough with three kingdoms."

The king and the entire court uttered long cries of joy and astonishment. The marriage was celebrated immediately, as well as those of the two princes, with the result that the entire court spent several months in diversions and pleasures. Everyone then departed to govern their estates. The beautiful White Cat is immortalized there, as much by her kindness and liberality as by her rare merit and her beauty.

> *That young prince was fortunate*
> *To find in his cat a august princess,*
> *Worthy of receiving his incense and his prayers,*
> *And ready to share his cares and tenderness;*
> *When two enchanting eyes want to be loved.*
> *One puts up little resistance,*
> *Especially when gratitude*
> *Also aids to inflame us.*
> *Shall I say nothing about that mother and her craving,*
> *Who caused White Cat so much ennui?*
> *In order to taste deadly fruits.*
> *She sacrificed her to the power of a fay.*
> *Mothers, who possess objects full of charms,*
> *Detest her conduct and do not imitate her.*

As he finished reading the tale, the prior cast his eyes upon La Dandinardière; he saw that his eyes were closed, and that he was no longer moving. He moved closer, and shouted at the top of his voice: "My friend, are you in this world or the other?"

The little man stared at him, and said: "I was so charmed by the White Cat that I seemed to be at the wedding, or picking up, as she made her entrance, the emerald horseshoes and diamond nails of her horses."

"You like these sorts of fictions, then?" said the prior.

"They're not fiction," added La Dandinardière. "All that happened once, and could still happen, except that it's no longer fashionable. Oh, if I had lived in those times, or they were this one, I'd have made a fine fortune."

"Undoubtedly," continued the prior, "You would have married some fay?"

"I don't know," said the little man. "They seem to me to be too ugly, and if I marry, I want my heart to find its satisfaction there."

"Which is to say," the prior interjected, "that you'd take a young woman of merit, beautiful, virtuous and intelligent; that with regard to wealth you'd make a concession, persuaded that it's difficult to encounter so many good things at the same time. Well, I like you better for it, and I'll make your panegyric to the future."

"You're misunderstanding me," cried La Dandinardière. "I intend that the young woman I marry should have all the qualities of body and mind that you've just mentioned, but I also intend that she should be rich, and in the time of the fays, I would certainly have found the means to have a queen; with all that, nothing was more convenient; one did everything by means of three magic words, with a wand, something trivial; whereas nowadays, if one is born poor and ne wants to enrich oneself, it's necessary to toil like the wolves, very often without success. *O tempora, O mores!* What do you say to that Monsieur le Prieur?" he continued. "That Latin isn't a conceit."

"I admire you as much," said the prior, "as you admired White Cat; you're marvelous, and one always learns something with you."

The little mortal felt an extreme joy at attracting praise; but in order to merit it, in his view, the wanted to tell a tale in his turn, with the consequence that he asked the prior to send someone to inform Alain about the accident that had happened to him, in order that he would come promptly. He thanked him for his kindness in reading to him for such a long time, and pretended to have a desire to sleep, in order to be entirely at liberty to dream.

He did, in fact dream, and it was much more about Virginie than fays. "What sublimity of spirit!" he exclaimed. "A young woman brought up on the edge of the sea, who ought not to have more genius than a sole or an oyster, writes like the most celebrated authors! I have good taste; when I approve of something, it must be excellent; I approve of White Cat, therefore White Cat is excellent, and I will sustain that against the entire human race. My valet Alain, whom I shall arm from head to toe, and who will fight for me, will man the barrier."

He could be heard in the antechamber talking thus, and making enough noise on his own as a dozen people. Someone went to inform Monsieur de Saint-Thomas; he was afraid that the fall had caused that species of delirium. He came to listen, and was surprised by the disparate things he was saying. Alain arrived, but he forbade him to enter his master's room for fear of making him talk more, and, in order to extract him from his anxiety, he told him to come back the following day.

La Dandinardière remained occupied all night with the desire to tell a tale; that prevented him from sleeping, he was in despair at not having his secretary in order to have him write. He asked before daybreak for a peasant to be sent to his château, because he wanted to see Alain at any price. The baron was woken up in order to tell him about the impatience of the bourgeois, and he sent for the faithful domestic immediately.

As soon as he appeared, La Dandinardière made two or three bounds in his bed and held out his arms to him. "Alain," he cried, "come, my friend, in order that I can recount the most astonishing things in the world to you."

"Permit me," said Alain, moved by seeing is head swathed in bandages, "to ask you how you are; that appears to me more urgent than anything in the world."

"I could be better," replied La Dandinardière, "but alas, my greatest wound is not the one you see on my head. I'm in love, Alain, and it's the most adroit shot that Cupid has launched since he began his career."

Alain made no reply; he knew as little about Cupid as the Koran, and was afraid of saying something stupid while wanting to say something good.

"You have nothing to say?" said La Dandinardière.

"No, Monsieur, I'm listening," Alain replied.

"Listen, then, to what has happened to me. I've pledged my liberty to a young princess."

"How much has she given you for it?" Alan interrupted.

"Do you think, great fool," cried La Dandinardière, "that it's a matter of a coat or some item of jewelry?"

"I don't know what I think," said the valet. "You're talking to me in terms that are new to me. For instance, where have you found a princess in these parts? Unless there's been a shipwreck and the sea has cast her up?"

"You reason very well," said the little bourgeois. "Princesses aren't abundant in this canton; but the person I adore merits being one, and so far as I'm concerned, it's exactly as if she were one. Her name is Virginie; that name comes from ancient Rome, and for love of the name alone, Virginie possesses my heart."

Alain opened his eyes and his mouth, marveling and his master's knowledge. He maintained a respectful silence, which gave the invalid time to talk without respite, but, making the reflection that nothing would advance less the tale that he wanted to write, he suddenly commanded Alain to go home, put all his books in one or two carts, and bring them to him.

"You're going to stay here then, Monsieur?" he said, sadly.

"No, my friend," replied the invalid. "I'll only stay for as long as I'm inconvenienced by my wounds. But I need to write a great work, and it's necessary that I leaf through the best authors. Run along promptly, and return with the same diligence."

Alain encountered the baron, the vicomte and the prior. He went past abruptly without looking at them and went out. The baron called to him several times; finally, he retraced his steps.

"Tell me, Alain, where has your master sent you?—for your urgency makes me curious."

"I'm going in quest of all his books," Alain replied, "and all his doctrine. He wants to write the most beautiful thing in the world; if you want to aid him, he has, I think, great need of it."

"I'm convinced of it," the baron replied, "But stay here; there are enough books to occupy him agreeably."

"Oh, I'm careful not to disobey him," said Alain. "He wants what he wants four times as much as anyone else, and he beats me when he's irritated. I don't want him to treat me again as he did with his quarrel of honor."

"I assure you," said the vicomte, stopping him, "that you shan't go until you've told us why you were beaten."

Alan liked talking too much to waste such a fine opportunity. He told them how his master had armed him, in order to pass him off as him, and everything that he had said to encourage him to the heroic action of combat.

The messieurs looked at one another, astonished by the little man's extravagances and Alain's simplicities. They tried in vain to deflect him from going in quest of his master's library; he told them that he was going, even if it were to throw all the books into the sea; and in fact, he quit them promptly.

"In truth," said Baron de Saint Thomas to his two friends, "would you advise me to think seriously about La Dandinardière for one of my daughters? It seems to me, given the visions they roll around in their heads, that they're made for one another, but a household goes very poorly when it's governed by such minds."

"Don't lose your appetite," replied the vicomte. "He's a rich man; he's a Don Quixote, but his extravagances will pass more easily, because he isn't as brave as him, and you can see that the name of Villeville alone makes him tremble. It's not easy to sustain that boastful attitude for long when one is always afraid."

"Add to that," said the prior, "that you could engage them to live with you, and you could set them to rights."

"I've more reason to dread," said the baron, smiling, "that they'd spoil my brain than I have to hope that my remonstrations might repair theirs. Look at my wife and my daughters, who each have their particular genius. La Dandinardière, with them, would complete the extravagance."

"No matter," said the prior. "He has ready money. I won't pardon you as long as I live if you let him escape; but in that regard, I'll go to see him; I need to know what he wants to write."

Immediately, he went up to his room, and after having asked him how he was, he said: "I've come to offer to be your secretary today, as I was your reader yesterday."

"You couldn't give me a more sensible pleasure," cried La Dandinardière, extending his arms to him, "for although I have Alain, his handwriting is so detestable that we'd need a third party to decipher what he scribbles. He has so little intelligence that all the good thoughts I say to him are lost, because he doesn't understand them, and how can one arrange what one doesn't understand?"

"Conclusion," said the prior, "I have all the qualifications to serve as your secretary, as long as you wouldn't be inconvenienced."

"Oh, Monsieur," cried La Dandinardière, "I'm your servant, your indebted valet."

"It's sufficient for you to be my friend," said the prior, interrupting him. "Tell me of what's a question, whether you want to treat the subject in verse or in prose."

"It's all the same to me," replied our bourgeois, "provided that I make up a tale, in order to convince Virginie that I have no less intelligence than her; all that chagrins me is that I've never seen fays and I don't even know where they live."

"It's unnecessary to be embarrassed," said the prior. "I'm entirely appropriate to aid you, and without racking your brains. There's one in my pocket that I've just finished, which no one in the world has seen."

"Oh, Monsieur!" cried La Dandinardière. "If you want to sell it, with an oath never to claim it for yourself and to leave the honor entirely to me, I'll gladly give you four louis."

"That's too little," said the prior. "It's better if it costs you nothing." At the same time, he showed him a thick note-book, by which La Dandinardière was so charmed that he wanted to get out of bed to throw himself at his feet. What delighted him more was the good bargain that he had made for something that, in his view, was priceless.

It is necessary to know that the tale in question was a pure larceny that the prior had committed in the room of Mesdemoiselles de Saint-Thomas; they had not even perceived it because they wrote so many that the majority of those little works were neglected before being finished. He refrained from making that confidence to La Dandinardière, not wanting to lose the merit of his liberality, and he imagined something rather humorous in the contestation that might arise between the veritable author and the plagiarist. Given the impatience in which he saw his listener to hear the reading, he did not delay the commencement.

BELLE-BELLE; OR, THE CHEVALIER FORTUNÉ

There was once a very amiable, very mild and very powerful king; but the Emperor Matapa, his neighbor, was even more powerful than he was. They had fought great wars against one another; in the last, the emperor had won a considerable battle, and after having killed or taken prisoner the majority of the king's captains and soldiers he came to lay siege of the capital city, and took it, with the result that he rendered himself master of all the treasures within. The king barely had time to escape with his sister, the dowager queen. That princess had been widowed at a young age; she had intelligence and beauty, but it is true that she was proud, violent and rather bad-tempered.

The emperor transported all the king's jewelry and furniture to his palace. He took away an extraordinary number of soldiers, young women, horses and all the other things that might be useful or agreeable to him. When he had depopulated the greater part of the realm, he returned triumphantly to his own, where he was received by the empress and the princess, his daughter, with a thousand testimonies of joy.

Meanwhile, the deprived king was not suffering the state he was in without impatience. He assembled a few troops, with which he composed a small army, and in order to swell its ranks in a short time he had an ordinance published by which he required the gentlemen of his kingdom either to come and serve him in person, or to send one of their children, well-equipped with arms and horses and disposed to second all his enterprises.

Near the frontier there was an old nobleman who was eighty years of age, and full of intelligence and wisdom, but he had been so poorly served by the favors of fortune that, having possessed a great deal, he found himself reduced to a kind of poverty, which he would have suffered patiently if it had not been shared with three beautiful daughters that remained to him. They were so reasonable that they made no murmur about their disgrace, and if they chanced to mention it to their father, it was to console him rather than to add anything to his troubles.

They were spending their life with him without ambition under a rustic roof when the king's ordinance reached the old man's ears. He summoned his daughters and looked at them sadly.

"What are we going to do?" he said to them. "The king is ordering all the distinguished persons in his realm to rally to him in order to serve him against the emperor, or he'll condemn them to a large fine if they fail. I'm not in a condition to pay the tax; these are terrible extremities, which will entail my death or our ruination."

His three daughters were afflicted with him, but they begged him nevertheless to have a little courage, because they were convinced that they could find some remedy for his affliction.

In fact, the following morning, the eldest went to find her father, who was walking sadly in an orchard that he tended himself. "Sire," she said, "I've come to beg you to permit me to depart for the army. I have an advantageous stature and am sufficiently robust; I'll dress as a man and pass for your son. If I don't perform heroic actions, at least I'll spare you the journey or the tax, and that's a great deal in the state we're in."

The count embraced her tenderly and initially wanted to oppose such an extraordinary design, but she told him with so much firmness that she could not envisage any other remedy that he finally consented to it.

It was then only a question of making clothes appropriate to the kind of person she was going to play. Her father gave her arms and the best of the four horses that served for plowing. The adieux and regrets were tender on both sides.

After traveling for a few days she passed alongside a meadow bordered by living hedges. She saw a very afflicted shepherdess who was trying to pull one of her sheep out of a ditch into which it had fallen.

"What are you doing there, good shepherdess?" she said to her.

"Alas," replied the shepherdess, I'm trying to save my sheep, which is nearly drowned, but I'm so weak that I don't have the strength to pull it out."

"I feel sorry for you," she said, and, without offering to help, she drew away.

The shepherd immediately shouted: "Adieu, beautiful woman in disguise."

Our heroine's surprise as indescribable. *What!* she said to herself, *is it possible that I'm so recognizable? That old shepherdess one saw me for a moment, and she knows that I'm in disguise. Where am I going, then? I'll be recognized by everyone, and if I am by the king, how ashamed and angry will I be? He'll believe that my father is a coward who are not put himself in danger.*

After all those reflections, she concluded that it was necessary to turn back.

The count and his daughters were talking about her and counting the days of her absence when they saw her come in. She told them about her adventure; the old man told her that he had foreseen it, and that if she had wanted to believe him she would not have departed, because it is impossible that people would not know that she was a young woman in disguise.

The whole family was in a new embarrassment, not knowing what to do, when the second daughter came in her turn to find the count. "My sister," she said to him, "had never ridden a horse. It's not surprising that she was recognized. As for me, if you'll permit me to go in her stead, I dare to promise you that you'll be content.

Whatever the old man could say to her to combat her design, he could not succeed. It was necessary that he consent to see her depart. She obtained another costume, other arms and another horse. Thus equipped, she embraced her father and sisters a thousand times, determined to serve the king well.

When she passed the same meadow where her sister had seen the shepherdess and the sheep, however, she found it in the ditch, and the shepherdess occupied in pulling it out.

"Calamity!" she cried. "Half my flock has perished in this manner; if someone helped me I could save this poor animal, but everyone flees me."

"What, shepherdess, have you so little care for your sheep that you let them fall in the water?" And without giving her any other consolation, she spurred her horse.

The old woman shouted at the top of her voice: "Adieu, beautiful woman in disguise."

Those few words afflicted our amazon in no uncertain terms. *What fatality*, she said to herself. *Now I've been recognized too; what happened to my sister has happened to me; I'm no more fortunate than her; it would be ridiculous if I were to go to the army with an appearance so effeminate that everyone recognized me.*

She returned immediately to her father's house, very sad at the poor success of her journey.

He received her tenderly and praised her for having had the prudence to come back, but that did not prevent the chagrin recommencing with all the more force because it had already cost the cloth of two useless costumes and several other small things. The worthy old man was desolate in secret, because he did not want to show all his dolor to his daughters.

Finally, the youngest came to beg him, with the utmost insistence, to grant her the same favor that he had done for her sisters. "Perhaps," she said, "it's presumptuous to hope to succeed any better than them, but I'll attempt the adventure nevertheless. I'm taller than them, you know that I go hunting every day; that exercise can't help giving some talent for war; and the extreme desire I have to relieve you in your troubles inspires me with an extraordinary courage."

The count loved her much more than her two sisters; she had so many cares for him that he regarded her as his unique consolation; she read agreeable stories to divert him, she watched over him when he was ill, and all the game she killed was only for him, with the result that he employed arguments to deflect her from her design even more forceful than those he had used with regard to her sisters.

"Do you want to leave me, my dear daughter?" he said to her, "Your absence will cause my death. Even if fortune favors your journey and you come back covered in laurels, I won't have the pleasure of seeing it; my advanced age and your absence will terminate my life."

"No, my father," said Belle-Belle—that was her name—"don't think I'll be gone for long. The war will necessarily end, and if I could see any other way of satisfying the king's orders I wouldn't neglect them, for I dare say that if my going away caused you pain, it gives me even more than you."

He finally consented to what she desired. She made herself a very simple costume; her sisters' had cost too much and the count's finances were insufficient, and she was obliged to take a very poor horse, because her two sisters had almost crippled the others; but all that did not discourage her. She embraced her father, received his blessing respectfully, and after having mingled her tears with her father's, she departed.

As she passed by the meadow I have already mentioned, she found the old shepherdess, who had not yet pulled out her sheep, or who was trying to pull another one out of a deep ditch.

"What are you doing there, shepherdess?" said Belle-Belle, stopping.

"I'm no longer doing anything, Sire," replied the shepherdess. "Since first light I've been occupied with this sheep; my efforts have been futile; I'm so tired that I can't breathe. Not a day passes when some new misfortune doesn't arrive and I haven't found anyone to help me."

"I feel very sorry for you," said Belle-Belle, "and to give evidence of my pity I want to help you." She descended immediately from her horse; it was so docile that she did not take the trouble to tether it in order to prevent it from running away. She leapt over the hedge and, after incurring a few scratches, she jumped into the ditch. She strove so hard that she pulled out the beloved sheep.

"Don't weep any more, my good mother," she said to the shepherdess. "Here's your sheep, and although it's been in the water for a long time, I still find it very frisky."

"You haven't obliged an ingrate," said the shepherdess. "I know you, charming Belle-Belle; I know where you're going and all your designs. You sisters went past this meadow; I know them too, and I'm not unaware that they have intelligence, but they appeared to me to be so harsh, and their behavior with me was so ungracious, that I found he means to interrupt their journey. It's a very different matter in your regard; you'll experience that, for I'm a fay and my inclination bears me to help those who merit it with benefits. You're horse is fearfully thin; I'll give you one."

Immediately, she touched the ground with her crook, and Belle-Belle heard whinnying behind a bush. She looked promptly and perceived the finest horse in the world. It started running and jumping in the meadow. Belle-Belle, who loved horses, was delighted to see one so perfect.

The fay called to the beautiful charger, touched it with her crook, and said: "Faithful Comrade, be better harnessed than the Emperor Matapa's best horse." Immediately, Comrade had a green velvet saddle-cloth embroidered with diamonds and rubies, as was the saddle, and the bridle with pearls, with a golden bit and blinkers. In sum, one could not see anything more magnificent.

"What you see," said the fay, "is the least admirable thing about this horse. He has many other talents, about which I want to tell you. First of all, he only eats once a week; it's unnecessary to take the trouble to groom him; he knows the past, present and future; he's been in my service for a long time; I've fashioned him as for myself.

"When you want to be informed about some matter, or you need counsel, you only have to address yourself to him, and he'll give you such good advice that sovereigns would be glad to have counselors that resemble him; it's necessary, therefore, that you regard him more as your friend than your horse. Furthermore, your costume isn't to my liking; I want to give you one that will suit you better."

She struck the ground with her crook, and a large chest emerged, covered with Levantine leather with golden nails. Belle-Belle's monogram was on it. The fay searched in the grass for a golden key made in England; she opened the chest with it; it was lined with embroidered Spanish hide. There were a dozen coats within, a dozen cravats, a dozen swords, a dozen plumed hats, and a dozen of everything else. The garments were so covered with embroidery and diamonds that Belle-Belle could hardly lift them.

"Choose the one that pleases you the most," the fay said to her, "the others will follow you everywhere; you have only to stamp your foot, saying: 'Leather chest, come to me full of clothes; leather chest, come to me full of underwear and lace; leather chest, come to me full of money and gems,' and you'll see it immediately, whether you're on campaign or in your bedroom. It's also necessary that you choose a name, for Belle-Belle doesn't suit the métier that you're going to follow; it seems to me that you could call yourself the Chevalier Fortuné. But it's only just that you know me, and I'll assume my ordinary form before you."

At the same time, she shed her old skin and appeared so marvelous that she dazzled Belle-Belle's eyes. Her costume was blue velvet lined with ermine; her hair was braided with pearls, and there was a superb crown on her head.

Transported with admiration, Belle-Belle threw herself at her feet and prostrated herself there with an inexpressible respect and gratitude. The fay lifted her up and embraced her tenderly; she told her to put on a costume of gold and green brocade. Belle-Belle obeyed her orders, and, mounting up, she continued her journey, so penetrated by all the extraordinary things that had just happened that she could not think about anything else.

In fact, she wondered by what unexpected good fortune she had been able to obtain the benevolence of such a powerful fay. *For after all,* she said to herself, *I wasn't necessary to her to pull out her sheep, since a single tap of her wand could bring an entire flock back from the Antipodes if they'd gone there. I've been very fortunate to find myself so disposed to oblige her, for nothing I've done for her is the cause of all that she's done for me; she knew my heart, and my sentiments were agreeable to her. Oh, if my father could see me now, so magnificent and so rich, what joy for him! But at least I'll have the pleasure of sharing the benefits that she has given me with my family.*

As she concluded those various reflections, she arrived in a beautiful, very populous city; she attracted everyone's gaze; people followed her and surrounded her, and they all said: "Has a more handsome, better made and more richly clad knight ever been seen? What grace he has in handling that superb horse!"

People bowed to him profoundly; he returned the salutes in an honest and civil fashion. When he wanted to enter the hostelry, the governor, who was out walking and had admired him in passing, sent a gentleman inviting him to come to his castle. The Chevalier Fortuné—for it is necessary to call him that—replied that, not having the honor of knowing him, he did not want to take that liberty; that he would come to see him, and that he begged him to give him one of his men in order that he could confide something of consequence to him for his father. The governor immediately sent him a very reliable man, and Fortuné engaged him to come back that evening, because he had not yet commenced his dispatches.

He shut himself in his room, and then stamped his foot and said: "Leather chest, come to me full of diamonds and pistoles." Immediately, the chest appeared, but there was no key. Where was it? What a pity it would be to break a lock made of gold enameled with several colors! Furthermore, what would he not have to fear from the indiscretion of a locksmith? Scarcely had he mentioned the chevalier's treasures than thieves would have assembled to rob him and perhaps kill him.

So he looked for the golden key everywhere, but the more he searched the less he found. *What desolation*, he exclaimed, *not to be able to take advantage of the fay's generosity or enable my father to share in the wealth she has given me*. As he mused thus, he thought that the best thing to do was to consult his horse.

He went down to the stable, and said to him in a low voice: "I beg you, my Comrade, to tell me where I can find the key to the leather chest."

"In my ear," the horse replied.

Fortuné looked in his horse's ear; he saw a green ribbon, pulled it, and saw the key that he desired so much to have. He opened the leather chest, where he saw more diamonds and more pistoles than a hogshead could have held. The chevalier filled three caskets with them: one for his father and the other two for his sisters; he charged the man the governor had sent him with them, and begged him not to stop by day or night until he reached the count's house.

That messenger made the utmost diligence, and when he told the old man that he had come on behalf of his son the chevalier and had brought him a heavy casket, he wondered what might be in it, for he had set out with so little money that he did not believe him to be in a state to buy anything, or even pay for the journey of the man he had charged with his present. He opened the letter first, and when he saw what his dear daughter had sent him, he thought he might expire of joy. The sight of the gems and the gold confirmed the verity of the words.

What was extraordinary is that Belle-Belle's two sisters, having opened their boxes, only found glass beads instead of diamonds and fake pistoles; the fay had not wanted them to feel her benefits, with the consequence that they thought their sister wanted to make fun of them and conceived an inexpressible chagrin. The count, seeing them distressed, gave them the greater part of the jewels he had just received, but as soon as they touched them they changed, like the others. They judged as a result that an unknown power was acting against them, and asked their father to keep what remained for himself alone.

The handsome Fortuné did not wait for the return of his messenger; he departed. His journey was too urgent, and it was necessary to render to the king's orders. He was in the governor's house; the whole city had assembled there to see him his person and all his actions had an air so honest that no one could help admiring and cherishing him. He did not say anything that was not a pleasure to hear, and the crowd around him was so large that he did not know to what to attribute something so extraordinary, for, having always been in the country he had seen very few people.

His continued on his way on his excellent horse, who entertained him agreeably with a thousand items of news, or what was most remarkable in ancient and modern history. "My dear master," he said, "I'm delighted to be yours; I know that you have a great deal of frankness and honor. I'm repelled by some people with whom I've lived for a long time and who made me hate life, so insupportable to me was their society. There was, among others, a man who made me a thousand amities, and raised me above Pegasus and Bucephalus when he spoke in my presence, but as soon as he no longer saw me he called me a worthless nag. He affected to praise me for my defects to give me reason to contract greater ones. It's true that one day, fatigued by his caresses, which, properly speaking, were treasons, I gave him such a terrible kick that I had the pleasure of breaking almost all his teeth, and I never saw him again except to say to him, with a great deal of sincerity: 'It's not just that a mouth that opens so often to speak ill of those who don't cause you any chagrin should be as agreeable as another.'"

"Oho!" cried the chevalier. "You're very sharp. Didn't you fear that the man might run you through with his sword, wrathfully?"

"It's of no importance," replied Comrade, "since I would have known his design as soon as he had formed it."

They were conversing thus when they arrived in a vast forest. Comrade said to the chevalier: "Master, there's a man here who might be very useful to us. He's a woodcutter; he's been endowed."

"What do you mean by that term?" asked Fortuné.

"*Endowed* means that he's received one of several gifts from the fays," the horse added. "It's necessary that you engage him to come with us." At the same time, he arrived at the place where the woodcutter was working.

The young chevalier approached him in a mild and insinuating manner, and asked him several questions about the place where they were, whether there were wild beasts in the forest, and whether it was permissible to hunt. The woodcutter replied to all of them as a man of good sense. Then Fortuné asked him where the people had gone who had aided him to chop down so many trees. The woodcutter said that he had felled them all himself, that it was the work of a few hours, and that it was necessary for him to fell many others in order to make up a load.

"What!" said the chevalier. "You intend to carry all this wood away today?"

"Oh, Sire," replied Strong-Back—that was his name— "my strength isn't ordinary."

"You earn a great deal, then," said Fortuné.

"Very little," replied the woodcutter, "for people are poor hereabouts. Here, everyone does his own work, without asking his neighbor to do it."

"Since you're in a country so scantly opulent," said the chevalier, "it's only up to you to go elsewhere. Come with me; you won't lack anything, and when you want to come back, I'll give you money for your journey."

The woodcutter thought he could do no better; he abandoned his ax and followed his new master.

As soon as he had traversed the forest he saw a man in the plain who was holding ribbons with which he was attaching his legs, leaving so little room that he hardly had enough in which to walk. Comrade stopped and said to his master:

"Sire, here's someone else endowed, of whom you have need. It's necessary to bring him."

Fortuné approached him, and with his natural grace he asked him why he was binding his legs like that.

"It's to prepare me for hunting," he replied.

"What!" said the chevalier, smiling. "Do you think you run better when you're tied up like that?"

"No, Sire," he replied. "I'm convinced that my pace will be less rapid, but that's also my design, for there's no red deer, roe deer or hare, that I can't easily overtake when my legs are free, with the result that, always leaving them behind me, they escape and I almost never have the pleasure of catching them."

"You seem to me to be a rare man," said Fortuné. "What is your name?"

"My name is Fleet," said the hunter, "and I'm well-known in this country."

"If you'd like to see another," said the chevalier, "I'd be very glad if you'd come with me; you won't have as much difficulty, and I'll treat you very well."

Fleet was not very happy; he gladly accepted the offer proposed to him, so Fortuné, followed by his new domestic, continued his journey.

The next day he found a man on the edge of a marsh with a blindfold over his eyes.

"Sire," the horse said to his master, "I advise you to take that man into your serve too."

Fortuné immediately asked him why his eyes were blindfolded.

"It's because I see too clearly," he said. "I perceive game further than four leagues away, and I never launch an arrow without killing more than I want. I'm therefore obliged to bandage my eyes and even though I can barely glimpse them, I depopulate a region of grouse and other small game in less than two hours."

"You're very adroit," replied Fortuné.

"People call me Sharpshooter," the man said, "and I wouldn't quit this occupation for anything in the world."

"I have, however, a strong desire to propose that of traveling with me," said the chevalier. "It wouldn't prevent you from exercising your talent."

Sharpshooter made some difficulty, and the chevalier had more trouble gaining him than the others, for he was ordinarily a friend of liberty, but he succeeded in the end and then drew away from the marsh where he had paused.

A few days later he was passing alongside a meadow and he perceived a man within it lying on his side. Comrade said to him: "Master, that man is endowed; I foresee that he is very necessary to you."

Fortuné went into the meadow and asked him what he was doing there.

"I need a few simples," the replied, "and I'm listening to the herbs that are about to grow, to see whether any of them are those I need."

"What" said the chevalier. "You have hearing subtle enough to hear the herbs under the ground and to divine which one is about to appear?"

"It's for that reason," said the listener, "that people call me Fine-Ear."

"Well, Fine-Ear," Fortuné continued, "are you in a humor to follow me? I'll give you wages large enough for you to be content."

The man, charmed by such an agreeable proposition, did not hesitate to add himself to the number of the others.

The chevalier, continuing his route, saw beside a highway a man whose inflated cheeks were making a rather humorous effect; he was standing up, facing a high mountain some two leagues away, on which there were fifty or sixty windmills. The horse said to his master: "Here's another of our endowed men. Don't miss the opportunity to take him with you."

Fortuné, who was able to engage anything as soon as it appeared or was mentioned to him, went up to the man and asked him what he was doing there.

"I'm blowing a little, Sire," he said, "in order to make all those windmills grind."

"It seems to me that you're a long way away," aid the chevalier.

"On the contrary," replied the blower. "I find that I'm too close, and if I weren't retaining half my breath I'd already have knocked the windmills over, and perhaps the mountain they're on. I cause a thousand mishaps in that manner, without wanting to, and I'll tell you, Sire, that once when I was badly treated by my mistress, and I went to sigh in the woods, my sighs uprooted the trees and made a strange disorder, with the result that no one in the district calls me anything any longer but Impetuous."

"If people have difficulty seeing you," said Fortuné, "and you want to come with me, there are people who will keep you company; they also have extraordinary talents."

"I have such a natural curiosity regarding things that aren't common," replied Impetuous, "that I accept your proposition."

Very content, Fortuné drew away from that place. As soon as he had traversed a rather open country, he saw a large pond into which several springs ran. There was a man on the edge who was looking at it attentively.

"Sire," said Comrade to his master. "Here's a man that your equipage lacks; if you can engage him to follow you, that won't be bad."

The chevalier immediately approached him.

"Would you care to tell me," he said "what you're doing here?"

"You'll see, Sire," the man replied. "As soon as the pool fills up I'll drink it in a single draught, for I'm still thirsty, even though I've already emptied it twice."

In fact, he bent down, and did not leave enough to regale the smallest fish.

Fortuné was no less surprised than the rest of his troop.

"What!" he said. "Are you always so thirsty?"

"No," said the water-drinker, "I only drink like that when I've eaten something too salty or it's a matter of a wager. I've been known for some time by the name of Tippler, which people have given me."

"Come with me, Tippler," said the chevalier. "I'll enable you to drink wine that will seem better to you than pond-water."

That promise pleased the man to whom it was made greatly, and he immediately started marching with the others.

The chevalier could already see the rendezvous point where all the king's subjects were to assemble when he perceived a man who was eating so avidly, that although he had more than sixty thousand Gonesse loaves in front of him, he seemed determined not to leave a single crumb. Comrade said to his master: "Sire, you only lack this man here; please oblige him to come with you."

The chevalier approached him. "Are you resolved to eat all that bread for your breakfast?"

"Yes," he replied. "My only regret is that here's so little of it, but the bakers are frank idlers, who don't care whether one is hungry or not."

"If you need as many every day," added Fortuné, "there's scarcely any land that wouldn't starve you."

"Oh, Sire, " replied Guzzler—that was his name—"I'd be very sorry to have so much appetite; neither my wealth nor that of my neighbors would be sufficient for it, but it's true that I'm very glad to regale myself in this fashion from time to time."

"Guzzler, my friend," said Fortuné, "attach yourself to me; I'll provide you with good cheer, and you won't be sorry to have chosen me for a master."

Comrade, who did not lack intelligence or foresight, warned the chevalier that it would be as well to forbid all his men to boast about the extraordinary gifts they had. He did not defer summoning them, and said to them: "Listen, Strong-Back, Fleet, Sharpshooter, Fine-Ear. Impetuous, Tippler and Guzzler; I warn you that if you want to please me, you'll keep the talents that you have an inviolable secret, and I assure you that I'll have as much care in rendering you happy that you'll be content."

Everyone swore to be faithful to his orders, and shortly afterwards, the chevalier, more adorned by his beauty and his fine manners than his magnificent costume, entered the capital city mounted on his excellent horse and followed by the best made men in the world. He did not take long to provide them with livery decorated with gold and silver; he gave them horses, and, having lodged in the best inn, he waited for daybreak in order to appear in the review. No one in the city was talking any longer about anything but him, and the king, forewarned of his reputation, had a strong desire to see him.

All the troops assembled in a great plain; the king came with his sister, the dowager queen, and their entire court. It was still pompous, in spite of the misfortunes that had befallen his State, and Fortuné was dazzled by so much wealth. But if they attracted his gaze, his incomparable beauty attracted that of the celebrated troop no less. Everyone was asking who the young chevalier was, so well made and so handsome, and the king, passing close to the place where he was, made him a sign to approach.

Fortuné immediately dismounted from his horse in order to make a profound reverence to the king; he could not help blushing, seeing the attention with which the king was looking at him; that additional color heightened the splendor of his complexion.

"I would be very glad," the king said to him, "to know from your own lips who you are, and what your name is."

"Sire," he replied, "my name is Fortuné, without having any reason thus far to bear that name, for my father, who is the Comte de la Frontière, spends his life in great poverty, although he was born with as much wealth as status."

"The fortune that you have from your godmother," replied the king, "has not served your interests poorly in bringing you here; I feel a particular affection for you, and I remember that your father rendered mine great services. I want to recognize them in your person."

"That is only just," added the dowager queen, who had not yet spoken, "and as I am your elder, my brother, and I know more particularly than you, all that the Comte de la Frontière did some years ago for the service of the State, I beg you to repose on me the care of recompensing this young chevalier."

Fortuné, delighted with the welcome he had been given, could not thank the king enough; he dared not, however, extend himself too much in his sentiments of gratitude, believed that it was more respectful to be silent than to talk too much. The little that he did say appeared so just and so appropriate that everyone applauded. Then he mounted up again and mingled with the lords who accompanied the king; but the queen summoned him continually to ask him a thousand questions, and, turning toward Floride, who was her dearest confidante, she said to her in a low voice: "Does it seem to you that any cavalier could have a nobler air and more regular features? I confess that I've never seen anything more likeable."

Floride had no difficulty in agreeing with what the queen said, and added great praise to it, for the cavalier seemed no less likeable to her than to her mistress.

Fortuné could not help casting his eyes upon the king from time to time; he was the best made prince in the world and all his manners were becoming. Belle-Belle, who had not renounced her sex in putting on clothes that concealed it, felt a veritable attachment for him.

The king said to him after the review that he feared that the war would be bloody, and that he had resolved to attach him to his person. The dowager queen, who was present, cried that she had had the same thought, that it was necessary not to expose him to the peril of a long campaign; that the position of first maître-d'hôtel in her household was vacant, and that she would give it to him.

"No," said the king, "I want to make him my chief squire." They disputed with one another thus the pleasure of advancing Fortuné; but the queen, fearing to reveal the secret emotions already stirring in her heart, ceded the satisfaction of having the chevalier to the king..

There were few days when he did not call upon is leather-bound chest and take a new set of clothes from within it. He was assuredly more magnificent then any prince in the court, with the consequence that the queen sometimes wondered by what means his father equipped him at such great expense. At other times she made war on him. "Admit," she said, "that you have a mistress; it's her who sends you all the beautiful things that we see."

Fortuné blushed, and responded respectfully to the various questions the queen asked him.

In other ways, he acquitted his charge admirably well; his heart, sensible to the king's merit, attached him more to his person than he would have wished. *What is my destiny?* he asked himself. *I love a great king, without being able to hope that he will ever love me, or take account of what I am suffering.*

For his part, the king heaped him with favors. He found nothing as well made as the handsome chevalier. The queen, deceived by his costume, thought seriously about means of contracting a secret marriage with him; the inequality of their birth was the only thing that created a difficulty for her.

She was not alone in feeling an inclination for Fortuné; the most beautiful women in the court were taken with him, in spite of themselves. He was bombarded with love letters, rendezvous, presents and a thousand gallantries, to which he responded with so much nonchalance that no one doubted that he had a mistress in his homeland; unless it were some fay, he would not appear so advantageously. He won the prizes in the tourneys; he killed more game in hunts than anyone else; he danced at balls with more grace than any courtier; in sum, it was a charm to see him and hear him.

The queen would have liked to spare herself the shame of declaring her sentiments to him; she charged Floride with making him perceive that so many marks of generosity on the part of a young and beautiful queen ought not to be indifferent to him. Floride found herself very embarrassed by that commission; she had been unable to avoid the fate of the majority of those who had seem the chevalier; he appeared too lovable to her to think of the interests of her mistress in preference to her own, with the consequence that every time the queen furnished her with an opportunity to talk to him, instead of talking about the beauty and the great qualities of the process, she only talked to him about her bad temper, how much her women suffered in her company, the injustices she had committed and the poor usage she made of the power she had usurped within the realm.

Then making a comparison of sentiments, she said: "I was not born a queen, but in truth, I should have been; I have a depth of generosity that bears me to do good to everyone; oh," she continued, "if I were at that august rank, how happy the handsome Fortuné would be! He would love me out of gratitude if he did not love me by inclination."

The young chevalier, utterly bewildered by that speech, did not know how to respond; that was why he carefully avoided being alone with her.

The impatient queen did not fail to ask Floride how she was governing Fortuné's mind. "He is so little prejudiced in his own favor," she told her, "and has so much timidity, that he cannot believe anything favorable that I say on your part, or pretends not to believe it, because he has some passion that occupies him."

"I believe that, like you," said the alarmed queen, "but is it possible that he would not cede everything to his ambition?"

"And it is possible," replied Floride, "that you want to owe his heart to your crown? When one is young and beautiful, like you, and has a thousand rare qualities, is it necessary to have recourse to the gleam of a diadem?"

"One has recourse to anything," cried the queen, "when it is a matter of a rebel heart that one wants to subjugate."

Floride knew full well that it was no longer possible to cure her mistress of the infatuation that had gripped her.

The queen was still waiting for some fortunate effect of her confidante's efforts, but the scant progress she made on Fortuné obliged her to seek the means of having a conversation with him herself. She knew that early every morning he went to a little wood that was visible from the windows of her apartment. She got up with the dawn and, looking in the direction from which he would come, she saw him, with a melancholy expression, walking nonchalantly.

Immediately, she summoned Floride. "You've spoken only too truly," she said. Fortuné is undoubtedly in love with someone in this court or his homeland; look at the sadness apparent in his features."

"I've also remarked it in all his conversations," replied Floride, "and if it were possible for you to forget him, in truth, Madame, you'd do well."

"It's too late," cried the queen, uttering a profound sigh, "but since he's entering that grove of trees, let's go there; I only want to be accompanied by you."

The young woman did not dare to stop the queen, however much desire she had to do so, for she feared that she might make Fortuné love her, and a rival of such rank is always very dangerous.

As soon as the queen had taken a few steps into the wood, she heard he chevalier singing; his voice was very agreeable, and he had made these words to a new tune:

Oh how difficult it is
To love tenderly and live tranquilly!
The more I see myself fortunate,
The more I fear the end of the joy that enchants me;
The fear of the future alarms me incessantly,
And comes to afflict me at the fullness of my prayers.

Fortuné had composed that verse of a song in relation to his sentiments for the king, the generosity that prince testified to him, and the apprehension of finally being recognized and obliged to quit a court where he would rather be than any-where else in the world.

The queen, who had stopped to listen to him, felt an extreme pain. "Whatever I attempt," she said, in a low voice, to Floride, "that young ingrate scorns the honor of pleasing me. He deems himself fortunate; he appears satisfied with his conquest, but he is sacrificing me to another."

"He's at a certain age," replied Floride, "over which reason does not yet have well-established rights; if I dared to give Your Majesty advice, it would be to forget a young scatterbrain who is incapable of savoring his fortune."

The queen would have liked her confidante to talk to her in another manner; she darted a furious glance at her and advanced precipitately. She entered abruptly into the grove of trees where the chevalier was reasoning. She pretended to be surprised to find him there and to have some difficulty because he was seeing her in a state of partial undress, although she had neglected nothing that might make her magnificent and elegant.

As soon as she appeared he wanted to withdraw out of respect, but she told him to stay, that he could aid her to walk. "I was awoken agreeably this morning by birdsong, the; cool weather and the purity of the air invited me to come and hear it at closer range. How fortunate they are, alas! They only know pleasures; chagrins do not trouble their life."

"It seems to me, Madame," said Fortuné, "that they are not absolutely exempt from trouble and anxiety; they always have to avoid murderous lead or the deceptive nets of bird-catchers; it is not only birds of prey that make war on those little innocents; when a harsh winter freezes the ground and covers it with snow, they die for lack of a few seeds of hemp or millet, and every year they have the embarrassment of finding a new mistress."

"You believe, then, Chevalier," said the queen, smiling, "that that is an embarrassment? There are men who like to do it a dozen times a year. Oh, good God," she continued, "you seem surprised. It seems to me that you have a heart turned in another manner, and have not yet entirely changed?"

"I cannot, Madame, know of what I am capable," said the chevalier, "for I have not loved, but I dare to believe that if I took an attachment, it would be for the rest of my life."

"You have not loved!" cried the queen, looking at him so fixedly that the poor chevalier changed color several times. "You have not loved? Fortuné, can you speak in that manner to a queen who can read in your face and in your eyes he passion that occupies you, and who has even just heard the words that you have made to the new tune that is running around at present?"

"It's true, Madame," he chevalier replied, "that the couplet is about me, but it is also true that I made it without any particular design; my friends engage me every day to make drinking songs for them, although I only drink water; there are others who want tenderness, so I sing about Amour and Bacchus without being either amorous or a drinker."

The queen was listening with so much emotion that she could hardly stand it, what he was saying reignited in her heart the hope that Floride had tried to take away from her. "If I could believe that you were sincere," she said, "I would have reason to be surprised that you have not found anyone in this court sufficiently lovable to fix you."

"Madame," replied Fortuné, "I attach myself so strongly to fulfilling the duties of my charge that no time remains to me to sigh."

"You don't love anyone, then?" she added, vehemently.

"No, Madame," he said. "I don't have a heart of sufficiently gallant character; I'm a misanthrope of sorts, who cherishes my liberty, and would not want to lose it for anything in the world."

The queen sat down, and darted obliging glances at him. "There are chains so beautiful and so gracious," she said, "that one ought to be glad to bear them; if fortune has destined such for you, I would advise you to renounce your liberty."

And, speaking in that manner, her eyes explained themselves too clearly for the chevalier, who already had very
strong suspicions, not to have every reason to confirm them.
In the dread that the conversation might go even further, he
took out his watch and, pushing the needle slightly, he said: "I
beg Your Majesty to permit me to go to the palace; it is the
hour when the king gets up; he has ordered me to go there."

"Go, handsome indifferent," she said, uttering a profound sigh. "You're right to pay your court to my brother; but
remember that you would not be wrong to dedicate some of
your duties to me."

The queen followed him with her eyes; then she lowered
them and, reflecting on what had just happened, she blushed
with shame and anger. What added even further to her chagrin
was that Floride had witnessed it, and that she remarked on
her face a hint of joy that seemed to be telling her that she
would have done better to listen to her advice that to speak to
Fortuné. She meditated for a time and, taking her notepad, she
wrote these verses, which she had set to music by the Lully of
her court:

> *You see, you finally see the torment I endure.*
> *My conqueror knows it, and is not touched by it;*
> *My heart in his presence has displayed its wound,*
> *And the arrow that ought always to remain hidden'*
> *Did you see his scorn, his inhumane rigor?*
> *He hates me; I would like to hate him in my turn;*
> *But that is a vain hope;*
> *I can feel nothing for him but amour.*

Floride played her role well with regard to the queen; she
did her best to console her and gave her a few returns of hope,
of which she had need in order not to succumb.

"Fortuné finds himself at a distance so remote from you,
Madame," she told her, "that he cannot comprehend what you
wanted to make him understand. It seems to me that it is al-

ready a great deal that he has affirmed to you that he does not love anyone."

It is so natural to flatter oneself that the queen finally recovered a little courage. She did not know that he malicious Floride, convinced of the distance of the chevalier from her, wanted to engage her to speak to him more clearly, in order that he could shock her further by the indifference of his responses.

For his part, he was in the utmost embarrassment. His situation appeared to him to be cruel; he would not have hesitated to quit the court if the fatal arrow that had wounded him for the king had not stopped him in spite of himself. He no longer went to see the queen except when she held her circle and in the king's retinue.

She immediately perceived that further change in his conduct; she gave him the opportunity several times to pay his court to her without him wanting to take advantage of it, but one day, when she went down into the gardens she saw him traversing a broad pathway and plunging promptly into the little wood. She called to him; he feared displeasing her and, pretending not to have understood her, he approached her in a respectful manner.

"Do you remember, Chevalier, the conversation we had, some time ago, in the grove of trees?"

"I am not capable, Madame," he replied, "of forgetting that honor."

"Doubtless the questions that I asked you caused you difficulty," she said, "for since that day, you have not put yourself in a position where I could ask you others."

"As hazard alone procured me that favor," he said, "it seemed to me that it would have been temerity to take others."

"Say rather, ingrate," she continued, blushing, "that you have avoided my presence; you know my sentiments only too well."

Fortuné lowered his eyes in an embarrassed and modest manner, and as he hesitated to reply, she said: "You're very

disconcerted; go, don't try to say anything to me; I understand
you better than I would like to understand you."

She might perhaps have said more if she had not perceived the king, who had come out for a walk. She advanced
immediately and, seeing him very melancholy, she implored
him to tell her the reason.

"You know," said the king, "that a month ago I was informed that a dragon of prodigious size was ravaging the entire country. I believed that it could be killed, and I gave the
necessary orders, but everything has been attempted in vain. It
is devouring my subjects, their flocks and everything it encounters; it is poisoning the rivers and springs where it slakes
its thirst and desiccating the grass and plants where it repos-
es."

While the king was speaking, the queen was rolling
around her irritated mind a sure mans of sacrificing the chevalier to her resentment.

"I'm not unaware," she replied, "of the bad news that
you've received; Fortuné, whom you sent to me, has just informed me of it, but, my brother, you will be surprised by
what remains for me to tell you, which is that he begged me,
with the utmost insistence, that you permit him to go and fight
the frightful dragon. It's true that he has such a marvelous skill
and handles weapons so well that I'm not at all surprised that
he presumes so much of himself. In addition to that, he tells
me that he has a secret for putting the most alert dragon to
sleep, but that it's necessary not to mention that, because there
wouldn't appear to be enough valor in his action."

"However he does it," said the king, "it would be very
glorious for him and very useful for us if he could succeed;
however, I fear that it might be the effect of a indiscreet zeal
and that it might cost him his life."

"No, my brother," added the queen, "have no anxiety
about that; he has told me surprising things; you know that he
is naturally very sincere, and then, what honor could he hope
for in dying stupidly? In any case," she continued, "I promised

him to obtain what he desires with so much passion that, if you refuse, he might die of it."

"I consent to what you wish," said the king, "but I confess to you, in spite of that, I'm reluctant to do it. Let's summon him."

Immediately, he made a sign to Fortuné to approach, and said to him, in an obliging manner: "I've just learned from the queen the desire that you have to combat the dragon that is desolating us. It's a resolution so bold that I can't believe that you have envisaged al the peril of it."

"I represented it to him," said the queen, "But he has so much zeal for your service and passion to signal himself that nothing could turn him away from it, and I take a fortunate augury from that."

Fortuné was surprised to hear what the king and the queen were saying to him. He had too much intelligence not to penetrate the malevolent intentions of that princess, but his mildness did not permit him to explain himself, and he let her speak, contenting himself with making profound reverences, which the king took for further pleas to grant him the permission he wanted.

"Go, then," he said to him, sighing. "Go where glory summons you; I know that you have so much skill in everything you do, and particularly with arms, that the monster will perhaps have difficulty avoiding your thrusts."

"Sire," said the chevalier, "in whatever manner I come out of the combat, I shall be satisfied: either I shall have delivered you of a terrible scourge, or I shall have died for you; but honor me with one favor that would be infinitely dear to me."

"Ask whatever you wish," said the king."

"I dare," he said, "to ask you for your portrait."

The king was very flattered that he could think of his portrait at a time when he had reason to be occupied with so many other things, and the queen felt a further chagrin that he had not made her the same request; but it would have been necessary to have an unusual good will to want the portrait of such a malevolent person.

The king returned to his palace and the queen to hers. Fortuné, very embarrassed by the word he had given, went to find his horse and said to him: "My dear Comrade, there is news."

"I know already, Sire" he replied.

"What shall we do, then?" Fortuné added.

"It's necessary to leave as soon as possible," replied the horse. "Obtain an order from the king by which he orders you to fight the dragon, and we shall do our duty."

Those few words consoled the young chevalier; he did not fail to go to see the king early the next morning, in a campaign costume as well-designed as all the others he had taken from the leather-bound chest.

As soon as the king appeared he cried: "What! You're ready to depart?"

"One cannot have too much diligence to execute your commands, Sire," he replied. "I have come to take my leave of you."

The king could not help being moved, seeing a knight so young, so handsome and so perfect on the point of exposing himself to the greatest peril in which a man could ever put himself. He embraced him, and gave him his portrait, enriched with large diamonds. Fortuné received it with an extraordinary joy; the great qualities of the king had touched him to such a point that he could not imagine anything in the world more lovable than him, and if he suffered in quitting him it as much less from fear of being swallowed by the dragon than the privation of a presence so dear.

The king wanted his specific order to Fortuné to go and fight the dragon to include a general one to all his subjects to aid him and to give him the assistance of which he might need.

Then he took his leave of the king, and in order that nothing untoward could be remarked in his conduct he went to see the queen, who was in her dressing-room surrounded by several ladies. She changed color when he appeared; had she not to reproach herself in his regard? He saluted her respectfully and asked whether she would honor him with her orders, as he was about to depart. That word completed disconcerting her, and Floride, who knew nothing about the scheme that the queen had woven against the chevalier, was quite bewildered. She would have liked to speak to him in private, but he fled such embarrassing conversations.

"I pray to the gods," said the queen, "that you will be victorious and that you will come back triumphant."

"Your Majesty does me too much honor," said Fortuné. "She knows well enough the peril to which I am exposed, and I am not unaware of it either; however, I am full of confidence; perhaps, on this occasion, I am the only one who is hopeful."

The queen understood very well what he wanted to say to her; doubtless she would have responded to that slight reproach had there been fewer people in the room.

Finally, the chevalier went home. He ordered his seven excellent domestics to mount up and follow him, because the time had come to prove what they could do; there was none who did not testify his joy at being able to serve him. They only took a hour to put everything in order, and departed with him, assuring him that they would neglect nothing for his satisfaction.

Indeed, when they were alone in the country and there was no danger of being seen, each of them gave proof of his skill. Tippler drank the water of ponds and fished up the finest fish for his master's dinner. Fleet, for his part, caught red deer on the run and grabbed a hare by the ears, cunning as it was. Sharpshooter gave no quarter either to grouse of pheasants, and when the game had been killed on the one hand, the venison on the other and the fish was out of the water, Strong-Back cheerfully loaded himself with it. Even Fine-Ear rendered himself useful; he listened for truffles, morels, mushrooms, salad vegetables and fine herbs emerging from the soil. Fortuné had almost no need, therefore, to put his hand into his purse to meet the expenses of the journey. He would have been sufficiently diverted by seeing so many extraordinary things if his heart had not been full of the person he had just quit. The merit of the king was always present to him, and the malice of the queen seemed so great that he could not help detesting her.

He was marching plunged in a profound reverie when he was extracted from it by the piercing creams of several people; they were poor peasants that the dragon was devouring. He saw some who, having escaped, were fleeing as fast as they could; he called to them without them wanting to stop he followed them and spoke to them. He found out from them that the monster was not far away.

He asked them what they did to protect themselves from it, and they told him that, water being scarce in the region, people only drank rain-water; they had made a pool of it and that the dragon, after many expeditions, came to drink there, that it made such loud cries when it arrived that it was audible for a league around, and then everyone ran to hide, closing the doors and windows of the houses.

The chevalier went into a hostelry, less to rest than to obtain the advice of his fine horse. When everyone had gone to bed he went down to the stable, and said to him: "Comrade, what are we going to do to vanquish the dragon?"

"Sire," he said, "I shall dream about it tonight, and I will render you an account of it tomorrow morning."

When he returned, Comrade said: "My opinion is that Fine-Ear should listen to discover whether the dragon is nearby."

Immediately, Fine-Ear lay down, and heard the cries of the dragon, which was still seven leagues away.

When the horse knew that, he said to Fortuné: "Order Tippler to go and drink all the water in the big pool, and have Strong-Back bring enough wine to fill it; it's necessary to put dried grapes, pepper and other things that create a thirst around it. Also order the inhabitants to shut themselves in their houses, and you, Sire, don't come out of the one you choose with all your men. The dragon won't take long to come to drink at the pool; the wine will seem good to it, and you'll see that it will have the desired effect,"

As soon as Comrade had finished regulating what they ought to do, everyone did as he was ordered. The chevalier went into a house whose windows overlooked the pool. He was scarcely there when the dragon arrived. It drank a little; then it ate the breakfast that had been prepared for it, and then it drank so much that it became drunk. It could no longer move. It was lying on its side, its head tilted and its eyes closed.

When Fortuné saw it thus, he judged rightly that there was not a moment to lose. He emerged, sword in hand and attacked with a marvelous courage. The dragon, feeling itself pierced in all sides, tried to get up and fall upon the chevalier, but it did not have the strength; it had lost too much blood, and the chevalier, delighted to have reduced it to that extremity, summoned his men to bind the monster with ropes and chains, wanting to preserve for the king the pleasure and the glory of putting it to death; with the consequence that, having nothing more to fear, they dragged it all the way to the city.

Fortuné marched at the head of his little cortege. When he drew near the palace, he sent Fleet to tell the king the good news of such an advantageous success; but it seemed incredible until the monster actually appeared, on a machine built expressly for that purpose, to which it was tightly bound.

The king came down and embraced Fortuné. "The gods reserved this victory for you," he said, "and I feel less joy at seeing that horrible dragon in the state to which you have reduced it than in seeing you, my dear chevalier."

"Sire," he replied, "Your Majesty can give it the final blows. I have only brought it here in order to receive them from your hand."

The king drew his sword and finished killing the cruelest of his enemies. Everyone uttered cries of joy and acclamations for such an unexpected success.

Floride, still anxious, did not take long to hear about the return of the handsome chevalier. She ran to announce it to the queen, who was so surprised, and so torn between her love and her hatred, that she could not respond to what her favorite said to her. She had reproached herself hundreds of times for the nasty trick she had played, but she preferred seeing him dead to seeing him indifferent, with the result that she did not know whether she was glad or sorry that he was returning to a court where his presence would once again trouble the repose of her life.

The king, impatient to tell her about the fortunate success of such an extraordinary adventure, came into her room, leaning on the chevalier. "Here is the vanquisher of the dragon," he said to the queen, "who has just rendered me the most signal service that I could ever wish from a faithful subject. It is to you, Madame, that he spoke first about the desire he had to combat the monster; I hope that you will take account of the peril to which he exposed himself."

The queen, composing her face, honored Fortuné with a gracious welcome and a thousand praises; she found him even more lovable than when he had departed, and her attention in looking at him made him understand only too well that her heart was still wounded.

She did not want to trust her eyes to explain themselves alone, and one day, when she was out hunting with the king, she pretended not to follow the dogs because she felt ill. Then turning to the young chevalier, who was not far away, she said to him: "You'll do me the pleasure of remaining with me; I want to dismount and rest for a while." To those who were accompanying him, she added: "Go; don't quit my brother."

Immediately, she dismounted with Floride and sat down on the edge of a stream, where she remained in a profound silence for some time, thinking about all that she would give to her discourse.

Finally, raising her eyes, she attached them to the chevalier and said to him: "As good intentions are not always manifest, I fear that you might not have penetrated the motives that engaged me to urge the king to send you to fight the dragon. I was sure, by virtue of a presentiment that has never deceived me, that you would emerge from it as a courageous man; and the envious were speaking so ill of you because you had not gone with the army, that an action as striking as that one was required close mouths. I might well have communicated to you what was being said in that regard," she continued, "and perhaps I should have done so, but for being persuaded that your resentment would have had consequences and that it was better to silence the ill-intentioned by means of your intrepid conduct in peril than by an authority that marks that one is a favorite rather than a soldier.

"You see now, Chevalier," she went on, "that I have taken a sensible interest in everything glorious that has happened to you, and that you were quite wrong to judge it in another manner."

"The distance that separates us is so great," he replied, modestly, "that I am not worthy of the clarification that you wanted to give me, nor of the care that you have taken to risk my life in order to protect my honor. Heaven has protected me with more generosity than my enemies wished, and I shall always esteem myself fortunate to employ in the service of the king, and yours, a life of which the loss is more indifferent than one might think."

Fortuné's respectful reproach embarrassed the queen; she sensed very clearly all that he meant to say to her, but she found him too lovable to seek to drive him away with too bitter a response. On the contrary, she pretended to enter into his sentiments and asked him to say with what skill he had vanquished the dragon.

Fortuné had been careful not to tell anyone that it was by means of the help of his men; he claimed to have gone to meet that redoubtable enemy, and that only his skill, or even his temerity, had got him out of the affair; but the queen, almost no longer thinking about what he was recounting, interrupted in order to ask him whether he was now convinced of the part that she took in everything regarding him.

That conversation was about to be pushed further when he said to her: "Madame, I have just heard the sound of the horn; the king is approaching; does Your Majesty not want to mount up in order to go to meet him?"

"No," she said, in a manner full of despair. "it's sufficient for you to go."

"The king would criticize me, Madame," he added, "if I left you in a place where you might run some risk."

"I dispense you of so much anxiety," she said, in an absolute tone. "Your presence importunes me."

At that order, the chevalier made her a profound reverence, mounted his horse and his himself from her view, anxious about the success that that new resentment might have. He consulted his beautiful horse on that subject.

"Tell me Comrade," he said, "whether that excessively tender and excessively angry queen will find another monster to which to deliver me."

"She will only find her," replied the pretty horse, "but she is more draconian that the dragon you have killed, and she will exercise your patience and your virtue sufficiently."

"Might she make me lose the good graces of the king?" he cried. "That's the only thing that I dread."

"I cannot reveal the future to you," said Comrade. "Let it suffice for you that I am watching over everything." He did not say any more, because the king appeared at the end of a path; Fortuné joined him told him that the queen had felt ill had and ordered him to remain with her.

"It seems to me," said the king smiling, "that you are sufficiently well in her good graces, and that it's her to whom you open your heart preferably to me; for after all, I have not forgotten that you asked her to procure you the glory of going to combat the dragon."

"Sire," replied he chevalier, "I dare not defend myself against what you say, but I can assure Your Majesty that I put a great difference between your good graces and those of the queen, and if it were permitted to a subject to have a sovereign for a confidant, I would have a very delicate joy in declaring all the sentiments of my heart to you."

The king interrupted him to ask him where he had left the queen.

While he went to join her she was complaining to Floride about Fortuné's indifference. "The sight of him has become odious to me," she cried. "It is necessary that he leaves the court, or I do; I can no longer suffer an ingrate who dares to testify so much scorn to me. And who is the mortal who would not esteem himself fortunate to please a queen omnipotent in this State? There is only him in the world. Oh, the gods have reserved him to trouble the repose of my life."

Floride was not sorry about the chagrin that her mistress had against Fortuné, and far from appeasing it, she aggravated it, by reminding her of a thousand circumstances that she might not have noticed. Her chagrin was further augmented, and made her conceive a new design to doom the poor chevalier.

As soon as the king was with her and had testified his anxiety for her health, she said to him: "I confess that I find myself rather poorly, but it is difficult not to be cured with Fortuné; he is so cheerful, his visions are so pleasant. Do you know," she continued, "that he has asked me to obtain another favor from Your Majesty? He has asked with the utmost confidence to succeed in the most temeritous enterprise in the world."

"What, my sister?" cried the king. "Does he want to combat some new dragon?"

"It's several of them at a time," she said, "that he is sure of vanquishing. Shall I tell you? In sum, he boasts of obliging the emperor to return our treasures to us, and that he needs no army for that purpose."

"What a pity," relied the king, "that the poor boy has fallen into such an extraordinary folly!"

"His combat against the dragon," added the queen, "only leaves him greater designs to conceive, and what would you be risking by giving him permission to gamble himself again in your service?"

"I would be risking a life that is dear to me," replied the king. "I would have extreme difficulty in making him perish with a glad heart."

"In whatever manner the thing turns out," she said, "it is therefore infallible that he will die, for I assure you that he has such a strong passion to recover your treasures that he will do more than languish if you refuse him the permission."

The king fell into a profound sadness. "I cannot imagine," he said, "what is filling his head with all these chimeras. I suffer from seeing him in this state."

"Fundamentally," said the queen, "he has fought the dragon, and vanquished it. Perhaps he will succeed again. I sometimes have accurate presentiments; my heart tells me that his enterprise will be successful; please, my brother, don't oppose his zeal."

"It's necessary to summon him," said the king, "And at least represent to him what he is risking."

"That's exactly the means of making him despair," replied the queen. "He'll believe that you don't want him to go, and I assure you with regard to retaining him by any consideration that concerns him won't work, for I've already said to him everything that can be imagined in such a occasion."

"Well, then," cried the king, "let him go; I consent to it."

Delighted by that permission, the queen summoned Fortuné. "Chevalier," she said to him, "thank the king; he has granted you the permission that you desire so much, to go and find Emperor Matapa and to force him to surrender, willingly or by force, the treasures that he has stolen from us; prepare yourself with the same diligence that you had to go and combat the dragon."

Fortuné, surprised, recognized in that dart the fury of the queen against him; however, he felt pleasure at being able to give his life for a king who was so dear to him, and without defending himself against that extraordinary commission, he put one knee on the ground and kissed the hand of the king, who, for his part, was very moved.

The queen felt a kind of shame on seeing with what respect he saw himself condemned to confront death. *Might it be*, she said to herself, *that he has an attachment for me, and that, rather than deny what I have advanced on his part, he will suffer the bad turn I have done him without complaint? Oh, if I could flatter myself with that, how I would wish upon myself the harm that I have done to him!*

The king did not say much more to the chevalier; he remounted his horse and the queen climbed into her caleche, still pretending to feel ill.

Fortuné accompanied the king as far as the edge of the forest; then, going back into it in order to talk to his horse, he said to him: "My faithful Comrade, it's all over; it's necessary that I perish. The queen has just taken advantage of an opportunity to ensure it that I would never have expected on her part."

"My amiable master," replied the horse, "cease to be alarmed; although I was not present at what has happened, I have known about it for a long time; that embassy is not as terrible as you imagine."

"You don't know, then," the chevalier continued, "that the emperor is the most wrathful of all men, and that if I propose to him that he return all that he has taken from the king he will make no other response than having a rope tied around my neck and having me thrown in the river."

"I'm informed of his violence," said Comrade, "but that doesn't prevent you from taking your men with you and departing; if you perish, we'll all perish; I hope, however, for a better success."

Slightly consoled, the chevalier returned home, gave the necessary orders and then went to obtain those of the king and his letters of credit.

"You'll say on my part to the emperor," he told him, "that I demand the return of all my subjects that he is holding in slavery, our imprisoned soldiers, my horses of which he is making use, and my furniture, with my treasures."

"What shall I offer him for all those things?" said Fortuné.

"Nothing," replied the king, "except my amity."

The young ambassador did not make any great effort of memory to retain his instruction. He departed without seeing the queen. She seemed offended by that, but he had little to protect with her; what could she do to him in her greatest anger that she had not done in the transports of her grand amour? A tenderness of that character seemed to him to be the most redoubtable thing in the world.

Her confidante, who knew the whole secret, was in despair against her mistress, for wanting to sacrifice the flower of all chivalry.

Fortuné took from his leather chest everything that was necessary for his journey; he was not content to dress himself magnificently; he wanted the seven men who were accompanying him to be very well-dressed, and as they all had excellent horses and Comrade seemed to fly through the air rather than running along the ground, they arrived in a very short time in the capital city where Emperor Matapa lived. It was larger than Paris, Constantinople and Rome put together, and so populous that the cellars, grain-lofts and roofs were inhabited.

Fortuné was very surprised to see a city of such prodigious extent. He requested an audience with the emperor, and obtained one without difficulty, but when he had declared to him the subject of his embassy, although he did so with a grace that added a great deal to his arguments, the emperor could not help smiling.

"If you were at the head of five hundred thousand men," he said to him, "one might have listened to you, but I'm told that you only have seven."

"I have not attempted, Sire," Fortuné said to him, "to make you render what my master wants by force, but by my very humble remonstrations."

"By whatever means," added the emperor, "you will not succeed unless you carry out a thought that has just occurred to me, which is that you find a man who has a good enough appetite to eat for breakfast all the warm bread cooked by the inhabitants of this great city."

At that proposal the chevalier was surprised by joy, and as he did not speak promptly enough, the emperor burst out laughing.

"You see," he said to him, "that it is natural to respond to an extravagance with an extravagant proposal."

"Sire," said Fortuné, "I accept what you offer me. I will bring a man tomorrow who will eat all the soft bread, and even all the hard bread, in the city. Order that it be brought to the main square; you will have the pleasure of seeing him take advantage of it, all the way to the crumbs."

The emperor replied that he consented to that. For the rest of the day he spoke of nothing but the folly of the new ambassador, and Matapa swore that he would put him to death if he did not keep his word.

Fortuné had returned to the ambassadors' hotel, where he lodged. He summoned Guzzler and said to him: "This time it's necessary to prepare to eat bread; everything depends on it for us." He told him what he had promised the emperor.

"Don't worry, Master," said Guzzler. "I'll eat so much that they'll weary of it before I will."

Fortuné feared nevertheless that he might not be able to do it, and forbade him to have any supper in order that he would have a better appetite for breakfast, although that precaution was unnecessary.

The emperor, the empress and the princess placed themselves on a balcony in order to get a better view of what was about to happen. Fortuné arrived in the main square with his little cortege, and when he perceived six mountains of bread higher than the Pyrenees he could not help going pale. Guzzler did not do the same, for the hope of eating so much good bread gave him great pleasure; he begged that not the smallest morsel be held back, saying that he did not want to leave anything for the mice.

The emperor joked with all his court about the extravagance of Fortuné and his men, but the impatient Guzzler asked for the signal to begin; it was given by the sound of trumpets and drums. At the same time, he threw himself upon one of the mountains of bread, which he ate in less than a quarter of a hour; and all the others were guzzled in the same manner.

There has never been such an astonishment; everyone wondered whether their eyes had not been fascinated, and they went to touch the place where the bread had been deposited. It was necessary that day for everyone, from the emperor to the cat, to dine without bread.

Fortuné, infinitely content with that success, approached the emperor and asked him, with a great deal of respect, whether he was agreeable to keeping the word he had given him. The emperor, a trifle irritated at having been taken for a dupe, said to him: "Sire Ambassador, it's too much to eat without drinking; it's necessary that you or one of your men drink all the water in the fountains, aqueducts and reservoirs in the entire city, and all the wine there is in its cellars."

"Sire," said Fortuné, "you want to make it impossible for me to obey your orders, but nevertheless, I would attempt the adventure if I could flatter myself that you will render to my master the king, that for which I have asked you on his behalf."

"I will do that," said the emperor, "if you can succeed in your enterprise."

The chevalier asked the emperor whether he would be present; he replied that he thing was rare enough to merit his curiosity; and, climbing into a magnificent carriage, he went to the fountain of lions; there were seven, of marble, which projected torrents of water through their mouths, of which a river formed on which the city could be traversed in gondolas.

Tippler approached the great basin, and without drawing breath, he drained that spring as dry as if there had never been water in it. The fish in the river cried vengeance against him, for they did not know what would become of them. He did no less at all the other fountains, aqueducts and reservoirs. In sum, he would have drunk the sea, salty as it was.

After such an experience, the emperor could scarcely doubt that he would drink the wine as well as the water, and everyone, in chagrin, had scant desire to contribute his own; but Tippler complained loudly about the injustice that was being done to him. He said that he had a stomach ache, and not only claimed the wine but that liqueurs were also part of his bargain, with the consequence that Matapa, fearing to appear too stingy, consented to everything that Tippler asked.

Fortuné, taking his opportunity, begged the emperor to remember what he had promised. At those words he adopted a severe expression, and said that he would think about it.

In fact, he assembled his council, in order to declare the extreme chagrin he was in, at having promised the young ambassador everything that he had gained from his master; that he had attached conditions to it the execution of which he had believed to be impossible; and asked what he could say to avoid something so prejudicial.

His daughter, the princess, who was one of the most beautiful women in the world, having heard him speak thus, said to him: "Sire, you know that until now I have defeated all those who have dared to dispute with me prizes for running. It's necessary to say to the ambassador that if he can arrive before me at a designated spot, you promise no longer to elude the word that you have given him."

He emperor embraced his daughter; he found her advice marvelous, and the next day he received Fortuné's duties agreeably.

"I have one more thing to demand of you," he said, "which is that you or one of your men run against the princess, my daughter. I swear to you by all the elements that if anyone wins the prize against her, I will give all sorts of satisfactions to your master."

Fortuné did not refuse that challenge; he told the emperor that he accepted it, and immediately, Matapa added that it would be in two hours. He sent word to his daughter to prepare herself. It was an exercise to which she had been accustomed since her most tender youth. She appeared in a huge avenue of orange trees that was three leagues long and had been so well sanded that no stone larger than the head of a pin could be seen there. She was wearing a light pink taffeta dress dotted with little stars embroidered in gold and silver; her beautiful hair was tied back with a ribbon and fell negligently over her shoulders. She was wearing very pretty small shoes without heels and a girls of gems that outlined her figure well enough to allow it to be seen that there had never been one more beautiful. The young Atalanta would never have dared to dispute anything with her.

Fortuné came, accompanied by the faithful Fleet and his other domestics. The emperor took his place with his entire court. The ambassador said that Fleet would have the honor of running against the princess. The leather-bound chest had furnished him with a garment of Dutch cloth garnished with English lace, stockings of flame-colored silk. plumes of the same color and beautiful underwear. In that state he was very good-looking.

The princess accepted him to compete with her, but before starting she had a liquor brought that aided her to become even faster and to give her strength. The runner cried that it was necessary that he be given some too, in order that the advantage should be equal. "Very willingly," she said, "I'm too just to refuse it to you." Immediately, she had some poured for him, but as he was not accustomed to the liquid, which was very strong, it went straight to his head; her spun around two or three times, collapsed at the foot of an orange tree and fell into a profound slumber.

Meanwhile, the signal was given to start; it had already recommenced three times. The princess was simply waiting for Fleet to wake up. She thought, finally, that it was of great consequence to her to get her father out of the embarrassment that he as in, with the result that she set off with a marvelous grace and lightness.

As Fortuné was standing at the end of the avenue with all his men he knew nothing of what had happened, when he saw the princess running in her own, no more than half a league from the finish.

"Gods!" he cried, speaking to his horse. "We're doomed! I don't see Fleet."

"Sire," said Comrade, "it's necessary that Fine-Ear listen; perhaps he can tell us what has happened."

Fine-Ear threw himself to the ground, and even though he was two leagues away from Fleet he heard him snoring. "Truly," he said "he won't come. He's sleeping as if he were in his bed."

"Eh! What shall we do?" cried Fortuné, again.

"My master," said Comrade "it's necessary that Sharpshooter loose an arrow into his earlobe, in order to wake him up."

Sharpshooter took his bow, and launched an arrow so accurately that it pierced Fleet's ear. The pain he felt brought him out of his slumber; he opened his eyes, saw the princess almost approaching the goal, and heard nothing behind him but cries of joy and applause. He was astonished at first, but quickly made up the ground that slumber had caused him to lose. It was as if he were borne by the wind, and eyes could not follow him.

In sum, he arrived first, with the arrow still in his ear, for he had not taken the time to remove it.

The emperor was so surprised by the three events that had occurred since the arrival of the ambassador that he thought the gods were taking an interest in him, and that he could not defer keeping his word any longer.

"Approach," he said, "in order to hear from my mouth that I consent to you taking from here whatever you or one of your men can carry of your master's treasures, for it's necessary that you don't think that I will ever be willing to give you more, or that I will release his soldiers his subjects and his horses."

The ambassador bowed profoundly; he told him that he still gave him many thanks and asked him to give his orders in that regard.

Matapa, full of chagrin, spoke to the guardian of his treasures, and went to a pleasure house he had near the city. Immediately, Fortuné and his men asked for entry to all the places where the king's furniture, rarities, silver and gems were contained. Nothing was hidden from him, but it was on condition that one single man could load himself with them. Strong-Back presented himself, and with his help, the ambassador took away all the furniture in the emperor's palace, five hundred golden statures taller than giants, carriages, chariots and all sorts of things, without exception, with which Strong-back marched so lightly that it did not seem that he had a heavy weight on his back.

When the emperor's ministers saw that the palace had been emptied of furniture to such an extent that not a chair, chest, cooking-pot or bed remained they went diligently to inform him, and one can imagine his astonishment when he knew that a single man had carried it all away. He cried that he would not suffer it, and commanded his guards and musketeers to mount up and follow the thieves of his treasures diligently.

Although Fortuné had covered more than ten leagues, Fine-Ear warned him that he could hear a large troop of cavalry riding at full tilt, and Sharpshooter, who had excellent eyesight, perceived them. There were on the bank of a river; Fortuné said to Tippler: "We have no boat; if you can drink some of his water, we can pass over." Tippler immediately did his duty.

The ambassador wanted to profit from the time to draw away, but his horse said: "Don't worry; let our enemies approach."

They appeared on the river's edge, and, knowing where the fishermen moored their boats, they embarked promptly, and were rowing with all their might when Impetuous inflated his cheeks and began to blow. The river became agitated; the boats capsized, and the emperor's little army perished without a single one saving himself in order to go and tell him the news.

Each of them, joyful at such a favorable event, no longer thought of anything but demanding the recompense that he thought he had merited. They wanted to render themselves masters of all the treasures they had carried away. A great dispute rose between them regarding the division.

"If I hadn't won the race," said the runner, you wouldn't have anything.

"And if I hadn't heard you snoring," said Fine-Ear, "where would we be?"

"Who would have woken you up without me?" retorted Sharpshooter.

"In truth," said Strong-Back, "I admire you with your contestations, but ought anyone to dispute with me the honor of choosing, since I had the trouble of carrying everything? Without my help you wouldn't be in the embarrassment of division."

"Say rather without mine," said Tippler. "The river, which I drank like a glass of lemonade, would have embarrassed you somewhat."

"We'd have been much more so if I hadn't overturned the boats," said Impetuous.

"I've kept silent until now," said Guzzler, "but I can't help representing that it was me who opened the stage to the great events that have occurred, and that if I'd have left a single crust of bread, all would have been lost."

"My friends," said Fortuné, in an absolute manner, "you have all worked marvels, but we must leave to the king the care of recognizing our services. I would be very sorry to be recompensed by any hand but his. Believe me, let us put everything at his disposal; he sent us to bring back his treasures, not to steal them. That idea is so shameful that my opinion is that it should never be mentioned, and I assure you that on my own part, I will give you so much wealth that you will have

nothing to regret even if it were possible that the king neglected you."

The seven endowed men were penetrated by their master's remonstration; they threw themselves at his feet and
promised to have no other will but his.

They finished their voyage thus, but the amiable Fortuné,
as he approached the city, felt agitated by a thousand different
troubles. The joy of having rendered a considerable service to
his king, the person to whom he felt such a tender attachment,
the hope of seeing him again, and that of being favorably received by him, all flattered him agreeably; on the other hand,
the dread of irritating the queen and experiencing further per-
secutions on her part and that of Floride threw him into a
strange dejection.

Finally, he arrived, and all the people, delighted to see all
the riches that he was returning, followed him with a thousand
acclamations, the noise of which reached all the way to the
palace.

The king could not believe such an extraordinary thing;
he ran to the queen to inform her of it. At first she was utterly
bewildered, but then, pulling herself together somewhat, she
said: "You see that the gods protect him; he has succeeded,
fortunately, and I am not surprised that he attempted something that appeared impossible to others."

As she finished speaking she saw Fortuné coming in; he
informed Their Majesties of the success of his voyage, adding
that the treasures were in the park because there was so much
gold, precious stones and furniture that there was nowhere
capacious enough to accommodate them. It is easy to believe
that the king testified a great deal of amity to such a faithful,
zealous and amiable subject.

The presence of the chevalier and all the advantages he
had brought back reopened a wound in the queen's heart that
had not yet scarred over. She found him more charming than
ever, and as soon as she was at liberty to speak to Floride she
resumed her usual plaints.

"You've seen what I've done to doom him," she said to her. "I could only imagine that means of forgetting him. An unparalleled fatality always brings him back to me, and whatever reasons I have for scorning a man who is so inferior to me and who repays my sentiments with a black ingratitude, I still love him, and I am finally resolved to marry him secretly."

"Marry him, Madame!" cried Floride. "Is that possible? Have I heard correctly?"

"Yes," replied the queen, "you have understood my design; it's necessary that you second it. I charge you to bring Fortuné to my cabinet this evening; I want to declare to him myself how far my generosity to him extends."

Floride, in despair at having been chosen to contribute to the marriage of her mistress and her lover, neglected nothing to prevent the queen from seeing it. She represented to her the anger of the king if he discovered the intrigue; that he might perhaps have the chevalier put to death; that at the very least he would be condemned to perpetual imprisonment, in which she would no longer see him. All of her eloquence failed; she saw that the queen was beginning to get annoyed and had no other course of action to take than that of obedience.

She found Fortuné in the gallery of the palace, where he was having the golden statues that he had bought back from Matapa arranged. She told him to come to the queen's apartment that evening; the order made him tremble. Floride understood his disturbance. "O gods," she said to him, "how I pity you! Why is it that the heart of that princess cannot escape you? Alas, mine is in a less dangerous condition than hers, which dare not declare itself."

The chevalier did not want to embark upon a further clarification; he had enough chagrin already.

As he was not seeking to please the queen, he put on a very negligent costume, in order that she could not think that he had any design to do so, but if he could easily neglect diamonds and embroidery, it was not the same for his personal charms; he was still lovable, still marvelous; whatever mood he was in, nothing equaled him.

The queen took great care to heighten her beauty with all the splendor that could be added by an extraordinary adornment; she remarked with pleasure that Fortuné seemed surprised by it.

"Appearances," she said to him, "Are sometimes so deceptive that I am very glad to justify myself with regard to what you have doubtless believed my sentiments to be. when I engaged the king to send you to the emperor, it seemed that I wanted to sacrifice you; believe, however, handsome Chevalier, that I knew everything that would happen, and that I had no other intention than securing you an immortal glory."

"Madame," he said, "you are too far above me to lower yourself as far as an explanation; I do not enter into the motives that made you act; it is sufficient for me to have obeyed the king."

"You have too much indifference for the clarification that I want to give you," she added, "but the time has finally come to convince you of my generosity. Approach, Fortuné, approach; receive my hand as a pledge of my faith."

The poor chevalier was so nonplussed that no one has ever been more so. Twenty times over he was ready to declare his sex to the queen. He dared not do it, and responded to the testimonies of her amity with an extreme coldness; he gave her infinite reasons regarding the anger that the king would be in if he learned that his subject, in the environment of his court, had dared to contract such an important marriage without his consent.

After the queen had tried in vain to cure him of the fear that seemed to alarm him, she suddenly took on the visage and voice of a Fury; she lost her temper; she made a thousand threats; she charged him with insults; she hit him; she scratched him; and then, turning her fury against herself, she tore out her hair, bloodied her face and her breasts, tore her veil and her lace, and crying "To me, guards, to me!" she made her people enter her cabinet and commanded them to put the unfortunate chevalier in a dungeon. Immediately, she ran to the king to demand justice against the violence of the young monster.

She told her brother that he had had the audacity to declare his passion for her a long time ago; that, in the hope that absence and rigors might be able to cure him, she had neglected no opportunities to send him way, as he had been able to remark; but that he was a wretch whom nothing could change, that he could see the extremity to which he had borne himself against her; that she wanted him to be tried, and that if he refused her that justice, she would hold him to account for it.

The manner in which she spoke astonished the king. He knew that she was the most violent woman in the world; she had a great deal of power and she was capable of turning the kingdom upside-down. The boldness of Fortuné demanded an exemplary punishment; everyone already knew what had happened, and it was his duty to avenge his sister. But alas, on whom was that vengeance to be exercised? On a knight who had exposed himself to the greatest perils for his service, to whom he was indebted for his repose and all his treasures, whom he loved with a particular inclination. He would have given half his life to save that dear favorite.

He represented to the queen the utility that he had, the services that he had rendered the State, his youth, and all the things that might engage her to pardon him. She did not want to hear any of it; she demanded his death. The king, therefore, no longer able to avoid giving him judges, appointed those he believed to be the mildest and the most susceptible to tenderness, in order that they might be the most disposed to tolerate his fault.

But he was mistaken in his conjectures; the judges wanted to reestablish their reputation at the expense of that poor unfortunate, and as it was an affair of great publicity, they armed themselves with the utmost rigor and condemned Fortuné without deigning to hear him. His sentence was to receive three dagger-thrusts in the heart, since it was his heart that was culpable.

The king dreaded that sentence as much as if it had been pronounced against him. He exiled all the judges that had pronounced it, but he could not save his lovable Fortuné, and the queen, triumphant at the torture that he was about to suffer, her eyes bloodshot, demanded that of the illustrious afflicted. The king made further attempts in her regard, which only served to aggravate her.

Finally, the day marked for the terrible execution arrived, when the chevalier was to be taken from the prison in which he had been put, and where he had remained without anyone at all having spoken to him. He did not know the crime of which the queen had accused him, only imagining that it was some new persecution that his indifference had attracted to him. What caused him more pain was that he believed that the king was seconding the fury of the princess.

Floride, inconsolable at the state to which her lover was reduced, made a resolution of the utmost violence, which was to poison the queen and to poison herself, if it were necessary that Fortuné experience the rigor of a cruel death. As soon as she knew the sentence, despair gripped her soul and she no longer thought about anything but executing her designs; but she was brought a slower poison that she desired, with the result hat even though she had made the queen take it, that princess, who had not yet felt its malignity, had the handsome chevalier brought to the middle of the main square of the palace in order to receive death in her presence.

The executioners took him from his cell with their usual custom, and conducted him like a tender lamb to the slaughter, The first object that struck his eyes was the queen on her chariot, who could not be close enough to him for her liking, wanting, if possible, his blood to spurt over her. As for the king, he had shut himself in his cabinet in order to lament at liberty the fate of his dear favorite.

When Fortuné had been attached to a stake, his robe and his shirt were removed in order to pierce the heart, but what was the astonishment of the numerous assembly when the alabaster breasts of the veritable Belle-Belle were uncovered!

Everyone knew that it was an innocent young woman, unjustly accused.

The queen, emotional and confused, was troubled to such a degree that the poison commenced to take surprising effect; she fell down in long convulsions, from which she only recovered in order to utter agonized regrets.

The people who cherished Fortuné had already set her free. People ran to announce the surprising news to the king, who had abandoned himself to a profound sadness. At that moment, joy took the place of dolor; he ran to the square, and was charmed to see the metamorphosis of Fortuné.

The last sighs of the queen suspended the transports of the prince briefly, but when he reflected on her malice he could not regret her, and resolved to marry Belle-Belle, in order to repay with a crown the infinite obligations that he had to her. He declared his intention to her; it is easy to believe that it fulfilled her dearest wishes, far less by virtue of her elevation than in regard to a king full of merit for whom she had always felt a extreme tenderness.

The day of the famous marriage of the king having been determined, Belle-Belle resumed her female costumes, and then appeared a thousand times more lovable than she had in those of the chevalier. She consulted her horse regarding the continuation of her adventures; he only promised her more agreeable ones, and in recognition of all the good offices that he had rendered her, she had a stable made for him paneled with ebony and ivory; he only lay down henceforth on satin mattresses. As for the men who had followed her, they were recompensed in proportion to their services.

However, Comrade disappeared; the news was brought to Belle-Belle. That loss troubled the queen, who adored him; she had people search for her horse everywhere, but it was in vain for three days. On the fourth her anxiety obliged her to get up before dawn; she went down into the garden, traversed the wood, and walked in a vast meadowland, calling from time to time: "Comrade, my dear Comrade, what has become of you? Have you abandoned me? I still have need of your sage advice; come back, come back in order to give it to me."

As she spoke thus she suddenly saw a second sun rising in the west; she stopped to admire that prodigy; her rapture was unparalleled on seeing that it was gradually drawing nearer to her, and recognizing after a moment her horse, whose equipage was covered in precious gems, prancing ahead of a chariot of pearls and topazes. Twenty-four sheep were pulling it; their wool was exceedingly brilliant gold and silver embroidery thread, their reins where crimson satin covered with emeralds; carbuncles were not lacking, they had them on their horns and their ears.

Belle-Belle recognized her fay protectress in the chariot, with her father, the Comte, and her two sisters, who shouted to her, while clapping their hands and making her a thousand signs of amity, that they had come for her wedding. She nearly died of joy; she did not know what to say in order to give them all the testimonies that she would have liked. She placed herself in the chariot, and that pompous equipage entered the palace, where everything was already prepared to celebrated the greatest fête that there could ever be in that realm.

Thus, the amorous king attached his destiny to that of his mistress, and that charming adventure has passed down the centuries as far as our day.

> *The cruelest lion of ardent Libya,*
> *Pressed by the hunter, whose arrows it feels,*
> *Is less redoubtable than a lover in fury*
> *Who sees her attractions scorned.*
> *Iron and poison are the slightest vengeance*
> *That her anger dares to demand,*
> *In order to calm its violence.*
> *You see here the deadly effects:*
> *Fortuné, in spite of his innocence,*
> *Was made to suffer the torments of the greatest crimes.*
> *His new metamorphosis*
> *Disarmed an entire people obstinate for his doom;*

And Belle-Belle was recognized
In the garments of Fortuné.
The queen demanded his torture in vain;
Heaven has always fought for innocence;
After having vice punished.
It has virtue crowned.

La Dandinardière had listened to the reading of the tale of Belle-Belle with great attention, and as he was susceptible to all the impressions that anyone wanted to give him, the prior remarked that he was weeping tenderly.

"What's the matter with you, then?" he said. "You seem to me to be very touched."

"Alas, who wouldn't be?" cried the little man. "You must have a heart harder that the stone that broke my head, to forbid yourself such a just affliction."

"If Belle-Belle had perished," replied the prior, "I believe that I would, in fact, have regretted her doom, but you're afflicting yourself inappropriately, and her marriage renders her too happy not to share her joy."

"Let's laugh, then," said La Dandinardière, wiping his eyes. "I also have reason to rejoice when I think of the generous gift that you are making me of this admirable tale; I have an obligation to you so pressing that I would sacrifice my life for you."

"Oh, you're too grateful," said the prior. "I don't ask any other recompense for the service I'm rendering you than to have the satisfaction of seeing you shine among all the tellers of tales as the sun shines on a beautiful day. By the same token, I shall announce to the charming Virginie and Marthonide that you surpass them in that literary genre, and that if they care to come to your room this afternoon, you will convince them of it."

"You delight me," he said, clasping him narrowly in his arms. "I'm convinced that such a work will immortalize me. I shall suffer nevertheless from the secret chagrin that those two beautiful young women will be in when they see that I have a hundred times more wit than them."

"It will be necessary for them to be patient," added the prior, "but adieu; I've read enough to need something to eat."

"And I've listened enough," replied our bourgeois, for my poor head to need a little repose."

The prior went out; he went to announce to Mesdemoiselles de Saint-Thomas that Dandinardière had written a masterpiece, and that he invited them to come and hear it.

"In truth," said Marthonide, "he has a physiognomy so intelligent that it's only necessary to see him to be convinced that he is capable of doing anything he wishes."

"It's a particular good fortune," added Virginie, "that a man like him, who has always been amid fire and carnage, who has played such an elevated role in the greatest European wars, conserves as much delicacy as men of letters who have never been away from their cabinets and alcoves."

The prior was dying of the desire to laugh when he heard them saying that La Dandinardière was a heroic general, and that he had made himself feared and admired in the army. He did not want to disillusion them, for that would have been very contradictory to the desire have him marry one of those two lovely young women. As he quit them, however, he went to tell the Vicomte de Berginville that before the end of the day there would be a rude war between the little bourgeois and Mesdemoiselles de Saint-Thomas over the tale of Belle-Belle.

"Is it possible," cried the vicomte, "that you want to make them quarrel at a time when we're thinking seriously about uniting them forever?"

"I'm wrong," said the prior, "but it seemed to me to be so amusing to listen to them assuring one another that they had composed that work, quarreling in that regard and producing their witnesses, that I was not the master of preventing myself from contriving it."

"I protest to you," he replied, "that, far from giving them dispositions of tenderness, you will give birth to an aversion in them that might last as long as they live."

"Well, what can be done?" added the prior. "He has the tale under his pillow; it would be easier to steal his soul than that little notebook."

"I'll think of a means to get it," replied the vicomte. "Since it's under his pillow, I'll steal it while he's being bandaged."

"That's the secret of getting him hanged," exclaimed the prior, "but he doesn't understand anything beyond the pleasure of persuading his mistress that he has intelligence; into what affliction will you cast him if he assembles the entire company to listen to him and finds that he has nothing to say?"

"The only remedy I know," replied the vicomte, "is to send someone to my house to ask my wife for one that one of her friends has sent her; for, in sum, he hasn't paid such great attention to the matter that he won't be easily deceived as long as he sees fays in it."

"I consent to that, said the prior, "provided that you conduct the affair well; otherwise you're a dead man."

The vicomte sent his valet de chambre diligently, and as he did not have far to go, he came back soon enough for his master to be able to make the projected exchange dexterously.

The impatient prior ran to Mesdemoiselles de Saint-Thomas's room. "I knew," he said to them, "that Monsieur de La Dandinardière is braver than Alexander and Caesar were, but I didn't know that he had a universal mind; he has just finished a tale that will enrage the storytellers, and if he commences thus for a first effort, one can say that the man will go far."

As he said that he rolled his two wide eyes and made mysterious grimaces that went as far as convulsion. Virginie and Marthonide maintained a profound silence, caused by the astonishment of such great news, and the prior, resuming speaking, said thirty times in succession, as if he were responding to his thoughts: "Yes it's a prodigy; yes, and yes again."

Virginie found an admirable savor in listening to him. "Oh, Monsieur," she said to him, "how well you praise, and how delicately you praise! You must be the panegyrist of the most illustrious of all men—I mean Monseigneur de La Dandinardière."

"But are we not to have the pleasure of hearing the reading of this marvelous work?" asked Marthonide, interrupting her sister.

"Undoubtedly," he replied. "I have come to invite you on his behalf."

"Oh, my sister, what a pleasure!" they said. "It's necessary to dress more appropriately than usual."

They each took a hunting costume, which they made from a green velvet skirt and a worn velvet hood, more gray than black. Their bonnets were covered in peacock plumes; each of them had a scarf of fine old lace full of tinsel, which fell elegantly in the firm hand of a bandolier, with a little horn that they did not know how to sound. In sum, however, such magnificence shone considerably in the village of Saint-Thomas,

What bizarre constellation meddled that day with the adornment of our heroines and our little hero? In the hope of seeing them he had sought what suited him most, for he could not resolve to appear before them with the napkins that enveloped his head, and removing them would be even worse. He made the decision to wrap a marigold and flax-gray jacket around them, which he made into a sort of turban, the two sleeves hang down at the sides. He had his burnished steel neck-guard, half-rusty and half-polished., and his gauntlets on his hands, with a pile of cushions to support them. It certainly required a depth of serious misanthropy to rest he desire to laugh caused by that strange figure, but the divine Virginie and Marthonide were only capable of admiration.

They dined with a frugality that did not astonish anyone; everyone knew that they regarded the necessity of eating as a defect of nature, which they wanted to remedy by resisting it stubbornly, and they often fell into a faint. As soon as they had left the table, the prior engaged Madame de Saint-Thomas to come and see the illustrious invalid; he promised her the reading of a tale. She was agreeable flattered, when she thought that she was being invited to hear a work of intellect; she retired immediately and went at a grave pace to the dying man's chamber; her daughters followed her, part-way between the appearance of amazons and that of provincial girls. The Messieurs lent them a hand, and La Dandinardière, transported by joy on seeing them, was so scarcely aware of what he was doing that he was ready and eager to leap out to bed to do the honors of his apartment.

After the initial civilities, everyone took their places; our little man, adopting a studied tone of voice, said to them: "I beg your pardon, Mesdames, for daring to attract you to this place; you would have reason to say that you were expecting the agreeable song of the nightingale and have only found an owl."

"We have never owled anyone," replied Madame de Saint-Thomas, who was fond of making up words and talking extraordinarily, "and we know that your nightingalery is marvelously sustained."

"I have as much desire to praise you as my mother," said Virginie "and I would perhaps do it in terms that would not dissonate the delicacy of your ears, but the passion that I have to read the tale that you have written imposes silence upon me."

"Ah, ah, Mademoiselle," said La Dandinardière, "you're going to spoil me if I'm not careful; the praises of a little crimson peck suffocate me."

"Don't fatigue yourself hearing it," added Marthonide, "A merit as splendid as yours is exposed to rude assaults."

"You overwhelm me with graces, charming persons," he cried. "In such circumstances, I can only respond by my silence, while Monsieur le Prieur de Richecourt reads my work. I made it what is called post-haste; it is necessary to know with what diligence I brocaded in that brushwood; I'm as ashamed of it as a dog."

"For an hour," said Madame de Saint-Thomas. I've been admiring the noble and easy expressions of which you make use; it must be admitted that people of the court have something that sets them above other mortals."

"Oh, Madame, said La Dandinardière, "There are courts and courts; the one in which I was brought up is so delicate that the slightest obscenity is not suffered there; anyone who committed a barbarity there would be proscribed; it is necessary to be purified or punctured."

Virginie, her sister and her mother would have let the invalid talk all day without interrupting him, so delighted were they by the grandiose verbiage that he was pronouncing, but a furious noise was suddenly heard in the courtyard; it was Alain who was bringing in a cart and three young donkeys laden with all his master's books; he was using his fists to batter the carter, whom he was accusing of having stolen a hymn-book. The peasant, indignant at the servant's injustice, was holding him by the hair, and on either side nothing could be seen but arms raised and lowered upon the faces or stomachs of the champions.

At that news, La Dandinardière jumped out of bed, enveloped in his sheet like a corpse; in that attire he ran to the window, delighted to see so much prowess on the part of his faithful Alain. Suddenly reflecting on the irregularity of his undress, however, he addressed himself to the ladies in order to make his apologies.

"I confess," he said to them, "that I have an inconvenient valor; it dominates me to such degree that I cannot hear the clash of weapons without being stirred; I have fought a hundred duels in my life, uniquely for the pleasure of clinking metal."

He was reasoning thus, with his sheet rather poorly wound around him, his turban askew and his feet bare, which he displayed without affectation, when Madame de Saint-Thomas begged him to go back to bed.

Someone was sent to separate Alain, who was already meditating an honorable retreat, because for every blow received the carter was giving him six, and in truth, he preferred his skin to all his master's books.

"Keep your hymn-book," he said to his adversary, "and let me go in peace."

"No," said the carter, "you have stolen my honor; unrob me, or you're dead."

The help that Madame de Saint-Thomas sent arrived them, just in time to remove him from the hands of the furious carter, but the dispute recommenced more heatedly when it was necessary to pay, for Alain, intent on his interests, wanted to withhold ten sols as compensation for the blows he had received, from which he was bleeding and which had blacked his eyes.

Finally, everything was pacified; the cart and the donkeys left, books remained piled up on the grass, and the rain was coming down so abundantly that whatever diligence could be employed to protect them, there was no means of saving them. La Dandinardière's regrets greatly amused those who knew how far his ignorance extended.

"Oh, my Greek texts!" he cried. "Dear delights of my solitude! Oh, my Hebrew books, of which I've commenced such an arduous translation! Oh, my Latin poets! Oh my algebra, all of you are drowned! If you had perished at sea or in the middle of a city on fire, or by some thunderbolt, your loss, being more honorable, would be less sensible to me, but by virtue of a wicked rain in the middle of a courtyard! No, I'll never be consoled for it."

Virginie, tenderly touched by the just dolor of the scholarly La Dandinardière, implored him to cease his plaints, unless he wanted to cause her death. She promised that everyone would occupy themselves in drying out the poor damp authors, and that enough would still remain to entertain him agreeably. Marthonide added further arguments to those of her sister.

The afflicted little man found that he would be wrong not to be consoled, since the most lovable young women in the universe were involved. He shook his head two or three times, saying: "Chagrin, black chagrin, I want you to dissipate." His turban fell off; he had a new chagrin in consequence; but in order to provide a diversion from so many subjects of pain, the prior demanded an audience with the entire company, in order to read the tale that he had mentioned to them. Everyone shut up, and he commenced thus.

THE PIGEON AND THE DOVE

There was once a king and a queen who loved one another so dearly that their union served as an example in all families, and it would have been very surprising to see a household in discord in their realm, which was known as the Realm of Deserts.

The queen had had several children, but the only one who remained was a daughter whose beauty was so great that if anything could console her for the loss of the others it was the charms that she observed in that one. The king and queen raised her as their unique hope, but the good fortune of the royal family did not last long. The king having gone hunting on an umbrageous horse, it heard a few shots fired; the noise and the fire frightened it, it took the bit between its teeth and departed like a flash of lightning; he tried to stop it on the edge of a precipice; it reared up and, having fallen on him, the impact was so rude that it killed him before anyone was able to help him.

News so catastrophic reduced the queen to the extremity, she was unable to moderate her grief; she sensed clearly that it was too violent to resist, and no longer thought about anything but putting order in her daughter's affairs in order to die with a sort of repose. She had a friend who was known as the Sovereign Fay because she had a great authority in all the empires and was very clever. She wrote to her, in a dying hand, that she wanted to render the last sigh in her arms; that she should hasten to come if she wanted to find her alive; and that she had things of consequence to tell her.

Although the fay had no shortage of affairs, she quit them all, and, mounting her chariot of fire, which went more rapidly than the sun, she arrived at the home of the queen, who was awaiting her impatiently. She talked to her about several things regarding the regency of the realm, begging her to accept it and to take care of little Princess Constancia.

"If anything," she added, "can soothe the anxiety I have in leaving her an orphan at such a tender age, it is the hope that you will give me in her person marks of the amity that you have always had for me; that she will find in you a mother who can render her happier and more perfect than I would have done; and that you will choose a husband for her lovable enough for her never to love anyone but him."

"You want all that it is necessary to want, great queen," the fay said to her. "I shall not neglect anything for your daughter, but I have drawn up her horoscope; it seems that destiny is irritated against nature for having exhausted all her treasures in forming her; it has resolved to make her suffer, and Your Royal Majesty must know that it sometimes pronounces sentences in such an absolute tone that it is impossible to avoid them."

"At the very least," said the queen, "soften her disgraces, and neglect nothing to thwart them; it often happens that great misfortunes can be avoided if one pays serious attention to them."

The Sovereign Fay promised everything that she wished, and the queen, having embraced her dear Constancia hundreds of times, died with sufficient tranquility.

The fay read the stars with the same facility that people read the new stories that are printed every day at present. She read that the princess was threatened by the fatal passion of a giant, whose estates were not very distant from the Realm of Deserts. She knew full well that it was necessary, above all, to avoid that, and she did not know any better way of doing so than to hide her dear ward at one of the ends of the earth, so far from the one where the giant reigned that there was no appearance that he would come there trouble her repose.

As soon as the Sovereign Fay had chosen ministers capable of governing the State that she wanted to confide to them, and had established laws so judicious that all the sages of Greece would have been unable to contrive anything approaching them, she went into Constancia's room one night, carried her away without waking her on her fiery camel, and then departed for a fertile land where people lived without ambition and without difficulty; it was a true Valley of Tempe; only shepherds and shepherdesses were found there, who lived in cabins of which each of them was the architect.

She was not unaware that if the princess reached sixteen years of age without seeing the giant, she would only have to return in triumph to her realm, but that if she saw him before then she would be exposed to great troubles. She was very careful to hide her from everyone's eyes, and in order for her to appear less beautiful, she had dressed her as a shepherdess, with an elaborate head-dress always lowered over her face. Such was the sunlight, however, enveloped in a cloud perceived by long shafts of sunlight, that the charming princess could not be so well covered that her beauty was not sometimes perceived, and in spite of all the fay's cares, Constancia was only talked about as a masterpiece of the heavens who stole all hearts.

Her beauty was not the only thing that rendered her marvelous; Sovereign had endowed her with a voice so admirable, and she played all instruments that she wanted to play so well that without having learned music, she could have given lessons to the muses, and even to celestial Apollo. Thus, she was not bored. The fay had explained to her the reasons she had for raising her in such obscure conditions. As she was full of intelligence, she entered into it with so much judgment that Sovereign was astonished that so much docility and intellect could be found at an age so little advanced.

It had been several months since she had been to the Realm of Deserts because she only quit her with difficulty, but her presence was necessary there; people only acted on her orders, and the ministers were not equally aware of their duty. She departed, recommending strongly that she shut herself away until she returned.

That beautiful princess had a little sheep that she loved dearly; she amused herself making garlands of flowers for him; at other times she covered him with knotted ribbons. She had named him Ruson. He was cleverer than all his comrades; he understood the voice and he orders of his mistress and obeyed her punctually. "Ruson," she said to him, "go and fetch my distaff." He ran to her room and brought it, making a thousand bounds. He jumped around her, no longer ate herbs except those she had picked, and would have died of thirst rather than drink elsewhere than from the hollow of her hand. He was able to close the door, beat the measure when she sang, and bleat in cadence. Ruson was lovable, and was loved; Constancia talked to him incessantly and made him a thousand caresses.

However, a pretty ewe in the vicinity pleased Ruson at least as much as his princess. Every sheep is a sheep, and the paltriest ewe was more beautiful in Ruson's eyes than the mother of the amours. Constancia often reproached him for his coquetries. "Little libertine," she said, "aren't you able to stay with me? You are so dear to me, I neglect my entire flock for you, but you don't want to leave that wretched ewe to please me. She attached him with a chain of flowers; then he seemed to become chagrined and pulled so hard that he broke it.

"Ah," Constancia said to him, angrily, "the fay has told me many a time that men are as willful as you, that they flee the slightest subjugation and that they're the most mutinous of animals. Since you resemble them, wicked Ruson, go seek out your beautiful ewe; if the wolf eats you, you'll be well eaten; I probably won't be able to help you.

The amorous sheep did not profit from Constancia's advice. He was with his dear ewe every day, near the small house where the princess as working all alone. One day, she heard him bleating so loudly and piteously that she had no doubt of his fatal adventure. She got up, very emotionally, went out, and saw a wolf that was carrying off poor Ruson.

She no longer thought about everything the fay had said to her when she left; she ran after the abductor of her sheep, crying "Wolf! Wolf!" She followed it, throwing stones at it with her crook, without making it release its prey; but alas, as it passed close to a bush, another wolf emerged therefrom; it was a horrible giant.

At the sight of that frightful colossus, the princess, paralyzed by fear, raised her eyes to the heavens to ask for help, and begged the earth to swallow her up. Neither the heavens not the earth listened to her; she merited punishment for not having believed the Sovereign Fay.

The giant opened his arms wide to prevent her from getting away, but, terrible and furious as he was, he felt the effects of her beauty.

"What rank do you hold among the goddesses?" he said to her, in a voice that made more noise than thunder. "For I don't think that I'm mistaken: you're not a mortal. Only tell me your name, and whether you're a daughter or a wife of Jupiter? Who are your brothers? What are your sisters? For a long time I've been searching for a goddess in order to marry her, and here you are, fortunately found."

The princess felt that fear had tied her tongue, and that the words were dying in her mouth.

As he saw that she was not responding to his gallant questions, he said: "For a divinity, you're not very intelligent." Without further discourse, he opened a large sack and threw her inside.

The first thing she perceived in the depths of the sack was the wicked wolf and the poor sheep. The giant had amused himself by caching them on the run. "You're going to die with me, my dear Ruson," she said, kissing him. "It's a small consolation; it would be better if we could escape together."

That sad thought made her weep bitterly; she sighed and sobbed loudly; Ruson bleated; the wolf howled. That woke up a dog, a cat, a cock and a parrot, which were asleep. They commenced for their part to make a desperate racket; there was a strange charivari in the giant's sack.

Finally, tired of hearing them, he thought about killing them all, but he contented himself with tying the sack and throwing it to the top of a tall tree, after having marked it in order to come back and collect it; he was on his way to fight a duel with another giant, and all that screeching displeased him.

The princess suspected that although he was walking he was covering a long distance, for a galloping horse could not have overtaken him when he was ambling. She took out her scissors and cut the canvas of the sack; then she brought out her dear Ruson, the dog, the cat, the cock, and the parrot; then she ran away, and left the wolf inside, to teach him to eat little sheep.

The night was very dark; it was a strange thing to find oneself alone in the middle of a forest without knowing which way to direct one's footsteps, unable to see either the sky or the ground, and always dreading the return of the giant.

She walked as rapidly as she could; she would have fallen hundreds of times, but all the animals she had rescued, grateful for the favor they had received from her, did not want to abandon her, and served her usefully in her journey. The cat had eyes so glittering that it illuminated the way like a torch; the yapping dog played sentinel; the cock crowed in order to frighten the lions; the parrot chattered so loudly that one might have thought, on hearing it, that twenty people were conversing together, with the result that thieves drew away to leave the way clear for our beautiful traveler, and the sheep, which walked a few paces ahead of her, protected her from falling into deep holes, from which it had trouble getting out itself.

Constancia went at hazard, recommending herself to her good friend the fay, from whom she hoped for some help, although she reproached herself abundantly for not having followed her orders. She would have liked her good fortune to take her back to the house where she had been secretly brought up, but as she did not know the way, she dared not flatter herself that she might encounter it without being particularly lucky.

At daybreak she found herself on the bank of a river that irrigated the most beautiful meadow in the world. She looked around, and did not see any dog, cat, cock or parrot; only Ruson was keeping her company.

"Alas, where am I?" she said. "I don't know this beautiful place; what will become of me? Oh, little sheep, how dearly you've cost me. If I hadn't run after you, I'd still be in the house of the Sovereign Fay; I wouldn't have to fear the giant or any other nasty adventure."

It seemed, to judge by Rison's attitude, that he was listening to her tremulously, and that he recognized his fault. In the end, the princess, dejected and fatigued, stopped scolding him; she sat down on the water's edge, and as she was weary and the shade of several trees shielded her from the ardor of the sun, her eyes closed slowly. She let herself fall on to the grass and slipped into a profound slumber.

She had no other guards than the faithful Ruson; he marched over her; he nudged her; but what was her astonishment to see, twenty paces away from her, a young man who was hiding behind some bushes? He was covering himself with them in order to look at her without being seen. The beauty of his figure, that of his face, the nobility of his appearance and the magnificence of his clothing surprised the princess so much that she got up abruptly, with the intention of running away. Some secret charm stopped her; she darted a fearful glance at the unknown man; he frightened her almost as much as the giant, but the fear departed from different causes; their expressions and their actions marked well enough the sentiments that they already had for one another.

Perhaps they would have remained a long time without speaking, except with their eyes, if the prince had not heard the sound of horns and that of dogs drawing nearer. He perceived that she was astonished by it. "Have no fear, beautiful shepherdess," he said to her, "You are safe in this place. I wish to heaven that those who see you could say the same!"

"Sire," she said, "I implore your protection; I am a poor orphan who cannot do anything other than be a shepherdess; procure me a flock; I will guard it with great care."

"Fortunate sheep," he said, smiling, "that you lead to pasture! But in sum, amiable shepherdess, if you wish, I will speak to my mother, the queen, about it, and I shall make it a pleasure to commence to render you my services today."

"Oh, Sire," said Constancia, "I beg your pardon for the liberty I am taking; I would not have dared to do it had I know your rank."

The prince listened to her with the utmost astonishment; he found that she had intelligence and politeness; nothing responded better to her excellent beauty, but nothing accorded more poorly with the simplicity of her clothing and her profession of shepherdess. He even wanted to enable her to make another decision. "Have you thought," he said, "about what you are risking, all alone in a wood or a meadow, having no company but your innocent ewes? Are the delicate manners that I remark in you adapted to solitude? Who can tell, besides, whether the rumor of your charms, which will spread through the region, will not attract a thousand importunate individuals to you? I myself, adorable shepherdess, would quit the court to attach myself to your footsteps, and what I would do, others will do also."

"Cease, Sire, to flatter me with praise that I do not merit," she said. "I was born in a hamlet; I have never known anything but rural life, and I hope that you will let me guard the queen's flock tranquilly, if she deigns to confide them to me. I will even beg her to put me under some shepherdess more experienced than I am, and as I would not quit her, it is certain that I would not be bored."

The prince could not respond; those who had followed him hunting appeared on a hill. "I'll leave you, charming person," he said, hastily. "It's not necessary that so many people share he god fortune that I have of seeing you. Go to the end of this meadow; there is a house there where you can live in safety after you have said that you have come on my part."

Constancia, who would have had difficulty finding herself in such a large company, hastened to walk toward the place that Constancio—that was the name of the prince—had indicated to her.

He followed her with his eyes; he sighed tenderly and, mounting his horse again, he put himself at the head of his troop without continuing the hunt.

When he went into the queen's apartment he found her very irritated against an old shepherdess who had rendered her a bad account of her lambs. After the queen had scolded her, she told her never to appear before her again. That opportunity favored Constancio's design. He told her that he had encountered a young woman who desired passionately to be in her service, that she had a neat appearance and did not appear to be interested. The queen liked what her son said; she accepted the shepherdess before having seen her and told the prince to give the order that she be taken to the crown pasturelands with the others.

He was delighted that she was dispensed from coming to the palace; certain urgent and jealous sentiments made him dread rivals, although there was no one who could dispute anything with him, either with regard to rank or merit; it is true that he feared great lords less than petty individuals, because he thought that she might have more inclination for a simple shepherd than a prince who was so close to the throne.

It would be difficult to recount all the reflections by which that one was followed; with what did he not reproach his heart, having not loved anyone until now and not having found any person worthy of him. He was giving himself to a young woman of birth so obscure that he could not even confess his passion without blushing; he tried to combat it, and, persuading himself that absence was an infallible remedy, particularly for a nascent tenderness, he avoided seeing the shepherdess again.

He followed his penchant for hunting and gambling; wherever he perceived sheep, he turned away as if he had encountered snakes, with the consequence that in a short time, the arrow that had wounded him seemed less sensible. But on one of the most ardent days of a heat-wave, Constancio, fatigued by a long hunt, finding himself on the edge of the river, followed its course into the shade of service trees that intermingled their branches with those of willows and rendered the spot as cool as it was agreeable. A profound reverie surprised him; he thought he was alone and was no longer thinking about the people who were waiting for him when he was suddenly struck by the charming tones of a voice that seemed to him to be celestial. He stopped to listen, and was not a little surprised to hear these words:

Alas, I had promised to live without ardor;
But Amour takes pleasure in rendering me perjured;
I feel myself torn by a painful wound,
Constancio has become the master of my heart.
The other day I saw him in this solitude,
Fatigued by the labor he finds in this forest;
He sang his anxiety,
Sitting under this cool shade.
Never was anything so handsome offered to my sight;
I remained still and bewildered for a long time;
From the hand of Amour I saw arrows depart.
Which I bear in the depths of my soul.
The hurt that I feel has too many charms;
I see by the ardor that inflames me,
That I shall never be cured of it.

His curiosity prevailed over the pleasure he had in hearing such fine singing; He advanced diligently; the name Constancio had struck him, for it was his own, although a shepherd might bear it as well as a prince, and thus he did not know whether it was for him or another that the words had been made.

He had scarcely climbed in to a small eminence covered in trees than he perceived the beautiful Constancia at the foot;

she was sitting on the edge of a stream, the precipitate fall of which made a sound so agreeable that it seemed to want to accord with his voice. Her faithful sheep, lying on the grass, was stationed like a favorite, much closer to her than the others. From time to time Constancia gave him little taps with her crook, and caressed him childishly, and every time she touched him he kissed her hand and looked at her with eyes full of intelligence.

"Oh, how fortunate you are!" the prince whispered. *If you knew the value of the caresses you're making! What! That shepherdess is even more beautiful than when I encountered her! Amour, Amour, what do you want of me? Must I love her—or rather, am I still in a state to forbid myself to do so? I've avoided her carefully because I sensed all the danger there is in seeing her; what impressions, great gods, those first movements have made in me! My reason tried to help me; I fled such a lovable object; alas I've found her, but the one of whom she speaks is the fortunate shepherd she has chosen!*

While he was reasoning thus, the shepherdess stood up in order to reassemble her flock and go to another part of the meadow where she had left her companions. The prince feared losing the opportunity to talk to her. He advanced toward her in an urgent manner.

"Lovely shepherdess," he said, "Would you object if I asked you whether the small service I rendered you has given you some pleasure?"

At the sight of him, Constancia blushed; her complexion seemed animated by the most vivid colors. "Sire," she said, "I would have taken care to come and render you my very humble thanks if it had been appropriate for a poor girl like me to make any to a prince like you; but although I have failed, Heaven is my witness that I am not ingrate, and I pray to the gods to fill your days with good fortune."

"Constancia," he replied, "if it is true that my good intentions have touched you to the extent that you say, it is easy for you to mark it to me."

"Oh? What can I do for you, Sire?" she replied, hastily.

"You can tell me," he added, "to whom the words refer that you just sang."

"As I did not make them," she replied, "it would be difficult for me to tell you anything about that."

While she was speaking he examined her; he saw her blush; she was embarrassed and kept her eyes lowered.

"Why hide your sentiments from me, Constancia?" he said to her. "Your face betrays the secret of your heart. You are in love?" He fell silent, and looked at her again with more application.

"Sire," she said, "the things in which I have an interest merit so little that a great prince should ask about them, and I am so accustomed to keeping silence with my dear ewes, that I beg you to pardon me if I do not reply to your questions."

She drew away so quickly that he did not have time to stop her.

Jealousy sometimes serves as a torch to reignite amour; the prince's gripped him at that moment with so much force that it was never extinguished; he found a thousand new graces in the young woman that he had not remarked the first time he saw her; the manner in which she quit him made him believe, as much as her words, that she was prejudiced for some shepherd. A profound sadness took possession of his soul. He dared not follow her, even though he had an extreme desire to converse with her. He lay down in the same place that she had just quit, and after trying to remember the words she had just sung, he wrote them in his notepad and examined hem attentively.

It is only a few days, he said to himself, *since she has seen the Constancio who is occupying her. Is it necessary that I am named like him and am so far away from his good fortune? How coldly she looked at me! She appeared more indifferent today than when I encountered her for the first time; her greatest care was to seek a pretext to draw away from me.*

Those thoughts afflicted him sensibly, because he could not understand how a simple shepherdess could be so indifferent to a great prince.

As soon as he returned, he summoned a young fellow who was involved in all his pleasures; he had birth, he was likeable. He ordered him to dress as a shepherd, to obtain a flock and to take it every day to the queen's pasturelands in order to see what Constancia was doing, without him being suspect. Mirtain—that was his name—had too much desire to please his master to neglect an occasion that seemed to interest him; he promised to acquit his orders very well, and the next day he was in a state to go into the plain. The man who took him would not have received him had he not shown him an order from the prince saying that he was his shepherd and had charge of his sheep.

Immediately, he was allowed to join the rural troop; he was gallant, he had no difficulty pleasing he shepherdesses, but with regard to Constancia he found her with a proud attitude so far above what she appeared to be that he could not accord so much beauty, intelligence and merit with the rustic country life that she led. He followed her in vain; he always found her alone in the depths of the woods, singing in a preoccupied fashion. He did not see any shepherds who dared attempt to please her; the thing seemed too difficult. Mirtain attempted that great adventure, rendered himself assiduous in her regard, and knew from his own experience that she did not want any engagement.

He rendered a account every evening to the prince of the situation of things; everything he told him only served to make him despair.

"Make no mistake, Sire," he said to him one day, "that beautiful girl is in love; it must be that he is in her homeland."

"If that were so," said the prince, "wouldn't she want to return?"

"How do we know," added Mirtain, "whether she might have some reason that prevents her returning to her homeland? Perhaps she's angry with her lover?"

"Oh," cried the prince, "She sings the words that I heard too tenderly."

"It's true," Mirtain continued, "that all the trees are covered with the initials of their names, and since nothing pleases her here, doubtless something elsewhere has pleased her."

"Test her sentiments for me," said the prince. "Speak well of me, speak ill of me; you'll know what she thinks."

Mirtain did not fail to seek an opportunity to speak to Constancia. "What's the matter, lovely shepherdess?" he said to her. "You seem melancholy, in spite of all the reasons you have for being more cheerful than another."

"What subjects of joy do you think I have?" she said. "I'm reduced to guarding sheep; far from my homeland; I have no news of my parents; is all that very agreeable?"

"No," he replied, "but you are the most amiable person in the world, you have much intelligence, you sing in a delightful manner and nothing can equal your beauty."

"If I possessed all those advantages, they would mean little to me," she said, uttering a profound sigh.

"So you have ambition," added Mirtain. "You think it is necessary to be born on a throne with the blood of the gods in order to live content? Oh, disabuse yourself of that error; I belong to Prince Constancio, and in spite of the inequality of our conditions, I nevertheless approach him sometimes; I study him, I penetrate what is happening in his soul, and I know that he is not happy."

"Oh! What troubles his repose?" said the princess.

"A fatal passion," continued Mirtain.

"He is in love," she said, anxiously. "Alas how I pity him—but what am I saying?" she continued, blushing. "He is too amiable not to be loved."

"He dare not flatter himself with that, beautiful shepherdess," he said, "And if you wanted to put him in repose in that matter, he would add more faith to your words than those of any other."

"It is not appropriate," she said, "for me to mingle in the affairs of such a great prince. Those of which you speak are too private for me to think of entering into them. Adieu, Mirtain," she added, quitting him abruptly. "If you want to oblige me, don't talk to me again about your prince or his amours."

She drew away, very emotional. She had not been indifferent to the merit of the prince; the first moment she had seen him was no longer effaced from her thought, and without the secret charm that stopped her, it is certain that she would have attempted everything to find the Sovereign Fay again.

It might seem astonishing, in fact, that that clever individual, who knew everything, had not come in search of her, but that no longer depended on her. As soon as the giant had encountered the princess, she was submissive to fortune for a certain time; it was necessary that her destiny be accomplished, with the result that the fay was content to come and see her in a ray of sunlight; Constancia's eyes could not look at it intently enough to perceive her within it.

That lovable individual had perceived, with chagrin, that the prince had neglected her greatly, that he would not have seen her again if hazard had not brought him to the place where she was singing; she wished a mortal harm upon the sentiments that she had for him, and if it is possible to love and hate at the same time, I can say that she hated him because she loved him too much. How many tears she shed in secret! Only Ruson witnessed them; she often confided her troubles to him as if he were capable of understanding them, and when he bounded in the meadow with the ewes she shouted: "Be careful Ruson, be careful that amour does not inflame you; of all misfortunes, that is the greatest, and if you loved without being loved, poor little sheep, what would you do?"

Those reflections were followed by a thousand reproaches that she made herself regarding her sentiments for an indifferent prince; she had had a great desire to forget him, when she found him, having stopped in an agreeable place to dream with more liberty about the shepherdess who fled him. Finally, overcome by sleep, she lay down in the grass; she saw him, and her inclination for him took on new force; she had not been able to prevent herself from making the words that had given rise to so much disquiet on the part of the prince. But with what annoyance was she not struck in her turn when Mirtain told her that Constancio was in love? Whatever attention she paid to herself, she had not been able to help changing color several times.

Mirtain, who had his reasons for studying her, had noticed that; he was delighted by it, and ran to render an account to his master of what had happened.

The prince was far less disposed to flatter himself than his confidant was. He believed that he could only see indifference in the behavior of the shepherdess, and he blamed for that the fortunate Constancio whom she loved. The next day he went to look for her.

As soon as she perceived him, she fled as if he were a tiger or a lion; flight was the only remedy she could imagine for her ills. Since her conversation with Mirtain she understood that she must not neglect anything to uproot him from her heart, and that the best means of succeeding in that was to avoid him.

What became of Constancio when the shepherdess drew away so abruptly? Mirtain was with him. "You see," he said to him. "You see the fortunate effect of your cares? Constancia hates me, and I dare not follow her in order to enlighten myself as to her sentiments."

"You have too much concern for such a rustic young woman," Mirtain replied, "and if you wish, Sire, I'll order you on your part to come to find you"

"Oh, Mirtain," cried the prince, "what a difference there is between the lover and the confidant! I only think of pleasing that lovable young woman. I have found a sort of politeness in her that would not accommodate that abrupt manner that you want to take; I consent to suffer rather than cause her chagrin." As he finished speaking he went in another direction, which might have caused pity in a person less touched that Constancia.

As soon as she had lost sight of him she retraced her steps, in order to have the pleasure of being in the place that he had just quit. *It's here*, she said to herself, *that he stopped; it's there that he looked at me; but alas, in all these places, he only has indifference for me; he comes here in order to dream at liberty of the person he loves, However*, she continued, *have I any reason to complain? By what hazard would he attach himself to a young woman he believes to be so far below him?*

Sometimes, she wanted to tell him about her adventures, but the Sovereign Fay had forbidden her so absolutely to talk about them that for now, her obedience prevailed over her own interests and she made the resolution to remain silent.

After a few days the prince came back again; she avoided him carefully; he was afflicted by that and charged Mirtain to reproach her for it. She pretended not to have made any reflection on the matter, but said that since he deigned to mention it, she would be more careful.

Mirtain, content to have extracted that promise from her, informed his mater of it. The next day, he went to find her.

When he approached, she seemed nonplussed; when he spoke to her about his sentiments, she was even more so; whatever desire she had to believe him, she feared being deceived, and that, judging her by what he saw, perhaps he wanted to make a pleasure of dazzling her with a declaration that was inappropriate to a poor shepherdess. That thought irritated her, she seemed prouder in consequence, and received the assurances that he gave her of his passion so coldly that it confirmed all his suspicions.

"You are touched," he said to her. "Another has been able to charm you, but the gods are my witnesses that if I knew who he is, he would experience all my wrath."

"I do not ask you for mercy for anyone, Sire," she replied. "If you are ever informed of my sentiments you will find them very different from those you attribute to me."

At those words the prince recovered some hope, but it was soon destroyed by the continuation of their conversation, for she protested that she had an invincible depth of indifference and that she felt strongly that she would never love as long as she lived. The last words would have thrown him into an inconceivable dolor, but he constrained himself in order not to show her the extent of his distress.

Either because of the effort he had made or the excess of his passion, which had taken on new force because of the difficulties he envisaged, he fell so dangerously ill that the physicians, knowing nothing of the cause of his malady, soon despaired of his life.

Mirtain, who had remained close to Constancia on his orders, told her the bad news; she heard it with a trouble and emotion difficult to describe.

"Do you not know some remedy," he said to her, "for fever and great aches of the head and the heart?"

"I know one," she said. "There are simples with flowers; everything consists of the manner of applying them."

"Will you not come to the palace for that?" he added.

"No," she said blushing. "I would be too fearful of not succeeding."

"What! You could neglect something to render him to us?" he continued. "I thought you very harsh, but you are a hundred times more so than I imagined."

Mirtain's reproaches gave Constancia pleasure; she was delighted that he pressed her to see the prince; it was only to procure herself that satisfaction that she had boasted of knowing a remedy appropriate to soothe him, for the truth is that she did not know any.

Mirtain went to him; he told him what the shepherdess had said, and with what ardor she wished for the return of his health.

"You're seeking to flatter me," Constancio said to him, "but I forgive you for it, and I would like, even if I were mistaken, to think that that beautiful young woman has some amity for me. Go and see the queen, tell her that one of her shepherdesses has a marvelous secret, that she might cure me, obtain permission to bring her. Run, fly, Mirtain; the moment will seem like centuries to me."

The queen had not yet seen the shepherdess when Mirtain went to speak to her; she said that she had no faith in what ignorant girls thought they knew and that it was a folly.

"Certainly, Madame," he said, "one can sometimes find more relief in simples than in all the books of Aesculapius. The prince is suffering so much that he wants to test what this young woman proposes."

"All right," said the queen, "but if she does not cure him, I shall treat her so rudely that she will no longer have the audacity to boast inappropriately."

Mirtain returned to his master; he gave him an account of the queen's ill humor and said that he feared its effects for Constancia."

"I would rather die," cried the prince. "Go back and tell my mother that I beg her to leave that beautiful young woman with her innocent ewes. What payment," he continued, "for the trouble she would take! I sense that that idea redoubles my illness."

Mirtain ran to the queen and told her on the prince's part not to send for Constancia; but as she was naturally quick-tempered she was angered by his irresolution.

"I've sent someone to fetch her," she said. "If she cures my son, I'll give her something; if she doesn't cure him, I do what I have to do. Return to him and try to divert him. He's in a melancholy that desolates me."

Mirtain obeyed her, and refrained from telling his master about the ill humor in which he had found her, for he might have died of anxiety for the shepherdess.

The royal pasturelands were so close to the city that she did not take long to arrive, also given the fact that she was guided by a passion that ordinarily causes great speed. When she reached the palace, the queen was informed but did not deign to see her, she contented herself with sending word to her to be careful of what she was about to attempt; that if she failed to cure the prince she would be sown into a sack and thrown in the river.

At that threat the beautiful princess went pale and her blood ran cold. *Alas*, she said to herself, *that punishment is my due; I told a lie when I boasted of having some science, and my desire to see Constancio is not reasonable enough for the gods to protect me.* She lowered her head meekly, letting her tears flow without responding.

Those who were around her admired her; she appeared to them to be a daughter of the heavens rather than a mortal. "Of what are you afraid, lovely shepherdess," they said to her. "You bear life and death in your eyes; a single glance from you might conserve our young prince; come into his room, wipe away your tears, and employ your remedies without dread,"

The manner in which they spoke to her, and the extreme desire she had to see him gave her some return of confidence; she asked that she be allowed to go into the garden in order to collect what she needed herself. She took myrtle, clover, herbs and flowers, some dedicated to Cupid, others to her mother, the feathers of a dove and a few drops of the blood of a pigeon; she called to her aid all the deities and all the fays. Then, more tremulous than a turtle-dove when it sees a merlin, she said that she could be taken to the prince's room.

He was lying down; his face was pale and his eyes languid, but as soon as he saw her he took on a better color; she remarked that with an extreme joy.

"Sire," she said to him, "it is already several days since I said prayers for the return of your health; my zeal even engaged me to tell one of your shepherds that I knew some petty remedies and would gladly try to relieve you, but the queen has commanded that if Heaven abandons me in this enterprise, she wants me to be drowned if you are not cured. Judge, Sire, the alarm that I am in, and be persuaded that I am more interested in your conservation for your sake than my own."

"Have no fear charming shepherdess," he said to her, "the favorable wishes you make for my life will render it so dear to me that I shall be very seriously occupied with it. I neglected my days alas! Can I be happy when I remember what I heard you sing for Constancio? Those fatal words and your coldness have reduced me to the sad state in which you see me; but beautiful shepherdess, you order me to live, so we shall live, and only live for you."

Constancia only hid with difficulty the pleasure that such an obliging declaration caused her; however, as she feared that someone might be listening to what the prince said, she asked him for permission to put in a headband and bracelets the herbs that she had collected. He held out his arms in such a tender manner that she promptly attached one of the bracelets, for fear that someone might penetrate what was happening between them. After having made little ceremonies to impose on all the prince's court, he shouted after a few moments that his illness was diminishing.

That was true, as he said it. His physicians were summoned; they were surprised by the excellence of a remedy whose effects were so prompt, but when they saw the shepherdess that had applied it, they were no longer astonished by anything and said in their jargon that one of her glances was more powerful than all of pharmacy combined.

The shepherdess was so unaffected by the praise that was given to her that those who did not know her mistook for stupidity what had a very different source. She stationed herself in a corner of the room, hiding from everyone except her patient, whom she approached from time to time in order to touch his head or his pulse, and in those brief moments they said a thousand pretty things in which the heart had far more part than the mind.

"I hope, Sire," she said to him, "that the sack the queen has had made in order to drown me, will not serve for such a deadly purpose. Your health, which is precious to me, will be reestablished."

"It will only depend on you, lovely Constancia," he replied. "A small place in your heart can do everything for me repose and the conservation of my life."

The prince got up and went to the queen's apartment. When she was told that he had come in, she did not want to believe it. She advanced abruptly and was very surprised to see him at the door of her bedroom.

"What! It's you, my son, my dear son!" she cried. "To what do I owe a resurrection so marvelous?"

"To your generosity, Madame," he said. "You sent for the cleverest person in the world for me; I beg you to recompense her in a manner proportionate to the service I have received from her."

"That isn't urgent," replied the queen, rudely. "She's a poor shepherdess, who will deem herself fortunate to keep guarding my sheep."

At that moment the king arrived; someone had gone to tell him the good news of the prince's cure, and when he went to the queen's apartment the first thing that struck his eyes was Constancia; her beauty, like the sun that burns with a thousand fires, dazzled him to such a degree that for a few seconds he was unable to ask those who were nearby what he saw that was so marvelous, and since when had goddesses been resident in his palace, Eventually, he collected himself, approached her, and, informed that she was the enchantress who has cured his son, he embraced her and said gallantly that he found himself very ill and implored her to cure him too.

He went in, and she followed him. The queen had not yet seen her; her astonishment was indescribable; she uttered a great cry and fell in a faint, darting furious glances at the shepherdess. Constancio and Constancia were frightened by that. The king did not know to what to attribute such a sudden illness, and the entire court was consternated.

Eventually, the queen recovered consciousness. The king asked her several times what she had seen that had distressed her so much. She dissimulated her anxiety and said that it was the vapors, but the prince, who knew her well, remained very anxious about it. She spoke to the shepherdess with a sort of generosity, saying that she wanted to keep her with her, in order to take care of her flower garden.

The princess felt joy, thinking that she would be in a place where she would be able to see Constancio every day.

However, the king obliged the queen to go into her cabinet. He asked her tenderly what could have caused her chagrin. "Oh, sire," she cried, "I have had a terrible dream. I had never seen that shepherdess when my imagination represented her to me so clearly that, on casting my eyes on her face, I recognized her. She married my son; I'm mistaken if that wretched peasant is not going to give me great pain."

"You are adding too much faith to the most uncertain thing in the world," the king told her. "I advise you not to act on such principles; send the shepherdess back to guard your flocks and don't afflict yourself so inappropriately."

The king's advice annoyed the queen; far from following it, she only applied herself to penetrating her son's sentiments for Constancia.

The prince took advantage of every opportunity to see her. As she was caring for flowers she was often in the garden, watering them, and it seemed that when she had touched them they were more brilliant and more beautiful for it. Ruson kept her company; she sometimes spoke to him about the prince, although he could not reply to her, and when the prince approached her she was so nonplussed that her eyes revealed the secret of her heart sufficiently. He was delighted by it, and said to her everything that the most tender passion can inspire.

Because of her faith in her dream, and even more because of Constancia's incomparable beauty, the queen could no longer sleep peacefully. She got up before daybreak; she hid behind palisades, and sometime in the depths of a grotto, in order to hear what her son was saying to the beautiful young woman, but they both took the precaution of speaking so quietly that she could only act on her suspicions. She was even more anxious by virtue of that; she only looked at the prince with scorn, thinking day and night that the shepherdess might mount the throne.

Constancio monitored himself as much as was possible, although, in spite of that, everyone perceived that he loved

Constancia, and that whether he praised her, by virtue of the habit he had of admiring her, or deliberately criticized her, he did both like an interested man. For her part, Constancia could not help speaking about the prince to her companions; as she often sang the words she had made for him, the queen, who heard them, was no less surprised by her marvelous voice than by the subject of her poetry.

"What have I done to you, just gods," she said, "for you to want to punish me by means of the thing in the world that is most sensible to me? Alas, I destined my son for my niece, and I see, with mortal pleasure, that he is attaching himself to a miserable shepherdess, who might render him rebellious to my will."

While she was afflicted, and she was making a thousand furious plans to punish Constancia for being so beautiful and charming, Amour was incessantly making further progress on the young lovers. Constancia, convinced of the prince's sincerity, could not hide from him the grandeur of her birth and her sentiments for him. A confession so tender and a confidence so particular delighted him to such a point that in any other place than the queen's garden he would have throw himself at her feet to thank her for it. It was only with difficulty that he prevented himself; he no longer wanted to combat his passion; he had loved Constancia as a shepherdess, so it is easy to believe that he adored her when she was his own rank, and if he had no difficulty in allowing himself to be persuaded of such a extraordinary thing as seeing a great princess adrift in the world, sometimes a shepherdess and sometimes a gardener, that is because those sorts of adventures were quite common in those days, and he found in her appearance and manners a guarantee of the sincerity of what she said.

Touched by amour and esteem, Constancio swore an eternal fidelity to the princess; she swore no less to him for her part; they promised to marry as soon as they had obtained agreement to their marriage from the persons of whom they depended.

The queen perceived all the force of that nascent passion. Her confidante, who strove no less than she did to discover something, in order to pay her court, came to tell her one day that Constancia sent Ruson to the prince's apartment every morning; that the little sheep carried two baskets; that she filled them with flowers; and that Mirtain conducted him. At that news, the queen lost patience; when poor Ruson passed by she waited for him herself, and, in spite of Mirtain's pleas, she took him into her room, tore the baskets and flowers apart, and searched so hard that she found a little piece in a large carnation that was not yet in blossom which Constancia had slipped into it very skillfully.

She made tender reproaches to the prince for the perils to which he exposed himself almost every day while hunting. Her note contained these lines:

> *Amid all my pleasures I experience alarms;*
> *Every day, my prince, you hunt in those places.*
> *Heaven! Where can you find charms*
> *To follow the furious guests of the forest?*
> *Rather turn your arms instead*
> *Toward tender hearts that cede to your thrusts,*
> *Avoid the anger of lions and bears.*

While the queen, was carried away with rage against the shepherdess, Mirtain had gone to tell his master about the sheep's misadventure. The anxious prince ran to his mother's apartment, but she had already gone to see the king.

"Look, Sire," she said. "See the noble inclinations of your son. He loves that miserable shepherdess who persuaded us that she knew remedies to cure him. Alas, she knew them only too well. In fact," she continued, "it's Amour who instructed her; she has only returned him to health in order to do him greater harm, and if we don't prevent the misfortunes that threaten us, my dream will be only too veritable."

"You're naturally rigorous," the king said to her, "you'd like your son only to think about the princess you destined for him. The thing isn't easy; it's necessary that you have a little indulgence for his age."

"I can't suffer your prejudice in her favor," cried the queen. "You can never criticize him. All that I ask of you, Sire, is to consent that I send him away for some time. Absence will have more power than all my arguments."

The king liked peace, he lent his hand to what the queen desired, and she returned to her apartment immediately.

She found the prince there, waiting for her with the utmost anxiety. "My son," she said to him, "the king has just shown me letters from his brother; he implores him to send you to his court, in order for you to get to know the princess destined for you since your childhood, and for her to get to know you. Is it not just that you judge her merit for yourself, and that you love her before being united forever?"

"I ought not to want particular rules for me, Madame," the prince said. "It is not the custom for sovereigns to go to one another's homes and that they consult their hearts rather than the reasons of State that engage them to make an alliance. The person whom you destine for me might be beautiful or ugly, intelligent or stupid, and I would obey you no less."

"I understand you, scoundrel," cried the queen, suddenly exploding. "I understand you; you adore an unworthy shepherdess, you fear quitting her. You will quit her, or I shall have her put to death before your eyes. But if you depart without hesitation, and strive to forget her, I will keep her with me and love her as much as I hate her."

The prince, as pale as if he were on the point of losing his life, consulted his intelligence as to what decision he ought to make. He could only see frightful penalties on either side; he knew that his mother was the cruelest and most vindictive princess in the world, he feared that resistance might irritate her and that his dear mistress might feel the repercussions. Finally, pressed to say that he would leave, he consented to do so, like a man consenting to drink a glass of poison that will kill him.

He has scarcely given his word than, leaving his mother's chamber he went to his own, his heart so constricted that he nearly died. He recounted his affliction to the faithful Mirtain, and in his impatience to make Constancia party to it, he went to find her.

She was in the depths of a grotto, into which she went when the ardor of the sun burned her in the flower garden. There was a little bed of grass there at the edge of a stream, which fell from the height of a rock-face. In that peaceful place she undid the braids of her hair; it was a silvery blonde, finer than silk, ad wavy; she put her bare feet in the water, the agreeable murmur of which, combined with the fatigue of labor, delivered her insensibly to the sweetness of slumber. Although her eyes were closed, they conserved a thousand attractions; long black lashes made all the whiteness of her complexion stand out; graces and amours seemed to be assembled around her, modesty and mildness augmented her beauty.

It was in that place that the amorous prince found her; he remembered that she had also been sleep the first time he had seen her, but the sentiments she had inspired in him since had become so tender that he would gladly have given half his life to spend the other half with her. He looked at her for some time with a pleasure that suspended his vexations; then, scanning her beauties, he perceived her foot, whiter than snow; he could not weary of admiring her, and, approaching her, he knelt down and took her hand. She woke up immediately, and seemed annoyed that he had seen her foot. She hid it, and blushed like a red rose blooming at the break of dawn.

Alas, that lovely color did not last long; she remarked a new sadness in the prince's face. "What's wrong, Sire?" she said, frightened. "I see in your eyes that you're afflicted."

"Ah, who wouldn't be, my dear princess?" he said to her, shedding tears that he did not have the strength to retain. "They are going to separate us; it's necessary that I leave, or I shall expose your life to all the violence of the queen. She knows the attachment I have for you, and she has even seen the note that you wrote to me; one of her women told me so,

and, without wanting to enter into my just dolor, she is sending me, inhumanely, to her brother."

"What are you telling me, Prince?" she cried. "You're on
the point of abandoning me and you believe that is necessary
to preserve my life? Can you imagine such a means? Let me
die before your eyes; I shall have less to lament than in living
apart from you."

A conversation so tender could not fail to be interrupted
frequently by sobs and tears; the young lovers did not know
the rigors of absence yet; they had not foreseen them, and that
added further vexations to those they had traversed. They
made one another a thousand oaths never to change. The
prince promised Constancia to come back with the utmost
diligence.

"I shall only go," he said, "in order to shock my uncle
and his daughter, so that he will no longer think of giving her
to me for a wife. I will work hard to displease that princess,
and I shall succeed."

"Don't show yourself to her, then," said Constancia, "for
you will be to her liking, whatever cares you take to the contrary."

They both wept so bitterly, they looked at one another
with such a touching dolor and they made reciprocal promises
so passionate that it was a subject of consolation for them to
be persuaded of all the amity they had for one another, and
that nothing would alter such tender and vivid sentiments.

Time had passed with so much rapidity in that sweet
conversation that the night was already very obscure before
they thought of separating, but, the queen wanting to consult
the prince regarding the equipage that he would take, Mirtain
hastened to come in search of him. He found him at the feet of
his mistress, holding her hand in his. When he approached
them they were seized to such an extent that they were almost
unable to speak. He told his master that the queen was asking
for him; it as necessary to obey her orders. The princess drew
away from his side.

The queen found the prince so melancholy and so changed that she divined the cause easily; she no longer wanted to talk to him about it; it sufficed that he was leaving. In fact, everything was prepared with such diligence that it seemed that the fays were involved. For himself, he was only occupied with matters that had some connection with his passion. He wanted Mirtain to remain at the court in order to send him news of the princess every day; he left her his most beautiful gems in case she had need of them, and his foresight neglected nothing in a matter that interested him so much.

Finally, it was necessary to depart. The despair of the young lovers was inexpressible; if anything could render it less violent it was the hope of seeing one another again soon.

Constancia understood then the full extent of her misfortune: to be the daughter of a king, to have considerable estates, and to find herself in the hands of a cruel queen who as sending her son away in the dread that he loved her, although she was not inferior to him in any way, and ought to have been desired by the foremost sovereigns in the world. But the stars had decided otherwise.

The queen, delighted to see her son absent, no longer thought of anything but intercepting the letters that were written to him. She succeeded in that, and knowing that Mirtain was his confidant, she had him arrested on a false pretext and sent to a castle where he suffered a rude imprisonment. At that news, the prince was greatly irritated; he wrote to the king and the queen to demand the liberty of his favorite; his pleas had no effect; and that was not the only thing that was done to cause him pain.

One day, when the princess got up with the dawn, she went in to pick flowers, with which the queen's dressing-table was ordinarily covered; she perceived the faithful Ruson, who was walking some way ahead of her, turn back, as if he were very frightened. As she ran forward to see what had caused him so much fear he caught hold of her dress in order to prevent her—for he was full of intelligence—and she heard the

shrill hissing of several snakes; she was immediately surrounded by toads, vipers, scorpions, asps and other snakes.
Encircling her without biting her, they hurled themselves into
the air in order to fall upon her, but always fell back in the
same place, unable to advance.

In spite of the terror that gripped her, she nevertheless
remarked that prodigy, and could only attribute it to a constel-
lated ring that her lover had given her. Whichever way she
turned, she saw those venomous beasts swarming; the path-
ways were full of them, they were on the flowers and under
the trees.

The beautiful Constancia did not know what would become of her; she perceived the queen at her widow, laughing
at her terror, and knew then that she ought not to expect to be
helped on her orders.

It's necessary to die, she said to herself. *These frightful
monsters have not come here of their own accord; it's the
queen who had them brought, and she wants to be the spectator of the terrible end of my life; thus far it has certainly been
so unfortunate that I have no reason to love it, and if I regret
its loss, the gods, the just gods, are my witnesses to what
touches me in this regard.*

After having spoken thus, she advanced. All the snakes
and their comrades drew away from her. as she marched toward them; she emerged in that manner, with as much astonishment as it caused the queen; those dangerous beasts had
been prepared over a long period in order to make the shepherdess perish by means of their bites; she thought that her son
would not be surprised by it, that he would attribute her death
to natural causes and she would be shielded from his reproaches, but, her project having failed she had recourse to
another expedient.

On the far side of a forest there was a fay, inaccessible of
access because she had elephants incessantly running through
the forest, which devoured poor travelers and their horses,
including the iron with which they were shod, such was their
appetite. The queen had agreed with her that if, by some unex-

pected hazard, anyone arrived at her palace on her behalf, she would provide them with something mortal to bring back.

She summoned Constancia, gave her orders, and told her to depart. She had heard all her companions talking about the peril there was in going into that forest, but an old shepherdess had told her that she had got out of it fortunately with the help of a little sheep that she took with her, because, furious as the elephants were, when they saw a lamb, they became as gentle as him. The same shepherdess had also said that, having been charged with bringing back a burning girdle for the queen, in the dread that she might make her put it on, she had circled trees with it, which had been consumed by it, and that afterwards, he girdle had no longer done the harm that the queen had expected of it.

When the princess had heard that tale she had not thought that it might be useful to her one day, but when the queen had pronounced her order, in a manner so absolute that the edict was irrevocable, she prayed to the gods to favor her. She took Ruson with her and departed for the perilous forest.

The queen was delighted. "We won't see the odious object of our son's amour again," she said to the king. "I've sent her to a place where a thousand like her wouldn't make a quarter of the elephants' breakfast."

The king told her that she was too vindictive, and that he could not help regretting the most beautiful young woman he had ever seen.

"Truly," she replied, "I counsel you to love her, and shed tears for her death, as the unworthy Constancio is shedding them for her absence."

Meanwhile, Constancia had no sooner entered the forest than she found herself surrounded by elephants. Those horrible colossi, delighted to see the beautiful sheep that was walking more boldly than his mistress, caressed him as gently with their formidable trunks as a lady would have done with her hand. The princess was so frightened that the elephants might separate her interests from those of Ruson that she took him in her arms, although he was already heavy. Whichever way she turned, she still saw them, so she advanced diligently toward the palace of the inaccessible old woman.

She reached it after a great deal of dread and difficulty; the place seemed very neglected to her, and the fay who lived there no less so. She hid a part of her astonishment on seeing her in her abode, for it had been a very long time since any creature had been able to reach it.

"What do you want, little girl?" she asked.

The princess gave her the queen's recommendations very humbly, and asked her on her behalf to send her the girdle of amity.

"She won't be refused," she said. "Doubtless it's for you."

"I don't know, Madame," she replied.

"Oh, for myself, I'm sure of it." And, taking from a casket a long belt of blue velvet, from which long cords hung down in order to attach a purse, scissors and a knife to it, she made her that beautiful present. "Here," she said to her, "this belt will render you completely lovable, provide that you put it on as soon as you're in the forest."

After Constancia had thanked her, she picked up Ruson, who was more necessary to her than ever. The elephants made a fuss of him and let her pass in spite of their devouring inclination. She did not forget to put the girdle of amity around a tree; immediately, it began to burn as if it had been in the most violent fire in the world. She removed the belt and took it from one tree to another until it no longer burned them. Eventually, she arrived at the palace, very weary.

When the queen saw her she was so surprised that she could not remain silent about it.

"You're a cheat," she said. "You haven't been to see my friend the fay?"

"Pardon me, Madame," the beautiful Constancia replied, "but I've brought you the girdle of amity for which I asked on your part."

"Haven't you put it on?" added the queen.

"It's too rich for a poor shepherdess like me," she replied.

"No, no," said the queen. "I give it to you for your trouble. Don't fail to adorn yourself with it. But tell me, what did you encounter on the road?"

"I saw elephants," she said, "so intelligent, and which are so clever that there's no land where one doesn't take pleasure in seeing them; it seems that the forest is their realm and that some of them there are more absolute than others."

The queen was very chagrined, and did not say everything that she thought, but she hoped that the belt would burn the shepherdess without anything in the world being able to protect her from it.

If the elephants have spared her, she said to herself, *the belt will avenge me; you'll see, wretch, what amity I have for you, and the profit you'll receive for having pleased my son!*

Constancia had retired to her little room, where she wept over the absence of her dear prince. She dared not write to him, because the queen had spies in the country who stopped the couriers and she had obtained her son's letters in that way. "Alas, Constancio," she said, "You'll soon receive sad news of me; you ought not to have departed, abandoning me to the fury of your mother; you could have defended me, or received my last sighs, instead of which I'm delivered to her tyrannical power, and I find myself without any consolation."

At daybreak she went into the garden to work, as usual. She found it full of venomous beasts again, from which her ring protected her. She had put on the blue velvet belt, and when the queen perceived her, picking flowers s tranquilly as if she only had a thread around her, there're has never been a chagrin equal to hers.

"What power is interested in that shepherdess?" she cried. "By means of her attractions she enchants my son and by means of her simples she returns him to health; serpents and asps crawl at her feet without biting her, elephants become gracious and obliging at the sight of her and the belt that should have served to burn her with the power of faerie only serves to adorn her. It's necessary, then, that I have recourse to more certain remedies."

She immediately sent for the captain of her guards, in whom she had a great deal of confidence, to ask whether there were any ships about to depart for the most distant regions. He found one that was to set sail at nightfall; the queen was overjoyed; she went to speak to the owner and proposed to sell him the most beautiful slave in the world. The delighted merchant agreed; he came to the palace and without poor Constancia knowing anything about it, he saw her in the garden. He was surprised by the charms of the incomparable young woman, and the queen, who was able to turn everything to profit because she was very miserly, sold her very dear.

Constancia was unaware of the new displeasures that were in preparation for her; she retired early to her little room in order to have the pleasure of dreaming about Constancio without witnesses and to reply to one of his letters, which she had finally received. She was reading it, without being able to quit such an agreeable reading, when she saw the queen come in. That princess had a key that opened all the doors in the palace; she was followed by two mutes and the captain of her guards. The mutes put a handkerchief in her mouth, bound her hands and took her away. Ruson tried to follow his dear mistress, but the queen threw herself on him and prevented him from doing so, for she feared that his bleating might be heard; she wanted everything to happen in complete secrecy and silence. Thus Constancia, having no help, was transported to the ship; as it was only waiting for her in order to depart, it immediately headed for the open sea.

It is necessary to leave her to make her voyage; such was her sad fate, for the Sovereign Fay had been unable to bend Destiny in her favor and all she could do was to follow her everywhere in a dense cloud in which no one could see her.

Meanwhile, Prince Constancio, occupied with his passion, did not retain any measure with the princess who had been destined for him; although he was naturally the most polite of men, he was nevertheless very abrupt with her; she complained about it frequently to her father, who could not prevent her from quarreling with his nephew, so the marriage was postponed indefinitely.

When the queen thought it appropriate to write to the prince that Constancia was at the last extremity, he felt an inexpressible dolor; he no longer wanted to maintain any reservation in a circumstance in which his life was at least as much at risk as that of his mistress, and he departed like lightning.

Whatever diligence he was able to make, he arrived too late. The queen, who had anticipated his return, told him that Constancia had been ill for several days; she had put with her women who were able to talk and keep silent as they were ordered. The rumor of her death soon spread, and a wax figure was buried, said to be her. The queen, who was seeking all possible means to convince the prince of that death, had Mirtain released from prison in order that he could witness her funeral, with the result than, the day of her burial having been known to everyone, everyone came to mourn the charming young woman. The queen, who composed her features as she wished, pretended to feel that loss with regard to the prince.

He arrived with all the anxiety imaginable; when he entered the city he could not help asking the first person he encountered for news of his dear Constancia; those who replied to him did not know her, and not being prepared in any way, told him that she was dead. At those catastrophic words he was no longer the master of his dolor; he fell from his horse, with no pulse or voice. People gathered, they saw that it was the prince; everyone hastened to help him and he was carried to the palace, almost dead.

The king felt the pitiful state of his son deeply. The queen was prepared for it; she believed that time and the loss of his tender hopes would cure him, but he was too afflicted to be consoled. His displeasure, far from diminishing, was augmented continuously. He spent two days without seeing or speaking to anyone; then he went to the queen's room, his eyes full of tears, his eyes wild and his face pale. He told her that she was the one who had caused his dear Constancia's death, but that she would soon be punished for it, since he was about to die, and that he wanted to go to the place where she was buried.

The queen, unable to turn him away from it, made the decision to take him herself to a wood planted with cypress where she had raised the tomb. When the prince found himself in the place where his mistress was reposing forever he said things so tender and so passionate than so one has ever spoken as he did. In spite of the queen's hardness, she dissolved in tears. Mirtain was as afflicted as his master, and everyone who heard him shared his despair. Finally, driven a sudden fury, he drew his sword and, approaching the marble that covered the beautiful body, he would have killed himself if the queen and Mirtain had not stopped his arm.

"No," he said, "nothing in the world will prevent me from dying and joining my dear princess."

The name of princess that he gave the shepherdess surprised the queen; she did not know whether her son was dreaming, and would have believed that he had lost his mind if he had not spoken precisely in everything he said.

She asked him why he called Constancia princess; he replied that she was one, that her realm was called the Realm of Deserts, that it had no other heir, and that he would never have said anything about it if he had still had measures to guard.

"Alas, my son," said the queen. "Since Constancia is of a birth appropriate to yours, console yourself, for she isn't dead. It is necessary to confess, in order to soften your dolor, that I sold her to merchants and they took her away as a slave."

"Ah!" cried the prince. "You're saying that to suspend the design I have formed to die, but my resolution is fixed; nothing can turn me away from it."

"It's necessary," added the queen, "To convince you by means of your eyes."

Immediately, she commanded that the wax figure be disinterred.

As he believed, when he first saw it, that it was the body of the lovely princess, he fell into a profound unconsciousness from which they had a great deal of difficulty bringing him round.

The queen assured him in vain that Constancia was not dead; after the bad turn that she had done him, he could not believe her; but Mirtain persuaded him that it was true. He knew the attachment that he had for him, and that he was incapable of telling him a lie.

He sensed some relief, because of all misfortunes death is the most terrible, and he still could flatter himself with the hope of seeing his mistress again. But where was he to look for her? No one knew the merchants who had bought her; they had not said where they were going; those were great difficulties, but there are scarcely any that a great amour cannot overcome. He preferred to perish running after the abductors of his mistress than to live without her.

He made the queen a thousand reproaches for her implacable harshness; he added that she would have time to repent of the bad turn she had done him, because he was about to depart, resolved never to return; thus, in losing one of them, she had lost both of them.

The afflicted mother flung her arms around her son's neck, moistened his face with her tears and implored him by the old age of his father, by the amity that she had for him, not to abandon them. She told him that if he deprived them of the consolation of seeing him, he would be the cause of their deaths; that he was their unique hope; that if they lacked him, their neighbors and enemies would take possession of their kingdom.

The prince listened coldly and respectfully, but he always had before his eyes the harshness she had had for Constancia; without her, all the kingdoms on earth would not have touched him; with the result that he persisted with a surprising firmness in the resolution to depart the following day.

The king tried in vain to make him stay; he spent the night giving orders to Mirtain; he confided the faithful sheep to his care. He took a large quantity of gems and told Mirtain to keep the rest, and that he was the only one who would receive his news, on condition of keeping it secret, because he wanted his mother to feel all the pains of anxiety.

Daylight had not yet appeared when the impatient Constancio mounted his horse, consecrating himself to fortune and praying that it would be favorable enough to enable him to find his mistress. He did not know which way to direct his steps, but as she had departed in a ship, he thought that he ought to embark in order to follow her. He went to the most famous port and, without being accompanied by any of his domestics or known to anyone, he sought information regarding the most distant places to which one might go, and then of all the coasts beaches and ports, wherever they were. Then he embarked in the hope that a passion as pure and powerful as his would not always be unfortunate.

As soon as he approached land, he went into the launch and traveled along the shore, shouting on all sides: "Constancia, beautiful Constancia, where are you? I'm searching for you and calling to you in vain; will you be apart from me for a long time?" His regrets and his plaints were lost in the vague atmosphere; he returned to the ship, his heat penetrated by dolor and his eyes full of tears.

One evening, when the anchor had been dropped behind a large rock, he came as usual to land on the shore, and as the country was unknown and the night very dark, those who accompanied him did not want to advance in the fear of perishing thee. As for the prince, who cared little about his life, he started marching, falling and getting up again a hundred times. Eventually, he discovered a bright light that appeared to be coming from a fire; as he drew closer to it he heard a great deal of noise, and the sound of hammers delivering terrible blows. Far from being afraid, he hastened to arrive at a huge forge open on all sides, where the furnace was so luminous that the sun seemed to be burning in its depths. Thirty giants, each of whom had only one eye in the middle of the forehead, were working there, making armaments.

Constancio approached them and said to them: "If you are capable of pity amid the iron and fire that surround you, if by chance you have seen landing in this place the beautiful Constancia, whom merchants took away captive, in order that I know where to find her, ask of me anything in the world; I will give it to you with all my heart."

He had barely finished that little speech when the noise, which had ceased when he arrived, recommenced with more force.

"Alas," he said, "you are not touched by my dolor, barbarians; I ought not to expect anything of you."

He was about to direct his steps elsewhere right away, when he heard a sweet symphony that enraptured him, and, looking toward the furnace, he saw the most beautiful child that the imagination could ever represent; he was more brilliant than the fire from which he emerged. When he had considered his charms, the blindfold that covered his eyes, the bow and the arrows that he carried, he had no doubt that it was Cupid.

It was, indeed him, who shouted to him: "Stop, Constancio, you are burning with a flame too pure for me to refuse you my help; my name is Virtuous Amour; it is me who wounded you for young Constancia, and it is me who is defending her against the giant who is persecuting her. The Sovereign Fay is my intimate friend; we have joined forces to protect her, but it is necessary that I test your passion before revealing to you where she is."

"Order, Amour, order anything you please," cried the prince. "I will omit nothing to obey you."

"Throw yourself into this fire," replied the child, "and remember that if you do not love uniquely and faithfully, you are doomed."

"I have no reason to be afraid," said Constancio. Immediately, he threw himself into the furnace.

He lost all consciousness, not knowing where he was, or what he was.

He slept for thirty hours, and when he awoke he found that he was the most beautiful pigeon in the world. Instead of being in the horrible furnace, he was lying in a little nest of roses, jasmine and honeysuckle. He was as surprised as one can ever be; his feather-legged feet, the different colors if his plumage and his fiery eyes astonished him greatly; he looked at himself in a stream, and, wanting to complain, he found that he had lost the usage of speech, although he had conserved it in his mind.

He envisaged that metamorphosis as the culmination of all his misfortunes. *Oh, perfidious Amour,* he thought, *what recompense do you give the most perfect of lovers? Is it necessary to be fickle, treacherous and perjured to find favor with you? I have seen many of that character whom you have crowned, while you afflict those who are veritably faithful. What can I promise myself,* he continued, *with a form as extraordinary as mine? I'm now a pigeon; even then, if I could talk as the Blue Bird—the tale of which I have always loved— could talk, I would fly so far and so high, I would search so many different climes for my dear mistress, I would ask questions of so many different people, that I would find her; but I do not have the liberty of pronouncing her name, and the unique remedy that it is permitted to me to attempt is that of precipitating myself into some abyss in order to die there.*

Occupied with that fatal resolution, he flew over a high mountain from which he tried to cast himself down; but his wings sustained him involuntarily. He was astonished by that, for, not having been a pigeon yet, he did not know what help feathers might be. He made the resolution to tear them all out, and he began to pluck himself without quarter.

Thus deprived, he was about to attempt a new somersault from the top of the rock when two young women arrived. As soon as they saw the unfortunate bird, one said to the other: "Where has that unfortunate pigeon come from? Has it emerged from the sharp talons of some bird of prey, or from the mouth of a weasel?"

"I don't know where it has come from," replied the younger, "but I know where it's going." And, throwing herself upon the pacific creature, she continued: "It's going to keep five of its species company, of which I want to make a pie for the Sovereign Fay."

The pigeon prince, on hearing her say that, far from fleeing, moved closer in order that she would do him the favor of killing him promptly; but what ought to have caused his doom saved him, for the young women found him so polite and tame that they resolved to nourish hm. The more beautiful of the two shut him in a covered basket in which she usually kept her needlework, and they continued their walk.

"For several days," said one of them, "It seems that our mistress has been very busy. She is continually mounting her fiery camel, and goes day and night from one pole to the other without stopping."

"If you were discreet," said her companion, "I'd tell you the reason for that, for she was kind enough to tell me."

"Go on, I'll keep quiet," cried the one who had spoken first. "Be assured of my secrecy."

"Know then," she replied, "that her Princess Constancia, whom she loves so much, is being persecuted by a giant who wants to marry her; he has put her in a tower, and in order to prevent him from completing that marriage, she has to do surprising things."

The prince listened to their conversation from the bottom of his basket. He had thought until then that nothing could augment his disgrace, but he knew with an extreme dolor that he had been greatly mistaken, as one can judge by everything I have related about his passion, and the circumstances in which he found himself, of having become a pigeon at the time when his help was so necessary to his princess, that he felt a veritable despair.

His imagination, ingenious in tormenting him, represented to him Constancia in the fatal tower, afflicted by the importunity, the violence and the rage of a redoubtable giant; he was afraid that she might be intimidated and might give her hand to that marriage. A moment later he was afraid that she might not be intimidated, and that she would expose her life to the fury of such a lover. It would be difficult to represent that state that he was in.

The young woman who was carrying him in her grip, having returned with her companion to the palace of the fay they served, found her walking in a somber pathway of her garden. They prostrated themselves at her feet, and then said: "Great queen, here is a pigeon we have found; it is gentle and tame, and if it had feathers it would be beautiful; we've resolved to nourish it in our room, but if you like it, it might perhaps amuse you in yours."

The fay took the basket in which he was contained, took him out of it, and made serious reflections on the grandeur of the world, because it was extraordinary to see a prince like Constancio in the form of a pigeon, ready to be roasted or boiled, and although it was her who had conducted that metamorphosis until then, and nothing happened without her orders, as she moralized gladly on all events, this one struck her forcefully.

She caressed the pigeon, and for his part, he neglected nothing to attract her attention, in order that she might be kind enough to relieve him in his sad adventure. He made her a reverence pigeon-fashion, drawing back his foot slightly; he pecked her in a caressant fashion; although he was a novice pigeon, he already knew more than the oldest fathers and the oldest wood-pigeons.

The Sovereign Fay carried him into her cabinet, shut the door and said to him: "Prince, the sad state in which I find you today does not prevent me from recognizing you and loving you, because of my daughter Constancia, who is as scantly indifferent toward you as you are for her. Don't blame anyone but me for your metamorphosis; I had you enter the furnace to test the candor of your amour; it is pure, it is ardent; it is necessary that you have all the honor of the adventure."

The pigeon lowered its head three times as a sign of gratitude, and listened to what the fay wanted to say to him.

"The queen, your mother," she said "had scarcely received the money and gemstones in exchange for the princess than she sent her with the utmost violence to the merchants who had bought her; and as soon as she was on the ship they set sail for great India, where they were sure to dispose with a great profit of the precious jewel that they were carrying. Her pleas and prayers did not change their resolution; she told them in vain that Prince Constancio would ransom her with everything he possessed in the world. The more she told them about the price that they could obtain from him the more rapidly they fled, in the fear that he might be informed of her abduction and come to snatch that prey away from them.

"Finally, after having traveled half the world, they were battered by a furious tempest. The princess, overwhelmed by dolor and the fatigues of the sea, was dying; they feared losing her, and ran for the nearest port, but as they were disembarking thy saw a giant of frightful grandeur coming toward them; he was followed by several others, who said all together that they wanted to see the rarest thing that there was on their ship.

"The giant having come aboard, the first thing that struck his eyes was the young princess; they recognized one another immediately. 'Ah little rascal,' he cried, 'the just and compassionate gods are returning you to my power, then. Do you remember the day when I found you and you cut my sack? I'm mistaken if you play more the same truck now.' In fact, he picked her up as an eagle clutches a pullet, and in spite of her resistance and the pleas of the merchants, he carried her away in his arms, running as fast as he could all the way to the great tower.

"That tower is on a high mountain; the enchanters who built it neglected nothing to render it beautiful and curious. It has no door; one enters it by means of windows that are very high; the diamond walls shine like the sun, and have a hardness proof against anything. In fact, everything that art and nature can assemble of the richest is below what one sees there. When the furious giant held the charming Constancia, he told her that he wanted to marry her and render her the most fortunate woman in the world; that she would be the mistress of all his treasures; that he would have the kindness to love her; and that he had no doubt that she would be delighted by the good fortune that had brought her to him.

"She made him know by her tears and her lamentations the excess of her despair, and as I was guiding events very secretly, in spite of destiny, which had sworn the doom of Constancia, I inspired in the giant sentiments of mildness that he had never known in his life, with the consequence that, instead of becoming annoyed, he told the princess that he would give her a year, during which he would not do her any violence, but that if she did not make the resolution in that time to satisfy him, he would marry her in spite of her, and that he would kill her afterwards; thus, she could see what suited her more.

"After that baleful declaration, he had the most beautiful young women in the world imprisoned with her, to keep her company and to extract her from the profound sadness in which she was plunged. He posted giants in the vicinity of the tower to prevent anyone from approaching it, and, in fact, if anyone had that temerity, they would soon receive the punishment for it, for they are very redoubtable and very cruel guards.

"In the end, the poor princess, seeing no appearance of being helped, and that only one day remains to complete the year, is preparing to hurl herself from the top of the tower into the sea. That Sire Pigeon, is the state to which she is reduced; the sole remedy that I have found for it is for you to fly to her, holding in your beak this little ring. As soon as she has put it on her finger, she will become a dove, and you will be able to escape successfully."

The pigeon was in the utmost impatience to depart, but he did not know how to make her understand that; he tugged the fay's sleeve and her trimmed apron; then he approached windows and tapped the glass several times with his beak. All that meant, in pigeon language: *I beg you, Madame, to send me with your enchanted ring to relieve our beautiful princess.*

She understood his jargon and responded to his desires. "Go, fly, charming pigeon," she said to him. "Here is the ring that will guide you; take great care not to lose it, for there is only you in the world who can extract Constancia from the place where she is."

The pigeon prince, as I have said, had no plumage; he had torn his feathers out in his extreme despair. The fay rubbed him with a marvelous essence, which returned him such beautiful and extraordinary ones that the pigeons of Venus would not have been worthy to enter into any comparison with him.

He was delighted to see himself replumed, and, taking flight, he arrived at dawn at the top of the tower, the diamond walls of which were so brilliant that the sun has less fire in its greatest splendor. It had a spacious garden at the top, in the middle of which was an orange tree laden with flowers and fruits. The rest of the garden was very curious, and the pigeon prince would not have been indifferent to the pleasure of admiring it if he had not been occupied with much more important matters.

He perched in the orange tree; he was holding the ring in his beak, and felt a treble anxiety when the princess came in. She was wearing a long white dress; her head was covered by a large black veil embroidered with gold; it as lowered over her face and trailing on both sides. The amorous pigeon might have been able to doubt that it was her if the nobility of her stature and her majestic attitude had been able to reach such a point of perfection in anyone else. She came to sit down under the orange tree, and suddenly lifted her veil; he remained dazzled for some time.

"Sad regrets, sad thoughts!" she exclaimed. "You are futile now; my afflicted heart has passed an entire year between dread and hope, but the fatal term has arrived. It is today, in a few hours, that it is necessary for me to die or marry the giant. Alas, is it possible that the Sovereign Fay and Prince Constancio have abandoned me so utterly? What have I done to them? But what use are these reflections? Is it not better to execute the noble design that I have conceived?"

She got up, with an air full of boldness, in order to precipitate herself; however, as the slightest sound frightened her and she heard the pigeon agitating in the tree, she looked up in order to see what it was; at the same time he flew toward her and deposited the important ring on her bosom. The princess, surprised by the beautiful bird and its charming plumage, nevertheless guessed what it had come to do. She considered the ring, remarked some mysterious characters, and she was still holding it when the giant came into the garden without her having heard him coming.

Some of the women who served the princess had gone to render an account to that terrible lover of the despair of the princess, and tell him that she wanted to kill herself rather than marry him. When he saw that she had gone up to the top of the tower so early he feared a fatal catastrophe; his heart, which until then had not been capable of barbarity, was so enchanted by the lovely woman's beautiful eyes that he had loved her delicately.

O gods, what became of her when she saw him! She feared that he might take away the means she sought of dying; and the poor pigeon's fear of the formidable colossus was not mediocre. In the disturbance she was in, she put the ring on her finger, and—O marvel!—she was metamorphosed into a dove, and flew away at top speed with the faithful pigeon.

No surprise ever equaled that of the giant. After having watched his mistress become a dove, which traversed the vast space of the atmosphere, he remained immobile for some time; then he uttered cries and howls that shook the mountains and only ended with his life; he terminated it at the bottom of the sea, where it was far more just that he drowned than the charming princess.

She drew away very diligently, therefore, with her guide, but when they had traveled a sufficiently long distance no longer to have anything to fear, they alighted gently in a wood, very somber by virtue of the quantity of its trees and very agreeable because of the green grass and flowers that covered the ground. Constancia still did not know that the pigeon was her veritable lover. He was very afflicted not to be able to talk in order to inform her of that when he felt an invisible hand that untied his tongue; he had a sensible joy, and immediately said to the princess: "Has your heart not told you, charming dove, that you are with a pigeon who burns with the same fires that set you ablaze?"

"My heart wished for the good fortune that has happened to me," she replied, "but it dared not flatter itself, alas with what it was able to imagine! I was on the point of perishing under the blows of my bizarre fortune; you have just snatched me from the jaws of death, or a monster that I feared even more."

The prince, delighted to be able to talk to the dove, and to discover her as tender as he desired her to be, told her everything that the most delicate and vivid passion can inspire. He told her everything that had happened since the sad moment of his absence, particularly the surprising encounter with the blacksmith Amour and the fay in her palace.

She had a great joy in knowing that her best friend was still acting in her interests. "Let us go find her, my dear prince," she said to Constancio, "And thank her for all the good she has done for us; she will render us our original form, and we can return to your realm or mine."

"If you love me as much as I love you," he replied, "I will make you a proposition in which amour alone has a part; but amiable princess, you are going to tell me that I'm extravagant."

"Don't conserve the reputation of your mind at the expense of your heart," she said, "Speak without fear; I will always hear you with pleasure."

"I would be of the opinion," he continued, "that we do not change form; you as a dove and I as a pigeon can burn with the same fires with which Constancio and Constancia burned. I am convinced that, rid of the care of our realms, having no council to hold, no war to make, no audiences to give, exempt from incessantly playing and importunate role on the great stage of the world, it would be easier for us to live in this pleasant solitude."

"Oh, cried the dove, "What grandeur and delicacy your design contains! Young as I am, alas, I have experienced so much disgrace; fortune, jealous of my innocent beauty, has persecuted me so stubbornly that I would be delighted to re-nounce all the possessions that it gives, in order only to live for you. Yes, my dear prince, I consent to it; let us choose an agreeable country and spend our finest days under this meta-morphosis; let us lead an innocent life, without any ambition or desires other than those that a virtuous amour inspires."

"It is me who wants to guide you," cried the Amour, de-scending from Olympus. "A design so tender merits my pro-tection."

"And mine also," said the Sovereign Fay, who appeared suddenly. "I have come to search for you in order to advance the pleasure of seeing you by a few moments."

The pigeon and the dove had as much joy as surprise at that new event. "We put ourselves under your guidance," Constancia said to the fay.

"Don't abandon us," said Constancio to the Amour.

"Come to Paphos," he said, "my mother is still respected there, and people there still love the birds that are consecrated to her."

"No, replied the princess, "We don't seek the commerce of humans; fortunate are those who can renounce it! We only need a beautiful solitude."

The fay struck the ground with her wand. The Amour struck it with a gilded arrow. At the same time they saw the most beautiful natural wilderness, and the most richly orna-mented with woods, flowers meadows and springs.

"Stay here for millions of years," cried the Amour. "Swear an eternal fidelity to one another in the presence of this marvelous fay."

"I swear it to my dove," cried the pigeon.

"I swear it to my pigeon," cried the dove.

"Your marriage," said the fay, "could not be made by a god more capable of rendering it happy. In any case, I promise you that if you weary of this metamorphosis, I will not abandon you, and I will render you your original form.

The pigeon and the dove thanked the fay, but they assured her that they would not call upon her for that; that they had experienced too many of the misfortunes of life. They only begged her to enable Ruson to come, if he was not dead.

"He has changed state," said the Amour. "It's me who rendered him a sheep. He caused me to take pity on him, and I have restored him to the throne from which I removed him."

At that news, Constancia was no longer surprised at the pretty things she had seen him do. She implored the Amour to tell her the adventures of a sheep who was so dear to her.

"I'll come back to tell you," he replied, obligingly. "For today, I'm awaited and desired in so many places that I don't know where to go first. Adieu, happy and tender spouses," he continued, "you can boast of being the sagest in my empire."

The Sovereign Fay remained with the newlyweds for some time. She could not praise enough the scorn they had for the grandeurs of the earth; but it is certain that they made the best decision for the tranquility of life. Finally, she quit them; it is known from her and from the Amour that the pigeon prince and the princess dove have always loved one another faithfully.

The reading of the tale had scarcely finished when Virginie and Marthonide stood up, clapping their hands and crying *"Hurrah, hurrah,* that is a perfect work!" La Dandinardière said to them in a composed and modest fashion that he begged them to spare him; that it was impossible that it could be good, because the diligence that he had made to commence it was almost incredible.

"What I tell you is true, he added, "that I did not have the time to read it, and that I find things in it, quite different from what I had wanted to put. For example, for the title, I would have sworn that it had "Belle-Belle; or, The Chevalier Fortuné," and in spite of that, there are sparrows."

"Say a pigeon and a dove," said the prior, interrupting.

La Dandinardière remarked that his memory had served him poorly, but in order to pay with wit, he cried: "I call any feathered animal a sparrow, be it a duck, a turkey, a grouse, a chicken or a pullet; I'm unable to give myself the fatigue of distinguishing them."

"You're right, Monsieur," said Madame Saint-Thomas, who was very satisfied with his tale. "It's not necessary for a man of intelligence like you to give in to vulgar rules."

"Oh, Madame," he continued, "I refrain carefully from that; I want to distinguish myself a little, and if everyone in the world took it into his head to talk like one another, to call a cat a cat and a wolf a wolf, what difference would there be between a clever man and an ignorant one?"

"Oh, Monsieur," said Marthonide, "how glad I am, in the denouement in which there are beautiful conversations and good models here, to have already thought what you have just said! Madame la Baronne, my mother, could render testimony that when I was hardly out of swaddling clothes I did not want talk like everyone else; for nurse, I said titty."

"What natural charm!" he cried. "If you were at court, statues would be raised to you and temples erected."

"Fie, Monsieur," said Madame de Saint-Thomas, "my daughters aren't pagans, they don't want temples or statues."

"Don't take him so literally, Mother," said Virginie. "We'd accept the temples of which he's speaking."

"Truly, you're joking, Mademoiselle," retorted the baronne, swelling up. "You're aspiring, I believe, to give me lessons and explain what it means to speak literally."

As the conversation between the mother and the daughter was becoming heated, Marthonide interrupted it and told La Dandinardière that she was struck by the title of the tale of Belle-Belle, which he thought he had put on his own.

"I don't know how that happened," he said, "unless the fays are mixed up in it, for surely I talked about Guzzler and Strong-Back, about…."

"You didn't say anything about them," the prior said, fearing that Marthonide might recognize her own property and reclaim it. "It's because I read that tale to you and you have a recent memory of it.

The little bourgeois believed it, and the precious amazon did not penetrate anything.

Alain was already cleaned up. He had a large wicker basket on his back full of books, and came into the room quite breathless. "My good mother," he said, "assured me that spirits were as light as air; if she were still alive I'd be able to put her right, for those I'm carrying on my shoulders are heavier the arms of the accursed carter who just knocked me about."

"Shut up, poltroon," cried the bourgeois. "I saw with shame the manner in which you were beaten, and I was on the point of going to aid you, to teach you whether it's written anywhere in the world that the valet of a master like me ought to let himself be knocked about by a ruffian like him."

"In fact," said Alain, a trifle heatedly, "I was wrong to risk receiving as much as a flick to defend your interests with so much zeal. It was a matter, Monsieur, of the book that you had such a great desire to sell to the parish churchwardens. I believed in good conscience that he had stolen it; I wanted to make him give it back. He's much stronger than me. If I suffered in that occasion, you're the cause of it, and for recompense, you're quarreling with me. Well, I'll…."

"Shut up, impudent chatterbox," cried La Dandinardière, redder than a firebrand. "If these illustrious ladies weren't present, I could pay you a part of what I owe you."

"But you wouldn't lose anything by it, Monsieur," he said. "I want to lose everything, or go away, for I'm not stupid enough to wait to be beaten with a stick. I've already received from your favor half as much again as I needed, for at present, I protest to you that I'm going to quit the jerkin unless you promise me before witnesses to leave me in peace."

The little bourgeois had lost more than half his patience. When he saw that Alain was taking advantage of the poor state to which his wound had reduced him in order to speak familiarly to him—all though he had not found it bad before—he got carried away, because he wanted to make a considerable impression on Madame de Saint-Thomas and her daughters. In order to repair the impertinence of his valet he committed a much greater one, for he leapt out of bed and ran after him.

Alain knew the peril to which he was exposed, but as he knew from long experience several tricks to avoid the hail of punches, he decided to employ one on his master, stopping close to him. La Dandinardière, delighted, raised his arms in order to bring them down vertically on his head; the valet dodged underneath, and our hero fell face down with so much force that the turban, the neck-piece and even the gauntlets, which were the only garments in which he was dressed, flew to the four corners of the room.

Alain did not wait for a second impact; he escaped while his poor master was being helped up, and if the scene had been less proximal to the door, Madame de Saint-Thomas would have run away with her daughters; but it would have been necessary to step over La Dandinardière's body. In that embarrassment there was no other course of action to take than to look out of the window.

While the petulant little man was put to bed, the vicomte begged them to approach him, in order to console him for his disgrace. The baronne had a strong desire not to do anything of the sort. "What!" she said. "Do you think, Monsieur de

Berginville that I can tolerate someone lacking the respect that is due to me? I want to teach him that in all my family, the women have never permitted that. Am I to be the only one to depart from that praiseworthy custom? No, no, I'd rather die."

She was beginning to get heated. La Dandinardière heard her grumbling anxiously; he begged the prior to make apologies for his indiscreet vivacity, and the latter, aided by the amazons, acquitted himself so well that the baronne forgave him, on condition that he would forgive the worthy Alain. The later peace treaty was no less difficult to conclude than the other. The bourgeois felt his heart very ulcerated against his valet; the tumble he had taken seemed difficult of digestion. However, he loved Virginie so much that, in order to see her near his bed again he promised her mother to grant Alain mercy.

The trick he had just played on his master was weighing heavily on his conscience; he had gone to hide in a grain-loft, and being covered by a thousand trusses of hay he was near to stifling when a valet, one of his friends, came to tell him the good news of his reconciliation and that he was being requested.

He hesitated for a few moments as to what he ought to do; he sent him to ask for Baron de Saint-Thomas's advice as to whether he ought to return to the bedroom or flee further away. Finally, he was assured so much that he could return that he was seen suddenly to appear at the foot of the bed with a suppliant expression. His posture mollified the company, and the baronne even wanted Alain not to be admonished. La Dandinardière, who prided himself on doing things with a good grace, told her that she could lay down the law with an entire certainty that he would always follow it.

"In order to appease the quarrel," said Virginie, "I ask you for a few moments' audience, in order to read you a tale in my turn that you might not find tedious, although it's very long."

"If it's yours, charming young woman," responded La Dandinardière, "I'm certain that you'll have the suffrage of everyone here."

"I won't tell you whose it is," she replied, "but in order to remove right away the prejudice you might have in my favor, I'll declare to you right away that it isn't mine."

"And whose might it be, then?" cried the bourgeois, putting on a capacious expression. "For I confess to you, Mesdemoiselles, that I only have a taste for your works, and that I'd go all the way to Rome to see one of them."

"Nothing is more flattering," replied Virgine. "You say things in the most obliging way in the world, but one must admit that the most beautiful terms, the noblest expressions, and the finest and best nurtured thoughts offer themselves in a host to your intellect; you're only ever embarrassed for choice, and you always make a good one."

"Ha ha, my princess!" riposted La Dandinardière, "Your thrusts are penetrating, and although you strike with gilded arrows, the wounds are no less profound. I ask you for quarter, beautiful amazon. I surrender; I'm dead, or very nearly, but dead of admiration, dead of a plenitude of gratitude. I'm….."

"Stop there, my friend," said the baron, laughing. "Both of you have just pronounced such fine compliments that we're all charmed, but the conversation is becoming too serious."

"To brighten it up," said the vicomte. "I'll propose a marriage to Monsieur de La Dandinardière."

"I want," he said, swelling up with a comical moue, "a beautiful and young woman, rich and of quality, but above all, that she has so much intelligence that she will be the admiration of our century and all the centuries to come, for I'd be mortally bored with an ordinary young woman."

"Tell us," said the prior, "what you exchange for so much merit?"

"It's not befitting for me to talk about that," he replied, "but since you force me to do so. I'm not sorry to tell you that in the matter of valor and birth, I cede nothing to Don Japhet of Armenia."[13]

The baron's seriousness abandoned him at that point. "There's a rich comparison," he said. "I've always remarked that he never makes any other."

"Since you're content on those two articles," said La Dandinardière, "you will truly be no less so on that of my wealth. I could show you a very tidy and very honest income. With regard to character, my intellect and my person, only modesty prevents me from speaking."

"It's true," said the vicomte, "that you have a great deal that is good, but one single fault suffices to spoil all that, and that is interest. It isn't fitting that one finds, in association with bravery, quality and all the delicacy in sentiments and manners that one could ever desire, a sordid passion for the wealth of this world; that would obfuscate the rest and soil the imagination."

"Yes, Monsieur," replied La Dandinardière, in a passionate tone of voice, "I'm of the opinion that one would never think solidly, and would upset the cooking-pot on the first day. Look at the sages of the century, who know that one and one make two; they weren't stupid enough to marry without having received large sums of money. I want to do as much or die in penury."

"Monsieur de La Dandinardière," cried the baron, "you'll spend the rest of your life in celibacy. It's a great pity; children in your fashion would be worth their weight in gold. Attach yourself, then, to the love of virtue, and detach yourself from that of riches."

"Ho ho, how you talk," he said. "That smacks of the country gentleman, who prefers an idea of generosity to the essential. I repeat again, if I don't encounter someone who is

---

[13] *Don Japhet d'Arménie* (1653) is a burlesque comedy in verse by Paul Scarron, the eponymous protagonist of which set new standards in ridiculousness.

worth as much as me, and who gives me supper when I've given her dinner, I'll be a bankrupt of amour."

A declaration so frank surprised the entire company. La Dandinardière laughed like a madman, and clapped his hands in his bed, making bounds that astonished the two precious beauties

"You're applauding yourself," said the baronne, "for having such refined taste."

"Ha ha, Madame, not at all," he said, "But as long as a gallant man knows the way of the world, he's protected from those will-o'-the-wisps that rise from the vulgar vapors of the earth. You understand sufficiently that the comparison is just."

"Oh, if we didn't understand it," cried Virginie "it would be necessary to have no intelligence."

"I have none, then," replied the prior, "for I protest to you that nothing seems murkier to me than your discourse."

"It's out of malice or envy that you say that," added Marthonide. "Who doesn't see that the the will-o'-the-wisps are the wispy inclinations of the heart, which rise into the median region of the head, as the others do into the air, and that all of that means that Monsieur is right?"

"Yes, right," said Virginie, "but a sublunar rightness of stellar nature, so brilliant is it."

Poor Baron Saint-Thomas was distressed to hear that pompous nonsense, in which his daughters were participating so wholeheartedly; he shrugged his shoulders and looked at the vicomte and the prior with a dark expression, which made them understand that he was suffering, in seeing the three women on the high road to poverty.

The prior, who was also beginning to tire of all that insipid discourse, said to the bourgeois: "I intended in my turn to propose to you the most charming person in the world, but you're too difficult, and if the King of Siam doesn't send you the princess queen or the great Mogul one of his daughters, we won't be dancing at your wedding."

"All joking apart, Monsieur le Prieur," said La Dandinardière, "I could aspire to the best matches in France if

I made the most of my quality and my valor, but I'd like, in spite of all my delicacy, to hear your propositions and humanize myself a little."

"I assure you," said Virginie, interrupting them, "that it's necessary not to talk about anything any longer, until the tale I've told you about is read."

"As my penance for having thought about something else," replied the prior, "I offer to read it."

Everyone assumed an attentive attitude, which invited him to begin. Virginie gave him a scroll of paper, extensively blackened—for it was a lady who had written it—and he commenced immediately.

PRINCESS BELLE-ETOILE AND PRINCE CHERI

There was once a princess to whom nothing any longer remained of her past grandeurs than her bed-canopy and her hair-grip; one was velvet embroidered with pearls, the other gold enriched with diamonds. She kept them as long as she could but the extreme necessity to which she found herself reduced obliged her from time to time to detach a pearl, a diamond, an emerald and sell it secretly in order to nourish her equipage. She was a widow charged with three very young and very amiable daughters. She understood that if she brought them up with an air of grandeur and suitable magnificence they would feel their disgrace more afterwards. She therefore made the resolution to sell the little that remained to her and go away with her three daughters, establish herself in a house in the country where their expenditure would be appropriate to their petty fortune.

While passing through a dangerous forest she was robbed, with the result that almost nothing remained to her. The poor princess, more chagrined by that last misfortune than all the ones that had preceded it, knew full well that it was necessary to earn her living or die of hunger. She had once loved good cheer, and knew how to make excellent sauces.

She never went anywhere without her little gold cooking-pot, which people came from far away to see. What she had once done to amuse herself, she now did in order to subsist.

She settled near a big city, in a very pretty house; she made marvelous stews there; people were very greedy in that region, with the result that everyone flocked to her house. There was no talk of anything but the good fry-cook; she was scarcely given time to breathe. Meanwhile, her three daughters grew up and their beauty would have made no less noise than the princess's sauces if she had not hidden them in a room from which they rarely went out.

On one of the most beautiful days of the year a little old woman came into her house who seemed very tired. She was leaning on a stick; her body was bent over and her face full of wrinkles. "I've come," she said, "in order for you to give me a good meal, for I want, before going to the other world, to treat myself in this one." She took a wicker char, placed it next to the fire, and told the princess to hurry up.

As she could not do everything, she summoned her three daughters. The eldest was named Roussette, the second Brunette and the youngest Blondine. She had given them those names with reference to the color of their hair. They were dressed as peasant girls, with bodices and skirts of different colors. The youngest was the most beautiful and the mildest. Their mother ordered one to go in quest of little pigeons in the aviary, another to kill pullets and a third to make the pastry. Finally, they set before the old woman a very proper place-setting, with a very white table-cloth and well-varnished earthenware crockery, and served her several courses. The wine was god, there was no lack of ice, the glasses were rinsed continually by the most beautiful hands in the world; all of that gave the little old woman an appetite. If she ate well, she drank even better. She complimented the wine and said a thousand things in which the princess, who seemed not to pay any heed to it, found a good deal of wit.

The meal finished as cheerfully as it had begun. The old woman got up, and said to the princess: "My good friend, if I had any money I'd pay you, but I was ruined a long time ago; I needed to find you to have such good cheer; all that I can promise you is to send you better custom than mine."

The princess smiled, and said, graciously "Go on, my good mother, don't worry about it; I'm always paid well enough when I give some pleasure."

"We've been delighted to serve you," said Blondine, "And if you'd like to sup here, we'd do even better."

"Oh, how fortunate one is," cried the old woman, "When one is born with a heart so benevolent! But do you believe that you won't receive the recompense? Be certain," she continued, "that the first wish you make without thinking of me will be granted."

At the same time, she disappeared, and they had no reason to doubt that she was a fay.

That adventure astonished them; they had never seen one before; they were fearful, with the result that for five or six months they talked about it, and as soon as they desired something they thought about her. Nothing succeeded, with the result that they were very angry against the fay.

One day, however, when the king had gone hunting, he went to the house of the good fry-cook, to see whether she was as skilful as people said, and as he approached the garden with a lot of noise, the three sisters, who were picking strawberries, heard him.

"Ah!" said Roussette, "if I were fortunate enough to marry Milord the Admiral, I could boast that I'd make so much thread with my spindle and my distaff, and so much cloth with that thread that he wouldn't have any more need to buy any for the sails of his ships."

"And I," said Brunette, "if fortune were favorable enough to enable me to marry the king's brother, could boast that I'd make so much lace with my needle that he'd see his palace filled with it."

"And I," added Blondine, "could boast that if the king married me, at the end of nine months I'd have two beautiful boys and a beautiful girl, that their hair would fall in ringlets, spread out with precious stones, with a brilliant star on the forehead and a neck circled by a rich gold chain."

One of the king's favorites, who had come in ahead in order to inform the hostess of his coming, having heard people talking in the garden, stopped without making any noise, and was very surprised by the conversation of the three beautiful young women. He immediately went to repeat it to the king in to order to amuse him; he did, in fact, laugh, and commanded that they be brought before him.

They appeared immediately, with a marvelous manner and grace. They curtseyed to the king with a great deal of re- spect and modesty, and when he asked them whether it was true that they had just been talking about the husbands they desired, they blushed and lowered their eyes. He pressed them to admit it; they agreed, and he immediately cried: "Certainly, I don't know what power is acting upon me, but I won't leave here until I've married the beautiful Blondine."

"Sire," said the king's brother, "I ask your permission to marry that pretty Brunette."

"Grant me the same favor," added the admiral, "for the redhead pleases me infinitely."

The king, very glad to be imitated by the noblest men in his realm, told them that he approved of their choices, and asked the mother if she was agreeable to it. She replied that it as the greatest joy she could ever have. The king embraced her, and the prince and the admiral did no less.

When the king was ready to dine, a table with seven gold place-settings was seen to come down the chimney, and every- thing that can be imagined of the most delicate to make a good meal. The king hesitated to eat, however; he feared that he meat might be the product of the Sabbat, and that manner of serving via the chimney seemed slightly suspect to him.

The sideboard was arranged; nothing could be seen but gold vases and bowls, the workmanship of which surpassed the material. At the same time a swarm of honey-bees ap- peared in crystal hives and commenced the most charming music that can be imagined. The whole room was filled with hornets, flies, wasps and midges, and other small creatures of that sort, which served the king with a supernatural skill. Three or four thousand gnats brought the drinks, without a single one daring to drown in the wine, and with astonishing discipline.

The princess and her daughters realized soon enough that everything that was happening could only be attributed to the little old woman; they blessed the hour when they had met her.

After the meal, which was so long that nightfall surprised the company at table, of which His Majesty felt slightly ashamed, because it seemed that in that marriage Bacchus had taken the place of Cupid, the king stood up and said: "Let's finish the feast as it ought to have begun." He took his ring from his finger and put it on Blondine's; the prince and the admiral imitated him. The bees redoubled their songs. They danced, they rejoiced, and the people who had followed the king came to salute the queen and the princess. For the admiral's wife they did not make as much ceremony, of which she was in despair, for she was older than Brunette and Blondine and found herself less well married.

The king sent his chief squire to inform the queen, his mother of what had happened and to summon his most magnificent carriages in order to bring back Queen Blondine and her two sisters. The queen mother was the cruelest of all women and the most ill-tempered. When she knew that her son had married without her participation, and, above all, a young woman of such obscure birth, and that the prince had done the same, she became so angry that she frightened the entire court. She asked the chief squire what reason had been able to engage the king in such an unworthy marriage. He told her that it was the hope of having two sons and a daughter in nine months, who would be born with long curly hair, stars in the forehead and golden chains around the neck, and that such rare things had charmed him. The queen mother was disdainful of her son's credulity; she said many offensive things about that, which gave sufficient evidence of her fury.

The carriages had already arrived at the little house. The king invited his mother-in-law to go with him, and promised her that she would be treated with every sort of distinction, but she immediately thought that a court is a perpetually agitated sea.

"Sire," she said to him, "I have too much experience of society to quit the repose that I have only acquired with great difficulty."

"What!" said the king. "You want to continue to keep a hostelry?"

"No," she said, "You can give me something on which to live."

"At least," he said, "suffer that I give you an equipage and servants."

"I thank you for that," she said, "but if I'm alone, I shall have no enemies to torment me; if I had domestics, I'd fear finding some among them."

He king admired the intelligence and moderation of a woman who thought and spoke like a philosopher.

While he was urging his mother-in-law to come with him, Admiral Rousse's wife hid in the back of her carriage all the beautiful golden bowls and vases from the sideboard, wanting to profit from them without leaving anything behind, but the fay, who saw everything although no one saw her, changed them into earthenware pitchers. When she had arrived and wanted to take them to her cabinet she found nothing worth the trouble of so doing.

The king and the queen embraced the sage princess tenderly, and assured her that she could dispose at will of everything they had. They quit the rural abode and came to the city, preceded by trumpets, oboes, timpani and drums, which could be heard a long way away. The queen mother's confidants had advised her to conceal her ill-humor, because the king would be offended by it, and that might have unfortunate consequences. She restrained herself, therefore, and only manifested amity to her two daughters-in-law, giving them gems and praising indifferently everything they did, well or badly.

The blonde queen and the brunette princes were closely united, but with regard to Admiral Rousse's wife, she hated them mortally. *Look at the good fortune of my two sisters*, she said to herself. *One is a queen, the other a princess of the blood; their husbands adore them, but I, the eldest, a hundred times more beautiful than them, only have an admiral for a husband, by whom I am not cherished as I ought to be.* The jealousy she had against her sisters caused her to ally herself with the queen mother, because she knew full well that the tenderness she manifested to her daughters-in-law was only feigned, and that she would be glad to have an opportunity to harm them.

The queen and the princess became pregnant. Unfortunately, a great war had broken out and it was necessary for the king to put himself at the head of his army. The young queen and the princess, being obliged to remain under the power of the queen mother, begged to be allowed to return to their mother, in order to console themselves with her for such a cruel absence. The king was unable to consent to that. He implored her to remain in the palace; he assured her that his mother would treat her well. In fact, he begged her with the utmost insistence to love her daughter-in-law and to take care of her. He added that she could not oblige him more sensibly, that he hoped that she would have two beautiful children, and that he would await news of them with great anxiety.

The malevolent queen, delighted that his son was confiding his wife to her, assured him that he could leave with an entire peace of mind. Thus, he left, with such a strong desire to return soon that he risked his troops in all encounters, and his good fortune not only ensured that his temerity always succeeded but that he advanced his affairs strongly.

The queen gave birth before his return. Her sister, the princess, gave birth to a beautiful boy on the same day, but died immediately thereafter.

The admiral's wife was very occupied with mans of harming the young queen. When she saw her with such pretty children, while she had none, her fury augmented. She made the resolution to speak to the queen mother promptly, for there was no time to lose.

"Madame," she said to her, "I am so touched by the honor that Your Majesty does me in giving me a part in her good graces, that I would gladly deprive myself of my own interests in order to further yours. I understand all the displeasure by which you have been overwhelmed since the unworthy marriages of the king and the prince. Now here are four children who will eternalize the fault that they have committed. Our poor mother is a poverty-stricken villager who had no bread when she took it into her head to become a fry-cook; believe me, Madame, make a fricassee of all those little brats and remove them from the world before they make you bluish."

"Oh, my dear Admirale," said the queen, embracing her, "how I love you for being so equitable and for sharing, as you do, my just displeasures. I had already resolved to execute what you are proposing to me; it is only the manner that embarrasses me."

"Don't let that trouble you," said Madame Rousse. "My mastiff bitch has just had three pups, two dogs and a bitch; they each have a star on the forehead and a mark around the neck that makes a chain of sorts. It's necessary to make the queen believe that she had given birth to those little beasts and to take her two sons, her daughter and the princess's son, and kill them."

"Your design pleases me infinitely," she cried, "And I've already given orders to that effect to Feintise, her maid of honor, so it's necessary to have the little pups."

"Here they are, said the admirale. "I've brought them." Immediately, she opened a large purse that she always had at her side, and took out three mastiff puppies, which she and the queen wrapped up as the queen's children would have been, all ornamented with lace and golden embroidery. They arranged them in a covered basket, and then the wicked queen, followed by the red-head, went to see the queen.

"I've come to thank you," she said to her, "for the beautiful heirs you've given my son; here are heads well made to wear a crown. I'm not astonished that you promised your husband two sons and a daughter with stars on their foreheads, long hair and gold chains around the neck. Here, nurse them yourself, for there's no woman able to suckle dogs."

The poor queen, overwhelmed by the misfortune she had suffered, nearly died of dolor when she perceived the three canines and saw that litter making a desperate howling on her bed; she started to weep bitterly. Then, putting her hands together, she said: "Alas, Madame, don't add reproaches to my affliction; it can surely be no greater. If the gods had permitted me to die before I had received the affront of seeing myself the mother of these little monsters, I would estimate myself too fortunate. Alas, what am I going to do? The king will hate me as much as he loved me."

Sighs and sobs stifled her voice; she no longer had the strength to speak, and the queen mother, continuing to heap her with insults, had the pleasure of spending three hours thus at her bedside. She went away thereafter and her sister, who pretended to share her displeasure, told her that she was not the first to whom a similar misfortune had occurred, that it was obvious that it was a trick of the old fay who had promised them so many marvels, but that, as it might be dangerous for her to see the king, she advised her to go to their poor mother's house with her three canine children.

The queen only responded with tears. It was necessary to have a very hard heart not to be touched by the state to which she was reduced; she suckled the wretched dogs, believing that she was their mother.

The queen mother ordered Feintise to take away the queen's children, with the son of the princess, to strangle them and bury them so well that no one would ever know anything.

As she was on the point of carrying out that order, and already had the cord in her had, she cast her eyes on them and found them so marvelously beautiful, and that they were marked in such an extraordinary manner by the stars that were shining on their foreheads, that she dared not put her criminal hands on such an august blood. She had a small boat brought to the edge of the sea, and she put the four children in the same cradle, along with a few strings of precious stones, in order that if fortune carried them into the hands of a women charitable enough to nourish them, she would be sufficiently recompensed.

The boat, pushed by a strong wind, drew away so rapidly along the shore that Feintise lost sight of it; but at the same time, the waves swelled, the sun was hidden, the clouds dissolved in the water and a thousand thunderclaps resounded all around. She had no doubt that the little boat had been submerged, and felt joy that the poor innocents had perished, for she would always have dreaded some extraordinary event in their favor.

The king, incessantly occupied with his dear wife and the state in which he had left her, having a brief truce, returned post-haste; he arrived twelve hours after she had given birth. When the queen mother saw him she went to meet him with a composed expression of dolor. She held him in her arms for a long time, moistening his face with tears; it seemed that dolor was preventing her from speaking. The king, trembling, dared not ask her that had happened, for he did not doubt that there were great misfortunes. Finally, she made an effort to tell him that his wife had given birth to the dogs. Immediately, Feintise presented them. The admirale, in tears, threw herself at the king's feet, and begged him not to put the queen to death, and to content himself with sending her back to her mother, which she had already resolved to do, and that she would receive that treatment as a great mercy.

The king was so bewildered that he could hardly breathe; he looked at the puppies, and remarked with surprise the star that each had in the middle of the forehead, and the different color circling the neck. He let himself fall into an armchair, rolling a thousand thoughts round his head, unable to make any firm resolution; but the queen mother pressed him so forcefully that he pronounced the exile of the innocent queen. Immediately, she was put in a litter with the three dogs, and without having any regard for her, she was taken to her mother's house, where she arrived almost dead.

The gods had looked with compassionate eyes upon the boat containing the three princes and the princess. The fay who protected them caused milk to fall instead of rain into their little mouths; they did not suffer from the frightful storm that had blown up so suddenly.

In the end, they floated for seven days and seven nights; they were as tranquil in the open sea was on a canal when they were encountered by a corsair ship. The captain having been struck, although from a distance, by the brilliant gleam of the stars they had on their foreheads, lowered a launch, convinced that the boat was full of gems. He found some, in fact, but what touched him more was the beauty of the four marvelous children. The desire to conserve them engaged him to return home, in order to give them to his wife, who had none and had wanted some for a long time.

She was very anxious on seeing him return so promptly, for he had gone to make a long voyage, but she was transported with joy when he put such a considerable treasure in her hands; they admired the marvel of the stars together, the golden chains that could not be removed from their necks, and their long hair. That was something else entirely when the woman combed it, for pearls, rubies, diamonds and emeralds of various sizes fell from it continually, all of them perfect. She talked about it to her husband, who was no less astonished than she was.

"I'm very weary," he told her, "of the profession of corsair. If the hair of these little children continues to give us treasures, I don't want to run the seas any longer, and my wealth will be as considerable as that of our greatest captains."

The corsair's wife whose name was Corsine, was delighted with her husband's resolution; she loved the children all the more for it. She named the princess Belle-Etoile, her elder bother Petit-Soleil, the younger one Heureux, and the son of the princess, Cheri. He was far above the other two for beauty, and although he had no star or chain, Corsine loved him more than the others.

As she could not raise them without the help of a nurse she asked her husband, who was very fond of hunting, to trap some little fawns; he found the means, for the forest where they lived was very spacious. When she had them, Corsine exposed them to the wind. The hinds, which scented them ran to suckle them. Corsine hid them, and put the children in their place, who adapted very well to hinds' milk. Twice every day four of them came in company to Corsine's house in search of the princes and the princess, whom they took for fawns.

It was thus that the tender infancy of the princes passed. The corsair and his wife loved them so passionately that they gave them all their care. The man had been well brought-up, it was less by inclination than the eccentricity of fortune that he had become a corsair. He had married Corsine in the house of a princess, where her mind had been fortunately cultivated; she knew how to live, and although she found herself in a kind of wilderness, where they had only subsisted on the larcenies he committed in his expeditions, she had not yet forgotten the usages of society. They had the utmost joy in no longer having the obligation to risk all the perils attached to the profession of corsair, and they became rich without that. Every three days, as I have said, considerable gems fell from the hair of the princess and her brothers, which Corsine went to sell in the nearest city, from which she brought back a thousand nice things for the four children.

When they had emerged from early childhood the corsair applied himself seriously to cultivating the fine nature with which Heaven had endowed them. As he did not doubt that there were great mysteries hidden in their birth and the encounter that he had had with them, he wanted to recognize by their education that present of the gods, with the consequence that, after having rendered his house more capacious, he attracted persons of merit there who taught them various sciences with a facility that surprised all those great masters.

The corsair and his wife had never told anyone about the adventure of the four children. They passed them off as their own, although they marked by all their actions that they emerged from a more illustrious blood. They were closely united with one another; they found that natural and polite; but Prince Cheri had sentiments more urgent and more vivid for Princess Belle-Etoile than the other two. As soon as she wanted something, he would even attempt the impossible to satisfy her; he hardly ever quit her; when she went hunting, he accompanied her; when she did not go, he always found excuses to forbid him to go. Petit-Soleil and Heureux, who were her brothers, spoke to her with less tenderness and respect. She noticed that difference, held it to Cheri's credit, and loved him more than the others.

As they advanced in age, their mutual tenderness increased; at first they had nothing but pleasure therein. "My tender brother," Belle-Etoile said to him, "if my desires were sufficient to render you fortunate, you would be one of the greatest kings on earth."

"Alas, my sister," he replied, "don't envy me the good fortune that I enjoy with you; I prefer spending an hour where you are to all the elevation you wish for me."

When she said the same thing to her brothers, they replied naturally that they would be delighted by it, and to test them further, she added: "Yes, I'd like you to occupy the finest throne in the world, even if I were never to see you."

Immediately, they said: "You're right, my sister, the one is far better than the other."

"You would consent, then," she replied, "to no longer seeing me?"

"Of course," they said. "It would be sufficient for us sometimes to hear your news."

When she was alone, she examined those different fashions of loving, and felt her heart disposed exactly like theirs, for even thought Petit-Soleil and Heureux were dear to her, she did not want to remain with them all her life, but with regard to Cheri, she dissolved in tears when she thought that their father might perhaps send him to roam the sea, or put him in the army. It is thus that amour, masked by the specious name of good nature, was established in their young hearts.

At fourteen years of age, however, Belle-Etoile began to reproach herself for the injustice she believed that she was doing her brothers by not loving them equally. She imagined that Cheri's cares and caresses were the cause of it. She forbade him to seek further means of making himself loved. "You've found too many of them," she told him, agreeably, "and you've succeeded in making me put a great difference between you and them."

What joy did he not feel when he heard her say that! Far from diminishing his eagerness, she augmented it; he made her a new gallantry every day.

They did not know as yet how far their tenderness went, and they did not know its species, until Belle-Etoile was brought several new books. She took the first one that came to hand; it was the story of two young lovers, whose passion had begun while believing themselves to be brother and sister; then they had been recognized by their relatives, and after infinite troubles they had married. As Cheri could read perfectly well, had a fine understanding and made himself understood in the same manner, she asked him to read the book to her while she finished some silk-floss needlework that she wanted to complete.

He read that adventure, and it was not without a great anxiety that he saw in it a naïve description of all his sentiments. Belle-Etoile was no less surprised, and it seemed that the author had read what was happening in her soul. The more Cheri read, the more touched he was; the more the princess listened, the more emotional she was; whatever effort she could make, her eyes filled with tears and her face was covered with them. Cheri made futile efforts on his part; he went pale, changed color and the tone of his voice; they both suffered all that one can suffer,

"Oh, my sister," he cried, looking at her sadly and dropping his book. "Oh, my sister, how fortunate Hippolyte was not to be Julie's brother!"[14]

"We would have a similar satisfaction," she replied. "Alas, is it any less due to us?" As she finished speaking, she knew that she had said too much; she remained nonplussed, and if anything could console the prince, it was the state in which he saw her.

From that moment on they fell into a profound sadness, without explaining themselves further; they penetrated a part of what was happening in their souls; they were careful to hide from everyone a secret that they would have liked not to know themselves, and which they did not discuss with one another. However, it is so natural to flatter oneself, the princess nevertheless took account of the fact that Cheri was the only one who did not have a star on his forehead or a chain around his neck, although, like his cousins, he had long hair with the gift of shedding precious stones when it was combed.

When the three princess went hunting one day, Belle-Etoile shut herself in a little cabinet, which she liked because it was dark and she could dream there with more liberty than elsewhere. She did not make any noise. That cabinet was only separated from Corsine's bedroom by a partition, and the woman thought she had gone out for a walk. She heard her say to the corsair: "Belle-Etoile is of an age to be married now; if we knew who she is, we could try to establish her in a manner appropriate to her rank; or if we could believe that those we represent as her brothers aren't, we could give her to one of them, for who could she ever find as perfect as them?"

"When I encountered them," the corsair said, "I didn't see anything that could instruct me as to their birth; the stones that were attached to their cradle made it known that the children belonged to rich people. What was singular about it is

---

[14] The coupling of these two names reveals that the book in question is Madame d'Aulnoy's historical romance *Hypolite, comte de Duglas* (1690).

that they were all twins, for they seem to be the same age, and it's not ordinary that there are four of them."

"I suspect too," said Corsine, "that Cheri isn't their brother; he doesn't have a star or a chain around his neck."

"It's true," replied her husband, "but diamonds fall from his hair, like that of the others, and after all the riches we've amassed by means of those dear children, nothing more remains for me to wish than to discover their origin."

"It's necessary to leave that to the gods," said Corsine. "They have given them to us, and doubtless when the time comes, they'll develop what is hidden from us."

Belle-Etoile listened attentively to that conversation. The joy she had in being able to hope that they came from illustrious blood was inexpressible, for although she had never lacked respect for those to whom she believed she owed the light of day, she had nevertheless felt the pain of being the daughter of a corsair. But what flattered her imagination was the thought that Cheri might not be her brother; she was burning with impatience to talk to him, and to tell them all about such an extraordinary adventure.

She mounted a light bay horse whose dark mane was attached with diamond buckles, for she had only had to comb her hair once to garnish an entire hunting equipage; its green velvet saddle-cloth was studded with diamonds and embroidered with rubies. Once mounted up, she set off into the forest to search for her brothers. The sound of horns and the barking of the dogs allowed her to hear where they were, and she joined them after a moment

At the sight of her, Cheri detached himself and came toward her more rapidly than the others. "What a pleasant surprise!" he shouted. "You've finally come hunting. You, whom we couldn't distract for a moment from the pleasures that music gives you, and the sciences you're learning!"

"I have so many things to tell you," she replied, "and wanting to do it in private, I came to look for you."

"Alas, my sister," he said, sighing, "What do you want with me today? It seems that for a long time you've no longer wanted anything from me."

She blushed; then, lowering her eyes, she sat on her horse, sad and pensive, without replying to him. Finally, her two brothers arrived; she woke up at the sight of them as if from a profound sleep, and leapt to the ground, walking ahead. They all followed her, and when they were in the middle of a small patch of grass shaded by trees, she said: "Let's sit down here and I'll tell you what I've just heard."

She related to them, exactly, the corsair's conversation with his wife, and how they were not their children. Nothing could be added to the surprise of the three princes; they debated between them what they ought to do. One wanted to depart without saying anything, another did not want to depart at all, and the third wanted to depart and tell them everything. The first sustained that it was the surest means, because the profit they obtained from combing their hair would oblige them to retain them; the second replied that it would be good to quit them if they knew of a definite place to go, and what condition they had, but that the title of vagabonds was not agreeable; the third added that it would be ingratitude to abandon them without their agreement, and stupidity to want to stay any longer with them in the middle of a forest where they could not learn who they were, and that the best course was to talk to them and make them consent to their going away. They all came round to that opinion. Immediately, they mounted up in order to go and find the corsair and Corsine.

Cheri's heart was flattered by all that hope could offer of the most agreeable to console an afflicted lover; his amour enable him to divine a part of future things; he no longer believed that he was Belle-Etoile's brother; his constrained passion, obtaining a new impetus, permitted him a thousand tender ideas, which charmed him.

They joined the corsair and Corsine with expressions mingling joy and anxiety.

"We haven't come," said Petit-Soleil—for he was the spokesman—"to deny you the amity, the gratitude and the respect that we owe you. Although we're informed of the manner in which you found us at sea, and that you're neither our father nor our mother, the pity that you had in saving us, the noble education you've given us, and all the cares and benevolence you've had for us are engagements so indispensable that nothing in the world can free us from your dependency. We've come to renew our sincere thanks to you, to beg you to recount such a rare event to us, and to advise us, in order that, guiding us by your sage advice, we'll have nothing for which to reproach ourselves."

The corsair and Corsine were very surprised that something they had hidden so carefully had been discovered. "You're too well informed," they said, "And we can't hide it from you that you're not our children and that fortune alone enabled you to fall into our hands. We have no illumination as to your birth, but the gems that were in your cradle could be evidence that your parents are either great lords or very rich. Apart from that, what can we advise you?

"If you consult the amity we've had for you, you'd doubtless remain with us and console our old age with your amiable company; if the château we've built in this place doesn't please you, or the abode of this solitude caused you chagrin, we'll go wherever you wish, provided that it's not to court; a long experience has disgusted us with that, and you'd probably be disgusted if you were informed of the continual agitations, feints, envy, inequalities, veritable evils and false goods that are found there. We could tell you more, but you'd believe that our counsels were interested; they are, too, my children; we desire to arrest you in this peaceful retreat, although you're free to quit us whenever you wish.

"Consider, however, that you're in port and you'll be setting forth on a stormy sea; that pains almost always surpass pleasures; that the course of life is limited; that one often quits it in mid-career; that the grandeurs of society are false diamonds by which one allows oneself to be dazzled by virtue of a strange fatality, and that the most solid of all goods is to know how to limit oneself, to enjoy tranquility and to become sage."

The corsair would not have finished those remonstrations so soon if he had not been interrupted by Prince Heureux. "My dear father," he said, "we have too much desire to discover something about our birth to bury ourselves in the depths of a desert. The morality that you establish is excellent, and I would like us to be capable of following it, but a kind of fatality is summoning us elsewhere. Permit that we fulfill the course of our destiny. We will come back to see you and render you an account of all our adventures."

At those words the corsair and his wife began to weep. The princes were moved to compassion, especially Belle-Etoile, who had an admirable nature and who would never have thought of leaving the wilderness if she were sure that Cheri would always remain with her.

That resolution having been made, they no longer thought about anything but preparing their equipage in order to embark; for having been found at sea, they had some hope that they might receive the enlightenment there regarding what they wanted to know.

They took aboard their small ship a horse for each of them, and, after having combed their hair to the point of skinning the scalp in order to leave gems for Corsine, they asked her to give them in exchange the diamond chains that had been in their cradle. She went to look for them in her cabinet, where she had kept them carefully, and she attached them to Belle-Etoile's garments. She embraced her incessantly, moistening her face with her tears.

No separation has ever been so sad; the corsair and his wife nearly died of it; their dolor did not come from an interested source, for they had amassed so much treasure that they did not want any more. Petit-Soleil. Heureux, Cheri and Belle-Etoile boarded the ship. The corsair had made it very good and quite magnificent. The mast was ebony and cedar, the rigging green silk mingled with gold, the sails cloth of gold and green, and the paintings excellent. When it set sail, Cleopatra with her Antony, and even all the oarsmen of Venus would have lowered the flag before it. The princess was sitting under a rich awning at the poop; her two brothers and her cousin were standing beside her, more brilliant than the stars, and their own stars projected long beams of dazzling light.

They resolved to go to the same place where the corsair had found them, and they did, in fact, go there. They had planned to make a grand sacrifice to the gods and the fays there in order to obtain their protection, and that they might be guided to their birthplace. They took a turtle-dove in order to immolate it, but the compassionate princess found it so beautiful that she saved its life, and to protect it from a similar accident, she released it. "Go, little bird of Venus" she said to it, "And if I have need of you some day, don't forget the good I've done for you."

The turtle-dove flew away; the sacrifice being finished, they commenced a concert so charming that it seemed that all of nature was keeping a profound silence in order to listen to them. The waves of the sea did not rise; the wind did not blow. Zephyr alone agitated the princess's hair and put her veil in slight disorder.

At that moment a siren emerged from the water, who sang so well that the princess and her brothers admired her. She turned toward them and cried to them: "Cease to worry; let your vessel go; descend where it stops, and let those who love one another continue to love one another."

Belle-Etoile and Cheri felt an extraordinary joy at what the siren had just said. They did not doubt that it was for them, and, making one another a sign of intelligence, their hearts spoke without Petit-Soleil and Heureux perceiving it. The ship sailed at the whim of the winds and the waves; their navigation had nothing extraordinary; the weather was always fine, and the sea always calm. Nevertheless, their voyage lasted three entire months, during which the amorous Prince Cheri often conversed with the princess.

"How many flattering hopes I have, charming Star!" he said to her one day. "I am not your brother; this heart, which recognizes your power, and which will never recognize another, was not born for crimes, although it would be one to love you as I do, if you were my sister; but the charitable siren who came to counsel us has confirmed what I had in mind in that regard."

"Oh, my brother," she said, "don't trust too much in something that is still so obscure that we cannot penetrate it. What would our destiny be if we irritate the gods by sentiments that could displease them? The siren explained herself so poorly that it is necessary to have a great desire to divine in order to apply what she said to us."

"You are forbidding yourself to do so, cruel woman," said the afflicted prince "much less because of the respect you have for the gods than by virtue of aversion for me."

Belle-Etoile made no reply, and, raising her eyes to the heavens, she uttered a profound sigh, which he could not help interpreting in his favor.

They were in the season when the days are long and hot; toward evening the princess and her brothers went up on deck in order to watch the sun set in the bosom of the waves; she sat down, the princes placed themselves beside her; they took up instruments and commenced their agreeable concert. Meanwhile, the vessel, impelled by a fresh wind, seemed to sail more lightly and hastened to double a little promontory that hid a part of the most beautiful city in the world; but suddenly, it was revealed; its aspect astonished our amiable young folk. All the palaces were marble, the roofs gilded, and the rest of the houses of very fine porcelain. Several evergreen trees mingled the enamel of their leaves with the various colors of the marble, gold and porcelain, with the consequence that they wished that their ship would enter the port; but they doubted that it could find a place there, there were so many others, the masts of which composed a floating forest.

Their desires were accomplished; they dropped anchor, and the shore was immediately covered with people, who had perceived the magnificence of the ship. The one that the Argonauts had constructed for the conquest of the fleece did not shine as much; the stars and the beauty of the marvelous children delighted those who saw them. Some ran to give the king the news; as he could not believe it, and the great terrace of the palace extended as far as the sea shore, he went there promptly. He saw that the Princes Petit-Soleil and Cheri, holding the princess in their arms, were carrying her ashore; afterwards, their horses were brought out, the rich harness of which responded well to everything else. Petit-Soleil was mounted on one blacker than jet; Heureux had one that was gray, Cheri one as white as snow, and the princess her light bay. The king admired all four of their horses, which were marching so proudly that all those who approached them moved aside.

The princes, having heard people say: "There's the king," looked up, and having seen him, his attitude full of majesty, they immediately made him a profound reverence, and passed by slowly, keeping their eyes fixed on him.

For his part, he watched them and was no less charmed by the incomparable beauty of the princess than the good looks of the young princes. He commanded his squire to go and offer them his protection and everything they might need in a country where they were apparently strangers..

They received the honor that the king did them with much respect and gratitude, and told him that they only needed a house where they could be in private, that they would be very glad if it were a league or two from the city, because they were very fond of walking. Immediately, the chief squire had them given one of the most magnificent, where he lodged them comfortably with all their retinue.

The king's mind was so full of the four children he had just seen that he went immediately to the room of the queen, his mother, to tell her about the marvel of the stars shining on their foreheads, and everything that he had admired about them.

She was utterly nonplussed; she asked without any affectation what age they appeared to be; he replied fifteen or sixteen years; she did not manifest her anxiety but she had a terrible fear that Feintise had betrayed her.

Meanwhile, the king was striding back and forth, and said: "How fortunate a father is to have sons so perfect and a daughter so beautiful! As for me, unfortunate sovereign, I am the father of three dogs; they are illustrious successors, and my crown is very secure!"

The queen mother listened to these words with a mortal anxiety. The brilliant stars and the approximate age of the foreigners had so much in common with that of the princes and their sister that she had strong suspicions of having been deceived by Feintise, and that instead of killing the children she had saved them. As she had great self-possession, she did not give any evidence of what was happening in her soul; she did not even send anyone that day to seek information about many things that she desired to know, but the next day she commanded her secretary to go there and, under the pretext of giving orders in the house for their comfort, to examine everything, and see whether they had stars on their foreheads.

The secretary left early in the morning; he arrived as the princess was dressing; at that time one's complexion could not be bought from merchants; what was white remained white and what was black did not become white, with the result that he saw her uncoiffed; her blonde hair, finer than gold thread, which was being combed, descended in curls all the way to the floor; there were several baskets around her in order that the stones that fell from her hair would not be lost; the star on her forehead projected fires that could hardly be sustained, and the gold chain around her neck was no less extraordinary than the precious diamonds that were tumbling from the top of her head.

The secretary had a great deal of difficulty believing what he saw, but the princess, having chosen the largest pearl, begged him to keep it as a souvenir of her; it is the same one that the kings of Spain esteemed so much under the name of

Peregrina, which means Pilgrim, because it came from a traveler.[15]

The secretary, confused by such great liberality, took his leave of her and saluted the three princes, with whom he stayed for a long time, in order to be informed of a part of what he wanted to know. He returned to give an account of it to the queen mother, who was confirmed in the suspicions that she already had. He told her that Cheri had no star, but that stones fell from his hair as from that of his brothers, that in his opinion he was the best made, that they came from far away, and that their father and mother had only give them a certain time in order to see foreign lands.

That article deflected the queen slightly, and she sometimes imagined that they were not the king's children. She was thus suspended between dread and hope when the king, who was very fond of hunting, went in the direction of their house. The chief squire, who accompanied him, told him in passing that it was there that he had lodged Belle-Etoile and her brothers, by his order.

"The queen has advised me not to see them," said the king. "She fears that they might have come from some country infected with the plague, and that they might bring bad air therefrom."

"That young foreign woman," said the chief squire, "is indeed very dangerous, but sire, I fear her eyes more than bad air."

"In truth," said the king, "I think as you do," and, immediately spurring his horse, he heard instruments and voices. He stopped close to a large drawing room, the windows of which were open, and after having admired the sweetness of the symphony, he advanced.

---

[15] The pearl known as La Peregrina became part of the Spanish crown jewels in 1558, having previously been worn by Queen Mary of England. In a more recent era, it was famously owned by the actress Elizabeth Taylor.

The noise of horses obliged the princes to look out; as soon as they saw the king they saluted him respectfully and hastened to come out, approaching him with cheerful faces and so many marks of submission that they embraced his knees and the princes kissed his hands, as if they had recognized him as their father. He caressed them abundantly and sensed his heart so emotional that he could not divine the cause of it. He told them that they should not fail to come to the palace, and that he wanted to converse with them and introduce them to his mother. They thanked him for the honor that he was doing them, and told him that as soon as their garments and equipages were complete, they would not fail to pay their court to him.

The king quit them in order to finish the hunt that had commenced; he sent them half of the kill, obligingly, and took the other half to his mother.

"What!" she said. "Is it possible that you have had such a meager hunt? You usually kill three times as much game."

"That's true," replied the king, "but I've regaled the handsome strangers; I feel an inclination for them so perfect that I'm surprised by it myself, and if you had less fear of contagious air, I would already have had them come to lodge in the palace."

The queen mother was very annoyed; she accused him of lacking regard for her and made him reproaches for risking himself so lightly.

As soon as he had left he she sent for Feintise to come and speak to her. She shut herself in her cabinet with her. She took her by the hair with one hand and held a dagger to her throat. "Wretch," she said. "I don't know what reserve of generosity prevents me from sacrificing you to my just resentment; you've betrayed me; you didn't kill the four children that I put into your hands to be rid of them. At least confess your crime, and perhaps I'll pardon you."

Feintise, half-dead with fear, threw herself at her feet and told her what had happened; that she believed it to be impossible that the children were still alive, because a tempest had blown up, so terrible that she had thought they would be crushed by the hail. In the end, though, she asked for time and said that she would find a means to get rid of them, one after another, without anyone in the world being able to suspect her.

The queen, who only wanted their death, was slightly appeased. And, in fact, old Feintise, who saw that she was in great peril, neglected nothing that depended on her. She waited for a time when the three princes were hunting, and, carrying a guitar under her arm, she went to sit under the princess's window, where she sang these words:

> *Beauty can overcome anything,*
> *Fortunate who can profit from it!*
> *Beauty is effaced,*
> *The age of ice*
> *Comes to tarnish all flowers;*
> *How painful it is*
> *When one remembers*
> *The attractions one has lost!*
> *One is in despair.*
> *And one takes, to please*
> *Superfluous cares.*
> *Young hearts, let yourselves charm,*
> *In the fine age one ought to love.*
> *Beauty is effaced,*
> *The age of ice*
> *Comes to tarnish all flowers;*
> *How painful it is*
> *When one remembers*
> *The attractions one has lost!*
> *One is in despair.*
> *And one takes, to please*
> *Superfluous cares.*

Belle-Etoile found those words rather pleasant; she advanced on to a balcony in order to see the person singing them. As soon as she appeared, Feintise, who had dressed very properly, made her a great reverence. The princes saluted her in her turn, and as she was cheerful, she asked her whether the words she had just heard had been made for her.

"Yes, charming person," Feintise replied, "they are for me; but in order that they will never be for you, I've come to give you some advice from which you ought not to fail to take advantage."

"And what is it?" said Bell-Etoile.

"As soon as you've permitted me to come up to your room," she added, "You'll know it."

"You can come up," the princess replied.

Immediately, the old woman presented herself, with a certain air of the court that one does not lose once one has it.

"My beautiful girl," said Feintise, without losing a moment—for she feared that they might be interrupted—"Heaven has made you very lovable; you are endowed with a brilliant star on your forehead, and many other marvels are recounted about you, but you still lack one thing that is essentially necessary to you; if you do not have it, I feel sorry for you."

"And what do I lack?" she replied.

"The dancing water," replied the malign old woman. "If I have had some of it, you wouldn't see a white hair on my head, not a wrinkle on my brow; I'd have the most beautiful teeth in the world, which a childish air that would charm. Alas, I knew the secret too late; my attractions were already effaced. Profit from my misfortunes, my dear child; it would be a consolation for me, for I sense movements of extraordinary tenderness for you."

"But where can I get this dancing water?" asked Belle-Etoile.

"It's in the luminous forest," said Feintise. "You have three brothers; does one of them not love you enough to go in search of it? Truly, they would scarcely be affectionate. In sum, there is no other means to be beautiful a hundred years after your death."

"My brothers cherish me," said the princess. "There is one of them who would not refuse my anything. Certainly, if that water does everything you say, I will give you a recompense proportionate to its merit."

The perfidious old woman retired diligently, delighted to have succeeded so well. She told Belle-Etoile that she would be careful to come to see her."

As the prior's voice was becoming a trifle hoarse, the baron took the notebook and said to him: "I'll interrupt you to read in my turn, for it seems to me that you wouldn't be sorry."

"Gladly," he replied. "These ladies will have more pleasure hearing you than me."

"That's what isn't yet decided," said the baronne. "You're quitting at a point where our curiosity is taking on new force."

"You're very obliging, Madame," La Dandinardière responded, "I would never have thought that a little work that is in the ultimate negligence, which lacks the most necessary things to give it value, would be so favorably received."

"I assure you," cried Virginie, "that it attracts all my attention; I want to render myself inseparable from Belle-Etoile."

"And me from Prince Cheri," added Marthonide. "The uncertainty of his birth puts me in a state so violent that I share all his anxieties."

"Eh! Not at all. *Finis coronat opus*."[16]

"Ho, Sainte-Barbe," said the baronne, very annoyed, "what are you saying there? I beg you to believe that we have ears as delicate as the women of the court, and that such words are inappropriate for us."

---

[16] *Finis coronat opus* [the end crowns the work] is routinely attributed to Ovid, but might have been an established proverb before his use of it. When Madame de Saint-Thomas mistakes it for an obscenity her reference to "Sainte-Barbe" [Saint Barbara] refers to the long use of that term to represent a powder-magazine or bomb.

La Dandinardière, uncertain of what he had just said, for he almost did not know himself, thought that Madame de Saint-Thomas understood better than he did, with the result that he made a thousand excuses for his liveliness, admitting that he had not thought that she understood Latin so well.

"Oh, Monsieur," she said, "women are as savant as men nowadays; the study, and are capable of anything; it's great pity that they can't take on charges; a parliament composed of women would be the prettiest thing in the world, and could there be anything more agreeable than a sentence of death pronounced by a beautiful mouth, rose-red and laughing?"

"That's true," said La Dandinardière—who wanted to efface the memory of his unfortunate *Finis coronat opus*—that's true, another coup; I wouldn't mind being doomed if a woman as lovely as Madame had condemned me."

"You're too gallant," she said, "but let's finish the reading of the tale; in truth, it's better than anything we might say."

The prior continued immediately.

The princes returned from hunting; one brought a young boar, another a hare and the other a red deer; all were laid at the feet of their sister. She gazed at that homage with a kind of disdain; she was occupied with Feintise's advice; she even seemed anxious about it, and Cheri, who had no other occupation than studying her, was not with her for a quarter of a hour without remarking it.

"What's the matter, my dear Star," he said to her. "Is the country where we are not to your liking? It that's the case, let's depart immediately. Perhaps, too, our equipage isn't large enough, the furniture beautiful enough, the table delicate enough. Speak, please in order that I have the pleasure of obeying you first and making the others obey you."

"The confidence that you give me to tell you what is passing in my mind," she replied, "engages me to declare to you that I can no longer live if I don't have the dancing water;

it's in the luminous forest. With it, I shall have nothing to fear from the years."

"Don't be upset, my lovely Star," he added. "I'll depart and bring it to you, or you'll know by my death that it's impossible to obtain."

"No," she said, "I'd rather renounce all the advantages of beauty; I'd rather be frightful than risk a life so dear. I implore you not to think any longer about the dancing water, and, if I have any power over you, I even forbid you to do so."

The prince pretended to obey, but, as soon as he saw that she was occupied, he mounted his white horse, which only went by leaps and curvets, he took money and a rich coat; of diamonds he had no need, for his hair would furnish enough, and three strokes of a comb sometimes caused a million's worth to fall. In truth, that was not always similar; they even knew that the disposition of their mind and that of their health regulated the abundance of the stones. He did not take anyone with him, in order to be more at liberty, and in order that, if the adventure were perilous, he could risk it without enduring the remonstrations of a zealous and fearful domestic.

When time for supper had come and the princess did not see her brother Cheri appear, anxiety gripped her to such a point that she could neither eat nor drink. She gave orders to search for him everywhere. The two princes, knowing nothing about the dancing water, told her that she was tormenting herself excessively; that he could not be far away; that she knew that he abandoned himself voluntarily to profound reveries; and the he had doubtless stopped in the forest. She acquired a little tranquility, therefore, until midnight, but then she lost all patience, and told her brothers, weeping, that she was the cause of Cheri having gone away, that she had testified an extreme desire to have the dancing water of the luminous forest, and he had doubtless taken the road there.

At that news they decided to send several people after him, and she charged them to tell him that she implored him to return.

Meanwhile, the malevolent Feintise was very intrigued to know the effect of her advice. When she learned that Cheri was already on campaign, she had a sensible joy, not doubting that he would have more diligence than those who were following him, and that he would be overtaken by misfortune. She ran to the palace, proud of that hope; she gave the queen mother an account of what had happened.

"I admit, Madame," she told her, "that I cannot doubt that they are the three princes and their sister; they have stars on the forehead, gold chains around the neck, their hair has a ravishing beauty, and precious stones fall from it continually. I've seen on the princess the jewels that I put in her cradle, with which she adorns herself, although they aren't worth as much as the ones that fall from her hair, with the result that it isn't possible for me to doubt their return, in spite of the care I believed I had taken to prevent it. But Madame, I'll rid you of them, and as that's the sole means that remains for me to repair my fault, I only beg you to grant me the time. One of the princes has already departed to go in search of the dancing water; he'll doubtless perish in that enterprise, as I've prepared several occasions to doom him."

"We shall see," said the queen, "whether the success responds to your expectations, but remember that that alone can save you from my just fury."

Feintise withdrew, more alarmed than ever, searching in her mind for everything that could make them perish.

The means that she had found with regard to Prince Cheri was one of the most certain, for the dancing water could not be drawn easily; it had cause so much rumor by virtue of the misfortunes of those who searched for it that no one know the route. His white horse went at a surprising speed; he spurred it without quarter, because he wanted to return to Belle-Etoile promptly and give her the satisfaction that she expected from his journey. Nevertheless, he traveled for a week without reposing anywhere but in the woods, under the first tree, without eating anything other than the fruits he found on the way, and scarcely leaving his horse time to browse the grass.

Finally, at the end of that time, he found himself in a region where the air was so hot that he began to suffer considerably. It was not that the sun had more ardor; he did not know to what to attribute the cause until, from the top of a mountain, he perceived the luminous forest All the trees were burning, without being consumed, and throwing flames into places so distant that the country was arid and deserted. The hissing of serpents and the roaring of lions could be heard in the forest, which astonished the prince greatly, because it seemed that no animal except the salamander could live in that kind of furnace.

After having considered such a frightful thing he descended, thinking about what he was going to do, and he said to himself more than once that he was doomed. As he drew nearer to the great conflagration he was dying of thirst. He found a spring that emerged from the mountain and fell into a large marble basin. He dismounted, approached it, and bent down in order to draw water in a small golden vase that he had brought in order to put the water that the princess desired into it.

He perceived a turtle-dove that was drowning in the spring; its feathers were soaked; it no longer had any strength, and sank to the bottom of the basin. Cheri took pity on it; he rescued it. First he suspended it by its feet; it had drunk so much that it was bloated by it. Afterwards, he warmed it up; he wiped its wings with a fine handkerchief. He helped it so much that after a while, the turtle-dove was more cheerful than it had ever been sad.

"Sire Cheri," it said to him, in a soft and tender voice, "you have never obliged a little animal more grateful than me. It's not only today that I have received essential favors from your family; I am delighted to be able to be useful to you in my turn. Don't believe that I'm unaware of the subject of your voyage. You've attempted it a trifle recklessly, for no one knows the number of people who have perished here. The dancing water is the eighth wonder of the world for the ladies; it embellishes, it rejuvenates and it enriches; but if I don't serve as your guide, you'll never be able to reach it, for the spring emerges seething in the middle of the forest and precipitates into a gulf there. The path is covered by tree branches that all hang down ablaze, and I can see no other means of going there than to go underground. Repose here without anxiety, therefore, and I will organize what is necessary."

At the same time the turtle-dove rose into the air, came and went, swooped and soared, again and again, so much that at the end of the day it said to the prince that everything was ready. He took the obliging bird, kissed it, caressed it, thanked it and followed it on his beautiful white horse.

He had scarcely gone a hundred paces when he saw two long files of foxes, badgers, moles, snails, ants and all sorts of creatures that hide underground. There was such a prodigious quantity of them that he could not understand by what power they were assembled thus.

"It's by my order," the turtle-dove told him, "that you see this little subterranean population in this place; they've just worked for your service and have done so with an extreme diligence. You'll give me the pleasure of thanking them."

The prince saluted them and told them that he would like to meet them in a less sterile place, that he would regale them with pleasure. Each small creature seemed content.

When he reached the entrance of the vault, Cheri left his horse there. Then, bent over, he went on with the benevolent turtle-dove, which led him safely all the way to the spring. It was making such a loud noise that would have deafened him if the bird had not given him two of its white feathers, with which he blocked his ears.

He was strangely surprised to see that the water was dancing with the same precision as if Favier and Pecout had taught it. It is true that they were only old dances, like the Bocane, the Mariée and the Saraband. Several birds that were fluttering in the air were singing the tunes to which the water wanted to dance.

The prince drew enough to fill his golden vase; he drank it in two draughts, which rendered him a hundred times more beautiful than before, and refreshed him so well that he scarcely perceived that of all the places in the world, the luminous forest is the hottest.

He departed by the same route by which he had come; his horse had drawn away but, faithful to his voice, as soon as he called it, it came at a fast gallop. The prince jumped on to it lightly, very proud to have the dancing water.

"Tender turtle-dove," he said to the bird he was still holding, "I still don't know by what prodigy you have so much power in this place; the effects that I have felt engage me to an enormous gratitude, and as liberty is the greatest of goods I return yours to you, to equal the favor that you have done me."

As he finished speaking, he let it go. It flew away as swiftly as if it had stayed with him against his will.

What inequality! he said to himself, then. *There is more of the human about you than the turtle-dove; one is inconstant, the other is not.*

The turtle-dove replied to him from up above: "Ah! Do you know who I am?"

Cheri, astonished that the turtle-dove had replied thus to his thought, judged that it was very clever; he was sorry to have let it go. *It might have been useful to me*, he said to himself, *and I could have learned many things from it that might have contributed to the repose of my life.* However, he agreed with himself that it is necessary never to regret a benefit accorded; he found himself greatly in debt when he thought about the difficulties that it had smoothed out for him in order to obtain the dancing water.

His golden vase was sealed in such a manner that the water could not escape or evaporate. He was thinking agreeably about the pleasure that Belle-Etoile would have in receiving it, and the joy he would have in seeing her again when he saw several horsemen riding at full tilt, who had no sooner seen him than they pointed him out to one another.

He was not afraid; his soul had an intrepid character that was not alarmed by perils; but he felt a great deal of chagrin that something was stopping him. He pushed his horse abruptly toward them, and was agreeably surprised to recognize a party of his domestics, who presented him with little notes, or, more accurately, orders, that the princess had given them for him so that he would not expose himself to the dangers of the luminous forest. He kissed Belle-Etoile's handwriting, sighed more than once, and, hastening to return to her, he extracted himself from the most sensible pain that one can experience.

When he arrived he found her under a few trees, where she had abandoned herself to all her anxiety. When she saw him at her feet she did not know what welcome to give him; she wanted to scold him for having departed against her orders and she wanted to thank him for the charming present he had brought her. In the end, tenderness prevailed, and the reproaches she made him had nothing unpleasant about them.

Old Feintise, who was not asleep, heard from her spies that Cheri had returned more handsome than he had been before his departure, and that the princess, having put the dancing water on her face, had become so exceedingly beautiful that there was no means of sustaining the slightest of her gazes without dying more than half a dozen deaths.

Feintise was quite astonished, and very afflicted, for she had expected that the prince would perish in such a great enterprise; but it was no time to be put off. She waited for a moment when the princess went to a small temple of Diana with little accompaniment. She approached her and said to her, in a manner full of amity: "How joyful I am, Madame, at the fortunate effect of my advice! It is only necessary to look at you to know that you now have the dancing water; but if I dare to offer you an advice, you ought to think of rendering yourself mistress of the singing apple. That is something else entirely, because it embellishes the mind to such a degree that there is nothing of which it is incapable. Does one want to be persuasive? It is only necessary to sniff the singing apple. Does one want to speak in public, make verses, write in prose, be diverting, makes people laugh or cry? The apple has all those virtues, and it sings so well and so loudly that one can hear it eight leagues away without being deafened by it."

"I don't want it!" cried the princess. "You nearly caused my brother to perish with your dancing water, your counsels are too dangerous."

"What, Madame!" replied Feintise. "You'd be sorry to be the most knowledgeable and intelligent person in the world? In truth, you're not thinking about it."

"Ah, what would I have done," Belle-Etoile continued, "if my brother's body had been brought back to me, dead or dying?"

"That one," said the old woman, "need not go again; the others can be obliged to serve you in their turn, and the enterprise is less perilous."

"It doesn't matter," said the princess. "I'm not in a humor to risk them."

"In truth, I feel sorry for you," said Feintise, "for losing such an advantageous opportunity; but you'll think about it. Adieu, Madame." She withdrew immediately, very anxious about the success of her speech, and Belle-Etoile remained at the feet of the statue of Diana, irresolute as to what she ought to do. She loved her brothers, and she loved herself too; she understood that nothing could give her a more sensible pleasure than to have the singing apple. She sighed for a long time, and then she started weeping.

Petit-Soleil was coming back from hunting; he heard the noise in the temple and went in. He saw the princess, who covered her face with her veil because she was shamed of having moist eyes. He had already remarked the tears and, approaching her, he implored her insistently to tell him why she was weeping. She would not do it, replying that she was ashamed of herself, but the more she refused her secret, the more desire he had to discover it.

Finally, she told him that the same old woman who had advised her to send someone to conquer the dancing water had come to tell her that the singing apple was even more marvelous, because it gave so much intelligence that one became a species of prodigy; that the truth was that she would have given half her life for such an apple, but that there was too much danger in going to search for it."

"You won't be afraid for me, I can assure you," said her brother, smiling, "For I don't have any desire to render you that good office. What! Don't you have enough intelligence? Come on, my sister," he continued, "and cease afflicting yourself."

Belle-Etoile followed him, as saddened by the manner in which he had received her confidence as the impossibility she found of possessing the singing apple.

Supper was served, and all four of them went to table. She could not eat. Cheri, the lovable Cheri, who only had attention for her, served her the best of what was there, and pressed her to taste it; at the first morsel her heart swelled, tears came to her eyes and she left the table, weeping.

Belle-Etoile weeping! O gods, what a subject of anxiety for Cheri! He demanded to know, therefore, what was wrong with her. Petit-Soleil told him, joking in a fashion that was rather disobliging to his sister. She was so piqued in consequence that she withdrew to her room, and did not want to speak to anyone all evening.

As soon as Petit-Soleil and Heureux had gone to bed, Cheri mounted his excellent white horse, without telling anyone where he was going. He only left a letter for Belle-Etoile, with an order to give it to her when she woke up, and all night long he rode at hazard, not knowing where he could obtain the singing apple.

When the princess got up, the prince's letter was presented to her. It is easy to imagine everything she felt of anxiety and tenderness on an occasion like that. She ran to her brothers' room in order to read it to them. They shared her alarm, and immediately sent almost all their men after him, to oblige him to return without attempting the adventure, which would doubtless be terrible.

Meanwhile, the king had not forgotten the beautiful children of the forest; his footsteps continually took him in that direction, and when he passed close to their house and saw them he reproached them because they had not come to his palace. They made excuses, first because they were working in their equipage, then because of their brother's absence, and assured him that when he returned they would be sure to take advantage of the permission he had given them to render their very humble respects to him.

Prince Cheri was too driven by passion to fail to make great diligence. At daybreak he found a young man reposing under trees, reading a book. He approached him in a civil manner and said to him: "Permit me to interrupt you, in order to ask you whether you know where the singing apple can be found."

The young man looked up, smiling graciously. "Do you want to make the conquest of it?" he asked.

"Yes, if it possible for me," the prince replied.

"Oh, Sire, you don't know all the perils then. This is a book that speaks about it, and it is frightening to read."

"It doesn't matter," said Cheri. "Danger is incapable of putting me off. Only tell me where to find it."

"The book indicates," the young man continued, "that it is in a vast desert in Libya; that one can hear it singing eight leagues away; and that the dragon guarding it has already devoured five hundred thousand people who have dared to go there."

"I'll be the five hundred thousand and first," the prince replied, smiling in his turn and saluting him.

He took the road that went in the direction of the deserts of Libya. His beautiful horse, which was of the zephyrian race—for Zephyr was his ancestor—went as rapidly as the wind, with the result that he made incredible diligence.

He listened hard, but he did not hear any singing from that direction; he was afflicted by the length of the road and the fruitlessness of the journey, when he perceived a poor turtle-dove that had fallen at his feet; it was not yet dead, but very nearly. As he could not see anyone who might have wounded it, he thought perhaps that it belonged to Venus and that, having escaped from her dovecot, the little mutineer Amour, in order to try his arrows, had launched one at it. He felt sorry for it; he dismounted from his horse, picked it up, and wiped its white feathers, already tinted with vermilion blood. He took a small golden flask from his pocket, in which he carried a balm admirable for wounds; he had scarcely applied some to the injured turtle-dove than it opened its eyes, raised its head, spread its wings and preened its feathers.

Then, looking at the prince, it said: "Handsome Cheri, you are destined to save my life, and perhaps I can render you great services. You have come to conquer the singing apple. The enterprise is difficult, and worthy of you, for it is guarded by a frightful dragon, which has twelve feet, three heads, six wings and a body of bronze."

"Oh, my dear turtle-dove," said the prince, "what a joy it is for me to see you again, and at a time when your help is so necessary to me. Don't refuse it to me, my little beauty, for I would die of dolor if I had the shame of returning without the singing apple, and since I obtained the dancing water by your means, I hope that you can find someone again to enable me to succeed in my enterprise."

"You have touched me," replied the turtle-dove, tenderly. "Follow me. I'll fly ahead of you, and I hope all will go well."

The prince let it go; after having traveled all day, they arrived near a mountain of sand.

"It's necessary to dig here," said the turtle-dove.

Immediately, without being deterred by anything, the prince started digging, sometimes with his hands and sometimes with his sword. After a few hours he found a helmet, a breastplate and the rest of a suit of armor, with the equipment for his horse, entirely made of mirrors.

"Arm yourself," said the turtle-dove, "and have no fear; the dragon, when it sees itself in all these mirrors, will be so frightened that it will flee, thinking that they are monsters like itself."

Cheri approved strongly of that expedient. He armored himself with the mirrors, and, picking up the turtle-dove, they went on together into the night. At daybreak, they heard a delightful melody. The prince begged the turtle-dove to tell him what it was.

"I'm convinced," it said, "that only the apple can utter such agreeable sounds, for it makes all the orchestral parts by itself, and, without making use of any instruments. It seems to be playing them in a delightful fashion.

They were still getting closer; the prince thought privately that he would like the apple to sing something appropriate to the situation he was in, and at the same time he heard these words:

> *Amour can overcome the most rebellious heart;*
> *Do not cease to be amorous.*
> *You who are following the laws of a cruel beauty,*
> *Love, persevere, and you will be happy.*

"Oh!" he cried, responding to those lines. "What a charming prediction! I can hope to be more content one day than I am; it has just been announced to me."

The turtle-dove said nothing about that; it had not been born loquacious, and only spoke about indispensably necessary things.

As they advanced further, the beauty of the music was augmented, and no matter what urgency he had, there was something so rapturous about it that he stopped without being able to think about anything but listening to it. The sight of the terrible dragon, however, which suddenly appeared with its twelve feet and more than a hundred claws, its three heads and its body of bronze, extracted him from that species of lethargy; it had scented the prince from far away, and was waiting for him in order to devour him like all the others, of whom it had made excellent meals. Their bones were distributed around the apple tree where the beautiful fruit was; they rose up so high that it could not be seen.

The frightful animal advanced, bounding. It covered the earth with an exceedingly dangerous poisonous foam. Fire emerged from its infernal maw, along with little dragonets, which it launched like darts into the eyes and ears of the knights errant who wanted to take away the apple. When it saw its terrifying figure, however, multiplied hundreds of times in all the prince's mirrors, it was frightened in its turn; it stopped, and, looking proudly at the prince charged with dragons, it no longer thought of anything but fleeing.

Cheri, perceiving the fortunate effect of his armor, pursued it all the way to the entrance to a profound cavern, into which it precipitated itself in order to evade him; he quickly sealed the entrance, and hastened to return toward the singing apple.

After having climbed over all the bones that surrounded it, he saw the beautiful tree with admiration; it was amber, with topaz apples, and the most excellent one of all, for which he had searched with so many cares and perils, appeared at the top, made of a single ruby, with a crown of diamonds above it. The prince, transported by joy to be able to give such a rare and perfect treasure to Belle-Etoile, hastened to break the amber branch, and, proud of his good fortune, he mounted his white horse; but he no longer found the turtle-dove. As soon as its cares were unnecessary, it had flown away.

Without wasting time in superfluous regrets, as he feared that the dragon, the hissing of which he could hear, might find some route to reach the apples, he returned with his own to the princess.

She had lost the usage of sleep during his absence; she reproached herself incessantly for her desire to have more intelligence than others; she dreaded Cheri's death more than her own.

"Oh, wretched woman!" she cried, uttering profound sighs. "Was it necessary that I had that vain glory? Was it not sufficient for me to think and speak well enough not to do and say anything impertinent? I shall be well punished for my pride if I lose the one I love! Alas," she continued, "perhaps the gods, irritated by the sentiments that I might be forbidden to have for Cheri, want to take him away from me by means of a tragic end."

There was nothing that her afflicted heart had not imagined when, in the middle of the night, she heard a music so marvelous that she could not help getting up and going to the window in order to listen better; she did not know what to think. Sometimes she believed that it was Apollo and the Muses, sometimes Venus, the Graces and the Amours. The symphony was still coming closer, and Belle-Etoile listened.

Finally, the prince arrived. The moonlight was bright. He stopped under the balcony of the princess, who had withdrawn when she perceived a rider in the distance. The apple immediately sang: "Wake up, beautiful sleeper."

Curiously, the princess looked out promptly to see who could be singing so well, and, recognizing her dear brother, she nearly leapt down from the window in order to be near him sooner. She shouted so loudly that the whole household woke up, and someone went to open the door to Cheri. He came in with an urgency that can easily be imagined. He was holding the amber branch in his hand, at the end of which was the marvelous fruit, and as he had often respired its scent, his intelligence was augmented to such a degree that nothing in the world was comparable.

Belle-Etoile ran to him with great precipitation.

"Do you think that I will thank you, my dear brother," she said to him, weeping with joy. "No, there is no possession that I am not buying too dearly when you risk your life in order to acquire it for me."

"There is no peril," he said, "that I do not always want to risk in order to give you the smallest satisfaction." He continued: "Receive, Belle-Etoile, this unique fruit; no one in the world merits it as much as you; but what can it give you that you do not have already?"

Petit-Soleil and his brother came to interrupt that conversation; they had a sensible pleasure in seeing the prince again. He recounted the story of his journey to them, and that relation took them all the way to daybreak.

The evil Feintise had returned to her little house after having talked to the queen about her projects; she was to anxious to sleep tranquilly; she heard the sweet song of the apple, which nothing in nature could equal. She had no doubt that the conquest had been made. She wept, she moaned, she scratched her face and she tore her hair; her dolor was extreme, for, instead of harming the beautiful children, as she had projected, she had done them good, even though nothing but perfidy had entered into her advice.

As soon as it was daylight, she learned that the return of the prince was only too true. She returned to the queen mother.

"Well, Feintise," that princess said, "are you bringing me good news? Have the children perished?"

"No, Madame," she said, throwing herself at her feet, "but Your Majesty should not be impatient; I still have an infinite number of means to deliver you from them."

"Oh, wretched woman," said the queen, "You're only in the world to betray me; you're sparing them."

The old woman protested that it was entirely the contrary, and when she had appeased her somewhat, she returned home in order to think about what it was necessary to do.

She let a few days go by without appearing, at the end of which she spied so well that she found the princess on a forest path where she was walking alone, awaiting the return of her brothers.

"Heaven is heaping you with benefits, charming Star," the rascally woman said, approaching her. "I've learned that you possess the singing apple; certainly, when news of that good fortune reached me, I could not have had more joy, for its necessary to confess that I have an inclination for you that interests me in all your advantages. However," she continued, "I can't help giving you a further advice."

"Oh, keep your advice!" cried the princess, drawing away from her. "Whatever benefits it brings me, they can't repay me for the anxiety for the anxiety it has caused me."

"Anxiety isn't such a great evil," she replied, smiling. "There are sweet and tender ones."

"Shut up," said Belle-Etoile. "I tremble when I think of it."

"It's true," said the old woman," that you have a great deal to lament, being the most beautiful and most intelligent woman in the world; I apologize for that."

"One more blow," replied the princess. "I have had enough of the state to which my brother's absence has reduced me."

"It's necessary, in spite of that," Feintise continued, "that I tell you that you still lack the little green bird that says everything; you would be informed of your birth, the good and bad successes of life; there is nothing so private that it could not reveal it to you. When everyone in the world says: 'Belle-Etoile has the dancing water and the singing apple,' they will say at the same time: 'but she does not have the little green bird that says everything,' and it would be almost as if she had nothing."

After having spoken thus what she had in mind, she withdrew.

The princes, sad and thoughtful, commenced to sigh bitterly. *That woman is right*, she said to herself. *What use to me are the advantages I receive from the water and the apple, since I do not know who I am, who my parents are, and by what fatality my brothers and I were exposed to the fury of the waves? It is necessary that there was something very extraordinary in our birth for us to be abandoned thus, and a very evident protection of Heaven to have saved us from so many perils. What pleasure I would have in knowing my father and my mother, in cherishing them if they are still alive, and honoring their memory if they are dead!*

With that, tears came in abundance to cover her cheeks, similar to the droplets of dew that appear in the morning on the lilies and the roses.

Cheri, who always had more impatience to see her than the others, had hastened to return from the hunt; he was on foot, his bow hanging negligently by his side, his hand holding a few arrows, his hair bound up. In that state he had a martial appearance that was infinitely pleasing. As soon as the princes perceived him, she went into a dark pathway, in order that he would not see the impressions of dolor that were on her face, but a mistress cannot draw away so rapidly that an urgent lover cannot overtake her.

He had scarcely cast his eyes upon her that he knew that she had some distress. He was anxious about that; he begged her and pressed her to tell him the reason for it, but she refused obstinately. Finally, he turned the point of one of his arrows against his heart. "You do not love me, Belle-Etoile," he said to her. "I have nothing more to do than to die."

The manner in which he spoke threw her into the utmost alarm; she no longer had the strength to refuse him her secret; but she only told him on condition that he would not seek as long as he lived the means of satisfying the desire that she had. He promised her everything she demanded, and gave no indication that he wanted to undertake that last journey.

As soon as she had retired to her bedroom and the princes to theirs, he went downstairs, took his horse out of the stable, mounted up and set forth, without speaking to anyone.

That news threw the beautiful family into a strange consternation. The king, who could not forget them, had sent an invitation to come and dine with him; they replied that their brother had just absented himself, and that they could not have any joy or repose without him, but that when he returned, they would not fail to go to the palace.

The princess was inconsolable; the dancing water and the singing apple had no more charms for her; without Cheri, nothing was agreeable to her.

The prince went forth, wandering through the world. He asked everyone he encountered where he might find the little green bird that says everything. Most of them did not know, but he encountered a venerable old man who, having invited him into his house, agreed to take the trouble to look into a globe that played a part in his study and his amusement. He said afterwards that it was in a glacial climate, on the summit of a frightful rock, and informed him of the route that he ought to take. The prince, full of gratitude, gave him a small bag of large pearls that had fallen from his hair, took his leave of him and continued his journey.

Finally, at dawn one day, he perceived the rock, very high and very steep, and on the summit, the bird that spoke like an oracle, saying admirable things. He understood that with a little skill it would be easy to catch, for it did not appear to be wild. It went back and forth, leaping lightly from one pinnacle to another. The prince dismounted, and, climbing silently in spite of the harshness of the mountain, he promised himself the pleasure of giving a sensible one to Belle-Etoile.

He was so close so the green bird that he thought he could catch it, when the rock suddenly opened up and he fell into a spacious hall; as motionless as a statue, he could no longer stir or complain of his deplorable adventure. Three hundred knights who had attempted the quest before him were in the same state. They looked at one another; it was the only thing that was permitted to them.

The time seemed so long to Belle-Etoile that, not seeing her Cheri return, she fell dangerously ill. The physicians knew full well that she was being devoured by a profound melancholy. Her brothers loved her tenderly; they talked to her about the cause of her malady; she confessed to them that she reproached herself day and night for Cheri going away; and that she sensed clearly that she would die if she did not receive news of him. They were touched by her tears, and in order to cure her, Petit-Soleil resolved to go in search of his brother.

The prince departed; he discovered where the famous bird was; he went there; he saw it; he approached it with the same hopes; and at that moment the rock engulfed him, he fell into the great hall, and the first thing that arrested his gaze was Cheri; but he could not speak to him.

Belle-Etoile was slightly convalescent; she hoped continually to see her two brothers return; but her hopes were disappointed; her affliction took on new force; she did not cease to lament day and night; she accused herself of her brothers' disaster, and Prince Heureux, having no less compassion for her than anxiety for the princes made the resolution in his turn to go in search of them. He said so to Belle-Etoile; immediately, she tried to oppose it, but he replied that it was only just that he risk himself in order to find the persons who were the dearest in the world to him. With that, he departed, having bid the princess tender adieux. She was left alone, prey to the sharpest dolor.

When Feintise heard that the third prince had set forth she rejoiced infinitely; she informed the queen mother, and promised her more than ever to doom the whole of that unfortunate family.

Indeed, Heureux had an adventure similar to Cheri and Petit-Soleil; he found the rock; he saw the beautiful bird; and he fell like a statue into the hall, where he recognized the princes for whom he was searching, without being able to speak to them. They were all arranged in crystal niches; they never slept, did not eat, and remained enchanted in a manner so sad that they only had the liberty to dream, and to deplore their adventure.

Inconsolable, Belle-Etoile, not seeing her brothers return, reproached herself for having waited such a long time to follow them. Without further hesitation, she gave orders to all her servants to wait for her for six months, but that if she or her brothers had not returned in that time they were to return to inform the corsair and his wife of their death. Then she put on male clothing, thinking that there was less risk for her, thus disguised, in her journey than if she had gone to travel the world as an adventuress.

Feintise saw her depart on her beautiful horse, and, at the culmination of her joy, she ran to the palace to regale the queen mother with that good news.

The princess was only armored by a helmet, the visor of which she hardly ever raised, for her beauty was so delicate and so perfect that no one would have believed, as she wanted them to, that she was a cavalier.

The rigor of the winter made itself felt, and the land where the little bird that says everything lived did not receive the fortunate influences of the sun in any season.

Belle-Etoile felt a strange cold, but nothing could deter her, when she saw a turtle-dove that was scarcely less white and scarcely less cold that the snow on which it was lying. In spite of her impatience to arrive at the rock, she did not want to let it die, and, descending from her horse, she took it in her hands, warmed it with her breath and then put it in her bosom. The poor little thing was no longer moving. Belle-Etoile thought it was dead; she regretted that. She took it out, looked at it, and said to it, as if it could understand her: "What can I do, lovely turtle-dove, to save your life?"

"Belle-Etoile," the small creature replied, "A soft kiss from your mouth can finish what you have so charitably begun."

"Not one," said the princess, "but a hundred, if necessary."

She kissed it, and the turtle-dove, recovering courage, said to her gaily: "I know you, in spite of your disguise; know that you are attempting something that would be impossible without my help; do as I advise you, then. As soon as you arrive at the rock, instead of seeking a means to climb it, stop at the foot, and commence singing the most beautiful and melodious song that you know. The green bird that says everything will listen to you and will remark where the voice is coming from. Afterwards, pretend to go to sleep. I will stay with you; when it sees me it will descent from the summit of the rock in order to peck me; it is at that moment that you will be able to catch it."

The princess, delighted by that hope, arrived at the rock almost immediately; she recognized her brothers' horses browsing the grass; that sight renewed all her dolors; she sat down and wept bitterly for a long time. But the little green bird said such beautiful things, so consoling for the unfortunate, that there was no heart that did not rejoice, with the consequence that she wiped away her tears and began to sing so loudly and so beautifully that the princes in the depths of their enchanted hall had the pleasure of hearing her. That was the first moment in which they sensed some hope.

The little green bird that says everything listened, and looked to see where that voice was coming from. It perceived the princess, who had taken off her helmet in order to sleep more comfortably, and the turtle-dove, which was fluttering around her. At that sight, it descended stealthily and came to peck it, but it had not plucked out three feathers when it was already captured.

"Ah! What do you want with me?" it said "What have I done to you to come so far to render me so unfortunate? Accord me my liberty, I implore you; say what you want in exchange, there is nothing I cannot do."

"I desire," said Belle-Etoile, "that you return my three brothers to me; I don't know where they are, but their horses, which are grazing near this rock, tell me whether you are retaining them in some place."

"I have a rose-red feather under my left wing," it said. "Pull it out and make use of it to touch the rock."

The princess was diligent in what she had been ordered to do; at the same time, she saw flashes of lightning and hard the sounds of wind and thunder mingled together, which caused her an extreme dread. In spite of her terror she kept hold of the green bird, fearful that it might escape. She touched the rock with the red feather again, and the third time, it split from the summit to the foot. She entered victoriously into the hall where the three princes were, with many others.

She ran to Cheri; he did not recognize her with his coat and her helmet, and the enchantment had not yet ended, with the consequence that he could nether speak nor act. The princess, who perceived that, asked further question of the green bird, to which it replied that it was necessary to rub the eyes and mouth of all those she wanted to disenchant with the red feather.

She rendered that good office to several kings and several other sovereigns, and especially to the three princes. Touched by such a great benefit, they threw themselves at her feet, naming her the liberator of kings. She perceived then that her brothers, deceived by her costume, did not recognize her, She took off her helmet promptly, held out her arms to them, embraced them a hundred times, and asked the other princes, with a great deal of civility, who they were.

Each one told her their particular adventure, and offered to accompany her wherever she wanted to go. She replied that, although the laws of chivalry might give her some right over the liberty that she had just rendered to them, she did not want to prevail upon it. With that, she retired with the princes, in order for them all to take account of what had happened to them since their separation.

The little green bird that says everything interrupted them to beg Belle-Etoile to set it at liberty; she immediately looked for the turtle-dove in order to ask its advice, but she no longer found it. She replied to the bird that it had cost her too many difficulties and anxieties for her to get such scant enjoyment from its conquest. All four of them mounted up, and left the kings and emperors to go away on foot, for in the two or three hundred years that they had been there, their equipages had perished.

The queen mother, rid of all the anxiety that the return of the beautiful children had caused her, renews her entreaties to the king to marry again, and importuned him so much that she chose a princess for him from among her relatives.

As it was necessary to break his marriage with poor Queen Blondine, who had always remained with her mother in their little house in the country, with the three dogs that they named Chagrin, Mouron and Douleur because of all the troubles they had caused them, the queen mother sent for her; she climbed into a carriage, dressed in black, with a long veil that fell to her feet, taking the dogs with her.

In that state, she appeared more beautiful than the day star, although she had become pale and thin, for she no longer slept and only ate out of complaisance. Except for the queen mother, everyone felt very sorry for her; the king was so moved by compassion that he dared not look at her, but when he thought that he was at risk of having no heirs but dogs, he consented to everything.

The day of the wedding having arrived, the queen mother, begged by Admirale Rousse—who had always hated her unfortunate sister—said that she wanted Queen Blondine to be present at the celebration. Everything was prepared to make it grandiose and sumptuous, and as the king would not be sorry for the foreigners to see that magnificence, he sent his chief squire to the house of the beautiful children to invite them to come, and ordered that if they could not come yet, he was to leave orders that they could be informed when they returned.

The chief squire went to search for them and did not find them, but, knowing the pleasure that the king would have in seeing them, he left one of his gentlemen to wait for them, in order to bring them without any delay.

The happy day arrived, which was that of a great banquet. Belle-Etoile and the three princes arrived; the gentleman told them the king's story: that he had once married a poor girl, perfectly beautiful and good, who had had the misfortune to give birth to three dogs, and that he had expelled her in order no longer to see her; that he had loved her so much that he had spent fifteen years without wanting to listen to any proposal of marriage; that the queen mother and his subjects had pressed him so forcefully that he had resolved to marry a princess of the court, and that it was necessary to come promptly to witness the whole ceremony.

At the same time Belle-Etoile put on a rose-colored velvet robe garnished with brilliant diamonds; she let her hair fall in long curls over her shoulders, and tied it again with ribbons. The star that she had on her forehead emitted so much light, and the golden chain that ran around her neck without her being able to remove it seemed to be of a metal far more precious even than gold. In sum, nothing so beautiful had ever appeared to mortal eyes. Her brothers were no less so, especially Prince Cheri, who has something about him that distinguished him very advantageously.

All four of them climbed into an ebony and ivory carriage, the interior of which was cloth of gold, with similar cushions, embroidered with gems; twelve white horses drew it; the rest of their equipage was incomparable.

When Belle-Etoile and her brother appeared, the delighted king came to receive them with his entire court at the top of the staircase. The singing apple made itself heard in a marvelous manner; the dancing water danced; and the little green bird that says everything spoke better than oracles. All four knelt down before the king, took his hand and kissed it with as much respect as affection.

He embraced them and said: "I am obliged to you, amiable foreigners, for having come here today; your presence gives me a sensible pleasure. As he finished speaking he went with them into a large drawing room, where musicians were playing all sorts of instruments and several splendidly-served tables left nothing to be desired of good cheer.

The queen mother arrived, accompanied by her future daughter-in-law, Admirale Rousse and all the ladies, among whom the poor queen was brought, with a long leather thong around her neck and the three dogs tethered in the same fashion. She was taken into the middle of the room, where there was a cauldron of bones and rotten meat, which the queen mother had ordered for their meal.

When Belle-Etoile and the princes saw her so unfortunate, although they did not know her, tears came to their eyes, either because the revolution of the grandeurs of the world touched them, or they were moved by the force of the blood, which made itself felt.

But what did the evil queen think of a return so unexpected and so contrary to her designs? She darted a furious glance at Feintise, who desired ardently then that the earth might open up in order to precipitate herself into it.

The king introduced the beautiful children to his mother, saying a thousand good things to her about them, and in spite of the anxiety by which she was gripped, she spoke to them nevertheless with a cheerful expression, and looked at them as favorably as if she had loved them, for dissimulation was customary in those days.

The feast passed very gaily, although the king was extremely pained to see his wife eating with her dogs, like the least of creatures. Having resolved to have complaisance for his mother, however, who was obliging him to remarry, he allowed her to organize everything.

At the end of the meal, the king addressed Belle-Etoile, saying: "I know that you are in possession of three treasures that are incomparable; I congratulate you, and I beg you to tell us what it was necessary to do to conquer them."

"Sire," she said, "I will obey you with pleasure. I had been told that the dancing water would render me beautiful and that the singing apple would give me intelligence; I wanted to have them for those two reasons. With regard to the little green bird that says everything, I had another; it is that we do not know our fatal birth; we are infants abandoned by our relatives, of whom we do not know any. I hoped that this marvelous bird might enlighten us on a matter that occupies us day any night."

"To judge your birth by you," replied the king, "it must be of the most illustrious; but speak sincerely, who are you?"

"Sire," she told him, "my brothers and I have deferred interrogating it until our return; on arrival we received you orders to come to your wedding; all that I have been able to do has been to bring you the three rarities in order to divert you."

"I am very glad," cried the king, "not to defer such an agreeable matter."

"You're amusing yourself with all these bagatelles that are proposed to you." said the queen mother, angrily. "They're clowns, with their rarities; the names alone ought to tell you that nothing is more ridiculous. Fie! I don't want petty foreigners, apparently from the dregs of the people, to have the advantage of abusing your credulity. All this consists of some tricks of sleight-of-hand and without you, they wouldn't have the honor of sitting at my table."

On hearing a discourse so disobliging, Belle-Etoile and her brothers did not know what would become of them; their faces were covered with confusion and despair at enduring such an insult before that great court. But the king, having replied to his mother that her procedure was exaggerated, begged the beautiful children not to be chagrined, and extended his had to them as a sign of amity.

Belle-Etoile took a crystal bowl, into which she poured all the dancing water; the water was immediately seen to leap in cadence, going back and forth, rising up like a little irritated sea, changing a thousand colors, and moving the crystal bowl along the king's table; then it suddenly threw a few drops in the face of the chief squire, to whom the children had some obligation. He was a man of rare merit, but his ugliness was no less so, and he had lost an eye. As soon as the water had touched him, he became so handsome that he was no longer recognizable, and his eye was cured.

The king, who loved him dearly, had as much joy in that adventure as the queen mother felt displeasure, for she could not hear anything but the applause that was given to the princes.

After the great noise had died down, Belle-Etoile put on the dancing water the singing apple, made of a single ruby crowned with diamonds, with its amber branch; it commenced a concert so melodious that a hundred musicians could not have done a much. That delighted the king and the entire court, and they only emerged from their admiration when Belle-Etoile took from her sleeve a little golden cage of marvelous workmanship, in which was the green bird that says everything. It was nourished on powdered diamonds and only drank the liquid of distilled pearls.

She took it, very delicately, and placed it on the singing apple; she fell silent out of respect, in order to give it time to speak. It had plumage of such great delicacy that it agitated when one closed one's eyes, and when they were reopened near to it, it was all the shades of green imaginable.

It addressed the king, and asked him what he wanted to know.

"We all want to know," said the king," who this beautiful young woman and these three young men are."

"O King," replied the green bird, in a strong and intelligible voice, "she is your daughter, and two of the princes are your sons; the third, named Cheri, is your nephew." With that, it recounted the entire story, with an incomparable eloquence, without neglecting the slightest detail.

The king dissolved in tears, and the afflicted queen, who had quit her cauldron and had approached slowly, wept with joy and amour for her husband and her children—for could the verity of the story be doubted, when all the marks that allowed them to be recognized were visible?

The three princes and Belle-Etoile got up at the end of their story; they came throw themselves at the king's feet; they embraced his knees and kissed his hands; He held out his arms to them, he hugged them to his heart; nothing could be heard but sighs and cries of joy.

The king got up and, seeing the queen, his wife, who was still fearful, lurking near the wall in a humiliated fashion, he went to her, made her a thousand caresses, presented her with an armchair next to his own and obliged her to sit in it. Her children kissed her feet and hands a thousand times; no spectacle was ever more tender or more touching.

Everyone wept on their own account, and raised their hands and eyes toward Heaven, to render thanks to it for having permitted such important and obscure things to be known.

The king thanked the princess who had had the design of marrying him, and gave her a large quantity of gems. But with regard to the queen mother, the admiral's wife and Feintise, what would he not have done to them if he had listened to his resentment? The thunder of his anger was beginning to rumble when the generous queen, her children and Cheri implored him to calm down and to render against them a judgment more exemplary than rigorous.

He had the queen mother imprisoned in a tower, but the admiral's wife and Feintise were thrown into a black damp dungeon, where they only ate with the three dogs named Chagrin, Mouron and Douleur, which, no longer seeing their good mistress, bit them continually. They ended their lives there, which were long enough to give them time to repent of all their crimes.

As soon as the queen mother, Admirale Rousse and Feintise had been taken away, each to the place that the king had ordered, the musicians recommenced playing their instruments and singing. The joy was unparalleled. Belle-Etoile and Cheri felt it more than everyone else put together; they saw themselves on the eve of being happy. In fact, the king finding his nephew to be the most handsome and most intelligent man in his court, said to him that he did not want such a great day to pass without celebrating his wedding, and that he would grant him his daughter.

The prince, transported by joy, threw himself at his feet, and Belle-Etoile testified no less satisfaction.

But it was only just that the aged princess, who had lived in solitude for so many years quit it in order to participate in the public joy. The same little fay who had come to dinner in her house and whom she had received so well, suddenly came in there again, in order to tell her what was happening at the court.

"Let's go," she continued. "I'll tell you on the way the cares I have taken for your family."

The grateful princess climbed into her carriage; it was brilliant with gold and azure, preceded by martial instruments and by a corps of six hundred guards, who appeared to be great lords. She told the princess the whole story of her grandchildren, and said that she had not abandoned them, that in the form of a siren, and that of a turtle-dove—in sum, in a thousand fashions—she had protected them.

"You see," the fay added, "that a benefit is never wasted."

The good princess wanted to kiss her hands continually to mark her gratitude; she could not find terms that were not below her joy.

Finally, they arrived. The king received them with a thousand testimonies of amity. As one can believe, Queen Blondine and the beautiful children hastened to testify amity to the illustrious lady, and when they knew what the fay had done in their favor, and that she was the gracious turtle-dove who had guided them, nothing could be added to what they said to her.

To complete heaping the king with satisfaction, she told him that his mother-in-law, whom he had always taken for a poor peasant, had been born Princess Souveraine. That was perhaps the only thing that the monarch's happiness lacked.

The celebrations finished with the wedding of Belle-Etoile and Prince Cheri. They sent in quest of the corsair and his wife, in order to recompense them for the noble education they had given the beautiful children. Finally, after long troubles, everyone was satisfied.

> *Amour, not to displease the censors*
> *Is the origin of glory,*
> *He can animate great hearts*
> *To brave peril and seek victory.*
> *He it is who, throughout the world,*
> *Has conserved the memory of Prince Cheri,*
> *And who made him attempt the various exploits*
> *That are marked in his story.*
> *As soon one wants to pay his court to the fair sex,*
> *One must be prepared to serve its caprices;*
> *But a heart does not fear the greatest precipices*
> *If it has to animate it glory and amour.*

The tale of Princess Belle-Etoile had given so much admiration to La Dandinardière that he would willingly have spent the rest of the evening praising it. He could not prevent himself, in the excess of his enthusiasm, from taking Virginie's hand and tugging it so abruptly that, not being prepared for it, she fell on to Vicomte de Berginville, and the vicomte fell rudely on to the floor. La Dandinardière appeared astonished by that disorder; he accused his star in pompous terms, said several times that he was persecuted, and that he had never expected to succeed so poorly in a petty gallantry to which admiration had engaged him.

"It is singular," the beautiful amazon said to him, "that one tears out the arm when one seeks to please; you've crippled me for several days."

"I'm no better treated, Monsieur de la Dandinardière," said the vicomte. "What annoys me most is that in falling, my wig also fell off, and as I give myself all the appearances of youth when I can, I find myself very embarrassed to justify my gray hairs before these ladies."

"I can see by Monsieur de La Dandinardière's expression that you're augmenting his pain by speaking to him thus," said the prior. "It's necessary to have some regard for a wounded knight like him, and I swear to you that he could have broken my neck and I wouldn't have said a word about it."

"I would expect that of you," he said, "but alas, the ladies have many other privileges; cruelty is their prerogative, and the beautiful Virginie is certainly sustaining her rights."

"Don't reproach me for my laments," she replied. "Another than me would have cried much louder, but to speak to you sincerely, I have the sentiments of an Alexander."

"And the rigors of an Alexandrette,"[17] said La Dandinardière, with an abundance of joy, for he believed that

---

[17] When the story was written Alexandrette was a small town in what was then part of Syria; it is now Iskenderun, a city in Turkey.

he had said the least common and prettiest thing. He was astonished that no one applauded him; he looked at all the company with a sly expression that gave the messieurs a strong desire to laugh. As for Marthonide, who was the most liberal of all your women in matters of praise, and refrained from leaving it unemployed for long, she commented with regard to Alexandrette on the finesse of the expression and the beauties it contained, even hidden beauties unknown to the vulgar.

Virginie spoke in her turn, to say that he had a superior mind, capable of polishing an entire kingdom, exiling obscenities therefrom and giving the utmost perfection to the language. That was followed by fifty more disparate compliments that were worth no more, for the beautiful provincials had an inexhaustible storehouse of them.

It was already late; Madame de Saint-Thomas thought that it was necessary to give the invalid the time to repose a little; she wished him goodnight, and all the company followed her. Only the good Alain remained with La Dandinardière; his attitude was still mortified and contrite because of the fall he had caused, and he was standing in a corner of the room, not daring to approach his lord and master, when the latter called to him benignly.

"Give me my night-cap," he said to him, "instead of this turban; it's becoming, but I find it very uncomfortable, and I don't know how the Turks can accommodate them, because mine keeps falling off."

"Oh, Monsieur," said Alain, with his usual simplicity, "don't be astonished; the demons are their friends, truly, when they get mixed up in it, they'll have something on their heads other than a turpin, and can't you see that the ladies, who aren't as Turkish as the Great Turk, wear I don't know how many ribbons on theirs."

"Say a turban, wretch," cried La Dandinardière. "I can't stand it when you speak improperly."

"Oh, if I'm improper," said Alain, who did not understand, "it's not my fault; it was raining when I had the punches in the courtyard; you've treated me roughly in your room since, and you now that plaster doesn't do a garment any good. I protest, Monsieur, that I'm heartbroken when I see you angry in a dirty place; it's as many stains on my coat, which won't blow away."

"I'm grateful to you," he said, "for having so much consideration for the clothes I give you; I promise you, Alain, that I'll be carefully to take off your undershirt every time I beat you."

"That's a nasty promise, Monsieur," he replied, "frankly, since you've been here, you've become ruder than our clothsbrushes. I've seen a time, not very long ago, when I was the faithful and beloved domestic. Alas, as my old grandmother used to say, to put them in our pot!"

"What pot are you talking about? We only like cabbages, rascal," replied his master

"I mean," Alain continued, "that you're the pot and I'm the cabbage, that you cultivate me and water me in order to eat me—which is to say, to make use of me and beat me; anyway, you don't love me. Oh la la, I'm very foolish to…but I'll say no more."

He did, indeed, shut up; his silence saved him a few blows that a longer argument would have attracted, for his master's head was already very heated.

Supper was served. La Dandinardière had been so tormented during the day that he ate like a starveling in the evening; his supper was followed by a profound slumber, and he was still asleep when Maître Robert, the village surgeon, came to knock on his door with his fists and feet.

"Ha ha! Monsieur de La Dandinardière," he shouted, at the top of his voice, "Do you want to depart without trumpets, then? The rumor's running around that you're returning home without paying me; haven't I taken good enough care of your head? If they'd let me go on when it was cracked, I would have put into it what it lacks; but I'll stand guard at your door, you'll only go out like a ghost. Make promises and don't keep any, that's the means of getting rich A good liar goes far; I don't care about all that; I'm a good trumpet horse; you'll pay me, or I'll lose my Latin."

La Dandinardière was very surprised and very indignant at Maître Robert's insolence. He listened to him spouting proverbs like Sancho Panza for a while; eventually he woke his valet, who was profoundly asleep, and having whispered to him approach, he went on: "Do you hear the impertinences of that rogue of a surgeon? He wants me to pay him for the care that he took to kill me. Doesn't it seem, to hear him, that I owe him a great deal, and that I could go bankrupt in honor and law and still have to satisfy him? Oh, he merits being thumped, but I'm not in a humor to commit myself with such a ruffian; that's your job. It's necessary that you make an abrupt and prompt sortie against him, throw him to the ground, then give him thirty punches at your leisure; I'll support you, and that will be his only payment."

"You'll support me?" replied Alain. "What will you do, Monsieur, to support me?"

"I'll go up quietly behind you," he replied, "and I'll bolt the door, for if you had the misfortune to be the weaker, he'd come into my room, and I've already said that I scorn him too much to beat him."

"Oh, Monsieur," Alain replied, "I also scorn him a great deal, and I ask you for permission not to have myself knocked down by a man so far beneath me."

"Since when have you become boastful?" added the bourgeois.

"I don't know what to call it," said the valet, "but to speak frankly. I still feel the broken ribs from yesterday's fight; would you really have the heart to send me against a fresh man that I scorn so much? Believe me, Monsieur, it's better that you take the trouble to beat him yourself; at least there won't be anything good or bad done except by you.

"I've already told him," said La Dandinardière, "that if someone demands money from me with so much noise, he'd be too inferior to me."

"Alas, Monsieur," said Alain, "You beat me every day, and I swear to you that he's from a family as good as mine; my father was the village farrier and he's the surgeon; it's more honorable to bandage people than horses; all that could well render him worthy of your blows."

"You can give me a hundred genealogies like that one," cried La Dandinardière, "without me getting any more heated, but I know you're a coward who only likes you're wretched skin."

"While he was saying these insults in a low voice to the prudent Alain, Maître Robert continued his racket, and La Dandinardière, in despair, unable to suffer it any longer or to expose himself to the vexing consequences of a quarrel, found a singular means of avenging himself. At the bottom of the door there was a rather large hole, by means of which the vigilant cat came in to make war on little mice. After getting up, as he had neither shoes nor slippers, and he was afraid of catching cold, he put on his boots and seized the fire-tongs, which he passed gently through the cat-hole, and with which he suddenly gripped Robert's leg.

The latter thought he had been bitten by a snake, and uttered frightful cries; he scarcely dared look at his leg, so fearful was he that the terrible snake might leap at his eyes. La Dandinardière neglected nothing for his part in order to pinch him hard; nothing has ever succeeded better; the noise was augmented as much by Maître Robert's plaints as by the bourgeois' bursts of laughter.

The vicomte and the prior, whose bedrooms were adjacent to his, knowing a part of what was happening—for those good folk had given the order for it—got up and came to appease the commencement of the most furious quarrel that has ever been seen in a peaceful village.

Maître Robert was a Norman; he liked lawsuits only slightly less than a broken head or dislocated arms. "Messieurs!" he cried. "I take you for witnesses; I assign you before all the judges in the world to declare that I am crippled and will never recover."

It was all that he could do to say those few words, for the tongs were playing their role so well that at that moment, when La Dandinardière tightening them more than he had before; Maître Robert lost his color and his speech.

The vicomte and the prior could not help laughing at so novel a means of combat; but as it was a question of pacifying the irritated spirits on either side, they begged La Dandinardière to declare a truce, withdraw the tongs and open the door. A soon as Maître Robert felt himself out of slavery, he went away, protesting that he would quarrel for as long as he lived against such a bad payer.

The little bourgeois had not yet had the pleasure of making an enemy quit the battlefield; he was so proud of it that, without reflecting on the irregularity of his undress, he appeared before the messieurs in a chemise and boots with his tongs over his shoulder, in a fashion almost reminiscent of Hercules carrying his club.

"You're very angry," said the prior. "Don't you fear that it might make you ill?"

"I fear nothing," he replied, proudly, "not even death when it arms itself with its most dangerous features."

"What has just happened," said the vicomte, with a serious expression, "marks your intrepidity clearly enough, but with all that, I think you ought to pay a poor unfortunate who has no step remaining."

"Say rather," cried La Dandinardière, "that he's a rogue who ought to pay me for all the harm he's done me; I'd be cured without him. That scoundrel wanted to cut my skin like a piece of leather."

"A little generosity would make peace," sad the prior. "He's ignorant, like many others; perhaps that's not his fault, but I advise you, as a friend, not to be obstinate in refusing him a few pistoles."

"You're joking, Monsieur le Prieur," said La Dandinardière. "I haven't come expressly from Paris to be the dupe of provincials; I've had more than one dispute in my life

from which I've emerged with drums beating and flags flying."

"Truly," said Alain, also playing the bravo, "I believe
that we're eaters of iron-bound handcarts; my master eats the
big ones and I the small ones."

"Don't play the villain so much, friend Alain," said the
vicomte. "If someone starts a lawsuit in which you're named,
beware the consequences."

"Why?" he said. "I didn't see anything; everything happened through the cat hole. I didn't even want to hand over the
tongs of which Maître Robert's leg might complain. Oh, let
him come with his lawsuit, to see if I can't defend myself. I
had an uncle who was the procurator fiscal of a good
seigneurie and I can scribble like anyone else."

"Courage, my lads," said the vicomte, laughing. "Here's
the Alexander and Barthole of our days united against Maître
Robert; for myself, as a friend of peace, I'll get dressed to go
in search of the olive branch."

"And I," said the little bourgeois, "am going back to bed,
for that rogue took care to irritate me at an early hour."

With that they separated.

No joy was ever greater than La Dandinardière on thinking about the exploits he had just performed; he talked about
them for a long time to his valet. "You see," he said, "now I
take action to punish insolence. Woe, woe betide anyone who
annoys me."

His valet repeated several times: "Woe, woe betide anyone who annoys us."

Although Alain had seen him do anything that that he
could not have done himself, he nevertheless looked at him in
a more respectful manner than usual "I confess, Monsieur," he
said to him, that you've repaired the dread that you testified in
regard to Monsieur de Villeville, and I don't doubt at present
that you'll have the goodness to fight him."

"That's an old quarrel," said the bourgeois, "of which
you can do without reminding me; I'm convinced that that
fellow has made his reflections and that he won't be suffi-

ciently devoid of common sense to measure his sword against mine."

"But at all hazard, Monsieur," said Alain, "Would you like to measure yours instead of mine?"

"I don't know," said La Dandinardière, shaking his head two or three times. "I don't know; once again, it's not lack of courage, I've said so a hundred times, I have that to spare, but when I think about the adventure that befell me on the sea shore, that demon who resembled a man like two drops of water, and who made me that wretched appeal that has bothered me since, I confess, Alain, that I'd rather see you do battle than do it myself."

"Oh, I'm not so stupid," said Alain. "You want to deliver me to the wolf's mouth, and that demon, if it is one, would carry me away still warm and fully dressed to the other world. Do you believe, Monsieur, that for having fewer pistoles than you, I like poor Alain any less? No, in truth the écus aren't sufficient to render one happy, health is necessary, or to die; if I go to fight with that magician and he gives me two or three sword-cuts, one of which makes my eyes pop out of my head, another cuts the whistle and the last punctures my heart, do you think in al conscience that I'll be well?"

"Where have you got the idea, wretch," replied La Dandinardière, "that Villeville would treat you thus?"

"It's very easy to believe," said Alain. "Don't demons have even more power than fays?" Don't you remember the fine tale that was read to us yesterday, in which apples sang like nightingales, birds talked like doctors and water danced like shepherds? After all that, Monsieur, aren't I right to fear for my skin?"

"You're a strange fellow," said La Dandinardière, "to torment yourself and torment me as you're doing; for, after all, at present there's no question of Villeville. Let me savor the pleasure of my victory, and go to sleep, disturber of my repose."

"Go to sleep yourself, Monsieur," said Alain. He drew his curtains and went to the window that overlooked the high road.

Alain had been killing flies there—for he was their sworn enemy—for more than an hour when he saw Villeville passing by on horseback, and who happened, by chance, to look up, saw him and recognized him.

Villeville knew the terrible fear that his name alone caused La Dandinardière and his valet; Baron Saint-Thomas, who was his friend, had informed him of it. He found that adventure very amusing, with the result, that in order not to belie his character of swashbuckler, he drew his pistol, as if he wanted to kill Alain.

"Oh, Monsieur!" the latter cried to him, putting his hands together. "Don't mistake me, please. Do you remember all the blows you gave me some time ago? I swear that I haven't conserved any rancor."

Villeville made no reply, but he continued to take aim, which augmented Alain's anxiety greatly.

"I can see, he said, that you want to kill someone; wait a moment. I'd rather it was my master than me; I'll go and wake him; he'll be very annoyed, but it's all I can do."

As he finished speaking he went to tug La Dandinardière's arm. "Monsieur," he said, "take the trouble to get up; there's someone under our windows who wants to see you."

The bourgeois was still asleep; he threw his dressing gown over his shoulder, put on his boots and ran to the window. But O gods, what a vision for him! A firearm in the hands of his enemy, the redoubtable Villeville! He certainly did not waste time complimenting him, as his valet had done; and without pushing reflection any further, he threw himself head first under the bed, where fear alone gave him the strength squeeze himself, for surely, at any other sight than that of a drawn pistol, he would not have been able to do so.

As soon as he had done it, however, he felt so pressed that, not understanding anything more dangerous for him than the violent state that he was in, he wanted to pull himself out, at the risk of the most unfortunate consequences.

He made futile efforts to do that; the bed was too low, he was crushed underneath it.

"Alain," he cried, "I'm going to die. Help me."

But his faithful domestic did not hear him; he was hiding in a cupboard that lowered by night to serve as a bed. He had quickly lifted it again and was holding on to it with both hands with all his might, as the thing most useful to his conservation in all the world. He was so occupied that he did not even feel his fingernails being torn out, which did him a great deal of harm.

Villeville, no longer seeing the bourgeois gentleman or his valet appear, fired two pistol shots in order to frighten them. In fact, La Dandinardière was so terrified by them that he lost his voice from some time, and Alain was so fearful that he suddenly dropped the front of the cupboard that he was clasping with so much fatigue; he fell too, full length, head first—gently, in truth, because he was on his bed, but he took a tumble that threw him to the other end of the room.

It would have been difficult for all that disorder to occur without making a lot of noise; Messieurs de Saint-Thomas, de Berginville and the prior were then in a room downstairs holding a little council, of which La Dandinardière was the subject. That room was underneath his bedroom; they thought that a thunderbolt had just struck it, or that Maître Robert, veritably angered by having been rudely seized by the tongs, was taking a memorable vengeance for it. They hastened to run upstairs in order to be spectators of that new scene.

They found Alain still lying on the floor. They went to his master's bed, where they could hear his plaintive voice and muffled cries, without being able to imagine where they were coming from. They asked his valet several times where he was, but Alain put his finger over his mouth, content to show them the window silently, without responding. They looked out, not knowing whether he might have been mad enough to try a somersault of that magnitude. Villeville was no longer here, and they could not understand what Alain meant by his mysterious signs.

The sad plaints continued; the poor bourgeois was suffering all that one can suffer. Finally, the baron looked under the bed, and was not a little astonished that he had been able to put himself under there.

Alain, encouraged by the sight of them, came to their aid; he took hold of his master by one foot and hauled with all his might; he pulled off his boot, which would not have been difficult to remove if it had not been wedged, like the rest of his body; but the valet was strong, and that only served to send him flying for twenty feet, the boot in his hand.

"Good," he said, rather comically. "The fays have endowed me with falling today, endlessly and incessantly, but I know a good remedy, which is not to get up again."

No one was listening to him; they were too occupied with saving the life of the bourgeois gentleman; they tried to pull him out, sometimes by one leg, sometimes the other, but he could not get out of the trap; and as his back and his shoulders were having a very bad time, they decided to throw the mattress on to the floor and give him a liberty of which he had great need.

He was extensively scratched, his face was bruised and his nose crushed; his skin was redder than scarlet. They laid him down. Hs valet was ordered to fetch some Spanish wine for drinking and some eau-de-vie for rubbing.

"I beg you," said Alain to the vicomte, "to take the trouble yourself, for, to conceal nothing from you, that terrible Monsieur de Villeville is prowling around the house, and I fear the sight of him more than thunder."

"Shut up, unworthy chatterbox," La Dandinardière shouted at him. Where have you got the idea that Villeville has just fired pistol shots under my window and that it scared me?"

"I didn't mention them," replied Alain, "but the cat's out of the bag now."

"Don't believe it," continued the bourgeois. "I wouldn't have been afraid of Hercules in the flesh and bone, much less so of that petty gentlemen whose income is very meager and far inferior to mine. It's true that this unworthy valet sometimes has visions so forceful that he believes them and cites them as truths. But to enable you to understand what obliged me to wedge myself so unfortunately under my bed, it's because I dreamed that, after fighting, I had put my enemy to flight; I jumped out of bed to pursue him and it seemed to me that he passed underneath it; the heat of combat and the courage that isn't astonishing in perils engaged me to do the same. As soon as I was there I woke up, chagrined to be there but not surprised to have put myself there, for I'm in the catalogue of sleepwalkers, and the whole court knows that for several years in succession I had myself bathed while asleep."

While he was speaking, Alain—whom he could not see—was making signs and muttering between his teeth to the contrary, but Monsieur de Saint-Thomas, who was seeking to oblige him, replied that everything that he had just said was true, that he knew that Villeville was not very well, and that even if he had been in good health he was not sufficiently hostile to life to come in search of doom with a man more dangerous in combats than Mars and Hercules.

La Dandinardière, thinking that he believed him, recovered a part of his good humor and was preparing to spout a few more lies when the messieurs decided that it was appropriate to give him time to drink the Spanish wine and rub himself with eau-de-vie.

As soon as they were at liberty to talk, Baron de Saint-Thomas, addressing the vicomte, said: "I protest to you that if you aren't as cowardly, you're at least as mad as our bourgeois gentleman if you want to persuade me to make him my son-in-law."

"Say anything you please," he replied. "I sustain that my vision isn't ridiculous, and if anything embarrasses me it isn't proprieties, for there aren't any in this affair, as we all know; it's the means of persuading that little miser to marry a young woman of quality for her lovely eyes."

"Did you notice yesterday," the prior said, interrupting, "the pretentions that he established on his fortune? Another blow—if we aren't clever, that's a marriage spoiled."

"That would be a great misfortune," said the baron, smiling, "And I'd be greatly afflicted by it."

"I assure you," said the vicomte, "that he's rich, and that for all his impertinent bragging—which always concludes with his self-preservation—he nevertheless understands his interest. By the way, it was me who had the idea of drawing the choleric Robert to him."

"I don't know your views on that," replied Monsieur de Saint-Thomas, "but it's necessary for you to let alone the conduct of an affair of which I'm not sufficiently fond to torment myself over much with it."

The arrival of other people interrupted the conversation.

The prior, having been told that La Dandinardière could not sleep, went to his room to keep him company. As he approached the door, he stopped, because he heard him talking to Alain.

"What!" he said. "You believe me to be capable of pardoning the affront that you've just attracted to me?"

"Do I even know what an affront is?" said Alain. "I spoke naively of what I'd just seen; any other valet in my place would have said the same. I saw you under the bed and I knew full well that you had good reasons for putting yourself there."

"You knew?" said the bourgeois. "Who told you, then?"

"My heart," said the worthy Alain, "which is flesh and bone like any other, and which was dying of fear; for without that cupboard in which I took shelter, certainly, Monsieur, I believe I wouldn't be alive at present."

"I find you very bold," cried La Dandinardière, "to judge my sentiments by yours. Heroes don't measure themselves by the yardstick of a rogue like you. If I put myself under the bed

it's because I didn't want to risk being shot by a traitor who
would only dare to attack me from a distance."

"You've forgotten, then," Alain replied, "that you'd been
hiding there for more than a quarter of an hour when Villeville
fired that terrible pistol shot, or cannon shot, for I don't know
which."

"Shut up, torturer," he replied. "Until now, I've counted
somewhat on your courage. I know you now, and I'm waiting
impatiently to return to my château in order to expedite a formal dismissal."

"Alas, Monsieur," he said, utterly afflicted, "how have I
merited it? I was afraid, like you—is that a crime? Ought I to
be braver than my master? If you'd taken me in order to beat
me, which I would have promised you without wanting to do
it, you'd have reason to complain, but there was no more question of that than the soul of the Wandering Jew."

La Dandinardière felt joy on seeing his valet so touched;
he liked people to love him. "Get down on your knees," he
said. "You're softening me."

Alain prostrated himself at the foot of the bed.

"I forgive you," he added. "And I'll do more; I'll give
you courage—here's a provision of it." As he finished speaking he boxed his ears with all his might. "You can count on
me," he said, "to put you in a state to fight anyone you like."

"What!" cried Alain. "Without being beaten?"

"Yes," said his master, "I assure you of it."

"Thank you," Alain relied, "but Monsieur, if you only
wanted to slap me a hundred écus of wages, I'd do it much
more easily; for all in all, I don't want to quarrel with anyone;
a little money would be better to obtain courage for you."

The prior could see by the appearance of the conversation that it would not finish soon; after having enjoyed it for a
while, he went into the room.

"I thought you were asleep," he said, "for it seems to me
that you went to bed with that intention."

"It's true," replied La Dandinardière, "and I would be
asleep, in fact, but for amour, which is a furious alarm-clock.

As soon as I want to close my eyes, it represents Virginie and Marthonide to me, more charming than the dawn."

"Oh, truly, you aren't inconvenienced by the excess of your tenderness," said the prior. "I haven't forgotten that you prefer wealth the merit and beauty. It's true," he continued, "that that declaration has put a veil over your good qualities, as eclipses veil the sun."

"I'm delighted by that good comparison," replied the little bourgeois, "but do you think me of a humor to reveal my amorous secrets in public? No, no, Monsieur, a little mystery is necessary."

"If you're speaking seriously," said the prior, "I offer you my cares to help your designs to succeed; remember that Virginie has a great deal of merit."

"Tell me," added La Dandinardière, "what would one be given in marriage to her?"

"What would one be given?" replied the prior. "Don't you know? A very large dowry, an income worth more that the most beautiful land in the region."

"You mean houses in Paris," said La Dandinardière, "or an income from the Hôtel de Ville?"

"Those are mere bagatelles," said the prior. "One would be given the gift of making up tales, and you don't know where that goes."

The bourgeois did not appear touched by that.

"Ha ha," he said, after a moment's meditation. "One could put that down for something in the marriage contract, but fundamentally, if she only brought that to a husband, I think the household would go badly."

"You're very materialistic," exclaimed the prior, "but intelligence has its price."

"I'm not so ignorant," he replied, "as to scorn intelligence; I only want a reasonable wealth with it, for I reply to you with regard to your much-vaunted tales that I can make them in my turn and put them to profit."

"I'd be glad to witness that," said the prior. "You doubtless think that it's only necessary to write hyperboles strewn here and there: *there was once a fay*, and the work is perfect. I declare to you that more art enters into it than you think, and I see some every day that have nothing agreeable about them."

"You're saying, then," said the bourgeois, angrily, "that mine would be in that class. Frankly, Monsieur, you're not obliging; but I intend to make one up, or die; we'll see you change your language afterwards."

"I would never refuse my praise," said the prior, adopting a gracious manner in order to appease him, "and if you take my advice, you'll start working on it today."

"I intend to," said La Dandinardière. "Do you think that I've brought my library with so much care and expense to leave it idle?"

"It only depends on you," said the prior, "for me to aid you as I've already done."

That proposition mollified him entirely. He took him by the arm and whispered in his ear for fear that Alain might hear: "I confess that the difficulty alarms me, and that I don't have the trivial mind that it's necessary to have to write all those pretty things. Am I fortunate enough, then, that you have another tale that can do me honor and make Virginie know that if she has that gift, I have it too?"

"That means," the prior continued "that you want to play a similar game and have as much advantage of her in the empire of literature."

"Ambition is always becoming," replied the bourgeois. "Serve me as a friend, I implore you."

The bell that was ordinarily rung to mark the hour of the midday meal having alerted the prior, he quit La Dandinardière, after having promised him all he desired.

When he went into the dining room he found two ladies of his acquaintance there, who had just arrived to pay a first visit to Baronne de Saint-Thomas. They were in slight disorder, because the apple-trees what were abundant in the area had inflicted a rude insult on their carriage, the imperial of which was shattered; they had been obliged to return from some distance away on foot in stifling heat.

The ladies had not been in the province for very long; they called themselves cousins, although they were nothing of the sort. One was a widow and very coquettish, the other had just married an elderly gentlemen who had been amassing wealth for a long time and who could boast, in espousing his wife, of having found a excellent means of spending it very rapidly.

The older of the two, whose name was Madame du Rouet, was the widow of a man of law who had scarcely rendered justice to his fellows. She liked gambling and good cheer, and spent a great deal on make-up, which consumed a part of her income. She was holding a pocket mirror and trying to take whitener from places where it was thickest or least necessary in order to put it in places where there was none at all; it was no mediocre task, and when she saw the prior she nearly despaired, for Monsieur and Madame de Saint-Thomas had not yet come in. The former was giving a few orders to his workmen; the latter was changing her clothes, and would not have appeared in a dressing-gown for the Empire of Trebizond.

But Madame de Lure—that was the newlywed—seeing her friend's complexion resembling a chessboard, black and white, in order to leave her the liberty that she needed, drew the prior into a corner mysteriously.

"My cousin wants to do some repairs," she said, "and I want to make you party to a tale that will delight you."

"Madame," he said, "no matter how short it is, we'd have difficulty finishing it before lunch."

"I only want to read you the name," she continued. "I'm certain that you'll want to hear it. It's 'Prince Marcassin'—what do you think of it?"[18]

---

[18] A *marcassin* is a young wild boar; the species was insufficient common in England for hunters there to establish a complex terminology to differentiate its various stages of devel-

"I'm so new to works of this sort," he said, "that I can't judge it very well by the title."

She criticized his ignorance, and having cast an eye covertly on her cousin du Rouet, who was replastered, she no longer cared about reading the tale.

Someone had gone to notify Baron de Saint-Thomas of the arrival of the ladies; he came promptly, with Vicomte de Berginville, and gave orders as he went past the kitchen to augment the meal. It was a question of killing, plucking and larding, and although such tasks are acquitted diligently in the country, he was nevertheless embarrassed with regard to finding something to amuse the ladies while waiting for the meal.

After he had greeted them and learned about the accident to their vehicle, he proposed that they go into a little wood full of springs, where they would find beds of moss, and even benches, on which to rest. They were delighted to go somewhere cooler than the dining room in order to reestablish their warmed faces, and as soon as they had chosen an agreeable spot, the prior, who suspected the delay that their arrival would cause the lunch, asked Madame de Lure to regale the company with her young wild boar.

The baron thought that they had brought one. "The ladies are right," he said, with a sort of chagrin, "to take precautions against the poor cheer that one finds in my home."

They found that misunderstanding so funny, that they laughed at it heartily, which would have caused the baron a certain chagrin if the prior had not told him that it was a matter of a tale; and, seeing the notebook in Madame de Lure's pocket, he took it.

---

opment. The tale in question is greatly elaborated from one found in Straparola's *Nights*, which was also elaborated—in a markedly different fashion, naturally—by the Comtesse de Murat in "Le Roi porc" (tr. as "The Swine King"), permitting an interesting comparison between the imaginative inclinations and narrative strategies of the two leading writers of *contes de fées*.

PRINCE MARCASSIN

There was once a king and a queen who lived in great sadness because they had no children. The queen was no longer young, although she was still beautiful, with the consequence that she dared not promise herself any. That afflicted her a great deal; she did not sleep much, and sighed incessantly, praying to the gods and all the fays to be favorable to her.

One day, when she was walking in a little wood, after having picked a few violets and roses, she also picked some strawberries, but as soon as she had eaten them she was gripped by a drowsiness so profound that she lay down at the foot of a tree and went to sleep.

She dreamed during her sleep that she saw three fays passing through the air, who stopped above her head. The first looked at her compassionately and said: "There's an amiable queen, to whom we could render a very essential service if we wanted to endow her with a child."

"Gladly," said the second. "Endow her, since you're our elder."

"I endow her," she continued, "with having a son, the most handsome, the most lovable and the best loved in the world."

"And I," said the other, "endow her with seeing that son successful in his enterprises, always powerful, full of intelligence and justice."

The turn of the third having come to endow, she burst out laughing, and muttered something between her teeth, which the queen could not hear.

That was the dream she had. She woke up after a few moments; she perceived nothing in the air or in the garden. *Alas*, she said to herself, *I don't have enough good fortune to hope that my dream will come true, whatever thanks I would offer to the gods and the good fays if I had a son.*

She picked more flowers, and returned to the palace more cheerful than usual. The king perceived it and begged her to tell him the reason; she resisted, but he pressed her harder.

"It's not something that merits your curiosity," he said. "It's only a question of a dream, but you'd think me very feeble to add any sort of faith to it." She told him that she had seen three fays in the air while sleeping, what two of them had said, and that the third had burst into laughter without her being able to hear what she muttered.

"That dream," said the king, "gives me satisfaction as well as you, but I'm anxious about the ill-humored fay, for most of them are malicious, and it's not always a good sign when they laugh."

"For myself," replied the queen, "I don't believe that it signifies anything either good or evil. My mind is occupied with the desire to have a son, and has formed a hundred chimeras on that subject. What could happen, anyway, in the case that there was something veritable in what I dreamed? He's endowed with all the most advantageous things possible—may it please Heaven that I have that consolation!"

With that she started weeping. He assured her that she was so dear to him that she took the place of everything in his regard.

After a few months the queen perceived that she was pregnant; the entire realm was alerted to pray for her; the altars no longer fumed except with sacrifices offered to the gods for the conservation of such a precious treasure. The estates appointed delegates to go and compliment Their Majesties; all the princes of the blood, the princesses and the ambassadors were at the queen's childbirth; the layette for the dear child was admirably beautiful, the nurse excellent.

But the public joy changed into sadness when, instead of a handsome prince, the queen was seen to give birth to a little pig! Everyone uttered loud screams, which frightened the queen badly. She asked what was wrong; nobody wanted to tell her, for fear that she might die of dolor. On the contrary, they assured her that she was the mother of a handsome boy and that she had reason to rejoice.

The king, however, was excessively afflicted. He commanded that the pig be put in a sack and thrown into the sea, in order to lose the idea of such a terrible thing entirely. Afterwards however, he took pity on it, and, thinking that it was only just to consult the queen on the matter, he ordered that it should be nourished and that nothing should be said to his wife until she was well enough for there to be no fear that she might die of such a great displeasure.

She asked every day to see her son; she was told that he was too delicate to be brought from his room to hers, and she was tranquilized by that.

As for Prince Marcassin, he was nourished like a pig possessed of a great desire to live; it was necessary to give him six nurses, three of whom were dry, in the English fashion. They continually gave him Spanish wine and liqueurs to drink, which taught him at an early age to know the best wines.

The queen, impatient to caress her child, told the king that she was well enough to go as far as his apartment and that she could no longer live without seeing her son. The king uttered a profound sigh; he commanded that the heir to the throne be brought.

He was swathed like a child in gold brocade sheets. The queen took him in her arms and lifted up a lace fringe that covered his snout. What became of her, alas, at that fatal sight? That moment was nearly the last of her life; she darted sad glances at the king, not daring to speak to him.

"Don't be afflicted, my dear queen," he said to her; "I don't impute any of our misfortune to you; no doubt this is a trick of some malevolent fay, and if you would like to consent to it, I shall follow the initial design I had to have the little monster drowned.

"Oh, Sire," she said, "don't consult me about such a cruel action. I'm the mother of the unfortunate pig; I sense my tenderness soliciting me in his favor; please don't do him any harm, he has suffered enough already, having been due to be born human and only being born a swine."

She touched the king so deeply with her tears that he promised her what she wished, with the result that the ladies who were bring up little Marcassin began to take even more care of him; for they had regarded him until then as a proscribed beast who would soon serve as nourishment for the fish. It is true that, in spite of his ugliness, a good deal of intelligence was remarked in his eyes; he had been accustomed to offer his little foot to those who salute him, as others gave their hand; diamond bracelets were put on him and he did everything with sufficient grace.

The queen could not help loving him; she often had him in her arms, finding him pretty in the depths of her heart, for she dared not say so for fear of being taken for a madwoman; but she confessed to her friends that her son seemed to her to be likeable. She covered him with a thousand knots of rose-colored nonpareil ribbon; his ears were pierced; he had a harness with which he was sustained, in order to accustom him to walk on his hind feet; shoes were put on them, and silk stockings attached at the knee, in order to make the leg seem longer; he was whipped when he wanted to grunt. In sum, as far as was possible, his swinish manners were removed.

One evening, when the queen was out walking and carrying him at her neck, she came to the same tree under which she had gone to sleep and had had the dream that I have described. The memory of that adventure came back to mind forcefully. "This, then," she said, "is that prince, so handsome, so perfect and so fortunate, that I was to have? O deceptive dream, fatal vision! O fays, what have I done to you for you to mock me?"

She was muttering those words between her teeth, when she suddenly saw an oak tree grow, from which an elaborately adorned lady emerged, who looked at her affably and said: "Don't be afflicted, great queen, to have given birth to little Marcassin; I assure you that a time will come when you will find him lovable."

The queen recognized her as one of the three fays who had passed through the air while she was asleep, had stopped and had wished her a son. "I have difficulty believing you, Madame," she replied. "Whatever negligence my son might have, who could love him in such a form?"

Once again, the fay replied: "Don't be afflicted, great queen, to have given birth to little Marcassin; I assure you that a time will come when you will find him lovable." Immediately, she returned to the tree, and the tree disappeared into the ground without leaving any appearance that it had been there.

Very surprised by that new adventure, the queen nevertheless flattered herself that the fays would take some care of His Bestial Highness. She returned to the palace promptly in order to talk to the king about it, but he thought that she had imagined that means to render his son less odious to him.

"I can see," she said, "by the way that you're listening to me, that you don't believe me. However, nothing is truer than what I've just told you."

"It's very sad," said the king, "to endure the mockery of the fays; what will they do to render our child anything other than a pig? I can't even think about it without falling into depression."

The queen withdrew, more afflicted than she had been before. She had hoped that the fay's promises might soften the king's chagrin, but he scarcely paid any heed to them. She retired, firmly resolved not to a anything further to him about their son, and to leave the care of consoling her husband to the gods.

Marcassin began to talk, as all children do. He stammered a little, but that did not prevent the queen from having a good deal of pleasure in listening to him, for she had feared that he might never talk in his life. He became very tall, and often walked on his hind feet. He wore long jackets, which covered his legs, and a black velvet English bonnet to hide his head his ears and a part of his snout. In truth, he grew terrible tusks; his bristles were furiously stiff, his gaze proud and his command absolute. He ate from a golden trough in which he was given truffles, scorns, morels and herbs, and nothing was neglected to render him clean and polite. He was born with a superior intelligence and an intrepid courage.

Knowing his character, the king began to love him more than he had thus far. He chose good masters to teach him everything that they could. He performed rather poorly in figured dances, but for the passepied and the minuet, in which he moved quickly and lightly enough, he contrived marvels. With regard to instruments, he knew full well that the lute and the theorbo did not suit him; he liked the guitar and played the flute nicely. He rode a horse with a surprising grace and disposition; he passed few days without going hunting, and inflicted terrible bites on the most ferocious and dangerous beasts. His masters found him to have a quick mind and all the facility possible in perfecting himself in the sciences. He felt very bitterly the ridiculousness of his swinish form, with the result that he avoided appearing at great assemblies.

He was spending his life in a happy indifference when, while in the queen's apartment, he saw a good looking lady come in followed by three lovely young women. She threw herself at the queen's feet and told her that she had come to beg her to receive them in her service; that the death of her husband and extreme misfortunes had reduced her to an extreme poverty; that her birth and misfortune were well enough known to Her Majesty for her to hope that she might have pity on her.

The queen was moved by compassion on seeing her at her knees thus; she embraced her, and told her that she would receive her three daughters with pleasure, the eldest of whom was called Ismene, the second Zelonide and the youngest Marthesie, and that she would take care of them. She told her not to be discouraged; that she could stay in the palace, where everyone would hold her in high regard; and that she could count on her amity.

The mother, charmed by the queen's generosity, kissed her hands a thousand times, and immediately found a tranquility that she had not known for a long time.

Ismene's beauty caused a stir in the court and touched a young chevalier named Coridon sensibly. He was no less brilliant than her; they were struck almost simultaneously by a secret sympathy that attached them to one another. The chevalier was infinitely lovable; he pleased people, and was loved. As he was a very advantageous match for Ismene, the queen perceived with pleasure the cares that he rendered to her and the account that she took of them. Eventually, there was talk of their marriage; everything seemed to concur in that regard. They were born for one another, and Coridon did not neglect anything in the gallant courtship and eager cares that strongly engaged a heart already prejudiced.

However, the prince had felt the power of Ismene as soon as he had seen her, without daring to declare his passion. "Oh, Marcassin, Marcassin," he cried, on looking at himself in a mirror, "is it possible that with a form so disgraced, you could dare to promise yourself some favorable sentiment on the part of the beautiful Ismene? It is necessary to cure yourself, for of all misfortunes, the greatest is to love without being loved."

He carefully avoided seeing her, but as he continued thinking about her nevertheless, he fell into a frightful melancholy. He became so thin that his bones pierced his skin; but he had a great augmentation of anxiety when he learned that Coridon was overtly seeking Ismene, that she held him in high esteem, and that before long the king and the queen would be celebrating their wedding.

At that news, he felt his amour increasing and his hope diminishing, for it seemed to him less difficult to please an indifferent Ismene than an Ismene prejudiced in favor of Coridon, He also understood that his silence would complete his doom, with the consequence that, having sought a favorable opportunity to talk to her, he found one.

One day, when she was sitting under an agreeable foliage, where she was singing a few words that her lover had made for her, Marcassin approached her, very emotionally, and having at down beside her, he asked her whether it was true, as he had been told, that she was going to marry Coridon. She replied that the queen had ordered her to receive his assiduities, and that apparently, that ought to have some consequence.

"Ismene," he said, calming himself, "you're so young that I didn't believe they would think of marrying you; if I had known, I would have proposed for you the unique son of a great king, who loves you and would be delighted to render you happy."

At those words, Ismene went pale. She had already remarked that Marcassin, who was naturally rather grim, talked to her with pleasure, that he gave her all the truffles that his swinish instinct enable him to find in the forest and that he regaled her with the flowers with which her bonnet was ordinarily ornamented. She had a great fear that he was the prince of whom he was speaking, and she replied to him: "I am glad, Sire, to have been unaware of the sentiments of the son of that great king; perhaps my family, more ambitious than I am, would have wanted to constrain me to marry him, and I confess to you confidentially that my heart is so prejudiced for Coridon that it will never change."

"What!" he replied. "You would refuse a crowned head that would apply his fortune to pleasing you?"

"There is nothing that I would not refuse," she told him, "and I implore you, Sire, since you have commerce with this prince, to engage him to leave me in repose."

"Oh, hussy!" cried the impatient Marcassin. "You know only too well who the prince is of whom I speak. His form displeases you; you would not want to have the name of Queen Marcassine; and you have sworn eternal fidelity to your chevalier. Think, however if the difference there is between us; I'm not an Adonis, I agree, but I'm a redoubtable boar;

supreme power is worth more than a few petty natural charms. Think about it, Ismene, don't make me despair."

As he spoke those words his eyes appeared to be all ablaze, and his long tusks made a sound in colliding with one another that made the poor young woman tremble.

Marcassin withdrew. The afflicted Ismene was shedding a torrent of tears when Coridon came to sit beside her. Until that day, they had only known the sweetness of a mutual tenderness; nothing had opposed its progress, and they had had reason to promise themselves that it would soon be crowned. What became of that young lover when he saw his beautiful mistress in tears? He pressed her to tell him the reason.

She did so, and the disturbance that the news caused him is indescribable.

"I am not capable," he said to her, "of establishing my happiness at the expense of yours; you are offered a crown, it's necessary that you accept it."

"Great gods, that I accept it!" she cried. "That I forget you and marry a monster? What have I done to you, alas, to oblige you to give me advice so contrary to our amity and our repose?"

Coridon was seized too such a degree that he could not respond, but the tears that flowed from his eyes marked the state of his soul well enough. Ismene, penetrated by their common misfortune, told him hundreds of times that she would not change, if it were a matter of all the kings of the earth; and he, touched by that generosity, told her hundreds of times that it was necessary to let him die of chagrin and mount the throne that was offered to her.

While that conflict was occurring between them, Marcassin was in the queen's apartment, telling her that the hope he had had of curing the passion he had acquired for Ismene had obliged him to keep quiet, but that he had combated it in vain; that she was on the point of being married; that he did not have the strength to sustain such a disgrace; and that, in sum, he wanted to marry her or die.

The queen was very surprised to hear that the boar was in love. "Have you thought about what you are saying" she replied. "Who could want you, my son, and for what children could you hope?"

"Ismene is so beautiful," he said, "that she could not have ugly children; and even if they were to resemble me, I am resolved to everything rather than see her in the arms of another."

"Have you so little delicacy," the queen continued, "as to want a young woman whose birth is inferior to yours?"

"And who is the princess," he replied, "indelicate enough to want a misfortunate pig like me?"

"You're mistaken, my son," the queen added. "Princesses have less liberty to choose than anyone else; we'll have you painted more handsome than Amour himself. When the marriage is made and we have her, it will be necessary for her to stay with us."

"I'm not capable," he said, "of contriving such a deception. I'd be in despair if I rendered my wife unhappy."

"Can you believe," she said, "that the woman you want will not be unhappy, with you? The man she loves is lovable, and if the rank is different between sovereign and subject, the difference is no less between a boar and the most charming man in the world."

"So much the worse for me, Madame," Marcassin replied, annoyed by the arguments she was putting to him. "I dare say that you ought to represent my misfortune to me less than another; why have you made me a pig? Is there not injustice in reproaching me for something that isn't my fault?"

"I'm not reproaching you," said the queen, compassionately, "I only want to represent to you that if you marry a woman who doesn't love you, you'll be unhappy and you'll be her torture. If you could understand what people suffer in these forced unions you wouldn't want to run the risk. Isn't it better to remain alone, in peace?"

"It would be necessary to have more indifference that I have, Madame," he said to her. "I'm touched for Ismene; she is meek, and I flatter myself that a good procedure with her, and the crown for which she can hope, will persuade her. At any rate, if it is my destiny not to be loved, I would have the pleasure of possessing a woman that I love."

The queen found him so strongly attached to that design that she forsook that of turning him away from it; she promised to work for what he wanted, and immediately went in quest of Ismene's mother. She knew her humor; she was an ambitious woman, who would have sacrificed her daughters to lesser advantages than that of reigning. As soon as the queen had told her that she wanted Marcassin to marry Ismene, she threw herself at her feet and assured her that it would be on the day that she chose.

"But her heart is engaged," said the queen. "We have ordered her to regard Coridon as the man for whom she is destined."

"Well, Madame," said the aged mother, "we'll order her to regard him in future as a man she won't marry."

"The heart doesn't always consult reason," added the queen. "Once it is determined, it's difficult to subjugate it."

"If her heart has other determinations than mine," she said, "I'll rip it out without mercy."

Seeing her so resolute, the queen believed that she could leave to her the care of making her daughter obey.

In fact, she ran to Ismene's room. The poor girl, having been told that the queen had sent for her mother, was waiting for her return anxiously, and it is easy to imagine how that was augmented when she told her with a stern and resolute expression that the queen had chosen her to be her daughter-in-law, that she forbade her ever to speak to Coridon again, and that if she did not obey she would strangle her. Ismene dared not respond to that threat, but she wept bitterly, and the rumor immediately spread that she was going to marry the royal swine, for the queen, who had made the king agreed to it, had sent her precious stones with which to adorn herself when she came to the palace.

Coridon, overwhelmed by despair, came to see her and talk to her in spite of all the prohibitions that had been made to allow him to enter. He reached her cabinet, and found her lying on a bed, her face covered in tears. He threw himself to his knees beside her and took her hand,

"Alas, charming Ismene," he said, "you're weeping for my misfortunes."

"They're common between us," she replied. "You know, my dear Coridon to what I am condemned; I can only avoid the violence that they want to do to me by my death. Yes, I shall be able to die, I assure you, rather than not be yours."

"No, live," he said to her, "you will be queen; perhaps you will become accustomed to that frightful prince."

"That isn't in my power," she said. "I cannot envisage anything in the world more terrible than such a husband; his crown will not soothe my dolors."

"The gods will preserve you from such a fatal resolution, lovable Ismene," he continued. "It only befits me; I am going to lose you; you are incapable of resisting my just dolor."

"If you die," she said, "I shall not survive you, and I shall feel some consolation in thinking that at least death will unite us."

They were talking in that fashion when Marcassin took them by surprise. The queen having told him what she had done in his favor, he had run to Ismene's apartment in order to testify his joy to her, but the presence of Coridon troubled him to the utmost degree. His humor was jealous and impatient. He ordered him, in a manner into which the wild boar entered considerably, never to appear in the court again.

"What are you trying to do, cruel prince?" cried Ismene, stopping the man she loved. "Do you think you can banish him from my heart as well as my presence? No, he is too deeply engraved there. No longer be unaware of your misfortune, then, you who are making mine; this is the only man who is dear to me; I have only horror for you."

"And I, barbarian," said Marcassin, "only have love for you. It is futile for you to reveal all your hatred to me; you will be my wife nonetheless, and you will suffer from it more."

Coridon, in despair at having attracted that new displeasure to his mistress, went out as Ismene's mother came to quarrel with her; she assured the prince that her daughter would forget Coridon forever, and that he ought not to delay such an agreeable marriage. Marcassin, who had no less desire for it than her, said that he would decide the day with the queen, because the king was leaving the care of the great celebration to her.

It is true that the king had not wanted to be involved in it, because the marriage appeared to him to be disagreeable and ridiculous, being convinced that the porcine race would be perpetuated in the royal house. He was afflicted by the blind complaisance that the queen had for her son.

Marcassin feared that the king might repent of the consent that he had given to what he wished, so they hastened to prepare everything for the ceremony. He had culottes, stockings and a perfumed doublet made, for he always had a slight odor that people sustained with difficulty. His mantle was embroidered with gems, his wig was an infantile blonde and his hat covered in plumes. Perhaps no figure more extraordinary than his had ever been seen, and unless they were destined to the misfortune of marrying him, no one could look at him without laughing. Young Ismene, alas, had no desire to do so; grandeurs were promised to her in vain; she scorned them, and only resented the fatality of her star.

Coridon saw her pass by to go to the temple; one might have taken her for a beautiful victim about to have her throat cut. The delighted Marcassin begged her to banish the profound sadness by which she appeared to be overwhelmed, because he wanted to render her so happy that all the queens in the world would envy her.

"I admit," he continued, "that I'm not handsome, but it's said that all men have some resemblance with animals; I resemble a wild boar more than any other, that's my beast; it's unnecessary for that to find me less lovable, for I have a heart full of sentiments, and touched by a strong passion for you."

Without replying, Ismene looked at him with an expression of the utmost disdain, shrugged her shoulders and left him to divine all the horror that she felt for him.

Her mother was behind her, who made her a thousand menaces. "Wretch! she said to her. "You want to doom us in dooming yourself, then. Do you not fear that the prince's amour might turn into fury?"

Ismene, occupied with her displeasure, did not pay the slightest attention to those words. Marcassin, who was leading her by the hand, could not help leaping and dancing, whispering a thousand sweet things in her ear.

Finally, the ceremony having finished, after people had cried three times: "Long live Prince Marcassin! Long live Princess Marcassine!" the husband brought his wife to the palace, where everything was prepared for a magnificent meal. The king and the queen having taken their places, the bride sat opposite the wild boar, who devoured her with his eyes, so beautiful did he find her; but she was buried in such a profound sadness that she did not see anything of what was happening, and did not hear the music, which was very loud.

The queen tugged her robe and whispered in her ear: "My daughter, quit this somber melancholy if you want to please us; it seems that this is not so much your wedding day as that of your burial."

"I wish to the gods, Madame," she said, "that it were the last of my life. You ordered me to love Coridon, he had soon received my heart from your hand and my choice; if you have changed for him, I have not changed likewise."

"Don't speak thus," replied the queen. "I blush with shame and chagrin at it; remember the honor that my son is doing you and the gratitude that you owe him."

Ismene made no reply; she allowed her head to fall upon her breast and buried herself in her reverie again.

Marcassin was very afflicted to know the aversion that his wife had for him; there were many moments when he

wished that his marriage had not been made; he even wanted
to break it immediately, but his heart opposed it.

The ball commenced; Ismene's sisters shone there; they
were unworried by her chagrins and conceived with pleasure
the brilliance that the alliance would give them. The bride
danced with Marcassin, and it was a frightful thing to see his
face, and even more frightful to be his wife. The entire court
was so sad that no one could manifest joy. The ball did not last
long; the princess was taken to her apartment; after she had
been undressed ceremoniously, the queen withdrew.

The amorous Marcassin immediately got into bed.
Ismene said that she wanted to write a letter, and she went into
her cabinet, the door of which she closed, although Marcassin
shouted to her to write promptly and that it was scarcely the
hour to commence dispatches.

Alas, on entering the cabinet, what a spectacle was suddenly presented to her eyes! It was the unfortunate Coridon,
who had bribed one of her women to open the door to a hidden
staircase to him, by which he had entered. He was holding a
dagger in his hand.

"No, charming princes," he said, "I have not come here
to make you reproaches for having abandoned me; you swore
at the commencement of our tender amours that your heart
would never change; in spite of that, you have consented to
quit me, but I blame the gods rather than you. Neither you nor
the gods, however, can make me support such a great misfortune; in losing you, princess, I must cease to live."

Scarcely had he pronounced the final words than he
plunged the dagger into his heart.

Ismene had not had time to respond to him. "You are dying, dear Coridon," she cried, dolorously. "I have nothing
more to keep me in this world; grandeurs are odious to me; the
light of day would become insupportable."

She only pronounced those few words; them, with the
same dagger that was still fuming with Coridon's blood, she
struck herself in the breast and fell, lifeless.

Marcassin was waiting for the beautiful Ismene to impatiently not to perceive that she was taking a long time to come back. He called to her with all his might, without any response. He became very irritated, and, getting up with his dressing gown, he ran to the door of the cabinet, which he ordered to be broke down.

He went in first; alas, what was his surprise to find Ismene and Coridon in such a deplorable state? He almost died of sadness and rage; his sentiments, confused between love and hatred, tormented him alternatively. He adored Ismene but he knew that she had only killed herself in order to break abruptly the union they had just contracted.

Someone ran to tell the king and the queen what had happened in the prince's apartment; the entre palace heard the cries. Ismene was loved, Coridon esteemed. The king did not get up; he could not enter into Marcassin's adventures as profoundly as the queen; he left the care of consoling him to her.

She had him put to bed; she mingled her tears with his; and when he left her time to speak and ceased his laments momentarily, she tried to make him conceive that he was fortunate to be delivered of a young woman who would never have loved him and who had a heart full of a strong tenderness; that it is almost impossible to efface a grand passion; and that she was convinced that he ought to be glad to be rid of her.

"It doesn't matter," he cried. "I wanted to possess her, even if she was infidel to me; I can't say that she sought to deceive me by feigned caresses; she always manifested her horror for me; I'm the cause of her death, and have I not to reproach myself for that?"

The queen saw that he was so afflicted that she left the women with him who were most agreeable to him, and returned to her room.

When she was in bed, she recalled mentally everything that had happened since the dream in which she had seen the three fays. *What have I done to them*, she said to herself, *to oblige them to send me such bitter afflictions? I hoped for a lovable and charming son; they have endowed him with swinishness; he's a monster in nature; the unfortunate Ismene killed herself rather than live with him. The king has not had a moment of joy since his birth, for myself, I'm overwhelmed with sadness every time I see him.*

As she was speaking to herself thus she perceived a great light in her bedroom, and recognized close to her bed the fay who had emerged from a tree in the wood, who said to her: "O Queen, why didn't you want to believe me? Have I not assured you that you will receive a great deal of satisfaction from your Marcassin? Do you doubt my sincerity?

"Well, who wouldn't doubt it?" she said. "I haven't yet seen anything that responds in the slightest to your words. Why didn't you leave me without an heir for the rest of my life rather than make me have one like that?"

"We are three sisters," replied the fay. "There are two good ones, the third almost always spoils what we do. It's her that you saw laughing while you were asleep; without us, your troubles would last much longer, but they will have a term."

"Alas, it will be at the end of my life, or that of my Marcassin," said the queen.

"I cannot inform you," said the fay. "It is only permissible for me to relieve you with some hope."

Immediately, she disappeared. The room remained perfumed by an agreeable odor, and the queen flattered herself with the idea of a favorable change.

Marcassin put on full mourning dress; he spent many days shut in his cabinet, scribbling in several notebooks, which contained sensible regrets for the loss that he had suffered. He even wanted these words to be engraved on his wife's tomb:

Rigorous destiny, cruel laws!
Ismene, you have descended into eternal night;
Your eyes, by which all hearts ought to be charmed,
Your eyes are forever closed.
Rigorous destiny, cruel laws!

Everyone was surprised that he conserved such a tender memory of a person who had testified so much aversion for him.

Gradually, he entered into the society of women, and was struck by the charms of Zelonide. She was Ismene's sister, who was no less agreeable than her, and who resembled her closely; that resemblance flattered him. When he conversed with her he found intelligence and vivacity; he believed that if anything could console him for the loss of Ismene, it was young Zelonide. She was always polite to him, for it did not enter her head that she he might want to marry her. Nevertheless, he made the resolution to do so.

One day, when the queen was alone in her cabinet, he went there with a more cheerful expression than usual. "Madame," he said to her, "I've come to ask you for a favor, and to beg you at the same time not to turn me away from my design, for nothing in the world can take away my desire to remarry. Lend your hand to it, I implore you. I want to marry Zelonide; speak to the king about it, in order that the affair is not delayed."

"Oh, my son," said the queen, "What is your design, then? Have you not forgotten the despair of Ismene and her tragic death? How can you promise yourself that her sister will love you anymore? Are you more lovable than you were, any less wild boar, any less frightful? Render yourself justice, my son, don't give new spectacles every day. When one is made like you, one ought to hide it."

"I consent to that, Madame," Marcassin replied. "It's in order to hide that I want a companion; long-eared owls find barn owls, toads find fogs and adders find grass snakes; am I then beneath those vile creatures? You're seeking to afflict me, but it seems to me that a young boar has more merit than all those I've just named."

"Alas, my dear child," said the queen, "the gods are my witnesses to the love I have for you and the displeasure by which I'm overwhelmed when I see your face. If I allege so many arguments it isn't because I'm seeking to afflict you; when you have a wife, I would like her to be capable of loving you as much as I love you, but there is a difference between the sentiments of a wife and those of a mother."

"My resolution is fixed," said Marcassin. "I beg you, Madame, to speak today to the king and to Zelonide's mother, in order that my marriage can take place as soon as possible."

The queen gave him her word, but when she talked to the king he told her that she had pitiful weaknesses for her son, that he was quite certain of seeing more catastrophes arrive by virtue of such a poorly regulated marriage. Although the queen was as convinced of that as he was, she did not give in because of it, wanting to keep the promise she had given her son, with the result that she pressed the king so hard that, being fatigued, he told her that she could do as she liked, but that if chagrin arrived in consequence, not to blame him for his complaisance.

Having returned to her apartment, the queen found Marcassin there, who was waiting for her with the utmost impatience. She told him that he could declare his sentiments to Zelonide, that the king consented to what he desired, provided that she consented to it herself, because he did not want the authority with which he was clothed to serve to make unhappiness.

"I assure you, Madame," Marcassin said to her, boastfully, "that you are the only one who thinks so disadvantageously of me. I see no one who does not praise me and does not make me perceive that I have a thousand good qualities."

"Such are courtiers," said the queen, "and such is the condition of princes; the former always praise, the latter are always praised; how can one know one's faults in such a labyrinth? Oh, how fortunate the great would be if they had friends more attached to their persons than their fortune!"

"I do not know, Madame," Marcassin retorted, "whether they are fortunate to hear disagreeable verities spoken; whatever condition one has, one does not like them. For example, what is the use of your always putting before my eyes that there is no difference between me and a wild boar, that I scare people, and that I ought to hide myself? Do I not have an obligation to those who soften my pain in that matter, who tell me favorable lies, and who hide the defects that you are so careful to reveal?"

"O source of self-esteem!" cried the queen. "In whatever direction one casts one's eyes, one always finds them. Yes, my son, you are handsome, you are pretty, and I advise you to give a pension to those who tell you so."

"Madame," said Marcassin, "I am not unaware of my disgraces; perhaps I am more sensible to them than another; but I am not the master of making myself either tall or upright, or of quitting my boar's snout in order to take on a human head ornamented with long hair, I consent to be given in return ill humor, inequality, avarice—in sum, all the things that might be corrected—but with regard to my person, you will agree, if you please, that I am to be pitied and not to be blamed."

The queen, seeing that he was chagrined, told him that since he was so determined to marry, he could see Zelonide and take measures with her.

He had too much desire to end the conversation to stay longer with his mother. He ran to find Zelonide; he entered her room without ceremony, and having found her in her cabinet he embraced her and said to her: "My little sister, I have just learned some news, which will doubtless not displease you; I want to marry you."

"Sire," she said, "if I am to be married by your hand I shall have nothing to wish for."

"It is a matter," he said, "of one of the greatest lords of the realm, but he isn't handsome."

"No matter," she said. "My mother has so much harshness for me that I shall be glad to change condition."

"The person of whom I am speaking," the prince added, "resembles me greatly."

Zelonide looked at him with attention, and seemed astonished.

"You're keeping silent, my little sister," he said to her. "Is that joy or chagrin?"

"I don't remember, Sire," she replied, "having seen anyone at court who resembles you."

"What!" he said. "Can't you divine that I'm talking about myself? Yes, my dear child, I love you, and I've come to offer to share my heart and my crown with you."

"O gods, what am I hearing?" cried Zelonide, dolorously.

"What you are hearing, ingrate," said Marcassin, "is something that ought to give you the greatest satisfaction in the world. Have you never hoped to be queen? I have the generosity to cast my eyes upon you; think about meriting my amour and don't imitate the extravagances of Ismene."

"No," she said, "don't fear that I'll attempt my days, like her; but Sire, there are so many women more lovable and more ambitious than me; can you not choose one who understands better than I do the honor for which you destine me? I confess to you that I only want a tranquil and retired life; leave me the mistress of my fate."

"You scarcely merit the violence I have done," he cried, "to raise you to the throne, but a fatality unknown to me is forcing me to marry you."

Zelonide only responded to him with tears.

He quit her, filled with dolor, and went to see his mother-in-law in order to reveal his intentions to her, in order that she dispose Zelonide to do as he desired with a good grace. He told her what had happened between them, and the repugnance she had testified for a marriage that would make her fortune and that of her entire family.

The ambitious mother understood well enough the advantages she might receive from it, and when Ismene had killed herself she had been more afflicted with regard to her own interests than the tenderness she had for her. She felt an extreme joy that the filthy Marcassin wanted to make a new alliance in her family. She threw herself at his feet, embraced him and rendered him a thousand thanks for an honor that touched her so sensibly. She assured him that Zelonide would obey him, or that she would put out her eyes with a dagger.

"I confess to you," said Marcassin, "that I have difficulty doing violence to her, but if I wait until hearts are thrown at my head, I shall wait for the rest of my life; all the beauties find me ugly; I am resolved however, only to marry a lovely girl."

"You're right, Sire," replied he malign old woman; "It's necessary to satisfy you; if they're discontented, it's because they don't know their veritable advantages."

She fortified Marcassin so much that he told her that it was a matter resolved, and that he would be deaf to Zelonide's tears and prayers. He returned to his apartment in order to choose everything he had of the most magnificent, and sent it to his mistress.

As her mother was present when she was offered golden baskets filled with jewels, she dared not refuse them, but she marked a great indifference for what was presented to her, except for a dagger, the hilt of which was garnished with diamonds. She picked it up several times, and put it in her belt, because the ladies of that country ordinarily wore one.

Then she said: "Am I mistaken or is this the same dagger that pierced the breast of my poor sister?"

"We don't know, Madame," said those to whom she was speaking, "but if you have that opinion it's necessary never to see it."

"On the contrary," she said. "I praise her courage; I would be fortunate if I had enough to imitate her."

"Oh, my sister," cried Marthesie, "What dark thoughts are passing through your mind? Do you want to die?"

"No," replied Zelonide, firmly. "The altar isn't worthy of such a victim, but I attest to the gods that....."

She could not say any more; her tears stifled her plaints and her voice.

Having been informed of the manner in which Zelonide had received his present, the amorous Marcassin became so indignant against her that he was on the point of breaking with her and not seeing her again as long as he lived. Either by virtue of tenderness or glory, however, he did not want to do it, and resolved to follow his initial design with the utmost fervor.

The king and the queen left the organization of the great celebration to him. He ordered a magnificent one; however, there was always something quite extraordinary in Marcassin's tastes; the ceremony was held in a vast forest, where tables were set up charged with venison for all the ferocious and savage beasts that wanted to eat it, in order that they could participate in the festivities.

It was in that place that Zelonide, having been conducted by her mother and her sister, found the king, the queen, their son the boar and the entire court, beneath dense and somber branches, where the newlyweds swore an eternal amour. Marcassin would have had no difficulty in keeping his promise. As for Zelonide, it was evident that she was obeying with a great deal of repugnance; although she was not unable to constrain herself and hide a part of her displeasures. The prince, liking to flatter himself, imagined that she would yield to necessity and would only think in future of pleasing him. That idea rendered him all the good humor that he had lost.

At the time when the ball began he hastened to disguise himself as an astrologer, with a long robe. Two ladies of the court wore an identical costume. He had wanted them to be so similar that they could not be recognized, and there was no small difficulty in making two well made ladies resemble an ugly pig like him.

One of those ladies was Zelonide's confidant; Marcassin was not unaware of that, it was only out of curiosity that he contrived that disguise. After they had danced a very short introductory ballet—for nothing fatigued the prince more—he approached his new wife and made certain signs, pointing at one of three masked astrologers, which persuaded Zelonide that it was her friend who was next to her and that she was indicating Marcassin.

"Alas," she said, "I understand only too well; that is the monster that the irritated gods have given me for a husband, but if you love me, we'll purge the earth of him tonight."

Marcassin understood by what she said that there was a conspiracy in which he had an important part. He said in a low voice to Zelonide: "I'm resolved to do anything for your service."

"Here, then," she said. "This is a dagger that he sent me; it's necessary that you hide in my room and help me to cut his throat." Marcassin said little in reply, for fear that she would recognize his speech, which was rather extraordinary; he took the dagger quietly and moved away from her. He came back afterwards without a mask in order to make amities to her; she received him in an embarrassed manner, for she was turning over in her mind the design to doom him, and at that moment, he had scarcely les anxiety than her

Is it possible, he said to himself, *that a person so young and beautiful can be so wicked? What have I done to her to oblige her to want to kill me? It's true that I'm not handsome, that I eat improperly, that I have a few faults, but who hasn't? I'm a man in the form of a beast. How many beasts there are in human form! Is not this Zelonide, whom I find so charming, a tigress and a lioness herself? Oh, how little one ought to trust appearances!*

He was muttering all that between his teeth when she asked him what was wrong. "You're sad, Marcassin. Are you not repenting of the honor that you're doing me?"

"No," he said, "I don't change easily. I was thinking about a means to end the ball soon. I'm tired."

The princess was delighted to see him drowsy, thinking that she would have less difficulty in carrying out her project.

The fête ended. Marcassin and his wife were taken away in a pompous carriage. The entire palace was illuminated by lamps, which formed little pigs.

Great ceremonies were made in order to take the boar and the bride to bed, She did not doubt that the confidante was behind the tapestry, with the result that she went to bed with a silk cord under her bed-head, with which she wanted to avenge the death of Ismene and the violence that had been done to constrain her to a marriage that displeased her so much.

Marcassin took advantage of the profound silence that reigned; he made a semblance of falling asleep, and snored to make all the furniture in the room tremble.

"You're finally asleep, vile pig," said Zelonide. "The time has come to punish your heart for its fatal tenderness. You'll perish in this obscure night"

She got up quietly and ran to all the corners, calling to her confidante, but she was not there, because she did not know about Zelonide's plan.

"Ingrate friend!" she exclaimed, in a low voice. "You've abandoned me; after giving me such a positive promise, you aren't keeping it; but my courage will serve me, at need. As she finished speaking she passed the silken cord around Marcassin's neck. He was only waiting for that to throw himself upon her. He thrust both of his huge tusks into her breast, and she expired shortly thereafter.

Such a catastrophe could not occur with making a great deal of noise. People came running, and they saw with the utmost surprise Zelonide dying. They tried to help her, but he set himself before her with a furious expression. And when the queen, of whom someone had gone in quest, had arrived, he told her what had happened, and what had driven him to the ultimate violence against that unfortunate princess.

The queen could not help regretting her. "I foresaw all too clearly," she said, "the disgraces attached to your alliance; let them at least serve to cure you of the frenzy you have to marry; that might be a means of not always seeing a wedding day conclude with funeral pomp."

Marcassin made no response; he was occupied with a profound reverie. He lay down without being able to sleep; he made continual reflections on his misfortunes; he reproached himself secretly for the two loveliest young women in the world, and the passion he had had for them reawakened constantly to torment him.

"Unfortunate that I am," she said to a young lord whom he loved. "I've never savored any sweetness in the course of my life. If anyone mentions the throne that I ought to fill, everyone replies that it's a great pity to see such a beautiful kingdom possessed by a monster. If I share my crown with some poor your woman, instead of deeming herself fortunate, she seeks the means of dying or killing me. If I seek some kindness from my father and mother, they abhor me and only look at me with irritated eyes.

"What ought I to do, then, in the despair that possesses me? I want to abandon the court. I'll go into the depths of the forests and lead the life that befits a well-meaning and honorable wild boar. I'll no longer be the gallant man. I'll only find animals that will reproach me for being uglier than them. It will be easy for me to be their king, for I have a share of reason that will enable me to find the means of mastering them. I shall live more tranquilly with them than I can live in a court destined to obey me, and I won't have the misfortune of being exposed to a sow who wants to stab herself or strangle me. Ah, let's flee, let's flee into the woods and scorn a crown of which people think me unworthy."

His confidant tried at first to turn him away from such an extraordinary resolution, but he saw that he was so overwhelmed by the continual blows of fortune that he no longer pressed him to remain; and one night, when no guard was set around the palace, he ran away without anyone seeing him, all the way to the depths of the forest, where he began to do all that his fellow young wild boars did.

The king and the queen were not untouched by a departure that only despair had caused. They sent hunters to search for him, but how were they to recognize him? Two or three furious wild boars were caught, which were brought back with a thousand peril, and which made so many ravages at court that it was decided no longer to risk such scorn. A general order was issued not to kill any wild boar, for fear of encountering the prince.

When he left, Marcassin had promised his favorite to write to him occasionally; he had taken a writing desk, and, in fact from time to time, a scribbled letter was found at the gate of the city, addressed to the young lord. That consoled the queen; she learned by that means that her son was alive.

The mother of Ismene and Zelonide resented the loss of her two daughters keenly; all her projects of grandeur had vanished with their deaths; she was reproached that without her ambition, they would still be in the world, that she had threatened them to oblige them to consent to marry Marcassin. The queen no longer had the same generosity for her. She made the resolution to go into the country with Marthesie, her unique daughter, who was even more beautiful than her sisters had been. Her mildness had something so charming about it that one could not look at her with indifference.

One day, she was walking in the forest followed by two women who served her—for her mother's house was not far away, when she suddenly saw a wild boar of frightful size twenty paces away from her. The two women who were with her abandoned her, and ran away. As for Marthesie, she was so terrified that she remained a motionless as a statue, without having the strength to run away.

Marcassin—for it was him—recognized her immediately, and judged by her trembling that she was dying of fear. He did not want to frighten her any more, but having stopped, he said: "Have no fear, Marthesie, I love you too much to do you any harm. It only depends on you for me to do you good; you know the reasons for displeasure that your sisters have given me; it's a sad recompense for my tenderness. I admit nevertheless that I merited their hatred by my obstinacy in wanting to possess them in spite of them. I've learned, since I've been an inhabitant of these forests that nothing in the world ought to be freer than the heart; I see that all the animals are happy, because they do not constrain one another. I didn't know their maxims then; I do now, and I felt that I would prefer death to a forced marriage. If the gods who are irritated against me finally consent to be appeased, I would like to touch you in my favor. I confess to you, Marthesie, that I would be delighted to unite my fortune with yours, but alas, what can I propose to you? Would you want to live with a monster like me in the depths of my cavern?"

While Marcassin was speaking, Marthesie recovered enough strength to respond to him. "What, Sire," she cried, is it possible that I see you in a state so ill-befitting your birth? The queen, your mother, does not let a day pass without shedding tears over your misfortunes."

"Over my misfortunes?" said Marcassin, interrupting her. "Don't call thus the state that I am in; I have made my decision; it has cost me, but it is done. Don't believe, young Marthesie, that it is always a brilliant court that makes our most solid felicity; there are more charming pleasures, and I repeat to you that you could enable me to find them if you were of a humor to become wild with me."

"And why," she said, "do you no longer want to return to a place where you are still loved?"

"I'm still loved!" he cried. "No, no, one doesn't love princes overwhelmed by disgraces. As two thousand good things are expected of them, when they aren't in a state to provide them, they're rendered responsible for their ill fortune; in the end, they're hated more than the others. But why am I wasting time?" he cried. "If a few bears or lions of my neighborhood passed this way and heard me speaking, I'd be a doomed boar. Resolve, then to come without any other goal that that of passing a few fine days in narrow solitude with an unfortunate monster, who will no longer be unfortunate if he possesses you."

"Marcassin," she said to him, "I have at present no reason to love you; without you I would have two sisters who were dear to me; leave me time to take such an extraordinary resolution."

"Perhaps you're asking me for time," he said, "in order to betray me?"

"I'm not capable of that," she replied. "And I assure you now that no one will know that I have seen you."

"Will you come back here?" he said.

"Don't doubt it," she continued.

"Oh. your mother will oppose it. She'll be told that you've encountered a terrible wild boar; she won't want you to risk yourself here again. Come, then Marthesie, come with me."

"Where will you take me?" she said.

"Into a profound grotto," he replied. "A stream clearer than crystal runs through it slowly; its edges are covered with moss and fresh grass; a hundred echoes respond there sometimes to the plaintive voices of amorous and maltreated shepherds. It's there that we'll live together."

"Or, to put it better," she said, "it's there that I'll be devoured by one of your best friends. They'll come to see you, they'll find me, that will be the end of my life. Add that my mother, in despair at having lost me, will search for me everywhere. These woods are too near her house; I'd be found there."

"Let's go wherever you wish," he said. "The equipage of a poor boar is soon made."

"I agree," she said, "but mine is more embarrassing; I need clothes for all seasons, ribbons, and gems."

"You need," said Marcassin, "a toilette full of a thousand bagatelles and a thousand futile things. When one has intelligence and reason, can one not put oneself above that petty attire? Believe me, Marthesie, they add nothing to your beauty, and I'm certain that they tarnish its splendor. Don't seek anything for your complexion except fresh and clear spring water; you have curly hair of a charming color, and finer than the webs in which spiders catch innocent flies; make use of them for your adornment; your teeth are better arranged and whiter than pearls; be content with their glam and leave trifles to women less lovely than you."

"I'm very satisfied with everything that you say to me," she replied, "but you can't persuade me to bury myself in the depths of a cavern, with no company but lizards and snails. Wouldn't it be better for you to come with me to the home of your father, the king? I promise you that if they consent to our marriage, I'll be delighted. And if you love me, don't you want to render me happy and put me in a glorious rank?"

"I love you, beautiful mistress," he said, "but you don't love me; ambition would engage you to receive me for your husband; I have too much delicacy to accommodate myself to those sentiments."

"You have a natural disposition," Marthesie riposted, "to judge our sex badly, but Sire Marcassin, it's something to promise you a sincere amity. Reflect on it. You'll see me in a few days in the same place."

The prince took his leave of her and retired into his gloomy grotto, very occupied by all that she had said to him. His bizarre star had rendered him so grateful to the women he loved, that until that day he had not been flattered by a gracious word. That rendered him more sensible to Marthesie's; and, his ingenuous amour having inspired in him the design to regale her, several lambs, red deer and roe deer felt the force of his carnivorous teeth. Then he arranged them in his cavern, awaiting the moment when Marthesie would keep her promise.

For her part, she did not know what resolution to make. Even if Marcassin had been as handsome as he was ugly, even if they had loved one another as much as Astrée and Celadon loved one another, it would be all that she could to pass her best days in a frightful solitude—and Marcassin would have had to be Celadon! However, she was not engaged; no one had yet had the advantage of pleasing her, and she was in the resolution to live perfectly well with the prince, if he wanted to quit the forest.

She slipped away in order to come to talk to him; she found him at the place of the rendezvous. He never failed to go there several times a day, in the dread of missing the moment when she came. As soon as he perceived her, he ran toward her, and, humiliating himself at her feet, he made her know that wild boars, when they wish, have very gallant fashions of saluting.

They retired together to an out-of-the-way place, and Marcassin gazed at her with little eyes full of fire and passion. "What ought I to hope," he said, "of your tenderness?"

"You can hope for a great deal," she replied, "If you are in the design to return to the court; but I confess to you that I don't have the strength to spend the rest of my life far from all commerce."

"Ah," he said, "that's because you don't love me. It's true that I'm not lovable, but I am unfortunate, and you ought to do for me, out of pity or generosity, what you would do for another by inclination."

"What tells you," she replied, "that that those sentiments have no part in the amity that I am testifying for you? Believe me, Marcassin, I am still doing great deal to want to go with you to the home of the king, your father."

"Come to my grotto," he said. "Come and judge for yourself what you want me to abandon for you."

At that proposition she hesitated slightly; she feared that he might retain her against her will.

He divined what she was thinking. "Oh, have no fear," he said. "I shall never he happy by violent means."

Marthesie trusted the world that he gave her; he took her down into the depths of his cavern. She found all the animals there that he had killed in order to regale her. That kind of butchery made her feel sick; immediately she turned her eyes away and wanted to leave, but Marcassin, taking the attitude and tone of a master, said to her: "Lovely Marthesie, I am not sufficiently indifferent to leave you the liberty to quit me. I swear by the gods that you will always be the sovereign of my heart; invincible reasons prevent me from returning to my father; accept my amour and my faith here; let this fugitive steam, these ever-green clusters, the rock, the woods and the guests that inhabit them be the witnesses to our mutual oaths.

She did not have the same desire as him to engage herself, but she was trapped in the grotto without being able to leave. Why had she gone there? Should she not have foreseen what had happened? She went, and made reproaches to Marcassin.

How can I trust your promises?" she said, "since you have broken the first one you gave me?"

"It's necessary," said Marcassin, smiling, "that there is a little human mingled with the wild boar. The breaking of the promise for which you reproach me, the little cunning with which I protect my interests, is just the human that is acting; for, to be frank, animals have more honor between them than humans do."

"Alas," she said, "you have the worst of both, the heart of a man and the form of a beast. Be, then, either entirely one or entirely the other; after that I'll resolve to do what you wish."

"But beautiful Marthesie," he said, "do you want to remain here without being my wife? For you can't expect that I will permit you to leave here?"

She redoubled her tears and her pleas; he was untouched by them. After arguing for a long time, she consented to receive him as a husband, and assured him that she would love him as dearly as if he were the most amiable prince in the world.

Those obliging manners charmed him; he kissed her hand a thousand times and assured her in his turn that perhaps she would not be as unhappy as she had reason to believe. He asked her afterwards whether she would eat the animals he had killed.

"No," she said, "That's not to my taste; if you could bring me fruits it would please me."

He went out, and sealed the entrance to the cavern so well that it was impossible for Marthesie to escape, but she had made her decision in that regard, and she would not have done it if she could.

Marcassin loaded three hedgehogs with oranges, sweet limes, lemons and other fruits, sticking them on the prickles with which they were covered, and the provisions came quite comfortably as far as the grotto. He went in, and invited Marthesie to eat them. "It will be a wedding feast," he said, "that will not resemble those made for your two sisters, but he hope that, although there is less magnificence in it, you will find it more pleasant."

"May the gods permit that it be so," she said. Then she drew water in the hollow of her hand and drank to the health of the wild boar, by which he was delighted.

The meal having been as brief as it was frugal. Marthesie gathered up all the moss, grass and flowers that Marcassin had brought her. She composed a rather hard bed with them, on which she and the prince lay down. She took great care to ask him whether he wanted to have his head higher or lower, if he had enough room and on which side he preferred to sleep.

The good Marcassin thanked her tenderly, and exclaimed from time to time: "I would not exchange my fate with that of the greatest of men; I have finally found what I was seeking; I am loved by the one I love." He said a thousand nice things, by which she was not surprised, for he had intelligence, but she was glad nevertheless that the solitude in which he lived had not diminished it.

They both went to sleep, and when Marthesie woke up it seemed to her that her bed was better than when she had made it. Then, touching Marcassin gently, she found that his boar's head was like a human head, that he had long hair, arms and hands; she could not help being astonished; she went back to sleep, and when it was daylight she found that her husband was as much a wild boar as before.

They spent that day like the previous one. Marthesie did not tell her husband what she had suspected during the night. The hour for bed arrived; she touched his head while he was asleep, and she found the same difference that she had found before. She was very distressed; she could was always incapable of sleep, she was in a continual state of anxiety and sighed incessantly.

Marcassin perceived that with a veritable despair. "You don't love me, my dear Marthesie," he said to her. "I'm an unfortunate whose form displeases you. You will cause my death."

"Say rather, barbarian," she replied, "that you will cause mine. The insult you offer me touches me so sensibly that I shall be unable to resist it."

"I offer you an insult?" he cried. "I am a barbarian? Explain yourself, for assuredly you have no reason to complain."

"Do you believe," she said to him, "that I do not know that you cede your place every night to a man."

"Wild boars," he told her, "especially those that resemble me, are not of such benevolent disposition; do not have a thought so offensive to you and me, my dear Marthesie, and believe that I would be jealous of the gods themselves; but perhaps, while asleep, you dream this chimera."

Ashamed of having mentioned something so implausible, Marthesie replied that she believed him to such an extent that although she had had every reason to believe that she was not asleep when she touched the arms, hands and hair, she would submit to his judgment and would not mention it again. In fact, she expelled from her mind al the subjects of suspicion that came to it.

Six months went by with few pleasures on Marthesie's part, for she did not leave the cavern, for fear of being seen by her mother or her servants.

Since that poor mother had lost her daughter, she never ceased to groan; she made the woods resound with her plaints and Marthesie's name. At those sounds, which reached her ears almost every day, she sighed in secret at causing her mother so much grief and not to be able to soothe it, but Marcassin had threatened her forcefully, and she feared him as much as she loved him.

As her mildness was extreme, she continued to manifest a great deal of tenderness to the boar, who also loved her with the utmost passion. She became pregnant, and when she imagined that the swinish race was going to be perpetuated she felt an unparalleled affliction.

One night, when she could not sleep and was weeping softly, she heard someone speaking so close by that, even though he was speaking in a whisper, she did not miss a word of what he was saying. It was the good Marcassin who was begging someone not to be so rigorous and to grant him the permission for which he had been asking for a long time. Someone always replied: "No, no, I don't want it."

Marthesie was more anxious than ever. *Who is able to enter this grotto?* She asked herself. *My husband hasn't revealed this secret to me.* She was careful to refrain from going back to sleep; she was too curious.

The conversation ended. She heard the person who had spoken to the prince leave the cavern, and shortly thereafter he was snoring like a pig. She got up immediately, wanting to see whether it as easy to move the stone that sealed the cavern, but she could not shift it. As she came back slowly, without any light, she felt something under her feet; she perceived that it was the skin of a wild boar. She took it and hid it; then she awaited the outcome of the affair without saying anything.

Dawn had scarcely broken when Marcassin got up; she heard him searching on all sides; while he was becoming anxious, daylight came; she saw him so extraordinarily handsome and well-made that no surprise had ever been greater or more agreeable than hers.

"Ah!" she cried. "Don't make a mystery of my happiness any longer; I know and I have penetrated it, my dear prince! By what good fortune have you become the most lovable of all men?"

At first he was surprised to be discovered, but he collected himself quickly. "I'll tell you, my dear Marthesie," he said, "and tell you at the same time that it's to you that I owe this charming metamorphosis. Know that my mother was asleep

one day in the shade of a few trees when three fays passed
through the air. They recognized her and stopped. The eldest
endowed her with being the mother of an intelligent and well
made son. The second overbid that gift, adding a thousand
advantageous qualities in my favor. The youngest said, burst-
ing out laughing: 'It's necessary to diversify the matter somewhat; spring would be less agreeable if it had not been preceded by winter. In order that the prince you want to be charming
should appear even more so, I endow him with being a wild
boar until he has married three women, and the third has found
his boar-skin.'

"With those words the three fays disappeared. The queen
had heard the first two quite distinctly, but with regard to the
one that did me harm, she was laughing so loudly that she was
incomprehensible. I didn't know myself what I've just told
you until the day of our marriage. As I was about to come in
search of you, fully occupied with my passion, I stopped to
drink from a stream that runs near my grotto; either because it
was clearer than usual, or I was looking at myself with more
attention because of the desire I had to please you, I found
myself so frightful that tears came to my eyes. Without hyper-
bole, I shed enough to swell the course of the stream, and,
speaking to myself. I told myself that it was impossible that I
could please you.

"Discouraged by that thought, I made the resolution not
to go any further. 'I cannot he happy,' I said, 'If I am not
loved, and I cannot be loved by any reasonable person.'

"I was muttering those words when I perceived a lady
who approached me with a boldness that surprised me, for I
have a terrible appearance for those who don't know me.
'Marcassin,' she said to me, 'the time of your happiness is
imminent if you marry Marthesie and she can love you as you
are; be sure that before long, you will be deswinized. As soon
as your wedding night you will quit the skin that displeases
you so much; but put it on again before daylight, and do not
mention it to your wife; be careful to prevent her from perceiving it, until the time when the great affair is revealed.

"She told me," he continued, "everything that I have already told you about my mother. I gave her very humble thanks for the good news she had given me. I came to find you with a joy mingled with hope that I had not experienced before; and when I was fortunate enough to receive evidence of your amity, my satisfaction was augmented in every manner.

"My impatience to be able to share my secret with you was great. The fay, who was not unaware of anything, came by night to threaten me with the greatest disgrace if I did not remain silent. 'Oh, Madame,' I said to her, 'you have doubtless never loved, since you are obliging me to hide something so agreeable to the person I love most in the world.' She laughed at my pain, and forbade me to be afflicted, because everything would be favorable to me. However," he added, "Return my boar-skin to me; it's necessary that I put it on, for fear of irritating the fays."

"Whatever you might become, my dear prince," Marthesie said to him, "I shall never change for you; I will always retain a charming idea of your metamorphosis."

"I flatter myself," he said, "that the fays will not want us to suffer for much longer. They take care of us; this bed, which appears to you to be moss, is excellent down and soft wool; they are the ones who put all the beautiful fruits you eat at the entrance to the grotto."

Marthesie never wearied of thanking the fays for so many favors.

While she was addressing her compliments to them, Marcassin made every effort to put his boar-skin on again, but it had shrunk so much that there was only enough to cover one of his legs. He pulled it this way and that with his teeth and hands, but nothing worked. He was very sad, and deplored his misfortune, for he feared, with reason, that the fay who had swinized him so thoroughly might put it back on him for longer.

"Alas, my dear Marthesie," he said, "Why did you hide this fatal skin? It's perhaps to punish us that I can't make use of it as I did. If the fays are angry, how will we appease them?"

For her part, Marthesie wept. It was a very singular subject for affliction, because he could no longer become a wild boar.

At that moment the grotto trembled; then the vault opened and they saw six distaffs fall, charged with silk, three white and three black, which danced together. A voice emerged from them, which said: "If Marcassin and Marthesie can divine what these black and white distaffs signify, they will be happy."

The prince thought for a little while, and then said: "I divine that the three white distaffs signify the three fays that endowed me at birth."

"And I divine," cried Mathesie, "That the three black ones signify my two sisters and Coridon."

At the same time, the fays appeared in the place of the white distaffs. Ismene, Zelonide and Coridon also appeared. Nothing has ever been as frightening as that return from the other world.

"We have not been as far as you think," they said to Marthesie. "The prudent fays have had the kindness to help us; and while you were mourning our deaths they took us to a castle where nothing was lacking for our pleasures except that of seeing you with us."

"What!" said Marcassin. "I did not see Ismene and her lover lifeless, and it was not by my hand that Zelonide lost hers?"

"No," said the fays; "your fascinated eyes were the dupe of our cares; these sorts of adventures happen every day. One man believes that he is with his wife at a ball while she is asleep in her bed; another believes that he has a beautiful mistress, who only has an ugly one; a third believes that he has killed his enemy, who is alive and well in another country."

"You are going to cast me into strange doubts," said Prince Marcassin. "It seems, to hear you, that it is not even necessary to believe what one sees."

"The rule is not always general," replied the fays, "but it is indubitable that one ought to suspend judgment on many things and think that a certain dose of faerie enters into what appears to us to be most certain."

The prince and his wife thanked the fays for the instruction they had just given them and for conserving the lives of persons who were so dear to them.

"But," added Marthesie, throwing herself at their feet, "may I not hope that you will no longer put that vile boar-skin on my faithful Marcassin?"

"We have come to assure you of that," they said, "for it is time to return to the court."

Immediately, the grotto took on the appearance of a superb tent, in which the prince found several valets de chambre, who dressed him magnificently. For her part, Marthesie found ladies-in-waiting, and a costume of exquisite workmanship, in which nothing was lacking to coif and adorn her. Then a meal was served, like any meal ordered by the fays, which is to say enough.

No joy has ever been more perfect; everything that Marcassin had suffered of pain did not equal the pleasure of seeing himself not merely as a man, but as an infinitely lovable man. After they had left the table, several magnificent carriages harnessed to the most beautiful horses in the world arrived at high speed. They climbed into them with the rest of the little troop. Horse-guards rode before and behind the carriages. It was thus that Marcassin returned to the palace.

No one at the court knew where that pompous equipage was coming from, and even less who was inside, when a herald published it in a loud voice, to the sound of trumpets and cymbals. All the delighted people ran to see the prince, and no one wanted to doubt the truth of an adventure that nevertheless appeared rather dubious.

When the news reached the king and the queen, they went down promptly into the courtyard. Prince Marcassin resembled his father so strongly that it would have been difficult not to be recognize him. There was no misunderstanding, so delight had never been more universal. After a few months it was further augmented by the birth of a son, who had nothing swinish in his form or his humor.

> *The greatest effort of courage,*
> *When one is very much in love,*
> *Is to be able to hide the object of one's desire*
> *Because duty engages us to do it;*
> *Marcassin was thus able to merit the advantage*
> *Of returning triumphant to a august court.*
> *I consent that his excessive tenderness be criticized;*
> *It is better to lack amour*
> *Than to lack wisdom.*

The tale had seemed so amusing to the entire company as to enable them to wait without impatience for lunch to be served.

Madame de Saint-Thomas arrived; she was audible at the end of the pathway for her stiff coffee-colored dress rustled loudly. As she always wanted something singular, and had seen women of quality going through the city with a little Moor, she thought that she ought to have one, but while waiting to find one, she chose the son of her farmer's wife, who could be called a white Moor, so much did he have the features of one.

The sun, to which he was often exposed in the fields, had already begun to give him a very brown complexion, but that was not sufficient; as she wanted him completely black, she had his face rubbed with soot steeped in ink; he had enough patience to allow it to be smeared over his entire face. It is true that when the soot was attached to his lips it intruded an insupportable bitterness into his mouth; it was necessary only to blacken the upper one and to leave the lower one red, and the effect was singular. There was an even greater quarrel over his hair; the baronne though it too long and wanted it cut; the farmer's wife and her entire family opposed it; threats were made on the one part and remonstrations on the other; thus, the young Moorized peasant conserved flat and greasy hair, and he had orders to carry Madame a Baronne's stiff skirt.

Her husband had never seen that extraordinary figure; when she appeared, everyone started to laugh uncontrollably; the Moor with the red lips and long hair was no more singular in his species than she was in hers.

The ladies from Paris, who prided themselves on having manners as free and familiar as the baronne's were prudish and formal, stood up immediately and ran to her with open arms. "Oh, good day my dear Madame," they said, embracing her as if to stifle her. "How we have desired to see you! Do you know that our carriage has been insulted by your apple trees and that at the present moment it is as motionless as Phaeton's chariot?"

"You'll permit me to tell you," the baronne replied, in a stern and serious fashion, "that Phaeton had no chariot; his father was foolish enough to lend him his, and we ought not to say Phaeton's chariot but Apollo's chariot driven by Phaeton."

"You have, Madame," said the widow, "an exactitude that I had not expected."

"I have," the baronne replied, "what we have in the provinces as well as in your great city of Paris."

"What!" sad Madame de Lure. "Have you then, Madame, a little common sense?"

"Madame," added the baronne, in a bitter tone of voice, "I pride myself that, although a countrywoman, one nevertheless has as much taste as anyone else for reading and talking sense."

Monsieur de Saint-Thomas, who knew that his wife was very delicate in ceremonial matters, suspected that she was chagrined that a bourgeois woman as well-dressed as Madame du Rouet had called her "my dear" in a familiar fashion, in the first words she had addressed to her in her life. He was afraid that they might fall out, and, giving his hand to the newlywed, he obliged the vicomte to offer his to the widow. The prior proposed to the baronne to aid her to walk, but that expression displeased her, because she was not in a good mood.

"Aid me to walk?" she said, proudly. "Am I so feeble? Do I need a walking-stick?"

He made no reply, for he knew that she had a strong tendency to become annoyed.

In fact, she was sulking somewhat, and, seeing that the ladies were looking at the new edition Moor with an unparalleled astonishment, and were moving their feet so forcefully that one of hers felt the repercussion, she said to them: "You are surprised, Mesdames, it seems to me?"

"It's true," said Madame de Rouet, "that a Moor of this species has never been seen in Paris."

"Oh, Paris, Paris," replied the baronne. "It seems to you that nothing that does not come from there is good for anything."

"But you'll agree," said Madame de Lure, "that the little boy is tinted with the most extraordinary complexion possible."

"The truth is," said the baronne, laughing in her turn, "that some people smear themselves with white and others with black."

Madame du Rouet took that malign joke a trifle personally, and returned it with interest.

The baron, who was very polite, was pained that a first visit was passing so bitterly; he tried to repair everything with praise, which, given appropriately, touched the ladies with a pleasure more sensible than the chagrin that the baronne's ill humor might have caused them.

She employed a pretext after lunch to return to her bedroom, where she had forgotten her box of beauty-spots and her snuff-box.

As they were talking about various things, La Dandinardière's turn came. The prior recounted very agreeably what had happened in recent days: his quarrels with his neighbor and Maître Robert, and his dispositions to become Don Quixote, provided that it was unnecessary to pay in bravery; the simplicities of Alain were not neglected. The newcomers had a strong desire to see him.

"That's very easy," said the baron. "It will only cost you the trouble of going up to his room."

"He would be well enough to come down," added the vicomte, "but for the adventure of the bed, when he grazed himself so rudely by hiding underneath it."

"Oh my charming cousin," cried Madame du Rouet, "that's a character who is too amusing; I'd go from Paris to Rome to see something similar; truly, let's not lose such a fine opportunity to divert ourselves."

The prior said that he would go to announce to La Dandinardière the visit that was being prepared for him, in order that he could arm himself."

"What, Monsieur," replied the widow. "Does he require weapons in order to receive us? Does he want to kill ladies?"

"No," he said, "he's very far from any such design; you have not yet seen the most courteous knight errant."

He quit them immediately and went up to La Dandinardière's bedroom in order to announce the visit of two utterly charming ladies. "And above all," he said, "Don't reproach them for speaking Norman, for they're from Paris, the city where it is only necessary to reside for twenty-four hours in order to acquire all the wit one needs for the rest of one's life. It's necessary not to seek any other evidence of that than you."

"Me!" said La Dandinardière. "I was born there; that's quite different."

"And that's exactly what renders you perfect, Monsieur," cried the prior; "you have suckled the spirit of politeness, science, grace and amour with your nurse's milk."

"You don't believe it," said the bourgeois, "but nothing is more true. "It seems to me that I think things that no one can have thought before me; that I have certain delicate sentiments that belong to a delicate soul, and that delicacy defines the interior and exterior man completely."

"I understand you," said the prior. "It means that since these ladies are from Paris, you desire passionately to see them; I'll go and fetch them."

"Oh, Monsieur, mercy, mercy!" cried La Dandinardière. "I'm like a guttersnipe in this bed; I feel a noble shame for that. You know that I haven't had time for anything; I've only been thinking about my books and my woes. In conclusion, permit me to turn my shirt, or lend me one of yours."

"I believe," said the prior, maliciously, "that you'd do better to put on your armor; that's imposing, and every armed man in his bed can boast of pleasing the ladies, for, make no mistake, that sex, so timid and so cowardly, esteems valor and cherishes heroes.

"Let's go, Alain," he said, "let's go: my armor, my arms."

"What!" replied Alain. "The turban?"

"Yes, great fool, the turban and everything else. I even want my breastplate."

"But Monsieur," replied his valet, "there's enough to cripple you. Alas, that accursed bed has already scraped you; when you're harnessed to these rags, you'll...."

"Oh, wretch!" said the bourgeois. "You'll only ever collect thistles on the field of Mars! To call military arms that ornament my like a Roman dictator *rags!* How can you speak in such an inept manner?"

"Oh, mercy Monsieur," said the prior. "A little fecundity in yours; the ladies are waiting."

"But what ears do you have, then?" replied La Dandinardière. "Nothing wounds them? My valet's absurdities don't deafen you like a tocsin? For me, I confess, it's impossible to hear inapt words. If I were taken to the throne with words so poorly organized, with such rude and savage barbarity, I'd be offended by my good fortune and would renounce everything rather than take such a path to glory."

"The French language is your very humble servant," said the prior, laughing. "I hope that you won't oblige an ingrate; I will even—but I ask you to keep it a secret—have a few measures taken among scholars to write your life."

"Oh, Monsieur, are you telling me the truth?" cried La Dandinardière, transported by the most sensible pleasure of which a man is capable. "Once again, I dare to doubt it, for I have never give any other benefit to those messieurs than to receive them at my table. It's certain that I've given lunch thirty times over to Homer, Herodotus, Plutarch, Seneca, Voiture, Corneille, and even Harlequin; they made me die of laughter, and I receive it as a favor to see them free and easy in my home. My butler had orders, when I was in the army or at Versailles, to serve them a table as proper as if I had been there; I never even boast about it, for does one boast about those sorts of things? And is it possible," he continued, "that they remember my amity with such slight marks of recognition? In those days I was paid only too well by the satisfaction of seeing them; frankly I doubt that there is at present a village philosopher like me."

"That is because you are the philosopher that they only think they are," replied the prior, dying of the desire to laugh. "I'm charmed to learn that you had table companions of such great merit. Admit that Cato is very amusing."

"I don't know who Cato is," the bourgeois replied. "It seems to me that he didn't come to my house as often as the others."

"No matter," said the prior. "He was one of your friends, and it's a matter agreed between them to write everything that concerns you; only one thing stops then, which is that you're too thrifty."

"Who isn't, these days?" said the bourgeois, with a chagrined expression. "If I threw money out of the window I'd have to throw myself out too. Believe me, Monsieur le Prieur, heroes don't know how to sew or spin; they only know the fortunate arithmetic that makes two into four, so they ought to conserve what they have."

"Prudence befits everyone," replied the prior, "and your historians won't forget yours; nevertheless, when it's a matter of talking about your marriage, how do you want them to represent it? Will they say: he was madly in love with a young woman of great quality and great merit, but because she didn't have great wealth, he didn't want to marry her? Oh, how nasty that would be! I suffer from it in advance."

"Oh," said La Dandinardière, "who asked them to write my life? If I'd been fond of praise, do you think I would have left Paris, where people heaped me with it from all directions, to bury myself in a province where people are only fond of praising no one, but like saying hard truths to one's face? I've sometimes swallowed some of that character; I would have been able to respond as vigorously as anyone else, but I avoid quarrels."

"I understand you, Monsieur La Dandinardière," said the prior; "my frank expression doesn't please you. What do you expect? I'm all of a piece; and as I honor you infinitely, I'd like you to be a perfect man, but you'll never be one with a depth of avarice that...."

The bourgeois interrupted him; he was annoyed. "Have you forgotten, then," he asked, "the beautiful lades who sent you here? Go in quest of them, if you please; we'll talk about various things."

The prior went to fetch them; they were waiting impatiently. He related a part of the conversation to them with a serious expression, for he dared not amuse himself too much at the little man's expense in front of Madame de Saint-Thomas, who might have taken exception to it, and there might have been further quarrels to endure.

The widow and the newlywed went up to La Dandinardière's room promptly. His appearance had something so funny about it that more serious people than them would have had difficulty preventing themselves from laughing. His nose was grazed and his cheeks a violet red; his face was swollen, with the result that, being naturally rather fat, he resembled a trumpeter who had been playing for a long time. His turban, like his armor, had nothing in common with any mortal.

Madame du Rouet was the first to approach him; she made him a profound reverence, but on casting her eyes upon him, what was her surprise to recognize him as her cousin

Cristoflet, merchant of the Rue Saint Denis! They each uttered a loud cry and embraced for a long time, saying to one another in low voices: "Shh! Shh!" for Cousine du Rouet had no more desire to be known in the province than Cousin Cristoflet, and they both wanted to pass for people of the highest quality.

In truth, she had known for a long time that he had excessive visions and that as soon as fortune had treated him favorably, he had set about making himself a man of quality, in spite of all his relatives. She had far more disposition to excuse him for that than anyone else, for if he was mad, so was she, and from morning till evening she spoke about nothing but her ancestors, the princes of Bredi Breda, whom she praised until she ran out of breath, who had as little foundation as the meals that La Dandinardière provided every week to the seven sages of Greece.

The whole company was very surprised by the intelligence there was between La Dandinardière and the widow. The baron was annoyed by what it told him, understanding that it might harm the marriage, for even though he pretended not to care about it very much, he nevertheless desired it. He expressed his joy that they had found one another in his house at the moment when it seemed that they least expected it.

"It's true," said La Dandinardière, "that in quitting the court, I took care to keep quiet about my retreat to my dearest friends; I knew that my absence would touch them, and I was touched myself by abandoning them."

"You can understand," the widow said to him, "how far that extended. I know more than one beauty, veritable *bellissima*, who spent the rest of the year without putting on ribbons and without wearing lace or colored fabrics."

"Alas," said La Dandinardière, uttering a profound sigh, "Poor women! That penetrates my heart."

"Mourning appeared general on their faces," she continued. "More than one husband divined the cause of it, and had a hammer in the head."

"Hey, hey!" cried the bourgeois. "What are you telling me? I fear for that young duchess with the blonde hair; I'd be inconsolable if I'd disturbed her marriage, for thus far, Madame, you'll admit that we had concealed our game so well that no one could have penetrated the secret of our hearts."

Madame de Saint-Thomas listened for some time to the conversation of the little man and the widow, but impatience seized her and moving closer to the vicomte she whispered to him: "What! You want to give us that man for a son in law? Can't you see that he has fifty intrigues? One could try to fix him but one would never be able to succeed."

"Don't be disgusted, Madame," he replied. "A little coquettish air isn't too ill-fitting in a courtier; don't believe that they love more than anyone else; they know the tricks of the finest gallantry, they sigh appropriately, they persuade, but they don't love any more for it."

"So much the worse, Monsieur," said the baronne. "This one's deceiving us."

"No, Madame," the vicomte continued, "he was born in a more sincere court."

"Wasn't he born in Paris?" said Madame de Saint-Thomas, again.

The vicomte was embarrassed as to how to characterize the court of the merchants of Saint-Denis, when he was relieved of the difficulty by the arrival of Mesdemoiselles de Saint-Thomas, whom the ladies had requested, and who had not been able to dress so early to come to dinner.

They were effectively beautiful, and if they had not taken it into their heads to be amazons and romantic princesses they would have appeared quite lovely. On seeing them, La Dandinardière made a sign to his cousin de Rouet, by which she understood that Virginie had made a deep impression on his heart; she graciously engaged her more than Marthonide, who would not have been content, if Madame de Lure had not made her a thousand caresses.

"One has nothing to lament, Mademoiselle," she said to her, when one quits the court, as I have, to come to a province where one finds a person as charming as you."

"Madame," she replied, "We try as much as possible to be your imitators, but our cares are futile in that regard."

"Oh, what are you saying, my beauty?" cried Madame de Lure. "You're utterly lovable, and I see a radiance of intelligence escaping from your eyes that enchants me."

The widow said many other things to Virginie; they both spoke at the same time with such great velocity that they choked.[19] Never had praise been distributed so cheaply. La Dandinardière was triumphant; he uttered fine sentiments until he ran out of breath; he was delighted that the widow applauded his nascent passion, and Virginie, for her part, deployed her finest eloquence.

The remainder of the company listened; the baronne found it difficult to accommodate anyone praising her daughters; she pretended to everything, and regarded as a larceny compliments addressed to anyone but her. She adopted a strange expression and only wanted to respond in monosyllables.

Meanwhile, the conversation, which did not revolve entirely around the advantages of beauty, fell upon those of intelligence; there was a further inundation of incense and excessive mutual compliments on the part of du Rouet and La Dandinardière. The messieurs looked at one another, admiring the inexhaustible spring of great words that signified little or nothing.

In order to try to create some diversion, the vicomte said to Madame de Saint-Thomas that they had both missed a great deal in not being in the little wood when the ladies had read the prettiest tale that had yet been made in memory of the fays.

"Do these demoiselles know that sort of amusement?" said the widow. "Has it reached the provinces already?"

---

[19] I have translated *s'engouèrent* [choked] in the more commonplace literal fashion, but it is not irrelevant to the subtext of this passage, and perhaps its relevance to the coterie of writers of *contes de fées*, that the verb also means "to become infatuated with."

"For what do you take us, Madame?" retorted Virginie. "Do you believe our climate to be so dispossessed of the favorable influences of a benevolent star that we're absolutely unaware of what is happening beneath the celestial vault? In truth, our sphere is not as limited as you think; we know the Carabosses and the Grognons, and we sometimes put some of them on stage, who would not make the author blush."

"I confess to you," said the newlywed, "that I was not expecting to see Norman muses and village fays. I would be delighted to know them and to hear them speak."

Marthonide, who did not lack merit, and who had an exceedingly high opinion of herself, offered to read the latest tale that she had written, in the middle of the night.

"It could scarcely be newer," said Virginie. "In truth, it's not yet corrected."

The entire company accepted her proposition; she had the notebook on her person, and commenced.

THE DOLPHIN[20]

There was once a king and a queen to whom Heaven had given several children, but they only loved them as much as they found them beautiful and amiable. Among others there was a younger one named Alidor, rather pleasant in his personality, although he was unbearably ugly. The king and queen could only suffer him with a great deal of repugnance; they were always telling him to get away from them. As he saw that all the caresses were for the others and all the harshness for him, he could not think of any other decision to make than that of departing secretly. He took effective measures to get out of the realm without anyone knowing where he was

---

[20] Like the previous tale, this one is an extensive elaboration of a tale in Straparola's *Nights*, and as with the previous one, the same tale was elaborated by the Comtesse de Murat, in a very different fashion, as "Le Turbot" (tr. as "The Turbot"), in an evident spirit of agreed competition.

going, hoping that fortune might perhaps treat him more favorably in another land than in his own.

His absence nevertheless troubled the king and the queen; they envisaged that he would not appear with the magnificence befitting a price and that he might attract disagreeable attention to them, in which they were more interested with regard to their reputation than his wellbeing. They sent a few courtiers after him, with orders to make him turn round, but he took so much care to use out-of-the-way roads that they followed him in vain, and those who received the order were unable to bring him back to court, where he was forgotten. Everyone was too well aware of the lack of tenderness that the king and queen had for him to love him as much as a prince ought to be loved. There was no longer any mention of Alidor; who was there who might have mentioned him? Fortune was contrary to him; his nearest relatives hated him, and little attention was paid to his merit.

Alidor was wandering randomly, without knowing himself in which direction he wanted to go, when he encountered a young man, well made and well mounted, who had the appearance of a traveler. They greeted one another and approached one another civilly; they spent some time together without talking about anything but general news, but eventually the traveler asked Alidor in which direction he was going.

"What about you?" he said. "Which way are you're going?"

"Sire," he replied, "I'm a squire of the King of the Woods. He has sent me to seek horses in a place distant from here."

"Is that king savage?" asked the prince. "Since you call him the King of the Woods, I imagine that he spends his life there?"

"His ancestors," said the squire, "did indeed spend their lives as you say, but for him there is a large court; the queen, his wife, is one of the loveliest women in the world, and Princess Livorette, their unique daughter, is endowed with a thousand charms that delight everyone who sees her. It's true that she's still so young that she doesn't perceive all the cares that are rendered to her, but one can't help rendering them."

"You give me a great desire to see her," said the prince, "And to spend some time in such an agreeable court, but do they look upon strangers with a kindly eye? I don't flatter myself; I know that nature hasn't favored me with a handsome face, but it has given me in recompense a good heart."

"That's a very rare item of furniture," said the traveler, "and I hold that it's far above the other. In our court, people are able to put a just price on everything, so you can go there with an entire certainty of being favorably received." With that, he informed him of the route that it was necessary to follow in order to reach the Kingdom of the Woods. As he was obliging and saw an air of nobility in him that all his ugliness could not conceal, he gave him the address of some of his friends, in order to be introduced to the king and the queen.

The prince felt such obliging manners keenly. He augured well of a realm where people were so polite, and, only seeking a place where he could live anonymously, he preferred to choose that one rather than another. He even found some particular determination of fortune to engage him to choose it. After parting from the traveler he continued on his route, sometimes dreaming about Princess Livorette, for whom he already felt a curiosity full of urgency.

When he had arrived at the court of the King of the Woods, the friends of the man he had encountered regaled him, and the king welcomed him. He was glad to have left his homeland, for although no one knew him, he nevertheless had reason to be grateful for all the regard that was shown to him. It is true that he did not find the same thing in the queen's apartment; he scarcely appeared there with hearing long bursts of laughter on all sides. Some women hid in order not to look at him, others ran away; but young Livorette above all, to whom those example of impoliteness were shown, let the prince see all that she thought of his ugliness.

It seemed to him that the princess, who laughed thus at the defects of a stranger, was not very well brought up; he lamented that in secret. *Alas*, he said, *that is how I was spoiled in my father's household; it's necessary to confess that princes are unfortunate when their defects are tolerated. I can now see the poison that we drank every day in long draughts. Ought that beautiful princess not to be ashamed of mocking me? I have come a long way to render my respects to her and swell her court. I might go further to publish her good qualities and her faults. I was not born her subject; nothing ties my tongue with regard to its honesty. However, she scarcely casts a glance at me except to insult me with mocking expressions. But alas*, he went on, gazing at her in admiration, *how safe she is from anything I might say; never has such beauty been offered to my sight; I admire her, I admire her too much, and I sense, too, that I shall admire her all my life.*

While he was making these sad reflections, the queen, who was obliging, had ordered him to approach, and wanting to soothe his mind, she said very favorable things to him and asked about his homeland, his name and his adventures. He responded to everything as a man of wit, and a man who was prepared for the questions. She liked his character, and told him that whenever he wanted to render his duties to her, she would always see him with pleasure. She even asked whether he ever played cards, and told him to come and play bassette.

As he was seeking to please, he made it a pleasure to play with the queen. He had a good deal of money and precious stones; people noted in all his actions an air of nobility that was no small help in enabling him to distinguish himself, and although no one knew anything about him and he took great care to hide his birth, he was nevertheless judged advantageously. There was only the princess who could not suffer him; she laughed in his face; she made grimaces and a thousand tricks appropriate to her age, which would not have caused him pain on the part of another, but were very different coming from her; he took the matter seriously, and when he was on slightly more familiar terms with her he made his complaints to her.

"Do you think, Madame," he said "that there is no injustice in your mocking me? The same gods who have made you the most beautiful princess in the universe have rendered me the ugliest man in the world, and I am their work as well as you."

"I agree, Alidor," she said, "but you're the most imperfect work that ever emerged from their hands." With that she studied him attentively without taking her eyes off him for a long time, and then she laughed until she felt ill.

The prince, who had time to study her then, drank long draughts of the poison that Amour had prepared for him. *It's necessary to die*, he thought, *since I cannot hope to please her and I cannot live without possessing Livorette's good graces.*

In the end he became so melancholy that everyone felt sorry for him. The queen perceived it; his card play was no longer proceeding as usual. She asked him what was wrong, but could not get anything out of him, except that he felt an extraordinary languor, that he believed that the change of climate might have contributed to it, and that he had resolved to go into the country frequently in order to take the air.

In fact, he could no longer stand seeing the process every day without hope, and flattered himself that he might be cured by avoiding her. Wherever he went, however, the passion followed him. He sought solitary places, and abandoned himself there to profound reveries.

The neighborhood of the sea engaged him to go fishing frequently, but he threw hooks and nets in vain; he did not catch anything. Livorette was almost always at her window every evening when he returned, and as she saw him coming back every evening she cried out, mischievously: "Well, Alidor, are you brining me a nice fish for my supper?"

"No, Madame," he replied, making a profound reverence, and he passed by with a chagrined expression.

The beautiful princess mocked him: "Of, how maladroit he is," she said. "He can't even catch a sole."

He was upset to be so unhappy and to have become the continual object of the princess's gibes, so he wanted to catch something worthy of being presented to her. Often he climbed alone into a small boat, where he took nets of all kinds, and, thinking about Livorette, he took enormous cares to make a good catch.

Am I not very unfortunate, he said to himself, *to find a new pain prepared in this amusement? I was only seeking to escape from the memory of the princess, and she has been seized by a desire to eat the produce of my fishing. Fortune is so contrary to me that it even refuses me this small pleasure.*

Penetrated by his chagrin, he advanced out to sea further than he had ever done before, and, throwing his nets determinedly, he felt them so heavily laden that he hastened to draw them into it again for fear that they might break. When he had hauled them all back into the boat, he looked curiously to see what was struggling therein, and found a beautiful dolphin, which he took in his arms, delighted to have succeeded so well.

The dolphin did what it could to escape; it made surprising leaps; then it played dead so that Alidor would no longer distrust it, but nothing succeeded for it.

"My poor dolphin," he said, "Don't torment me anymore; I shall take you back very resolutely to the princess, and you shall have the honor of being served at her table this evening."

"You're making a design that is very fatal for me," it replied.

"What! You can talk!" cried the prince, utterly astonished. "Just gods, what a prodigy!"

"If you are good enough and generous enough to give me my liberty," the dolphin continued, "I will render you services so essential in the course of my life that you will have no reason to repent of it as long as you live."

"And what will the princess eat for her supper?" said Alidor. "Don't you know the ironic airs she takes with me? She calls me maladroit and stupid, and gives me certain other names that engage me to sacrifice you to my reputation."

"So, because of a princess who amuses herself with knowing jokes," said the dolphin, "if you don't fish well, you think yourself degraded of honor and nobility? Let me live, I implore you; replace your very humble servant the dolphin in the water; there are benefits whose recompense is not far away."

"Go on," said the prince, throwing it back in the water. "I don't expect either good or evil from you, but it appears that you have a strong desire to live. Livorette can add, if she wishes, further insults to the ones she has already made me. No matter, I find you an extraordinary animal, and I want to content you."

The dolphin disappeared from the prince's sight; he saw the hope of his fishing vanish suddenly. He sat down in the boat, withdrew the oars, which he set beneath his feet, and had abandoned himself to a profound reverie when he heard a very agreeable voice that seemed to curl the waves as they emerged from the sea.

"Alidor, Prince Alidor," said the voice, "look at one of your friends."

He bent over and saw the dolphin, which was making a thousand capers on the surface of the sea. "It is only just," it said, "that everyone has his turn. Only a quarter of an hour ago, you obliged med me sensibly; now wish for a few services for me and you'll see what I can do."

"I would like," said the prince, "a small recompense for a great benefit. Send me the best fish in the sea."

At the same time, without him casting his nets, salmon, soles, turbots, oysters and other marine mollusks began hurling themselves into the boat in such large quantities that Alidor feared perishing, with reason, so heavily was it loaded.

"Hey, hey!" he cried. "I'm ashamed of all that you're doing in my favor, but I'm afraid that your profusion might become harmful to me; save me, for you can see that this is serious."

The dolphin pushed the boat all the way to the shore, and the prince arrived there with his entire catch. Four mules could not have carried it; he sat down and was choosing the best when he heard the voice of the dolphin. "Alidor," it said, showing its large head, "are you a little satisfied with my cares?"

"It would be difficult," he said, "to do any more."

"Oh," said the fish,[21] "know that I'm as sensible to the way you behaved toward me as to the life you conserved for me. I've come to tell you, therefore, that every time you'd like to command me to do something. I'll always be ready to obey you. I have more than one sort of power; if you don't believe me, you can test it."

"Alas," said the prince, "What have I to wish for? I love a princess who hates me."

"Would you like to stop loving her?" said the dolphin.

"No," replied Alidor. "I can't resolve myself to that; rather enable me to please her, or to die."

"Can you promise me," the dolphin continued, "never to love any other woman than Livorette?"

"Yes, I promise you that," cried the prince. "I've sworn that I'll be faithful to my passion and that I will neglect nothing that depends on me to please her."

"It's necessary to deceive her," the dolphin said, "for she doesn't want to marry you, because she finds you ugly and she doesn't know you."

"I consent to deceiving her," said the prince, "although I know, personally, that she will never put her heart in the possession of a heart like mine."

"Time might persuade her to do it," added the dolphin, "but find it good that I metamorphose you into a canary; you'll be able to quit the form whenever you wish."

"You're the master, my dear dolphin," said Alidor.

"Well, then," the fish continued, "be a canary. I want it."

---

[21] Aulnoy did not know, as everyone now does, that a dolphin is not a fish, so it would be inappropriate to correct her use of the term.

Immediately, the prince saw that he had feathers, splayed feet and a small beak; he whistled and spoke admirably well; he admired himself. Then, making a wish to become Alidor again, he found himself as he had always been.

No man had ever been so joyful; he was extremely impatient to be with the young princess. He called his men, loaded them with all his fish, and resumed the road to the city.

Livorette did not fail to come on to her balcony and shout to him: "Hey, Alidor, have you been luckier than usual?"

"Yes, Madame," he said to her. At the same time he showed her the large baskets, all filled with the finest fish in the world.

"Oh!" she cried, in an infantile fashion. "How sorry I am that you've made a grand catch, for I won't be able to mock you any longer."

"You'll always find enough reasons when it pleases you, Madame," he said, and going on his way, he sent all the fish to her. Then, after a moment, he took the form of a little canary and flew to her window.

As soon as she saw him, she advanced slowly, and stretched out her hand to grasp him—at which moment he drew away, fluttering in the air.

"I've come from one of the ends of the earth," he said, "where your beauty causes a great deal of talk; but, lovely princess, it isn't just that I've come so far to be treated like a canary in a dozen; it's necessary that you promise me never to lock me up, to let me come and go, and never to give me any other prison than your beautiful eyes."

"Oh, cried Livorette, "lovely little bird, make your conditions as you wish; I promise not to fail in any of them, for nothing has ever been seen as pretty as you. You talk better than a parrot, you whistle marvelously; I love you so much that I'm dying of the desire to hold you."

The canary swooped down and alighted on Livorette's head, and then on her finger, where he did not merely whistle

tunes; he sang words with as much propriety and clarity as the
most skillful musician.

Nature has made me inconstant and flighty,
But I am too charmed to live in your court.
I require no other cage
Than the two bonds of Amour.
With what pleasure one engages
To wear your lovable irons!
One ought to prefer that slavery a thousand times more
Than the empire of the universe.

"I'm charmed," she said to all her ladies, "by the present
that fortune has just sent me."

She ran to the queen's bedroom to show her the lovely
canary; the queen was dying to hear him talk, but he only
talked for the princess and did not care at all about complaisance for others.

Night having fallen, Livorette went into her apartment
with the beautiful canary, which she had named Biby.[22] She
sat down at her dressing table; he perched on her mirror,
sometimes taking the liberty of pecking the tip of her ear and
sometimes her hand. She was transported with joy. As for
Alidor, who had not savored any kind gestures before, he felt
this one as the sovereign good and never wanted to be anything but the canary Biby. It is true that he was sad to see
when he was left in a room where Livorette's dogs, monkeys
and parrots ordinarily slept.

"What!" he said, with an afflicted air, "you value me so
little that you're abandoning me?"

---

[22] In the *Cabinet des fées* version of the story, this name is
initially given as Byby, which is repeated several times before
being changed to Biby. I have unified the spelling using the
more frequent usage.

"Is it abandoning you, dear Biby," she said, "to put you with what I like the best?" She went out, and the prince remained on the mirror.

*

As soon as he perceived daylight he flew to the sea shore. "Dolphin, dear dolphin," he called, "I have two words to say to you; don't refuse to hear me."

The obliging fish appeared, cleaving the waves in a serious fashion. On seeing him, Biby flew toward him and alighted gently on his head.

"I know everything that you've done and I know everything that you want of me." said the dolphin. "I declare to you that you won't go into Livorette's bedroom until you've married her, and the king and queen have consented to it; then I'll regard you as her husband."

The prince had so much regard for the fish that he did not persist at all. He thanked him a thousand times for what the charming metamorphosis had procured him, and asked him for the continuation of his amity.

He returned to the palace in his feathered form. He found the princess in a dressing gown; she had been searching for him everywhere and, not finding him, weeping bitterly.

"Oh, little traitor," she said, "have I not received you well enough? What caresses have I not given you? I've given you biscuits, sugar and bonbons."

"Yes, yes," said the canary, who was listening through a little hole, "you've given me a few marks of amity, but you've given me plenty of indifference. Do you think that I can accustom myself to sleeping with your nasty cat? He would have eaten me fifty times over if I hadn't taken the precaution of staying awake all night to preserve myself from his paw."

Touched by that story, Livorette looked at him tenderly and offered him her finger. "Come on, good Biby," she said to him, "come and make peace."

"Oh, I'm not so easily appeased," he said. "I want the king and the queen to be involved in it."

"Willingly," she said. "I'll carry you to their chamber."

Immediately, she went to find them. They were still in bed, and talking about an advantageous marriage that concerned her.

"What do you want this morning, my dear child," said the queen.

"It's my little bird," she replied, flinging her arms around her neck, "who wants to speak to you."

"The thing is rare," said the king, laughing "but are we in a state to give him a serious audience?"

"Yes, yes, Sire," replied the canary, "although I haven't appeared in your court with all the pomp I ought to have, for having heard talk of the beauty and charms of this young princess, I have come promptly to beg you to give me to her in marriage. Such as you see me, I am the sovereign of a little wood of orange trees, myrtles and honeysuckle, which is in the most delightful location in the Canary Isles. I have a large number of subjects of my species, who are obliged to pay me a large tribute of gnats and worms; the princess will be able to eat her fill of them. She will have no lack of concerts; I am even related to several nightingales, who will render her eager cares. We shall live in your court for as long as you please. Sire, I only ask you for a little millet, rapeseed and fresh water. When you order us to go to our estates, the leagues of distance will not prevent us for having your news and giving you ours; flying couriers will be an admirable aid to us, and I believe, without vanity, that you will receive a good deal of satisfaction from a son-in-law like me."

He concluded this discourse by singing two or three tunes, and then twittering very agreeably.

The king and the queen laughed to the point of making themselves ill.

"We have refrained," they said, "from refusing Livorette to you. Yes, amiable bird, we will give her to you provided that she consents to it."

"Oh, with all my heart," she said. "I've never been so glad as I am to marry Prince Biby."

Immediately, he extracted one of his most beautiful wing-feathers, which he offered to her as a wedding present. Livorette received it graciously, and put it in her hair, which was admirably beautiful.

As soon as she had returned to her bedroom she told her ladies that she wanted to inform them of some great news, which was that the king and queen had just married her to a sovereign prince. Everyone hearing her speak thus threw themselves, some at her knees in order to embrace them, and others at her hands in order to kiss them. They asked with eager expressions who the fortunate prince was for whom the most beautiful princess in the world was destined.

"Here he is," she said, taking the little canary from the depths of her sleeve and showing them her husband. At the sight of him they laughed wholeheartedly, and made a few jokes about the perfect innocence of their beautiful mistress.

She hastened to get dressed in order to return to the apartment of the queen, who loved her so dearly that she wanted to have her with her. Meanwhile, the canary flew away, and, resumed the ordinary form of Alidor into order to come and pay his court to her.

As soon as the queen perceived him, she cried to him: "Approach to compliment my daughter on her marriage to Biby; don't you think that we've given her to a great lord?"

Alidor entered into the joke, and as he was more cheerful than he had ever been in his life, he said a hundred agreeable things, which amused the queen greatly. As for Livorette, however, she continued to mock him and always to contradict him. He would have felt the pain of seeing her in that humor if he had not thought at the same time that his friend the fish would aid him to overcome that aversion.

When the princess went to bed, she wanted to leave her canary in the animal room, but he began to complain and flutter around her; he followed her into her bedroom and perched neatly on a porcelain, from which she dared not expel him for fear that he might break it.

"If you sing too early, Biby," said Livorette, "and you wake me up, I shan't pardon you."

He assured her that he would be mute until she ordered him to sing his little song, and on that promise, they retired tranquilly. Scarcely was the princess lying down than she fell deeply asleep, to which there was no doubt that the dolphin contributed; she even snored like a little pig, which is not natural to a child. Biby did not snore in the same way; he knew full well that it was necessary that he had not yet closed his eyes. He quit the porcelain, and came to place himself next to his charming wife, so gently that she did not wake up.

As soon as he saw the daylight again, he resumed the form of a canary and flew to the sea shore, where, becoming Alidor again, he sat down on a rock that was smooth enough and covered in samphire; then he looked in all directions to discover the fish dear to his heart. He called several times, and while waiting, he made agreeable reflections on his good fortune.

O fays who are praised so much, he said to himself, *and whose power is so extraordinary, could you render any other mortal as content as me?*

That thought gave way to these lines:

Obliging friend dolphin, whose help
Has allowed me to savor the fruit of my tender amours,
I dare not divulge the joy that enchants me.
I enjoy the sweetest fate.
But a black presentiment haunts me;
I tremble that the gods might become jealous.

As he was muttering those words, he felt the rock agitating forcefully; then it opened up to let out an aged waddling female dwarf, who was leaning on a crutch. It was the fay Grognette, who was no better than Grognon.

"Truly, Sire Alidor," she said, "I find you very familiar to come and sit down on my rock; I don't know what prevents me from throwing you into the sea, to teach you that if the fays can't render any mortal happier than you, they can at least render him unhappy as soon as they wish."

"Madame," relied the prince, astonished by the adventure, "I didn't know that you lived here, or I would certainly have refrained from lacking the respect that is due to your palace."

"You apologies can't please me," she continued. "You're ugly and presumptuous; it's necessary that I have the pleasure of seeing you suffer."

"Alas, what have I done to you?" he said.

"I don't know of anything myself," she added, "but I'll treat you as if I knew."

"The antipathy you have against me is quite extraordinary," he said, "and if I didn't hope that the gods would protect me against you, I'd anticipate that the harm with which you threaten me would cause my death."

Grognette muttered more threats, and then plunged back into the rock, which closed up.

The prince, very chagrined, did not want to sit down on it; he had no desire to start a further quarrel with an inopportune dwarf. *I was too satisfied with my lot*, he thought. *Now a little Fury has come to trouble it. What does she want to do to me, then? Oh, doubtless it isn't upon me that she'll exercise her wrath but rather on the beauty that I love Dolphin, dolphin, I implore you to race here to console me.*

At the same moment the fish appeared close to the shore. "Well, what do you want of me?" he said.

"I came to thank you for all the good you've done me. I've married Livorette, and in the excess of my joy, I ran toward you, to make you party to it, when a fay....."

"I know that," said the dolphin, interrupting him. "That's Grognette, the most malign of all creatures, and the oddest. Its only necessary to be content to displease her; what troubles me more she has power, and she's going to thwart me in the good that I've resolved to do you."

"She's a strange Grognette," replied Alidor. "What displeasure have I rendered her?"

"What!" cried the dolphin. "You're human and you're astonished by human injustice? In truth, you can't think so; it's all that you could do if you were a fish, although we're not exactly equitable in our briny empire, and one sees the largest swallowing the smallest every day; it ought not to be tolerated, for the smallest herring had its rights of citizenship acquired in the sea, as well as a frightful smell."

"I'll interrupt you," said the prince, "to ask whether Livorette will ever know that I'm her husband."

"Enjoy the present time," replied the dolphin, "without seeking information about the future."

As he finished speaking he hid himself on the sea bed and the prince became a canary and flew back to his dear princess, who was looking for him everywhere.

"What! Do you always intend to worry me, little libertine?" she said, as soon as he appeared. "I dread your loss, and I'd die of displease in consequence."

"No, my Livorette," he replied, "I'll never doom myself for you."

"How can you answer for that?" she continued. "Everyone knows that traps and nets are set for you everywhere. If you fell into those of a beautiful mistress, how do I know you'd come back?"

"Oh, what an insulting suspicion," he said. "You don't know me at all."

"Pardon me, Biby," she said, smiling. "I've heard it said that no one cares about fidelity to one's wife, and as I'm yours, I dread your change."

The canary found something to his advantage in conversations of that sort; he discovered that he was loved, albeit only in the quality of a little bird. The delicacy of his heart was sometimes wounded by that.

"Is the trick that I've played permissible?" he said to the dolphin. "I know that the princess doesn't love me, that she finds me ugly and that none of my defects has escaped her. I have every reason to believe that she wouldn't want me for her husband; in spite of that, I've become her husband. If she finds out one day, with what reproaches will she not heap me? What could I say to her? I'd die of dolor if I displeased her/"

Your reflections accord poorly with your amour," the fish replied. "If all lovers were similar, there would never be any abducted or discontented mistresses. Take advantage of the present time; less happy ones will arrive for you."

That threat afflicted Alidor greatly; he understood that the fay Grognette still wished to harm him for sitting on her rock when she was underneath it; he implored the dolphin to continue to render him good offices.

There was much talk of marrying the princess to a young and handsome prince whose estates were not far away; he sent ambassadors to ask for her; the king received them very well, and that news alarmed Alidor greatly. He went diligently to the sea shore, called to the fish that served him so well and told him about his alarm.

"Consider the extremity in which I find myself," he said. "Either losing my wife and seeing her married to someone else, or declaring my marriage and seeing myself separated from her for the rest of my life."

"I can't prevent Grognette from causing you pain," said the dolphin "I'm no less in despair than you are, and you can't be more occupied with your affairs than me. Have a little courage; I can't tell you anything at present, but count on my amity as a benefit that you will never lack."

The prince thanked him with all this heart and returned to his princess.

He found her in the midst of her women; one was holding her head and another her arm; she was complaining of pain in her heart. As he was not metamorphosed into a canary at that moment he dared not approach her, although he was very disturbed by her illness. As soon as she perceived him she smiled, in spite of all that she was suffering.

"Alidor," she said to him, "I believe I'm going to die; I'm very annoyed by that, now that the ambassadors have arrived, for a thousand good things are said about the prince who is asking for me."

"What, Madame!" he replied, striving to smile. "Have you forgotten that you have chosen a husband?"

"What, my canary!" she said. "I know that he'll be annoyed by it, but it wouldn't prevent me from loving him tenderly."

"Perhaps a divided heart isn't his affair," replied Alidor.

"It doesn't matter," added Livorette. "I'll be very glad to be queen of a great kingdom."

"But Madame," he said, again, "he has offered you one."

"That's a pleasant empire," she said. "A little jasmine wood; it could accommodate a bee or a linnet; in my regard, it's not the same thing."

The princess's women feared that she might inconvenience herself by talking too much; they begged Alidor to withdraw, and they put her on her bed, where Biby came to make her agreeable reproaches for her infidelity.

As her illness was not violent, she went to see the queen, but from that day on scarcely one passed without her feeling ill. Her languor changed her; she became thin and nauseated.

Several months went by; no one knew what to do; and what caused the court more chagrin is that the ambassadors who had come to ask for her were pressing for her to be put in their hands. One of them told the queen that there was a very skillful physician who might be able to relieve her. She sent him an equipage and forbade that he be informed of the quality of the invalid, in order that he could speak more freely.

He examined her for a while and said smiling: "Is it possible that your court physicians haven't discovered the inconvenience of this little lady? Truly, she will soon add a handsome boy to her family...."

He was not allowed time to finish; all the ladies heaped him with insults, and he was expelled by the shoulders with loud jeers.

Biby was in Livorette's room. He did not judge, like the others that the country physician was an ignoramus; it had come to his mind several times that the princess was pregnant.

He went to the sea shore in order to consult his friend the fish, who did not appear to have another sentiment. "I advise you to depart," he said, "for I fear that someone might surprise you when she's asleep, and you'd both be doomed."

"Oh," said the afflicted prince, "do you think I could live separated from the person who is most dear to me in the world? What does it matter to me to protect my life? It is going to become odious to me. Let me see Livorette, or let me die."

The dolphin felt sorry for him; he wept a little, although dolphins hardly ever weep; nevertheless, he consoled his dear friend. Grognette was blamed for everything.

The queen told the king about the physician's vision. Livorette was summoned; she was asked questions to which she responded with as much sincerity as innocence. They even spoke to her women, whose testimony was what it had to be. Thus, Their Majesties were tranquilized, until the day when the princess brought into the world the most beautiful baby there had ever been.

To express the astonishment and anger of the king, the dolor of the queen, the despair of the princess, the anxiety of Alidor, the surprise of the ambassadors and that of the entire court, would be impossible. Where had the child come from? Who was his father? No one could say, and young Livorette was as ignorant as the child himself; but the king did not intend to be mocked; her tears and her oaths were of no use. He made the resolution to have her hurled with her son from the top of a mountain into a precipice bristling with pointed rocks, where she would find a very cruel death. He said so to the queen, who was so violently afflicted that she fell at his feet as if dead.

He softened on seeing her in such a state, and when she had recovered slightly he tried to console her; but she told him that she would never have joy or health until he had revoked such a deadly sentence. She threw herself at his knees, and in tears, she begged him to kill her and to let Livorette and her son live, whom she summoned expressly in order to touch the king by means of her innocence.

The queen's lamentations and the baby's tears moved him to compassion; he threw himself into an armchair and, covering his eyes with his hand, he meditated and sighed for a long time without being able to speak. Then he said to the queen that he wanted, in her favor, to defer the death of the princess and her son, but that she had to understand that it was only deferred, and that blood was necessary to wash away such a shameful stain from their house.

The queen thought that she had already gained a great deal in having the death of her dear daughter and her grandson deferred, with the result that she was no obstinate and consented to the princess being imprisoned in a tower, where she would not even enjoy the light of the sun.

In that sad place she deplored her barbaric destiny. If anything could soften her chagrin it was her perfect innocence; she never saw her child and never received any news of him. "Just Heaven," she cried, "What have I done to be crushed by such bitter displeasures?"

Alidor, overwhelmed by the sharpest dolor, could not find the strength to sustain it any longer; his mind was gradually troubled, and in the end he went completely mad He was heard lamenting and crying in the woods; he threw his money and his gems away in the middle of roads; his clothes were in tatters, his hair unkempt and his beard long—which, combined with his natural ugliness, rendered him almost frightful. Everyone felt extremely sorry for him, and more attention would have been paid to his misfortune if that of the princess had not occupied the entire kingdom.

The ambassadors who had come to ask for the princess did not wait to be dismissed; they wanted to return home urgently, feeling a kind of shame at having come to ask for her.

For his part, the king saw them depart without displeasure; their presence caused him pain.

The dolphin, on the other hand, having plunged in the abysms of the sea, no longer appeared. leaving the field free for the fay Grognette to exercise all the malice she wished against the prince and the princess.

Although the little prince became more beautiful than a beautiful day, the king had only conserved his life in order to discover by that means who the father was. He had said nothing about it to the queen, but one day he issued an edict that all the courtiers should bring his grandson a present that might delight him. Everyone came immediately, and when the king was told that a large crowd had assembled he came with the queen into the large audience hall. The nurse followed them, carrying the lovable infant in her arms, clad in gold and silver brocade.

Everyone came to kiss his little hand, and to present him with a rose of precious stones, artificial fruits, a golden lion, an agate wolf, an ivory horse, a spaniel, a parrot or a butterfly. He took all that indifferently.

The king, without seeming to be doing anything, studied what happened and remarked that the child did not caress anyone more than any other. Then he had notices posted that if anyone failed to come he would be culpable and punished as such.

At that threat, everyone hastened more than they had before, and the king's squire, who had encountered Alidor during his journey and was the cause of his coming to the court, having found him in the depths of a cave, where he usually retreated since he had lost his mind, said to him: "Hey, Alidor, are you going to be the only one who doesn't give anything to the little prince? Don't you know about the edict that has been published? Do you want to king to have you put to death?"

"Yes, I want that," relied the poor prince, utterly distraught. "Why are you interfering, coming to trouble my repose?"

"Don't be annoyed," said the squire. "I'm only talking to you with a view to making you appear."

"Oh, I'm pleasantly dressed," said Alidor, laughing, "to go and see the royal brat."

"If it's only a question of furnishing you with clothes," said the squire, "I'll give you with rich ones."

"Let's go, then. It's a long time since I've seen myself in pompous apparel."

He emerged from his cave and went meekly enough to the home of the king's squire. The latter, who was one of the most magnificent men of the court, gave him a choice of several rich coats, but he only wanted a black one, and whatever anyone could say to him or do, he went without a cravat, a hat and shoes.

When he reached the door he had forgotten that it was necessary to give something to the prince, but he was no more troubled about that, and, seeing a pin on the ground, he picked it up in order to present it. He went hopping into the room, rolling his eyes and letting his tongue hang out in a fashion that, in addition to his natural ugliness, caused the sight of him to be unsustainable.

The nurse, thinking that the little prince would be frightened, tried to turn him away, and made a sign to Alidor to go away, but as soon as the child perceived him, he held out his arms to him laughing and making such an extraordinary fuss that it was necessary that he be brought to him. Then the child threw his arms around his neck, kissed him a thousand times, and could no longer resolve to be separated from him. In spite of his madness, Alidor showed him no less amity.

The king was transfixed by astonishment by such a surprising adventure. He hid his wrath from the entire assembly, but as soon as it was finished, without communicating his design to the queen, he ordered two noblemen in whom he had a particular confidence to go and take Princess Livorette from the tower where she had been languishing for four years, to put her in a barrel with Alidor and the little prince, to add a jug full of milk, a bottle of wine, a loaf of bread, and to throw them thus into the sea.

The noblemen, afflicted by such a barbaric order, prostrated themselves at his feet and begged him humbly to grant mercy to his daughter and his grandson. "Alas, Sire," they said to him, "if Your Majesty had deigned to inform himself of how she has been suffering for four years, he would find that she has been sufficiently punished without adding such a cruel death to it, Consider that she is your unique daughter, reserved by the gods to wear your crown one day. You are accountable for her blood to your subjects; her son promises great things; do you still want to stifle him in the cradle?"

"Yes, I want it," cried the king, very irritated by the resistance that his will encountered, "and if you refuse to make her perish, I'll make you perish with her."

The noblemen knew, dolorously, that they would gain nothing on the firmness of the king; they withdrew with heads bowed and tears in their eyes. They ordered a barrel large enough to contain the princess, her son, Alidor and the petty provisions. Then they went to the tower, where they found her lying on a bed of straw, with irons on her feet and hands, not having seen daylight for four years. They approached her with profound respect and told her the order they had received from her father, the king; they were sobbing so forcefully that she could hardly hear them. She understood them well enough, however, and started weeping with them.

"Alas," she said to them, "the gods are my witnesses that I am innocent. I'm only sixteen years old; I was destined to wear more than one crown, and you're going to throw me into the sea like the most criminal of all creatures. But have no fear that I'm trying to corrupt your fidelity and that I'm begging you to find some temperament that might save me life; it's a long time since my father has accustomed me to wish for death; I am prepared to suffer it, provided that my dear child is saved. Of what crime is he guilty? Can his innocence not serve to protect him from the king's fury? Is it possible that he has condemned him to perish with me? Is it not sufficient for my father to take my life? Does he want more than one victim?"

The noblemen who were listening to her had no response to make; it was necessary to obey, they told the princess.

"Well," she said, "break the chains that retain me; I'm ready to go with you."

The guards came and filed through the irons with which her hands and feet were charged; they did her a great deal of harm in the process, but she suffered everything with a marvelous constancy. She emerged from her prison as charming as the sun emerging from the bosom of the waves; all those who saw her admired her courage no less than her ravishing beauty; it had augmented further in spite of her displeasures, and her languid air was worth just as much as her ordinary vivacity.

Alidor and the little prince were waiting on the sea shore, where guards had brought them; they knew as little as one another about the evil that was about to be done to them. When the princess saw her son she took him in her arms and kissed him a thousand times with an extreme tenderness, and when she was told that she was being drowned because of Alidor she said that she was glad that the man she liked least in the world had been chosen, and that in wanting to doom her, she was nevertheless being justified

As for him, he started laughing as soon as he perceived her. "Hey, where have you come from, little princess?" he said. "Truly, there's a great deal of news since your departure. Livorette is no longer in the palace and I've gone mad enough to be tied. It's said," he continued, "that we're going to make a voyage together to the bottom of the sea. Listen, princess, wake me up every day, for I'll sleep until midday if you aren't careful."

He would have said more if Livorette, making a final effort, had not entered the barrel first, holding her son at her neck. Alidor jumped in recklessly, leaping and rejoicing in going to the kingdom of the soles, where the turbots were kings. In sum, disparate things swarmed in his mouth.

The barrel was tightly sealed, and from the top of a rock that jutted out over the sea, it was dropped into it. Everyone sobbed and uttered long cries full of despair; they returned to the court penetrated with the most veritable dolor.

As for Alidor, he was marvelously tranquil; he began by seizing the loaf of bread, which he ate entirely; then he found the bottle of wine, and began to drink gaily, singing songs as if he were at a celebratory feast.

"Alidor," said the princess, "at least let me die quietly, without deafening me with your impertinent joy."

"What have I done to you, Princess," he replied, "for you to want me to have chagrin? Do you want to know a secret that I'll confide to you? Somewhere, in a corner unknown to me, there is a certain fish whose name is Dolphin; he's the best of my friends; he has promised to obey me in everything I command. That's why, beautiful Livorette, I'm not worried, for I'll call him to our rescue as soon as we're hungry or thirsty, or we want to sleep in some superb palace, which he'll build expressly for us."

"Call him then, innocent," said the princess. "Why defer the most urgent thing in the world? If you wait until I'm hungry, you'll wait a long time; my heart is too sad, alas, for me to think of eating; but my son is dying, he's stifling in this horrible barrel. Hurry up, I beg you, in order that I can see whether you're telling the truth, for a man without reason, like you, might well be mistaken."

Alidor immediately called the dolphin.

"Dolphin, my fishy friend, I command you to come immediately in order to obey me in all the things I want to order you to do."

"Here I am," said the dolphin. "Speak."

"Are you there?" said the prince. "This barrel is so tightly sealed that I can't see."

"Only say what you want," added the dolphin.

"I would like," he replied, "to hear an agreeable music."

"Oh, god God!" cried the princess, impatiently. "You're assuredly mocking with your music. Isn't it a very useless thing to hear fine singing when one is drowning?"

"But what do you want, then?" he said. "You aren't hungry or thirsty."

"Give me the power that you have to command the dolphin," she said.

"Ho, Dolphin!" cried Alidor. "I order you to do whatever Princess Livorette wishes, without fail."

"Well, then," said the dolphin, "I'll do it."

At the same time, she told him to carry them to the most agreeable island on earth and to build in that location the most beautiful palace there had ever been; that she wanted ravishing gardens there, with rivers around them, one of wine and the other of water; a a flower-bed full of blooms, in the middle of which there would be a tree, the stem of which would be silver and the branches gold, with three oranges on it, one of the diamond, another of ruby and the third of emerald; that the palace be painted and gilded; and that the entirety of history should be represented in a great gallery."

"Is that all you want?" said the dolphin.

"It's a great deal," she replied.

"Not too much," he said, "for everything is already done."

"I want you," she said, "to tell me something that I don't know and you might."

"I understand you," said the dolphin. "You're asking who the father of your little prince is. It's the canary Biby, and the canary Biby is none other than Prince Alidor, who is with you."

"Ah, Sire Dolphin," cried Livorette, "you're mocking me."

"I swear to you," he said, "by Neptune's trident, by Scylla and Charybdis, by all the lairs of the sea, by its mollusks, by its treasures and by the Tritons, by the Naiads, and by the fortunate auguries that the desperate pilot obtains by following me; finally, I swear to you by yourself, charming Livorette,

that I am a fish of benignity and honor, and that I am not lying
to you."

"After so many oaths," she said, "I reproach myself for
not believing you, although, to tell the truth, what I'm hearing
is the most surprising thing in the world. I order you, therefore, to return Alidor's reason and to give him all the intelligence one can have and all the charms of an agreeable conversation. I also want you to make him a hundred times more
handsome than he is ugly and I want you tell me why you
named him prince, for that title sounds agreeably in my ears."

The dolphin, obeyed in all that, as he had in everything
else. He told Livorette about the prince's adventure, who his
father was, who his mother was, his ancestors and his relatives, for he had an infinite knowledge of the past, the present
and the future, and he was a great genealogist by profession.
Such fish are not caught every day; it is necessary that Dame
Fortune is mixed up in it.

While they were chatting thus, the barrel came to rest
against an island; the dolphin, having gradually lifted it, threw
it on to the shore. As soon as it was there, it opened. The princess, the prince and the child were free to emerge from their
prison.

The first thing that Alidor did was to throw himself at the
feet of his dear Livorette. He had recovered all his reason and
an intelligence a thousand time more charming than he had
had before; he had become so well made, all his features having been changed for the better, that she had difficulty recognizing him. He begged her pardon tenderly for his metamorphosis into the canary Biby; he apologized for it in a respectful
and passionate manner. Finally, she pardoned him for a marriage to which she might perhaps not have consented if he had
adopted other means to obtain her consent. It is also true that
the dolphin had rendered him so lovable that she had never
seen anything to equal him at her father's court.

He confirmed everything that the dolphin had said about
his quality; that was an essential thing for the satisfaction of
the princess, for, after all, one might well be a friend of the

fays but one cannot change one's birth; when Heaven dies not give us the one we would have liked, only virtue and merit can repair it; but often it is with so much interest that one has the wherewithal to console oneself.

The princess was in the best humor in the world; she had been in a peril so frightful that the pleasure she felt in having escaped it was by no means mediocre. She rendered thanks to the gods; then she looked out to sea in order to see their good friend the dolphin; he was still there, and she thanked him, and she ought, for having saved her life. The prince did no less. Their son, who could speak so prettily and had more intelligence than children of his age usually have, also complimented him in a fashion that delighted the gallant dolphin. He performed a hundred somersaults in favor of the little boy.

Suddenly, they heard a loud noise of trumpets, fifes and oboes, with the neighing of several horses; it was the equipages of the prince and the princess, and all their guards, magnificently dressed. Several ladies came in the carriages; they got down promptly as soon as they saw them and came to kiss the hem of the princess's robe. She did not want to suffer that, finding an air of quality about them that merited her attention. They told her that they had received orders from the fish Dolphin to recognize them as the king and queen of the island, and that they would find many submissive subjects there, and a great deal of satisfaction.

Alidor and Livorette testified a great joy at seeing themselves honored by such polite and obliging persons. They responded to them with as much generosity as grace and majesty. Then they climbed into an uncovered caleche drawn by eight winged horses, which lifted them up from time to time all the way to the clouds. Then they descended so gradually that it was scarcely perceptible. That manner of travel has its conveniences, because there are no jolts and no risk of traffic jams.

They were still in mid-air when they perceived on the slope of a hill overlooking the sea a palace so marvelously constructed that even though all the walls were silver, it was nevertheless possible to see through them all the way to the interior of the rooms. They remarked that they were furnished with everything imaginable of the most superb and the most tasteful. The gardens surpassed the beauty of the palace; one could not count the springs and pools that nature has assembled in that location in order to render it delightful. The prince and his wife did not know to which to give the prize, so perfect did everything seem.

When they had entered it, they heard from all sides: "Long live Prince Alidor! Long live Princess Livorette!" Numerous instruments and charming voices made an enchanted symphony.

It was not long before they were served a excellent repast; they needed it because the sea air and the manner in which they had been embarked had fatigued them terribly. They sat down at table and ate with a good appetite.

When they left the table the guardian of the royal treasure came in and asked whether they would like, while they digested the meal, to stop into the adjacent gallery. When they did so they saw, along the walls, great wells with seals of perfumed Spanish leather garnished with gold; they asked what they were for, and the guardian replied that metallic springs ran through the wells and that when money was wanted it was only necessary to send down a bucket and say: "My intention is to draw louis,"—or pistoles, quadruples, écus, or other coins—and at the same time, the water took the form that one had wished and the bucket came up full of gold or silver coins, without the spring ever running dry for those who made good usage of it; but it had been seen several times that when misers sent the buckets down with the design of merely amassing gold and keeping it locked away, the buckets came up filed with toads and snakes, which gave them a great fright, and sometimes great harm, in proportion to their avarice.

The prince and princes admired the wells as one of the best and rarest things there were in the world; they sent down a bucket in order to make the experiment; it immediately came up full of little gold nuggets. They asked why it was not ready-minted coins, and the guardian told them that it must be the lack of the arms of the prince and the princess, because they had not said what they wanted to be put on them.

"Oh," said Alidor, "We have too much obligation to the generous dolphin to want any other effigy but his." At the same time, all the nuggets changed into gold coins, stamped with a dolphin.

The hour to retire having arrived, Alidor went to bed in his apartment, timid and respectful, and the princess in hers with her son.

At eleven o'clock, the princess was still asleep. The prince had got up early in order to go hunting, and returned before she was awake. When he was able to see her without inconveniencing her, he went into her room, followed by several gentlemen carrying large golden bowls filled with all the game he had just killed. He presented it to his dear princess, who received it graciously, and thanked him several times for his attention for her. That gave him the opportunity to say that he had never loved her with more passion than he did then, and that he implored her to mark the time when they would celebrate their marriage with pomp.

"Oh, Sire," she said, "my design in that regard is fixed, I will only ever consent to it, as long as I live, with the permission of the king, my father, and the queen, my mother."

Never had a man in love been so afflicted. "To what are you condemning me, beautiful princess?" he said. "Do you not know that what you want is impossible? We have only just emerged from the fatal barrel in which we were imprisoned in order to doom us, and you can imagine that they will consent to what I desire. Oh, undoubtedly you want to punish me for the violent passion that I have for you; I know full well that you destined your hand and your heart for the prince who sent you ambassadors while I became a canary."

"You judge my sentiments poorly," she said. "I esteem you, I love you, and I have pardoned you for all the harm that you attracted to me by a metamorphosis that you ought not to have attempted; for, being the son of a king, could you not believe that my father might have deemed it a pleasure to see you in his alliance?"

"A grand passion does not reason so coldly," he said. "I took the first course that has led me to happiness; but you have so much harshness that I shall be inconsolable if you do not revoke the barbaric sentence that you have just pronounced."

"It is impossible for me to revoke it," she said. "You should know that last night, while I was sleeping tranquilly, I felt someone tugging me rather rudely. I opened my eyes and I saw, by the light of a torch that was casting a somber light, the most frightful little creature in the world. She was staring at me with furious eyes. 'Do you know me?' she said.

"'No, Madame,' I replied, 'and I do not have any desire to know you.'

"'Aha!' she continued, 'you're jesting!'

"'No, I swear it,' I replied, 'I'm telling the truth.'

"'My name is the fay Grognette,' she said, 'I have essential reasons for complaint against Alidor; he sat down on my rock and he has the gift of displeasing me. I forbid you to regard him as your husband until the king, your father, and the queen, your mother, consent to it. If you disobey my orders I shall exercise my vengeance on your son; he will die, and his death will be followed by a thousand other misfortunes that you will be unable to avoid.'

"With those words she blew flaming brands over me, by which I was covered; I thought they were going to burn me, when she said: 'I will grant you mercy, as long as you obey my will.'"

The prince knew by the name and depiction of Grognette that the princess's story was sincere. "Alas," he said, "why did you ask our friend the fish to cure me of my madness? I had less to lament than I have now. What use are intelligence and reason to me, except to make me suffer? Permit me to go and implore him to take away my judgment; it's a possession that is a burden to me."

The princess felt very compassionate; she loved the prince veritably and found a thousand good qualities in him. He said everything and did everything with a particular grace. She wept, and allowed him to enjoy the pleasure of seeing tears flow of which he was the cause.

He found even more satisfaction in knowing the sentiments that she had for him than he had found in her company when he was a canary, with the result that his dolor was eased to such a degree that he threw himself at her feet, kissed her hands and said: "Know, my dear Livorette," he said, "that I have no will where you are; I render you the absolute mistress of my fate."

She sensed all the merit of such a great complaisance, and incessantly meditated means of obtaining the permission so necessary to their happiness. In fact, that was the only thing it could lack, for there were no pleasures that the inhabitants of the island did not try to give them. Their rivers were full of fish, the forests with game, the orchards with fruits, the fields with wheat, the meadows with grass and the wells with gold and silver; there was no war, no lawsuits; there were youth, health, beauty and intelligence, books, clean water, excellent wine and inexhaustible snuff-boxes; Livorette did not love Alidor any less than Alidor loved Livorette.

From time to time they went to render their duties to the fish, who always saw them with pleasure, and when they spoke to him about the fay Grognette and the orders he had given the princess, and begged him to serve them as a friend, he always gave them a few words of consolation in order to soften their pains; but he never promised them anything positive.

Two years passed thus. Alidor consulted the dolphin about the desire he had to send ambassadors to the King of the Woods, but he told him that Grognette would surely make them perish, and perhaps the gods were working themselves in order to do something in their favor.

Meanwhile, the queen had learned about the deplorable adventure of her daughter, her grandson and Alidor; no dolor was ever greater than hers; she no longer had any joy or health; all the places where she had seen the princess reminded her of her misfortune, and she could not help making continual reproaches to the king.

"Cruel father," she said to him, "is it possible that you were able to resolve to have that poor child drowned? We only had her; the gods had given her to us; we ought to have waited for the gods to take her away from us."

For some time, the king sustained those words philosophically, but in the end, he sensed the grandeur of his crime himself. He felt the absence of his daughter no less than his wife. He reproached himself secretly for having given everything to his glory and so little to his tenderness. He did not want the queen to know the full extent of his affliction; he hid his pain under an air of firmness, but as soon as he was alone he cried: "My daughter, my dear daughter, where are you? Unique consolation of my old age, have I lost you, then? And I have lost you because I wanted it."

Finally, overwhelmed one day by the queen's grief and his own, he admitted to her that since the unfortunate day when he had had Livorette and her son thrown into the sea he had not had a moment of repose; that her plaintive shade followed him everywhere; that he heard the innocent cries of her son; and that he feared that he might die of the chagrin. The news added greatly to that of the queen.

"I am going, therefore," she cried, "to have your grief as well as mine! What shall we do, Sire, to soothe them?"

The king told her that someone had mentioned to him a fay who had recently taken up residence in the Forest of Bears, and that he would go to consult her.

"I would be very glad," she told him, "to be in the expedition, although I don't know yet what I want to ask of her, for the death of our dear Livorette and the little prince is only too certain."

"No matter," said the king, "it's necessary to see her." He immediately ordered that the large caleche be prepared, and everything necessary for a journey of thirty leagues.

They departed early the next day, and did not take long to reach the abode of the fay, who, having read in the stars the visit that the king and queen were about to render her, advanced purposefully to meet them.

As soon as Their Majesties perceived her, they descended from the caleche and, after embracing her with great testimonies of amity, they could not help weeping bitterly.

"Sire," said the fay, "I know the subject of your visit. You are very afflicted to have procured the death of the princess, your daughter. I know no other remedy for that than to advise both of you to embark on a good ship and go to Dolphin Island; it is a long way from here, but you will find a fruit there that will enable you to forget your grief. I advise you not to lose a moment in that; it's the unique means of your relief. In your regard, Madame," she added, addressing the queen, "the state in which you are in touches me so sensibly that it seems to me that your troubles are my own."

The king and the queen thanked the fay for her good advice; they made her considerable presents and asked her to be so kind, in their absence, as to take particular care of their realm, in order that their neighbors would not attempt to make war on it. She promised everything they desired. They returned to the capital city with a sort of consolation, in being able to hope that their dolor might diminish.

They had a ship equipped, embarked on it, and headed out to sea, guided by a pilot who had been to Dolphin Island. The wind was favorable to them for several days, but then became absolutely contrary, and the tempest was augmented to such an extent that, after having been battered by it, the ship was opened up by a rock, without any remedy being possible. All the people who had been on the vessel found themselves drawn apart in a moment; they did not know how to escape such a great peril.

Throughout that time, the king was only thinking about his dear daughter. *I have thoroughly merited*, he said to himself, *the punishment that the gods have sent me, because I exposed Livorette and her son to fury of the waves*. These reflections tormented him to such a point that he was to longer thinking of prolonging his life when he perceived the queen on a dolphin, which had received her as she fell from the ship. She held out her arms to the king, dying of the desire to join him and pleading with the charitable dolphin to reach him and save them both.

That is what happened, for at the moment when the king was about to sink to the bottom, the amiable fish approached him, and with the queen's aid, he placed himself on his back. She was charmed to see him again, and begged him to have a little courage, since there was every appearance that Heaven was interested in their conservation.

Indeed, toward the end of the day, the obliging fish carried them as far as an agreeable shore, where they landed as little fatigued as if they had just emerged from the poop cabin.

It was precisely the island where Livorette and Alidor commanded as sovereigns. They were walking along the shore; Livorette was holding her son by the hand, and they were followed by a numerous court, when they were astonished to see two people being carried to land on the back of a dolphin. That obliged them to advance toward them in order to offer them hospitality. But how surprised the prince and the princess were when they recognized the king and the queen!

They saw clearly that they had not been recognized in the same way; that was not extraordinary, for it had been six years since the king and queen had seen their daughter; a young woman changes a great deal in such a long space of time. Alidor having been ugly and mad, had become handsome and reasonable. As for the child, he had grown. Thus, Their Majesties were far from thinking that they were seeing their lovely daughter and their dear grandson.

Livorette only held back her tears with great difficulty; at every word she spoke to her father and her mother, or that she heard the say, her heart swelled. Her voice changed tone continually, emotional and tremulous.

"Madame," the king said to her, "see at your feet an afflicted monarch and a desolate queen; we have been shipwrecked far from here, all those who were with us have perished; we are alone, deprived of treasures and aid, sad examples of the inconstancy of fortune."

"Sire," the princess said to him, "you could not have landed on any shore where people would have more pleasure in helping you; please forget your troubles. And you, Madame," she said to the queen, "permit me to embrace you." At the same time, she flung her arms around her neck, and the queen hugged her in her arms with movements of tenderness so extraordinary, because she found her so similar to her dear Livorette that she was on the point of fainting.

Prince Alidor invited them to climb into his carriage with him; they were glad to do so, and allowed themselves to be taken to the palace, all the beauty and magnificence of which surprised the king greatly.

There was no moment when people did not take care to give them some pleasure, but what caused them an infinite amount was that the prince's ships, which were not far from the place where the king's had broken up, had saved the crew and all the passengers, and had brought them to Dolphin Island while the king was deploring their death.

After having spent several days with the prince and princess, the king finally asked them one day to give them the means of returning to their realm. "Alas," added the queen "I will not conceal from you the most dolorous adventure than could ever happen to a father and a mother." With that, she told them the story of Livorette, the troubles that had oppressed them since the cruel torture to which the king had condemned them, the advice of the fay who lived in the Forest of Bears, and their plan to go to Dolphin Island.

"It is here," she continued, "that we have arrived by means of the most extraordinary navigation there has ever been. However, apart from the pleasure of seeing you, we have found nothing here to soothe us, and the fay who made us come here has not made a good prediction."

The princess had listened to her mother with so much pity and emotion that she could not arrest the flow of her tears. The queen had a veritable gratitude in finding her so sensible to her chagrins; she prayed to the gods to compensate her for it and embraced her a thousand times, addressing her as her daughter and her child, without knowing why she was doing so.

Finally, the ship being equipped, the departure of the king and the queen was fixed for the following day. The princess had always reserved one of the greatest beauties of her palace in order to show it to them when they were about to go. It was the beautiful tree in the flower garden, the stem of which was silver, the branches gold and the fruits diamond, ruby and emerald. Three guardians were commissioned to watch over it night and day, for fear that someone might try to steal the fruits and succeed in doing so.

When Alidor and Livorette had taken the king and queen to that place, they left them there for some time to admire the beauty of the marvelous tree, which had no parallel in the world, at their leisure.

After having spent more than four hours examining it, they returned to where the prince and the princess were waiting for them to give them a superb meal. There was only one table in the room with two places set. When the king asked the reason they told him that they wanted to have the honor of serving them. Indeed, they invited Their Majesties to sit down. Livorette and Alidor, with their son, gave drinks to the king and the queen, which they served on their knees; they carved all the meat and arranged it neatly on Their Majesties' plates, choosing the best and most delicate morsels.

An agreeable and soft symphony was heard, which was giving them a great deal of pleasure, when the three guardians of the beautiful tree came in, with wild eyes, and said that they had terrible news: that the beautiful oranges of diamond and ruby had been stolen, and that it could only be the people who had come to see them. That indicated the king and the queen. They were offended, as they had to be, and, both rising from the table, they said that they wanted to be searched before the entire court. At the same time, the king unfastened his sash and opened his jacket, while the queen unlaced her corset. But how surprised they both were when they saw the diamond and ruby oranges fall out!

"Oh, Sire!" cried the princess. "What recompense are you giving us for the obliging and respectful manner in which we have received you on our island? That is a poor repayment for a good welcome and hosts who respect you."

The king and the queen, confused by such an affront, sought all sorts of means to justify themselves, protesting that they were incapable of carrying out that theft; that they did not know anything about the oranges, and they could not understand how it had happened.

At those words, the princess prostrated herself at the feet of her father and her mother. "Sire," she said, "I am the unfortunate Livorette whom you had put in a barrel with Alidor and my son; you accused me of a crime to which I never consented; that misfortune happened to me without my having any more knowledge than Your Majesties when the oranges were hidden in their bosom. I dare to beg you to believe me and to pardon me."

Those words penetrated the hearts of the king and the queen. They lifted their daughter up and nearly stifled her, so tightly did they hold her in their arms. She presented them to Prince Alidor and her son. It is easier to imagine the satisfaction of those illustrious persons than it is to depict it.

The wedding of the prince and the princess was celebrated magnificently. The dolphin appeared there in the form of a young monarch, infinitely amiable and witty. Ambassadors were dispatched to Alidor's father and mother with considerable presents. They were charged with telling them everything that had happened.

The life of the prince and princess was as long and a happy thereafter as it had been sad and troubled at the outset.

Livorette returned with her husband to her father's realm, and her son remained on Dolphin Island

> *What would that deplorable prince have done,*
> *Who was persecuted by destiny,*
> *Without the help of the benevolent dolphin*
> *Who was always favorable to him?*
> *The richest treasure that one can possess*
> *Is a tender and faithful friend,*
> *Who aids us appropriately,*
> *When to cruel fortune*
> *One is ready to cede.*
> *One sees friends flee when fortune deserts us;*
> *There are few true ones, and the sage was right,*
> *Who, seeing his house condemned*
> *Which everyone thought too small,*
> *Cried "Alas, in this little abode,*
> *How worthy of envy I would be,*
> *Nothing would be lacking the happiness of my life*
> *If I could only fill it with sincere friends!"*

Marthonide had difficulty finishing her reading, so eager was everyone to praise the tale of the dolphin. One would like to make his friends serve him in the same fashion; one envied the beauty of Livorette and another the merit of Alidor.

"Oh!" cried La Dandinardière, "will you never stop with these trivia? Is there anything in the world that can equal the beauty and utility of those wells from which one extracts gold in buckets of Spanish leather? I confess to you that that place enchants me. If I knew where to find that delightful island, I'd depart immediately to make a pilgrimage there."

"Monsieur," said Alain, hastily, "I'd also have the benevolent devotion to go with you; when I heard those beautiful things read, my mouth watered two or three times. You couldn't, in all conscience, make such a beautiful voyage; the bucket would be very heavy if I didn't pull it up; I have the strong arms."

"Get away," said La Dandinardière. "You're too cowardly to follow me into such a dangerous place."

"I'm not a coward," said Alain, "as witness my combat
with the carter and fifty other encounters when I've been
showered with blows."

"Well," said La Dandinardière, in a very serious tone,
"it's necessary to see on the map where we can fish up that
island, and then we'll draw from it to our honor."

"For myself," said Madame du Rouet, "I confess that I'm
charmed and very surprised by the gallant turn that
Marthonide has given that new tale."

"I'm not so unfortunate in coming to this region as I
thought I'd be," added Madame de Lure in a precious tone,
"for in sum, I couldn't imagine that there was an ounce of
good sense in the provinces, except in the ones where the ardor of the sun warms the brain."

"Truly, truly," said Madame de Saint-Thomas, impatiently, "you're very hard on us, Mesdames from Paris, when you
think we're so stupid."

"It's the most erroneous opinion there is in the world,"
said La Dandinardière; "it's only necessary to see and hear
you to judge more sanely, and everyone I knew at court ought
to lower the flag before these illustrious individuals."

"I have some slight design, my dear relative," added the
widow, "to establish myself here. I'd like to find a large estate
to buy."

"How much, Madame" said the baron, "would you like
to invest in it?"

"Well," she said, that depends on the title. "I'd be glad if
it were a marquisate; in that case I'd go as far as seven thousand francs."

"As far as seven thousand francs, Madame?" said the
vicomte. "You can't think so."

"What!" she cried. "Can a provincial marquisate be
worth anymore? They're being given away in Paris; people
throw them at your head, one doesn't know what to do with
them. For myself, I admit that I'd almost be ashamed to be a

marquise, and I could only resolve myself to it at a low price. But in sum, if you know of one, I'd be obliged if you'd inform me, because I have money with which I don't know what to do. It's true that I could buy a town house in Paris; one is glad to be lodged in one's own home and as I see all the court and all the city, that puts me in certain engagements that many others don't have."

"Is it possible, Madame," said the prior, "that you expect to have a town house for seven thousand francs? I assure you that we couldn't get a thatched cottage here for such a modest price."

"Oh, Monsieur le Prieur," said Madame de Lure, "I can see that you don't know what things are worth; it's a waste of effort to tell you."

"Constantly," said La Dandinardière, with the most malign air he could contrive, "abbés mingle in everything, and often they don't know what they're saying."

"Your account is settled, Monsieur le Prieur," said the vicomte, smiling.

"It's true," he replied. "I wouldn't have expected it on the part of my friend Monsieur de La Dandinardière, but we're in a time when one sacrifices one's best friends for the pleasure of making a quip."

"Personally," said Virginie, "that's not my character; I want people to be attentive to the essential and the trivial."

"Oh, beautiful Virginie," said the bourgeois gentleman, "I'm doomed, and more than doomed, if you're against me; the ascendancy that Heaven has given you is such, in my regard, that I no longer find myself capable of self-defense if you attack. That has been obvious, alas, since I've been in this château." Addressing Madame du Rouet, he went on: "I was led here, my dear cousin, by the strangest and most surprising adventure that could ever happen to a man of quality. I'll tell you about it in private, for it wouldn't be just to fatigue these ladies with such a story. All that I can tell you is that I have an enemy in the canton who is employing iron and fire, enchantments and demons against me."

"What are you telling me, cousin?" said the widow. "I'm frightened by such a prelude."

"These Mesdames and Messieurs," said the gentleman, "can render testimony to what I advance, and at the same time to the vigor with which I've sustained such assaults. Rock— yes, rock—is not firmer than me, and that's what has put my enemy in despair. In sum, he's seeking the means to make me succumb by unusual treasons."

"In truth, Monsieur," said Madame de Lure, "I would like now never to have seen you. I dread so strongly that some misfortune might overtake you that I won't sleep tonight."

"My fate is worthy of envy," riposted La Dandinardière, gallantly. "It seems to me that I no longer have anything to fear since you're interested in my fortune."

"These demoiselles," said the vicomte, indicating Virginie and Marthonide, "assuredly have no less part in it, and if Monsieur de Villeville intends ill-usage, perhaps they will have enough power to arrest his violence."

"About whom are you talking to me?" asked the widow.

"A gentleman," the vicomte continued, "who would have merit if he weren't our friend's enemy."

"Truly," she said. "I've seen him; he pleases me immensely."

"He pleases you?" said La Dandinardière, frowning. "Are you making fun of me? He's a countryman with whom I wouldn't care to make a comparison, and I'm surprised that a woman as well dressed as you can admit that a fellow of that stripe might not displease you."

Madame du Rouet, who had a secret penchant for Villeville, found herself strangely wounded by what her cousin said. "And who are you, then, Monsieur de La Dandinardière?" she replied, dryly. "Does it seem that your transplantation from the Rue Saint-Denis to the seaside authorizes you to jeer at the whole human race?"

"Ah, petty lady of new edition," he cried, red with anger, "it truly befits you to take sides against me; without my money, your late father of glorious memory would have seen the pillory at close range."

"What insolence!" she said. "My father only suffered from the bankruptcy of yours."

The dispute commenced in such a vigorous tone that the listeners judged that it was about to go too far, and that Madame de Saint-Thomas, always on the alert to discover the veritable origin of the bourgeois gentleman, might learn more than was desirable from the insults that were on the point of being hurled; everyone intervened in order to reestablish peace between them. Madame de Lure was not one of the last to conciliate the embittered spirits. She did not want it said in the province that she was accompanied by a bourgeois. The bitterness between the widow and La Dandinardière was already very violent, but they maintained silence in order to oblige the company, and at the plea of their common friends. The indignation that they had for one another was, however, legible in their eyes; from time to time they made little digressions, and without naming anyone, it was obvious that they were not sparing one another.

The baron judged that the best thing to do was to separate them, like two dogs ever ready to bite. "Perhaps you wouldn't be sorry, Mesdames," he said, "to return to the little wood that you visited this morning?"

"It's true that the situation is infinitely agreeable," said the widow. "I love the sea madly, and I approve wholeheartedly of the custom of the Venetians, who marry her ever year. But if I were the wife of the Doge, I'd want to marry her too, or at least make some alliance of amity with her." As she spoke she stood up, without looking at La Dandinardière, and taking Madame de Saint-Thomas, under the arm, said to her: "Let's go my good lady, we'll recuperate a little on the shore of the indocile element."

Madame de Saint-Thomas withdrew her arm rudely and told her that she could sustain herself perfectly well without leaning on her.

The widow, who was already in a bad mood because of the little bourgeois, felt very offended by the manner that the baronne was employing with her. "In truth," she said, "there are people so ungracious that they only offer thorns."

"I understand you," said the baronne, taking offense and raising herself up to her full height, "You're claiming to be the rose and I'm the thorn? Oh well, if you're a rose, it's assuredly a faded rose."

"Your manners are insulting, Madame," retorted the widow blushing. "If I'd believed I'd be received in such a fashion, I'd gladly have done without doing you the honor of visiting your home."

"And I'd gladly have done without seeing you," said the baronne, who did not want to be outdone.

"Oh, my God, what a slanging match!" cried Madame de Lure. "Is it possible that women of quality and good sense amuse themselves like this?"

"I beg you, Madame," said the baronne, "to speak on your own account. I don't use slang."

"In good faith, wife," said Monsieur de Saint-Thomas, "you have a great desire today to cause me chagrin."

"I advise you, Monsieur," she said, raising her voice by a factor of three, "not to play the part of the Great Turk against me; I've stood it for many years, but a good separation of bodies and possessions would put me in repose for the rest of my life; if my grandfather were still alive, he'd weep tears of blood to see me so provoked by a husband. The poor man always said that he wanted to make me a bailiff's wife or a duchesse." With that she started to weep as if all her relatives and friends had been buried.

Discord with bristling spines seemed to have taken up residence in Baron de Saint-Thomas's house; everyone was grumbling, everyone was sulking. He did not make any response to his wife, for it would never have finished. He engaged the ladies to go down into the wood.

The baronne stayed with La Dandinardière; they found themselves at that moment in a mind to confide in one another, which would never have come about without their chagrin against Madame du Rouet.

"Would you mind if talked to you with an open heart?" said the baronne.

"You'd do me a great honor," replied the bourgeois.

"I find that your cousin is an impertinent creature," she said.

"My cousin!" he replied. "Oh, Madame, she is nothing to me; she is one of those cousins….well, you understand what I mean."

"Yes, I understand," she said. "I have more wit and intelligence than any woman in Europe; a word, a trivial detail, enables me to divine a whole story without missing a single vowel."

"How fortunate one is," cried La Dandinardière, "to have a wife of such great merit. If Heaven had provided me with a similar one, I'd worship her as the Chinese worship their pagodas; I'd kiss her little feet; I'd eat her little hands."

"You see, however," said the baronne, "the attitude my husband takes with me. It's necessary that I tell you, Monsieur de La Dandinardière, that there has never been a man less obliging than him; he pretends to be mild and agreeable, but the bottom of the sack is very bitter. For myself, I was born with a sort of politeness that adapts poorly to abruptness."

"I can match you in that," said La Dandinardière. "One could have my soul by means of certain engaging manners, but when someone takes another tone, I become iron. All the demons, follet spirits, sorcerers, magicians, enchanters, werewolves and the rest wouldn't get to the bottom of me."

"Oh, how I love you!" she claimed. "You and I have been made on the same model, and then the mold was broken. That's my humor; I recognize myself in it; but to return to what you told me a moment ago—that widow isn't your relative?"

"Oh, my God, no," he replied, impatiently. "I said it and I'll say it again; it was to one of her uncles that I had confided the stewardship of my house. She was young and pretty; she often came to see him; I was young too, and I was always saying a thousand silly things."

"Fie, Monsieur!" she cried. "I don't want a woman like that to be able to boast that she knows me. I'll go tell her right away that if she ever mentions my name, we'll have a bone to pick with one another."

"You're taking things too literally," replied the bourgeois. "I have no intention of attacking the virtue of Madame du Rouet; everything that I've said relates to the difference between her quality and mine. Fundamentally, Madame, if one prided oneself on such rigidity, and women, in order to be practiced, were obliged to give proof of their life and mores, as Malta was made to prove its nobility, the century is so corrupt that the majority of virtuous women would be obliged to spend their lives alone. It's necessary to relax a little in what's said about it."

"Your maxims are mine, Monsieur de La Dandinardière," said the baronne, "relating to different principles, so you'll permit me not to believe you."

"My God, Madame," he said. "Do you want to cause a racket that would desolate your husband?"

"That's what I'm seeking," she said. "You've seen yourself the attitude he took with me regarding that bourgeois woman; I intended to clarify the matter, for I believe that he's known her for a long time."

As they were speaking thus in good amity, Alain came to interrupt them, with a distraught expression that surprised his master. He approached his ear, and whispered to him: "Monsieur, it's necessary to pack the luggage for the other world. Villeville is in the wood, laughing and chattering as if he had no fear of you. I was hidden behind a tree, from where it was easy for me to see; he's even bigger than he was before, by a cubit."

The baronne remarked that Alain's news altered La Dandinardière's tranquility. She went out immediately with a "Perhaps I'm inconveniencing you," and the little man, delighted to find himself at liberty, asked him whether he was quite certain that he had seen Villeville.

"Make no mistake about that, Monsieur," he said. "I saw him like I see my foot. I'll tell you the whole story. When the ladies came out of your room I was in the little dark passage, where one can hardly see a thing, and I heard one of them say to the messieurs: 'He's a dirty fellow who used to be my merchant in the Rue Saint-Denis; in those days he had a particular inclination for counterfeiting men of quality; people made fun of him every day, as I bought a lot from him on credit I enjoyed myself at his expense more often than most, and I called him my cousin in order to have time to pay, for we women of the court don't always have ready cash.' She said a hundred other things that I can't remember."

"I'm not sure I find your memory good with regard to that one," said his master, "for I know by the style that you've put something of your own into it."

"Me, Monsieur," said Alain. "I'd rather be hanged as a forger than tell a lie. I repeat to you the words I hear like a magistrate's clerk. But to get back to those ladies, I followed them quietly, and hid close by; each one was chatting in her fashion when a horse was heard going *pit-a-pat*; everyone looked, and it was that curmudgeon Villeville, who jumped down to salute them, and I withdrew on all fours, all a-tremble, to come and warn you."

"This is an affair that merits much attention," cried La Dandinardière. "My enemy is accustomed to appear in this vicinity; he passed through this morning, he's come back in the evening; he's telling tales to the window, she has a grudge against me. Why don't you have any courage, Alain?"

"And if I had, Monsieur," he replied, "what would we do?"

"All that we won't do," said the bourgeois, "because I know you lack any. What's the point of my forming projects with you? The best of all is to think about retreat."

"That's not too badly said, Monsieur," added Alain. "That desperado Maître Robert might play some trick on us too."

"But how can we do it?" said La Dandinardière. "If anyone sees us on the road, we're doomed!"

"A little patience, Monsieur," said Alain. "I'll put you in my handcart, with your livery on top, which will hide you marvelously."

"Library, fool," La Dandinardière interrupted. "That's not a bad idea, but return to the same place where you saw Villeville, in order to come and tell me where he is."

Alain quit him, and went along an obscure pathway as far as the company whose members were still in the wood. He saw that his master's enemy had gone; he looked carefully in all directions and then came back to tell him that there was no longer anything to fear, because the eater of little children had gone.

At those words he cried: "Let's go, let's go combine new laurels with those I have already. Give me my armor, my boots and my little Bucephalus. Ah, the impudent fellow, he comes to where I am; I'll teach him what wood I warm myself with."

Alain looked at him, quite astonished. "Is it a good idea, Monsieur," he said, "to want your armor? Your head is still very poorly, and the adventure of the bed has damaged your poor shoulders badly."

La Dandinardière pretended not to be listening to Alain and, as if he were talking to himself, he said: "But for well-born souls, virtue doesn't await the number of years." Then, continuing, he cried in a lively and courageous fashion: "Appear Navarrois, Moors and Castilians!" He continued thus to repeat parts of *Le Cid*, grateful for the fortunate fecundity of his memory.

While he was exciting himself for battle, he found himself armored, and then mounted his palfrey, which was much more cheerful than him, because it had been a long time since it had eaten such good oats. It bucked and was restive. Nevertheless, La Dandinardière took the route to the wood, lance in hand, with which he delivered such terrible thrusts against the branches that he brought down more cockchafers than leaves in autumn. The great racket that he made caused all the ladies to turn round; his equipage surprised them and they burst out laughing, particularly the widow, who, having rather beautiful teeth, opened her mouth wide in order to show them off while they all reverberated her *ha ha ha*s.

La Dandinardière, who had a grudge against her, found it very bad that she was mocking him. He sought to signal that to her, and seeing that her head-dress was rather tall and garnished with rose-colored rubies he lifted off her bonnet with his lance, as the rogue is lifted when one tilts at heads.

Madame du Rouet's remained bald; she had no hair, because hers had been a trifle russet, but she had metamorphosed that overly ardent color into infantile blonde. Her chagrin and affliction can be imagined. She uttered long screams after her hairpiece, the dearest and healthiest part of herself.

The umbrageous and spirited little horse was frightened by the headgear that was dangling in front of its eyes and the racket that the lady who had lost it was making; it took off at a gallop, in spite of its master, and got the bit between its teeth; La Dandinardière's attempts to stop it would have been futile if Villeville, who had just quit the company and had stopped to talk to Maître Robert, had not looked round.

He was surprised to see the bourgeois gentleman in such great peril; he stopped his horse, and, taking advantage of the opportunity to execute the project that he had just formed with the vicomte and the prior, he drew his sword and said: "Let's go, Monsieur de La Dandinardière. It's necessary for us to cut throats now."

The poor man was already so frightened that he did not have the strength to speak, but when he saw a sword glittering before his eyes, it is certain that he nearly died

After a quarter of an hour of silence and reflection, he replied: "I don't fight when I'm armed; I have too much advantage and I'm too honest a man.

"A truce on considerations," said Villeville, putting the tip of his sword to his throat.

"Oh, Maître Robert, I'm dead," cried La Dandinardière, letting himself fall. "Come and bleed me. Oh, my good Monsieur de Villeville," he continued, "don't kill me; I ask you for my life; if my warrior attire displeases you I'll renounce it for the rest of my life."

"Only one thing can save you from my fury," said Villeville. "I'll let you live provided that you give me your word to marry Mademoiselle de Saint-Thomas."

"Name which one," replied poor La Dandinardière, promptly, "for, if you order it, I'll marry them both, and the father and mother as well."

"I'll let you choose between them," Villeville continued, "but if you fail to take advantage of the honor I'm procuring for you, count on me killing you, even if you hide a hundred feet underground."

The bourgeois reckoned himself the happiest of all men to have got out of it so cheaply. He got up, trembling, and prostrated himself at the feet of his redoubtable enemy, assuring him that he would go as far as the impossible to obey him. He requested to kiss his victorious hand, and Villeville gave it to him with a grave expression

"I'm willing," he said, "to ask Monsieur de Saint-Thomas on your behalf for Virginie; he'll have more disposition to grant her to you when he sees that I've forgiven you and that we're going to be friends."

"You're the master," replied the bourgeois. "I'll abide by anything you agree with him."

Furnished with that promise, Villeville retraced his steps and took the vicomte and the prior to one side. "It required no more," he said, "than putting Maître Robert on the stage and contriving an encounter between La Dandinardière and me; hazard has done by itself what we could only have done with a great deal of care." With that, he recounted the adventure he had just had and what had followed it. The two messieurs had no less joy in it than him.

"Let's not lose a moment," they said, "in concluding the marriage. What embarrasses us is the widow, who might prefer no longer to be angry with her cousin, and then to meddle in counseling him against our interests."

"Don't worry about that," said Villeville, "I have some slight ascendancy over her; I'll talk to her about our designs; she'll be delighted with that confidence, and will support us marvelously."

He was not mistaken. While he approached her, the vicomte spoke to Monsieur de Saint-Thomas, who received the proposal agreeably. Madame de Saint-Thomas lent her hand to it, as an effect of caprice, which rarely left her in the same situation for long, and Virginie consented to it joyfully, anticipating that La Dandinardière was a little hero who would carry out great exploits of bravery, and that she would have the pleasure of making Apollo and the Muses sing in his favor.

Thus, all the minds that had been in discord a few hours before found themselves reunited when the good La Dandinardière arrived, still very emotional and tremulous; he was received with open arms; everyone worked to enable him to forget the catastrophe of his combat; they even had the discretion not to mention it in his presence and to praise his merit excessively.

He made the formal request for Virginie; he was heard favorably; the vicomte proposed to return to the house to draw up the articles.

But with what astonishment was the faithful Alain struck when he saw the lambs and the wolves bounding together in the meadow! I mean La Dandinardière and Villeville, who were embracing continually, and shaking hands like the best friends in the world. He opened his eyes and his mouth wide, and stood with one foot in the air, neither advancing or retreating; in sum, he was in the utmost surprise. It was something else when he was told that his master was going to marry Virginie, and that it was Monsieur de Villeville who had organized that good fortune. He immediately sang, and danced the branle and the mariée, and rejoiced the entire company with his simplicities.

La Dandinardière was disarmed; Mesdemoiselles de Saint Thomas acquitted themselves almost as the Dulcineas of whom Don Quixote spoke; he was crowned with roses; everyone named him the Anacreon of our days, the joy of good companies, the annealed fop; but the baron, who was beginning to be veritably interested in him, did not laugh to loudly at those jokes. He even asked the vicomte, the prior and Villeville to regard him as a man who was going to be his son-in-law. They understood what he was trying to say to them, and spared him a little more.

That very evening the poor pullets in the chicken-run and the pigeons in the dovecot were put to death in order to serve for the meal. All the hunters in the region gave no quarters to the grouse. The baron paid the expenses of the wedding; the dowry went no further; the gift of making up tales was extolled and future hopes assigned thereto.

La Dandinardière was satisfied by that, or at least pretended to be, for he feared Villeville, and without him, the marriage would never have succeeded.

Virginie took her sister into her new household. The day it was concluded, the cart of books, with the three donkeys, which were laden with them, set off at the head of the cortege. The bourgeois mounted his little horse and Alain followed him, bearing his arms in a trophy. Virginie and her sister, with an amazon air, came afterwards, mounted as best they could. The widow, who did not hate Villeville, was riding on the rump behind him. The precious baronne and Madame de Lure were in a little rolling chaise, pulled by a brood-mare. The cavalcade was closed by the rest of the messieurs, and several relatives who had rendered to the celebration.

It would take some time to describe everything that happened on the way. I fear having abused the patience of the reader and I am stopping before I am told to stop.

CLASSIC FRENCH FANTASY

Honoré de Balzac. *The Last Fay*
Gabrielle-Suzanne Barbot de Villeneuve. *The Naiads / Beauty and The Beast*
Chevalier de Béthune. *The World of Mercury*
Jean Carrère. *The End of Atlantis*
Charlotte-Rose Caumont de La Force. *The Land of Delights*
Comte de Caylus. *The Impossible Enchantment*
Félicien Champsaur. *Pharaoh's Wife*
Jacques Collin de Plancy. *Voyage to the Center of the Earth*
Gaston Danville. *The Perfume of Lust*
Comtesse D.L. *The Tyranny of the Fays Abolished*
Marie-Antoinette Fagnan. *The Enchanter's Mirror*
Paul Féval. *Anne of the Isles*
Charles de Fieux. *Lamékis*
Judith Gautier. *Isoline and the Serpent-Flower*
Nathalie Henneberg. *The Green Gods*
Gustave Kahn. *The Tale of Gold and Silence*
Edmond Haraucourt. *Dieudonat*
Françoise Le Marchand. *Florine and Boca*
Marie-Jeanne L'Héritier de Villandon. *The Robe of Sincerity*
André Lichtenberger. *The Centaurs; The Children of the Crab*
J-M. & Randy Lofficier. *The French Fantasy Treasury 1-3*
Charles Lomon & P.-B. Gheuzi. *The Last Days of Atlantis*
Maurice Magre. *The Marvelous Story of Claire d'Amour; The Call of the Beast; Priscilla of Alexandria; The Angel of Lust; The Mystery of the Tiger; The Poison of Goa; Lucifer; The Blood of Toulouse; The Albigensian Treasure; Jean de Fodoas; Melusine; The Brothers of the Virgin Gold*
Marie-Madeleine de Lubert. *Princess Camion.*
Camille Mauclair. *The Virgin Orient*
Hippolyte Mettais. *Paris Before the Deluge*
Victor-Emile Michelet. *Superhuman Tales*

Henriette-Julie de Murat. *The Palace of Vengeance*
Charles Nodier. *Trilby / The Crumb Fairy*
Edgar Quinet. *The Enchanter Merlin*
Henri de Régnier. *A Surfeit of Mirrors*
Restif de la Bretonne. *The Fay Ouroucoucou* (2 vols.)
J.-H. Rosny Aîné. *Pan's Flute*
Marie-Anne de Roumier-Robert. *The Voyage of Lord Seaton
to the Seven Planets*
Nicolas Ségur. *Penelope's Secret*
Brian Stableford (ed.). *Funestine; The Queen of the Fays; The
Origin of the Fays*
Kurt Steiner. *Ortog*
C.-F. Tiphaigne de La Roche. *Amilec / Giphantia*
Simon Tyssot de Patot. *The Strange Voyages of Jacques
Massé and Pierre de Mésange*